Old Mission, San Diego, Cal.

Souvenir Folder of
CALIFORNIA MISSIONS

POSTAGE 1½¢ WITHOUT MESSAGE

The Heart Has Its Reasons

Also by María Dueñas

The Time In Between

THE HEART
HAS ITS
REASONS

A Novel

MARÍA DUEÑAS

Translated by Elie Kerrigan

ATRIA BOOKS

NEW YORK   LONDON   TORONTO   SYDNEY   NEW DELHI

ATRIA BOOKS

A Division of Simon & Schuster, Inc.
1230 Avenue of the Americas
New York, NY 10020

First Atria Books hardcover edition November 2014

ATRIA BOOKS and colophon are trademarks of Simon & Schuster, Inc.

For information about special discounts for bulk purchases, please contact Simon & Schuster Special Sales at 1-866-506-1949 or business@simonandschuster.com.

The Simon & Schuster Speakers Bureau can bring authors to your live event. For more information or to book an event, contact the Simon & Schuster Speakers Bureau at 1-866-248-3049 or visit our website at www.simonspeakers.com.

Jacket art © Giovan Battista D'Achille/Trevillion Images
Endpaper art by Pasquale Caprile/Photogaleria, SL

Manufactured in the United States of America

10 9 8 7 6 5 4 3 2 1

Library of Congress Cataloging-in-Publication Data

Dueñas, María, date.
[Misión olvido. English]
The heart has its reasons : a novel / María Dueñas ; [translated by Elie Kerrigan]. — First Atria Books hardcover edition.
pages cm
I. Kerrigan, Elie, translator. II. Title.
PQ6704.U35M5713 2014
863'.7—dc23
2014014023

ISBN 978-1-4516-6833-9
ISBN 978-1-4516-6836-0 (ebook)

To my brother, Pablo Dueñas Vinuesa,
in return for everything he knows I owed him.
To those who, against all odds, teach every day with passion
and dedication: my colleagues, my teachers, my friends.

The Heart Has Its Reasons

Chapter 1

———————

Sometimes life comes crashing down, heavy and cold as a dead-weight.

This is how I felt on opening the office door. It had all felt so cozy, so intimate, so mine. Before.

And yet to the naked eye there was no reason for apprehension; everything remained just as I had left it. Shelves crammed with books, bulletin board full of schedules and reminders. Folders, filing cabinets, old playbills, envelopes addressed to me. The calendar frozen two months back, July 1999. Everything stood intact in that space which for fourteen years had been my haven, where semester after semester I'd welcomed countless students lost in doubt or searching for something. The only thing that had changed were the props that supported me. Shattered.

Several minutes went by, perhaps even ten. Sufficient time, in any event, for me to come to a decision. My first order of business was to dial a telephone number. In reply I only got the icy courtesy of a voice mail. Hesitating whether or not to hang up, I decided to leave a message.

"Rosalia, it's Blanca Perea. I have to get out of here, I need your help. I don't know where I could go; it's all the same to me. Somewhere

I don't know a soul and no one knows me. I realize it's the worst timing, with the semester about to begin, but call me as soon as you can, please."

I felt better after leaving the message. I knew I could trust Rosalia Martin, both her understanding and her goodwill. We had known each other since our early days at the university, when I was a young professor with a meager temporary contract and she was responsible for running a recently established department of international relations. Although our friendship had diluted somewhat with the passing of time, I knew Rosalia's mettle and was sure that my cry for help would be answered.

Only after the phone call could I muster enough energy to face my duties. My e-mail in-box opened like an overflowing dam of messages, and I dove into its current for a good while, answering some and discarding others that were outdated or of no import. Until the telephone interrupted me, and I answered with a curt "Yes . . . ?"

"What's the matter with you, madwoman? Where do you want to go at this point? And what's with all the rush?"

Rosalia's impassioned voice brought back the memories of so many shared experiences. Hours on end sitting in front of the black-and-white screen of a prehistoric computer. Shared visits to foreign universities in search of exchange programs and partnerships, double rooms in nondescript hotels, dawns spent waiting in empty airports. With the passage of time we'd gone our separate ways, but the traces of an old complicity remained alive, and that is why I told her everything. Without reservation, with brutal honesty.

In a couple of minutes she knew all she needed to know. That Alberto had left me. That the assumed solidity of my marriage had vanished during the first days of summer; that my kids had already flown the nest; that I'd spent the last couple of months awkwardly trying to adjust to my new reality. And that now, facing the new semester, I lacked the stamina to stay afloat in the setting I'd lived comfortably in for years, simply latching onto my responsibilities and routines as if my life hadn't undergone a swift sure gash like a knife through flesh.

With a dose of pragmatism equal to her body's considerable size,

Rosalia immediately absorbed the situation and realized that the last thing I needed was well-meaning sugarcoated advice. So she did not delve into details or offer me her soft shoulder as solace. She only made a comment that, as I might have expected, bordered on bluntness.

"Well, I'm afraid it won't be that easy for us, honey." She spoke in the plural, immediately taking on the matter as something we were in together. "The deadlines for interesting things passed months ago," she added, "and the next fellowship application deadlines are still some months away. But the semester is just beginning, and I don't know if we've received anything new in the last couple of weeks. Give me until the end of the day to see if I can come up with something."

I spent the rest of the morning wandering around the university. I took care of pending paperwork, returned books to the library, and had coffee afterwards. Nothing sufficient to distract me while waiting for Rosalia's call. I was overanxious and lacked confidence. At a quarter to two I rapped on her office door, which was ajar. Inside, serene as always, and with violet-tinted hair, Rosalia was busy at work.

"I was just about to call you," she announced, without even giving me time to greet her. Pointing to the computer screen, she proceeded to reel off what she'd found. "Three things came in during the holidays. They're not that bad—more than I expected, to tell you the truth. Three universities and three different activities. Lithuania, Portugal, and the United States. California, specifically. None are cushy jobs, mind you, and they all promise to work your ass off without contributing much to your curriculum vitae, but it's better than nothing, right? Where would you like me to start?"

I shrugged, pursing my lips slightly to stifle a smile: this was my first glimpse of optimism in a long time. In the meantime, Rosalia adjusted her chewing-gum-green glasses and redirected her gaze to the computer, scrutinizing its contents.

"Lithuania, for instance. They're looking for specialists in linguistic pedagogy for a new teacher training program. Two months. They have a European Union subsidy, which requires an international group. And this is in your line of work, right?"

Indeed it was. Applied linguistics, language pedagogy, curriculum design. I'd been treading that path for the last two decades of my life. But before succumbing to the first siren's song, I chose to inquire a bit further.

"And Portugal?"

"University of Espirito Santo, in Sintra. Private, modern, loaded. They've put together a master's program in teaching Spanish as a foreign language, and are looking for experts in methodology. The deadline is this Friday—in other words now. A twelve-week intensive course, with enough teaching hours to choke a horse. The salary isn't too bad, so I imagine they must have loads of applications. But in your favor you have all those years of slogging away, and we've got a wonderful relationship with Espirito Santo, so it might not be too hard for us to get it."

That offer seemed infinitely more tempting than the Lithuanian one. Sintra, with its forests and palaces, so close to Lisbon, and yet near to home. Rosalia's voice brought me out of my reverie.

"And lastly, California," she resumed, without ungluing her eyes from the screen. "I see this possibility as more iffy, but we can take a look at it, just in case. University of Santa Cecilia, north of San Francisco. The information we have is rather scant right now: the proposal has just come in and I haven't had time to ask for more. At first glance, it seems like a grant financed by a private foundation, although the work will be carried out on campus. The endowment offered is nothing to write home about, but you'd be able to survive."

"What does the work consist of, basically?"

"It has something to do with the compilation and classification of documents, and they're looking for someone of Spanish nationality with a PhD in any area of the humanities." Removing her glasses, she added: "Normally this type of grant goes to people with a lower professional standing than you, so you'd certainly stand out from the rest when it comes to evaluating the candidates. And California, dear, is a real temptation, so, if you wish, I can try to get further information."

"Sintra," I insisted, refusing the third offer. Twelve weeks. Perhaps enough time for my wounds to stop stinging. Far enough away to distance me from my immediate reality, close enough for me to return frequently in the event that my situation resolved itself suddenly and everything returned to normal. "Sintra sounds perfect," I stated categorically.

Half an hour later I left Rosalia's office, the electronic application sent. I had a thousand details in my head, a handful of papers in my hand, and the feeling that perhaps luck, in a haphazard fashion, had finally decided to take my side.

The rest of the day went by in a sort of limbo. I ate a grilled vegetable sandwich, without much appetite, in the faculty cafeteria and went on working distractedly all afternoon. At seven I attended the presentation of a new book by a colleague in the Ancient History Department. I tried to get away as soon as it was over, but afterwards a few colleagues dragged me with them in search of a cold beer and I didn't have the strength to decline. It was close to ten when I finally reached home. In the semidarkness before I turned on the light I could see the answering machine blinking insistently in the far corner of the living room. Then I remembered that I'd turned my cell phone off when the presentation began and had forgotten to switch it back on.

The first message was from Pablo, my younger son. Charming, incoherent, and vague, with loud music and laughter in the background. I had difficulty understanding his rushed words.

"Mother, it's me, where the hell are you? . . . I've called your cell phone a bunch of times to tell you . . . I'm not coming back this week either, I'm staying at the beach, and . . . and . . . well, I'll keep on trying you, okay?"

"Pablo," I whispered, pausing the machine to search for his face amid the bookshelves. There it was, photographed a dozen times. Sometimes alone but almost always with his older brother, so alike the two of them. The eternal smiles, the black bangs covering the eyes. Rowdy sequences from their twenty-two and twenty-three years of life. Indians, pirates, and Flintstones in school plays, blowing out an ever-increasing number of candles on cakes. Summer camps, Christmas scenes. Fragments printed on Kodak paper, memory cutouts of a close-knit family that, as such, no longer existed.

With my son Pablo still lingering in my mind, I pressed the Play button to listen to the next message.

"Uh . . . Blanca, it's Alberto. You don't answer your cell phone, I don't know if you're home. Uh . . . I'm calling you because . . . um . . . to tell you that . . . uh . . . Well, it's better if I tell you afterwards, when I reach you. I'll call you later. Good-bye, talk to you later. Bye."

My husband's blundering voice left me restless. Or rather, my ex-husband's. I was clueless as to what he wanted to tell me, but from his tone I hardly expected good news. My first reaction was, as usual, to think that something must have happened to one of my kids. From the previous message I knew that Pablo was fine; I then quickly rescued the cell phone from my bag, switched it on, and called David.

"Are you okay?" I inquired impatiently as soon as I heard his voice.

"Yes, of course I'm okay. How about you?"

He sounded tense. Perhaps it was only a false perception due to the phone connection. Perhaps not.

"Me, well, more or less . . . The thing is that Dad called and—"

"I know," he interrupted me. "He just called me too. How did you take it?"

"How did I take what?"

"About the kid."

"What kid?"

"The one he's going to have with Eva."

Without the power of thought or sight, impenetrable as a marble mausoleum or a sidewalk curb, I remained suspended in a void for an indeterminate time. When I was again conscious of reality, I heard David's voice screaming from the telephone, which had fallen on my lap.

"I'm still here," I finally answered. And without giving him more time to inquire any further, I ended the conversation. "Everything's fine; I'll call you later."

I sat still on the sofa, gazing into nowhere while trying to digest the news that my husband was going to have a kid with the woman he'd left me for barely two months ago. Alberto's third kid: that third child he never wanted to have with me despite my long insistence. The one who would be born from a belly that wasn't mine and in a house that was not our own. I felt anguish rising unchecked from my stomach, announcing waves of nausea and distress. With hurried staggering steps, bumping against the doorway to the hall, I managed to reach the bathroom. I flung myself over the toilet and, down on my knees, began vomiting.

I remained kneeling there for a long while, my forehead glued to the wall's cold tiles as I tried to find a shred of coherence in the midst of the confusion. When I was finally able to stand up, I washed my hands slowly, deliberately, allowing the lathery water to run between my fingers. Then I brushed my teeth methodically, giving my brain time to work in a parallel manner, unhurriedly. Finally I returned to the living room with a clean mouth and hands, an empty stomach, a clear mind, and a numb heart. I found my cell phone on the carpet and dialed a number, but no one answered. Once more, I left my message on the answering machine.

"It's Blanca again, Rosalia. Change of plans. I have to go farther away, longer, immediately. Please find out whatever you can about that California fellowship."

Nine days later I landed at the San Francisco airport.

Chapter 2

_____

The abrupt cessation of hammering brought me back to reality. I looked to see what time it was. Noon. Only then was I conscious of the number of hours I had spent rummaging through papers without the slightest idea what to do with them. I rose from the floor with difficulty, noticing that my joints were numb. While dusting off my hands, I stood on tiptoe and peered out the small window close to the ceiling. The only thing I saw was a building under construction and the sturdy boots of a handful of workers bustling about with their lunch pails amid stacks of wooden planks. I felt a sharp pain in my stomach: a mixture of weakness, bewilderment, and hunger.

I had reached California the previous evening after three planes and countless hours of flight. After picking up my luggage and feeling momentarily disoriented, I spotted my name written in thick blue letters on a small piece of cardboard. It was held up by a robust woman with a lost look and of indeterminate age, thirty-seven, forty, forty-something, perhaps, with a vanilla-colored dress and a blunt haircut that ended at the jawline. I went up to her, but not even when I was standing in front of her did she seem to notice my presence.

"I'm Blanca Perea, I think you're looking for me."

I thought I was mistaken: she was not looking for me. Not for me nor for anyone else. She simply remained static and absent, apart from the moving mass, immune to the terminal's hectic bustle.

"Blanca Perea," I repeated. "Professor Blanca Perea, from Spain."

She finally reacted, opening and closing her eyes quickly, as if she had just returned hastily from an astral voyage. Extending her hand, she shook mine with an abrupt jolt; then, without a word, she took off without waiting for me while I made an effort to follow, juggling two suitcases, a handbag, and a laptop bag dangling from my shoulder.

The white 4x4 vehicle awaiting us in the parking lot had been parked diagonally, brashly invading two adjacent parking spots. JESUS LOVES YOU could be read on a sticker in the rear window. With a sudden powerful acceleration that belied the stolid appearance of its driver, we headed into the humid night along San Francisco Bay. Destination: Santa Cecilia.

She drove glued to the wheel and focused. We hardly spoke during the entire journey; she simply answered my questions with monosyllables and brief scraps of information. All the same, I learned a few things. Her name was Fanny Stern, she worked for the university, and her immediate objective was to drop me off at the apartment that, along with a modest stipend, was part of the fellowship granted to me. I still had only a vague idea of what my new assignment entailed, since the suddenness of my departure had prevented me from obtaining more detailed information. That didn't worry me, however, for there would be plenty of time to find out. In any case, I expected my job to be neither stimulating nor rewarding. For the time being, I was just happy to be able to flee my reality like a bat out of hell.

In spite of my lack of sleep, when the alarm clock surprised me at seven a.m. the next day, I was reasonably awake and clear-minded. I got up and immediately jumped into the shower, preventing the fresh consciousness of morning from revisiting the dark road I'd traveled in recent days. With the sunlight I was able to confirm what I had intuited the previous night: that this nondescript apartment intended for visiting professors would turn out to be a suitable refuge for me. A small living room and basic kitchen were integrated at one end.

A bedroom, a plain bathroom. Bare walls, sparse and neutral furniture. An anonymous shelter, but decent. Livable. Acceptable.

I roamed the streets in search of a place to have breakfast while absorbing what Santa Cecilia had on display. In the apartment I'd found a folder bearing my name with all the necessary information to help orient me: a map, a pamphlet, a writing pad with the university's logo. Nothing else was needed.

I found no trace of the Californian scenery familiar from television series and the collective imagination. No coast, no swaying palm trees or mansions with ten bathrooms. That superwealthy California, a paradise of technology, nonconformity, and showbiz, was clearly elsewhere.

Ravenous, I finally sat down at a nearby coffee shop. While devouring a blueberry muffin and drinking a watery cup of coffee, I slowly took in the scenery. There was a large square clotted with trees and surrounded by renovated buildings with an adobe appearance that gave the whiff of a past halfway between America and Mexico, with a residue of something vaguely Spanish. Lined up on the opposite side of the square were a First National Bank branch, a souvenir shop, the all-important post office, and a CVS pharmacy.

My next goal was to reach Guevara Hall, where I would find the Modern Languages Department. This was to serve as my work environment for a still undetermined number of months. Whether this interval would turn out to be an effective balm or a simple Band-Aid for my wounds remained to be seen, but in any case I would at least stop feeling trapped. Entering the campus, I remained vigilant so as not to get lost in that maze of paths where throngs of students were making their way by bike or on foot to their classrooms.

The noise of the department's photocopying machine masked the sound of my steps and prevented Fanny, who was working there, from noticing my arrival until I was right beside her. She raised her eyes and stared at me again for several seconds with her inexpressive face. Extending her right arm with an automaton's precision and pointing to the open door of an office, she announced: "Someone is waiting for you." Having nothing further to say, she turned and went off with that same dull gait as on the previous evening at the airport.

I took a quick glance at the sign on the door as I entered. Rebecca Cullen, the name on almost all e-mails I'd received prior to departure, finally had a tangible place and presence. In addition to all the files and transcripts in her office were paintings saturated with color, family pictures, and a bouquet of white lilies. Her greeting was an affectionate, warm handshake. Her clear eyes lit up a pretty face from which the wrinkles did not detract. A large lock of silvery hair fell over her forehead. I figured she was in her sixties, and I had a feeling that she must be one of those indispensable secretaries who, with a third of their superiors' salaries, are usually three times as competent.

"Well, Blanca, finally . . . It's been a total surprise to learn that we have a visiting researcher this semester. We're delighted . . ."

To my relief, we were able to communicate without a problem. I had laid the groundwork for my English during stays in the U.K. and had strengthened it through years of study and frequent contact with British universities. However, my experience regarding North America had only been sporadic: a few conferences, a family celebration in New York after my son Pablo passed his university entrance exam, and a brief research stint in Maryland. So I was reassured to confirm that I'd be able to cope on the West Coast without any great language barrier.

"I think I told you in one of my last messages that the head of our department, Dr. Luis Zarate, would be at a conference in Philadelphia, so in the meantime I'll be the one in charge of orienting you in your work."

Rebecca Cullen explained in general terms what I more or less knew I was expected to accomplish: to order and assess the legacy of an old faculty member who had died decades earlier. It was financed by SAPAM, the newly created foundation for Scientific Assessment of Philological Academic Manuscripts.

"His name was Andres Fontana and, as you know, he was a Spaniard. He lived in Santa Cecilia until his death in 1969, and was much beloved, but the usual thing happened afterwards. Since he didn't have any family in this country, no one came forward to claim his things and, awaiting someone to decide what to do, they've sat here all these years, stacked in a basement."

"Nothing has been moved since then?"

"Nothing, until SAPAM finally endowed a grant to carry out this project. To be perfectly honest," she added in a knowing tone, "I think it's rather shameful that three decades have already gone by, but that's how things are: everyone's always busy, the faculty comes and goes. And of all the people who were familiar with and esteemed Andres Fontana in his day, hardly anyone is left here except a few veterans like myself."

I made an effort to disguise the fact that, if his own colleagues weren't interested in that expatriate who had fallen into oblivion, I was even less so.

"And now, if it's okay with you," she continued, getting back to practical matters, "first I'm going to show you your office and then the storeroom where all the material is kept. You'll have to forgive us: the news of your arrival has been rather sudden and we haven't had a chance to find you a better spot."

I pretended to look in my bag for a tissue to blow my nose, waiting for Rebecca Cullen to change subjects, hoping she'd move on to another matter quickly and not delve into the reasons why a Spanish professor with a secure professional career, an impressive CV, a good salary, family, and contacts had decided so swiftly to pack a couple of suitcases and move to the other end of the world like someone fleeing the plague.

My new office turned out to be a remote cubbyhole, with no comforts and a single window—narrow, off to one side, and not too clean—overlooking the campus. There was a desk with an old computer and a heavy telephone supported by two sturdy outdated telephone books. Relics from other times and other hands; decrepit surplus that no one wanted any longer. We'd get along well, I thought. After all, we were both in a state of depreciation.

"It's important that you know how to find Fanny Stern: she'll be in charge of supplying you with any materials you may need," Rebecca announced, making way for me to navigate the turn that led into Fanny's working space.

On sticking my head in Fanny's cubicle, I was overcome by a feeling of confusion but one that existed somewhere between tenderness and hilarity. There was not an inch of empty space on the walls, which were covered with playbills, calendars, posters of sunsets among snowy mountaintops, and sugary, optimistic messages like *Don't lose heart, you can make it; The sun always shines after a storm;* and *There's always a helping hand nearby.* In the middle of all this, beatific and absent, sat Fanny, gobbling up a white chocolate bar as greedily as a five-year-old.

Before Fanny managed to finish swallowing and greet us, Rebecca went over to her and stood behind her. Holding Fanny by the shoulders, she gave her an affectionate squeeze.

"Fanny, you already know Professor Perea, our visiting researcher, and you know what office we've assigned her, right? Remember that you must help her with everything she asks for, okay?"

"Sure, Mrs. Cullen," she answered with a full mouth. To emphasize her willingness, she nodded several times vigorously.

"Fanny is very eager and a hard worker. Her mother was also part of this department for decades." Rebecca spoke slowly, as if carefully choosing her words. "Darla Stern worked here many years, and for a while she held the position that I later took over. How is your mother, Fanny?" she asked.

"Mother is very well, Mrs. Cullen, thank you," Fanny replied, nodding once more as she swallowed.

"Give her my regards. And now we're off: I must show Professor Perea the storeroom," she concluded.

When we left, Fanny was again sinking her teeth into the chocolate bar, surrounded by her blissful posters and perhaps even some devil lurking somewhere in a drawer.

"Before retiring from the dean's office about four years ago, her mother saw to it that Fanny remained in the department as a kind of inheritance," Rebecca explained with no trace of irony. "She doesn't have a great many tasks, because, as you may have noticed, her abilities are somewhat limited. But her responsibilities are well-defined and she manages reasonably well: she hands out the mail, is in charge of making photocopies, organizes supplies, and carries out small errands. She's an essential part of this house. And she can be counted on whenever you need her."

A labyrinth of hallways and stairs took us to a remote section of the basement. Rebecca, in front, moved about with the familiarity of someone who had trod these floors for ages. I, behind, tried in vain to commit to memory all the twists and turns, anticipating how often I'd get lost before finding my way around. Meanwhile, Rebecca reeled off some facts about the university. More than fourteen thousand students, she said, almost all from out of town. Initially it was a college and eventually evolved into its present-day status of small, somewhat prestigious university. She mentioned that it currently created the most jobs and the greatest revenue of any institution in the community.

We reached a narrow hallway flanked by metallic doors.

"And this, Blanca, is your storeroom," she announced, turning the key in one of the locks. When she finally opened it, with some difficulty, she flipped several switches on and the fluorescent lights sputtered to life, blinding us.

I saw before me a long, narrow room like the corridor of a train. The cement walls, which had not been painted, were lined with industrial shelving whose contents spoke of dislocation and oblivion. Through two horizontal windows located at a considerable height, some natural light filtered in and the sound of hammering from a nearby construction site could be heard. At first it seemed like a rectangular space; however, after we had taken a few steps forward, I realized that the apparent shape and size were somewhat deceiving. At the back end, to the left, the storehouse had an L-shaped space that unfolded into another room.

"*Et voilà*," she announced, flipping on another switch. "Professor Fontana's legacy."

I was filled with such a terrible feeling of discouragement that I was about to tell her not to leave me there, to take me with her, to shelter me in any corner of her hospitable human office, where her calm presence would mitigate my anxiety.

Perhaps aware of my thoughts, she tried to rally my spirits.

"Daunting, right? But I'm sure you'll be making your way through it in no time, you'll see . . ." she said as she took her leave.

My eagerness to flee my domestic demons had led me to imagine that a radical change of work and geography would anchor me. But on seeing that chaos—piles of papers, folders strewn on the floor, and boxes stacked one upon the other without a trace of coherence, I felt I'd made a huge mistake.

Even so, there was no turning back. Too late, too many bridges burned. And there I was, marooned in the basement of a campus at the farthest reaches of a foreign country, while thousands of miles away my sons ventured forth alone in the first stretch of their adult lives, and the man who until then had been my husband was about to relive the passionate adventure of paternity with a blond lawyer fifteen years younger than me.

I leaned against the wall and covered my face with my hands. Everything seemed to be getting worse and I was running out of strength to endure it. Nothing seemed to be sorting itself out; nothing moved forward. Not even the immense distance had brought me a glimmer of hope. Even though I had promised myself to be strong, to endure courageously and not surrender, I began to notice that salty, murky taste of saliva that precedes weeping.

Somehow I was able to hold back, to calm down and thereby halt the threat of succumbing. One step before descending into the void, some mechanism beyond my will kicked in and transported me via memory to a time far in the past.

There I was, with the same chestnut-colored hair, the same slender body, and two dozen fewer years, facing adverse circumstances that were nonetheless unable to knock me down. My promising college studies were truncated in their fourth year by an unexpected pregnancy, intolerant parents who were unable to accept the blow, and a sad emergency wedding. An immature counterpart as a husband. A freezing subterranean apartment as a home. A scrawny baby that cried inconsolably and all the uncertainty of the world before me. Times of mackerel sandwiches for dinner, cigarettes of dark tobacco, and lousy tap water. Poorly paying private classes and translations on the kitchen table seasoned with more imagination than exactitude; days short on sleep with lots of rushing, shortages, anxiety, and confusion. I didn't have a bank account; all I had was the unconscious strength provided by my twenty-one years, a recently born baby boy, and the closeness of the person I thought was going to be my life mate.

Suddenly, everything had turned upside down and now I was alone, no longer struggling to bring up that skinny crying little kid, nor his brother, who came into the world barely a year and a half later. I no longer had to fight for that young rash marriage to work out, to help my husband in his professional aspirations, to achieve my own career by studying at dawn with borrowed notes and a stove at my feet. To pay for babysitters, day care, baby food, and a thirdhand Renault 5, to finally move to a rented apartment with central heating and two terraces. To prove to the world that my existence was not a failure. All this had been left behind and in this new chapter only I was left.

Impelled by the sudden lucidity that the memories had brought, I removed my hands from my face, and as my eyes grew accustomed to the cold ugly light, I rolled my shirtsleeves up past my elbows.

"Greater heights than this have been scaled," I whispered.

I had no idea about where to start organizing the disastrous legacy of Professor Andres Fontana, but I rushed headlong to work as if my entire life depended on the task.

Chapter 3

The first few days were the worst: submerged in the storeroom, trying to find a thread of congruity amid the chaos. Dozens of notepads were scattered among folios, reams of yellowing papers, and countless letters and cards. Everything stacked on shelves that risked collapsing or in ramshackle piles on the verge of toppling over.

After the first week I gained a certain confidence, and despite the snail's pace I began to negotiate that shapeless mess more efficiently, giving each document a quick glance to ascertain its contents and assign it a corresponding category according to my rudimentary organizational scheme: literary criticism, prose and poetry, history of Spain, history of California, and personal correspondence.

I'd begin work before nine a.m. and wouldn't stop until past five o'clock in the afternoon, with a short lunch break in some corner of the campus cafeteria when I would absentmindedly leaf through the university's newspaper. Usually it was rather late, toward two o'clock, when the cleaning crew would begin their perfunctory mopping of the floor and when only a few students were left scattered among the tables, some busy reading, others dozing off, still others wearily underlining in their books before finishing off their lunch.

I finally met Luis Zarate, the department chairman, one day when

I needed scissors to cut the tape from some bundles and mine were nowhere to be found, lost no doubt beneath some pile or other. Unable to locate Fanny to borrow a pair, I went to Rebecca's office, where I bumped into her and Zarate going over a course syllabus together. She, seated, speaking deliberately. He, standing beside her with hands leaning on the table as he bent over the syllabus, seemed to be listening to her attentively. My first glance registered a slender, well-groomed man of roughly my own age with brown hair and rimless eyeglasses, wearing dark gray pants, a black shirt, and a light-gray tie.

Once we had exchanged pleasantries, he invited me to accompany him back to his office. I inwardly regretted the deplorable state of my attire. My overly casual clothes, resistant to grime and cobwebs, would hardly make a professional impression on the person who was in effect my new boss. I looked dusty and disheveled, with a ponytail that could barely restrain my hair and dust-covered hands that I was forced to rub against the seat of my trousers before extending one to greet him.

"Well, I'm delighted to welcome you to our department, Professor Perea," he said, pointing to an armchair in front of his desk. "Or Blanca, if you'll allow me," he added while taking his seat.

His cordiality sounded authentic and his Spanish excellent: polite, modulated, with a slight accent that I was not quite able to pinpoint.

"Blanca, please," I agreed. "I'm equally delighted, and thankful to have been accepted."

"It's always a pleasure to receive visiting professors, although we're not used to having many from Spain. So your visit pleases us all the more."

I took advantage of that initial exchange of pleasantries to take a quick look around his office. Adjustable steel table lamp, modern prints, books and papers enviably in order. Without being altogether minimalist, it came quite close to it.

"For us," he went on, "it has been very gratifying to strike this deal with SAPAM to subsidize your work. Any initiative that involves attracting research from other institutions is always welcome. Although we weren't expecting someone with your background . . ."

His words put me on guard. I did not want to discuss the reasons that had pushed me to apply for this position so far from my area of expertise. I had no intention of being sincere, nor did I feel like inventing an awkward lie. So I chose to change the course of the conversation instead.

"SAPAM and the department have been incredibly efficient in making all of the arrangements, and here I am, already immersed in my work. Santa Cecilia is turning out to be a very pleasant change of scenery to finish out the momentous year of 1999. Perhaps the world will come to an end as well while I'm here," I said, trying to be clever.

To my relief, he smiled at my clumsy joke.

"What paranoia, this business of the end of the millennium! And in Spain all this madness must be affecting you all the more so now that the euro is about to become the new currency. How is it progressing, by the way? When will the old pesetas cease to function?"

The reasons behind my applying for this fellowship turned out to be of less interest to the department chairman than a superficial conversation about recent events in my country on the threshold of the new century. We talked of Spain in general, of the situation in Spanish universities, of everything and nothing. In the interim, I moved out of harm's way and, while I was at it, took advantage of the chance to have a thorough look at him.

I figured he must be three or four years younger than myself; recently turned forty, no doubt, but no older than that. There were the unmistakable signs of gray streaks at his temples and small creases at the corners of his eyes, which did not in any way diminish his appeal. He was the son of a Chilean psychologist, he explained, and a trauma surgeon from Santander who had been living in the U.S. for a long while but with whom he didn't seem to have much contact.

Luis Zarate clearly enjoyed talking, and I selfishly took advantage of the situation, giving him free rein. The less I had to explain about my own matters, the better. I was already familiar with his academic career, but discovered that he had been in Santa Cecilia only a couple of years and that his intention was to leave as soon as possible in pursuit of a position at some prestigious East Coast university. To my relief, after having spent more than half an hour chatting with him, I was convinced that this specialist in postmodern cultural studies couldn't have cared less about the yellowing bits of paper belonging to an old professor who'd been dead for three decades. Thus I would be able to continue working at ease without having to give explanations to anyone.

I was already in the hallway, about to make my way back to the storeroom, when, as if not quite willing to let me go, he called me back from his office door.

"I think it would be a good idea to organize a little get-together to introduce you to the rest of our department colleagues." He did not wait for my answer. "At noon on Thursday, for instance," he added. "Next door in the conference room."

Why not? It would do me good to climb out of my hole and socialize a little, I thought. It would also be a convenient way to put names to some of the faces I had been coming across in hallways and on campus.

The proposed lunch date finally rolled around. The conference room was quite large, with several windows, a bookcase full of old leather-bound books, and a collection of photos displayed on the wall. The university's catering service had prepared a cold buffet of meats, cheeses, fruit, and salads. Hardly anyone sat down: we all served ourselves standing, chatting away in small groups that varied according to the flow of conversation.

The department chairman kept pulling me from one group of professors to the next. There were Americanized Hispanics, Hispanicized Americans. Chicano literature professors; experts on Vargas Llosa, Galdos, and Elena Poniatowska; specialists in comparative linguistics and Andalusian poetry as well as enthusiasts of all things mestizo or alternative. The great majority I knew by sight. Rebecca was also at the luncheon, participating in conversations while overseeing the event with a keen eye. Fanny, meanwhile, alone in a corner, feasted on roast beef and Diet Pepsi, absorbed in her own world as she chewed away industriously.

The lunch lasted exactly sixty minutes. At one o'clock sharp the diaspora took place, whereupon a couple of students dressed in blue and yellow—the university's colors—began to clear out the leftovers. When almost everyone had gone, I was finally able to center my attention on a wall that was covered with photos.

Some were older, others more recent, individual and group photos, in color and black-and-white. The great majority commemorated institutional events; the conferring of diplomas, graduation speeches, conferences. I was in search of some familiar face among them when I noticed Rebecca approaching me.

"The history of your new home, Blanca," she said with a trace of nostalgia.

She fell silent for a couple of seconds, then pointed to four different photos.

"And here you have him: Andres Fontana."

A strong, energetic bearing. Dark eyes, intelligent beneath bushy eyebrows. An abundant head of curly hair combed back. A thick beard and a serious expression when he was apparently listening to someone. A man of flesh and blood despite the motionless images.

I was overwhelmed. With a pang in my stomach, I backed away from the wall.

I needed space, distance, air. For the first time since my arrival I decided to give myself a break.

Without even going back to the storeroom to turn off the lights, I wandered around Santa Cecilia, discovering places I'd never encountered before. Streets through which an isolated car or a solitary student on a bicycle appeared once in a while; deserted residential neighborhoods; remote areas I'd never set foot in, until my erratic steps took me to a unique spot: a large expanse of woodland, a mass of pine trees ascending a slope and disappearing into the horizon. By that time of the day, close to dusk, the effect was overwhelming. Though it lacked the drama of many picture-perfect sites that could be captured within the confines of a postcard, it possessed a rare atmosphere of solace and serenity.

I soon realized, however, that this piece of paradise was in imminent danger. An immense billboard full of photos of apparently happy faces and lettering a foot and a half high announced the area's new fate: LUXURY SHOPPING CENTER. EXCITING SHOPPING, DINING AND ENTERTAINMENT, FAMILY FUN.

Nailed on sticks at the foot of the billboard like so many tiny Davids before a looming Goliath were several homemade placards repeating the word "NO." No to the exciting shopping, no to the specialty stores, no to that type of family fun. I recalled seeing several editorials and letters in the university newspaper objecting to the construction of a new mall.

I moved away from the billboard and decided it was time to return home.

On my way back I stopped to buy something for dinner at Meli's Market, which was on a side street off the main square. Despite the place's apparent lack of pretense—rustic wooden floors, bare-brick walls, and the air of an old establishment out of a Western—its numerous delicacies and organic products labeled with elegant simplicity were evidence that it catered to sophisticated palates and deep pockets, not students and middle-income families with tight budgets that had to stretch to the end of the month.

With my arrival at Santa Cecilia, I'd left behind most of my old routines, including the large bimonthly shopping spree in a superstore with a deafening public-address system, discounts in the frozen sections, and three-for-two special offers. Like so many other things in my life, the shopping carts overflowing with part-skim milk and dozens of rolls of toilet paper had become a thing of the past.

Closing time was nearing and the last clients were hurriedly making their purchases. The employees, dressed in long black aprons, seemed anxious to put an end to the day's work. In the cheese section I decided, without much thought, to go for a chunk of Parmesan. Then I added a can of dried tomatoes in olive oil to my basket along with a bag of arugula before heading to the bakery section, figuring there wouldn't be much choice left. Suddenly I felt a tap on my left shoulder, little more than a grazing of two fingers and a slight pressure. In the middle of my absurd dilemma—a small round loaf of bread with bits of olive or a baguette topped with sesame seeds—I looked up, and to my surprise there stood Rebecca Cullen.

As we greeted each other, someone appeared behind her back. A tall, distinctive man with slightly long, grayish-blond hair and a beard that contrasted with his tan skin. He was holding a bottle of wine, and the reading glasses perched on his nose suggested that he'd been scrutinizing its label just a couple of seconds earlier.

"My friend Daniel Carter, an old professor from our department" was all Rebecca volunteered.

He offered me a large hand and I noticed he was wearing a sizable black digital watch on his right wrist, something I associated more with athletes than university types. I held my hand out and readied a greeting in English that I never uttered, a standard greeting I'd been repeating since my arrival: "How do you do, a pleasure meeting you." But he took the lead. Surprisingly, disconcertingly, that athletic-looking American, almost juvenile despite his obvious maturity, took my hand in his while regarding me with blue eyes, and burst into flawless Spanish, throwing me completely off guard.

"Rebecca has spoken to me about your presence in Santa Cecilia, dear Blanca, of your mission to rescue the legacy of our old professor. I was looking forward to meeting you, as lovely ladies of regal Spanish lineage do not abound in these remote places."

I couldn't help laughing at the stilted flair in his parody of an old-fashioned gallant scene, as well as the hidden warmth behind his spontaneity—not to mention the soothing sensation, after weeks of obscure seclusion, of hearing an accent so familiar and impeccable in someone so alien to my universe.

"I've spent much of my life in your country," he added, without letting go of my hand. "Great affections, wonderful Spanish friends, Andres Fontana among them. More than half a lifetime coming and going from here to there—great moments. What a place. I always go back—always."

We hardly had the chance to continue talking: the shutters were being pulled down and the lights turned off; they were expected for dinner someplace, while an empty apartment awaited me. As we headed toward the cashiers and then outside, I was able to learn only that he was a professor at the University of California at Santa Barbara who was enjoying a year's sabbatical and that his friendship with Rebecca had temporarily brought him back to Santa Cecilia.

"I'm still not sure how long I'll be here," he concluded while holding the door to let us through. "I'm finishing a book and it's good for me to keep away from daily distractions. Turn-of-the-century Spanish prose; I'm sure you're familiar with the whole crew. We'll see how it comes along."

We said good-bye on the street with a vague promise of meeting up on some other occasion and took off in opposite directions as the first stars became visible.

On reaching my apartment I was again overwhelmed by that uncomfortable and hard-to-define feeling that I'd been dragging along like a deadweight ever since the department luncheon. I slept poorly that night, restless and preoccupied with Andres Fontana. Seeing a photo of the actual man, his face and his forceful presence, had somehow destroyed all my preconceived ideas, creating a new anxiety. Toward dawn my dreams were filled with vintage photographs among which I tried to identify a face as the images began dissolving and then disappeared.

· · ·

I woke up thirsty and hot, my head throbbing. Daylight was advancing timidly. I threw open the window, seeking fresh air. Hardly any cars could be heard and only the silhouettes of a few joggers broke the stillness with their rhythmic pace. I grabbed a glass mechanically, turned on the faucet, and filled it. As the water ran down my throat, the previous day's images came back to my mind. Then and only then did I understand.

I had approached my task from the wrong angle. After my self-imposed discipline of long hours locked up in the storeroom, struggling before a ton of old documents, something was still lacking. I had been dealing with Andres Fontana's papers as if they were so many boxes of nuts and bolts, turning my task into a disrespectful invasion of a human being's privacy.

Between the archival material and the conference room's old snapshots I began to see something more than a tenuous common thread. The connection linking the legacy's contents and the four images of the dead professor, whose name was all I knew at that point, grew sharp and powerful.

I could no longer confine myself to simply classifying the work Professor Fontana had left behind upon his death. My task had to be approached from a human stance, up close. I had to make an effort to grasp the person hidden behind the words—someone whose soul I had until then failed to seek out. Seeing those photos the day before made me realize that I had handled my new assignment with a coldness verging on hostility, as if I were dealing with a mere commercial product. Absorbed by my own miseries, forcing myself to work compulsively to evade my problems, I hardly bothered to take into account the human being hidden among the pages of his legacy: crouching between the lines, concealed within sentences, suspended amid the strokes of each word.

My job had suddenly become clear to me: to rescue and bring to life the buried legacy of a man who had been long ago forgotten.

Chapter 4

His father was a miner, basically illiterate. His mother served as a maid to a wealthy family and was able to string a few letters together and add and subtract with moderate speed. Her name was Simona and she had given birth to Andres at the age of thirty-seven, after more than fifteen years of infertility and the consecutive births of her first two daughters and a stillborn child who had been quickly buried and virtually forgotten. They lived in a village south of La Mancha in a dwelling known as a barrack, two small connecting rooms with dirt floors and no running water or electricity. The untimely arrival of that last child was received with little joy: another mouth to feed, a little less space. Simona had continued to work until the afternoon prior to delivery; the luster of her lady's floor made no allowances for an aging maid's pregnancies. The following day, mother and son were back at Doña Manolita's house: she, mopping the patios and feeding the furnace with coal; the baby boy, wrapped in rags and tucked in a basket in a corner of the kitchen.

Doña Manolita must have been fifty-something at the time. A decade earlier she had been a rich spinster, partially lame and ugly, and had fallen for one of the workers from the oil mills that she'd inherited from her late father. And so Ramon, the swarthy young man with broad shoulders and a luminous smile who worked for her during the olive season, became Don Ramon Otero at the age of twenty-one as a result of the whimsical wish of his patroness. No one had foreseen such a fate for that handsome, quick-witted lad who each autumn fled his mountain village's harsh winters along with his brothers in search of work as a seasonal laborer in other parts of the country. But Doña Manolita liked younger men, all the more so if they were vigorous, with an impudent stare and skin the color of a cinnamon stick. Winter nights were cold and she hadn't the slightest intention of becoming the richest woman in the cemetery, so with the shamelessness of someone fully aware of her power, she made brazen advances to Ramon. First came the stares, afterwards the encounters, grazings, and lewd exchanges hidden behind seemingly trivial words. In less than three weeks they were frolicking on the three fluffy mattresses of her mahogany bed in their first carnal encounter, which turned out to be immensely gratifying to them both, although for different reasons. To her, because she had finally calmed her lust with the youth's muscular body, which had been driving her crazy for weeks. To the young man, because never before in his miserable life had he known the intense pleasure provided by acts as simple as brushing one's naked skin against cotton sheets, walking barefoot on a carpet, or submerging one's weary body in a hot bath.

To the satisfaction of both parties the meetings lasted for months, although Ramon was convinced that such an incompatible relationship would be terminated once the season came to an end, and he'd have to return to his native soil. His prediction, however, quickly vanished one stormy night when he was immersed in Doña Manolita's porcelain bathtub. As she was pouring pitchers of steaming water on his back, she proposed marriage. Since he was a clever kid and knew full well that hunger is the best sauce, he quickly assessed the benefits of the transaction: to become the dependent consort of a rich woman, no matter how withered and malformed she might look, was certainly more profitable than a wandering life of felling pine trees in his native mountains or harvesting and pressing olives on other people's farms. He accepted her proposal swiftly.

The unexpected news caused an equal measure of rejoicing and envy among his brothers and fellow workers, and triggered unrelenting gossip in the village. But it didn't bother the couple in the least. Doña Manolita had no need to explain her arrangements to anyone but herself, so after a short ceremony in the Church of the Assumption they became husband and wife without any reproaches for their twenty-three-year difference in age.

Besides her never having to sleep alone again and his never having to break his back working from dawn to dusk, two other things became evident before long, just as the neighbors had foretold. First was that they did not have any offspring. And second was that the young husband—now Don Ramon—began to be unfaithful to his wife with any pretty girl that crossed his path, just as he had on the very first day of their engagement. Because of such realities, Doña Manolita adopted the approach of accepting in her house the presence of her maids' children while barring any young lady eager to join her domestic staff. Of course, other people's children never replaced those she was unable to have, just as the absence of women of legal age did not dissuade her horny husband from having dozens of extramarital adventures beyond their now common hearth.

The maid Simona's son was baptized with the name Andres, that of the lady's late father, who had bequeathed her a fortune along with a snub-nosed face and some other unattractive features. She was god-mother to Andres and gave the child a Mother of Grace gold medal, which the infant's father promptly sold that same afternoon to invest the profits in liquor. Perhaps Doña Manolita saw something special in that dark-complexioned child who a year later began to wander about the house on his own, or perhaps she was simply getting old; the fact is that she displayed a solicitude toward him that, without being remotely maternal, must have come close to the love of a bored and grumpy great-aunt who was nonetheless affectionate. With remarkable insensitivity to the miner family's financial straits, the lady got in the habit of making expensive gifts that neither the boy nor his mother was able to appreciate for their true worth: velvet suits so that he could accompany her to noon Mass, a small pianola, a patent-leather-covered album for stamp collecting, and even a sailor's cap that would have made him the laughingstock of his neighborhood.

It was of little use to Simona that on occasion her son donned those ostentatious garments while on a daily basis he wore rope-soled sandals and clothes full of patches—just as she found it useless that Doña Manolita insisted on teaching him to use silver cutlery at the table when in his poor home they all shared the same gruel, bringing the spoonfuls directly from the common pan to their mouths. Doña Manolita never did take care of the boy's real needs, just as she never seemed to be conscious that each of the fancy things she ordered for him from the capital cost more than the weekly salary of both his parents. But Simona never said a word about her lady's whimsical behavior or the cruel absurdity of her acts. She simply let her carry on and, at the end of each workday, usually around dusk, took her son by the hand; then, chilled to the bone and walking in silence amid the dampness, they returned to their miserable dwelling for the night.

As soon as Andres turned six, however, the situation changed. He started attending one of the Ave Maria schools for the poor, and before long both he and his mother began to appreciate the most positive aspects of that tutelage: the privilege of reading. Simona was not an intelligent woman, but for decades she had observed how the rich lived and was smart enough to realize that, besides money and property, education and culture mattered in that milieu. This was why, when Doña Manolita began to furnish her son with children's books that otherwise would have been out of his reach, Simona recognized that her lady was finally contributing something valuable.

By the age of fourteen, Andres had given up his schooling and was busy running errands for a local packaging company. His father insisted that it was time for him to go down into the mine: he could not conceive of any other occupation for his son except continuing in his footsteps. Simona, on the other hand, tried to postpone for as long as she could that sad fate she feared was inevitable. When he turned fifteen, Doña Manolita gave him *The Treasure of Youth,* an encyclopedia for youngsters that immediately became his only window to the larger world. For his sixteenth birthday he did not get anything because his godmother was on the verge of death. She passed away on Christmas Eve 1929, and her husband was, naturally, the beneficiary of her will.

To everyone's surprise, however, she left a handwritten letter addressed to Simona and her son, and another one to a man named Eladio de la Mata. Without any gratuitous display of affection, in the first she stipulated a fixed income in the name of her godson, exclusively devoted to his education, the conditions of which were clearly spelled out. If he were to accept them, the youngster would move to Madrid, where he would live as a guest in the house of the caretaker of a building belonging to her on Calle Princesa. He would then have to prepare for the baccalaureate exam and, if he were to pass, enroll in the university, where he'd pursue the degree of his choice. Don Ramon Otero would take on all the expenses on account of his inheritance. If Andres never attended university, there would be no possible way of receiving compensation either in the form of hard cash or by any other means. The ironclad proposal left no room for interpretation other than getting the boy as far away as possible from the miserable future that awaited him extracting coal from the depths of a mine. The objective of the offer was, in the words of Doña Manolita, to turn the lad into what back then was referred to as a useful man.

That enlightened despotism left Andres and his mother full of hope and the father and husband extremely angry. Unable to decipher the meaning of such an unexpected stipulation, the miner cursed his foul luck while he damned the deceased lady without realizing that by behaving in such a manner he was only confirming her prediction. And thus, while continuing to heap insults upon both the lady and all her ancestors, he got so plastered that he ended up passing out in the middle of the street and two mining blasters from the North Well hauled him off home.

Simona disagreed with her husband and confronted him with the same energy with which she'd cleaned other people's homes since childhood. But the miner Fontana remained obstinate, and each time his wife tried to make him understand the benefits of the situation, she received more blows than understanding. So she decided to do the smart thing instead. Without saying a word to anyone, on the last night of the year she put together a small bundle consisting of a change of clothes and half a loaf of bread with cheese, and waited. At three o'clock in the morning on New Year's Day her husband once again returned home totally plastered. When she finally was able to put him to bed, she sat down on a wicker chair, moved closer to the charcoal brazier, and remained staring at the coals, absorbed in thought.

An hour later she woke up Andres and quietly ordered him to get dressed. Seized by the early-morning frost, they picked up their pace on their way to the station. Once there, Simona handed Andres the envelope with papers and money that she'd received from Don Ramon Otero and hugged him with all the force of her skinny body. And so, at 5:10 on the morning of January 1, 1930, Andres Fontana took the mail train to an alien world from which he would not return. He never saw his mother again.

Simona made her way back home wrapped in her black tattered shawl, carrying in her bosom all the grief of the world. But she didn't shed a tear. There were none left in her sad, exhausted eyes.

Chapter 5

The Mediodia railway station of Madrid with its majestic wrought-iron structure dazzled the young Fontana. He was unaware that the station had also served as the staging point for the Spanish troops' deployment to the African War or of the tumultuous welcoming of the toreador Joselito's dead body ten years earlier in the Plaza de Talavera. But then, the young man was unaware of practically everything. For starters, he found it difficult to get out of that place full of steam, noise, and a swarm of people loaded with luggage who were moving hurriedly between platforms.

He wore a shabby corduroy suit and an old cap, and at the age of sixteen had already surpassed in shoulder width many a hardened man who on a daily basis descended into the mines in the village he'd left behind. In his left hand he carried the parcel that his mother had put together for him, now lighter without the bread and cheese he'd eaten on the train. His right hand in his pants pocket was clutching the envelope that Don Ramon Otero had given Simona the previous day, which contained the caretaker's address, a little money for his initial expenses, and the letter that would clear his path to knowledge. The rest of the allowances would be duly given to him by Señora Antonia, the caretaker in whose house he would reside. How the money from Doña Manolita would get to that woman was not his place to know.

Following the brisk pace of the pedestrians, he finally managed to leave the station and penetrate the immense unknown city. There was plenty of sun, but it was bitterly cold. He pulled down his cap, raised his coat lapels, and took off without the slightest idea of where he was headed. Driven by his young legs and an equal measure of anxiety and euphoria, he soon found his way.

It took him three hours to reach his destination, not out of necessity, but rather because he kept stopping, amazed by the wonders displayed before his eyes: the grandeur of the buildings, the speed of automobiles, the opulence of storefronts, the elegance of women trotting along in their high heels on the brand-new sidewalks of the Gran Via. Finally, following the directions given to him by some passersby, he managed to reach number 47 Calle Princesa, located near a statue of Don Agustin de Argüelles, a nineteenth-century politician.

Señora Antonia turned out to be a smallish woman with a lilting voice, much younger than he had imagined, married to a militant construction worker of the then-illegal CNT (National Confederation of Labor) by the name of Marcelino. Their entire family consisted of two boys, Joaquin and Angelito, both under ten years old. The room that Andres was to share with them in the caretaker's place was dark and rickety, with a twenty-five-watt bare bulb hanging from the ceiling and a few furnishings cowering near the flaking walls: a nickel-plated bed, a dilapidated closet, and a butcher block table that would serve as a desk. Its small window opened onto an interior patio, where Señora Antonia washed and hung the clothes, and which contained a few potted geraniums, a couple of canaries in their cages, and the primitive toilet that the family shared with a cabinetmaker neighbor. Daily personal washup took place at the kitchen sink; for hygiene of greater scope there was a zinc washtub.

In the following days Marcelino, who at the time was unemployed, devoted himself to showing Andres around the neighborhood to familiarize him with his new surroundings. In less than a week he had already introduced Andres to most of the neighbors; moreover, being a staunch anarchist and an indefatigable speaker, he readily updated Andres on recent historical events. Andres, however, fascinated by his immediate reality, didn't much care. In fact, it would barely register on him toward the end of that month of January 1930 that when King Alfonso XIII accepted Prime Minister Primo de Rivera's resignation, General Berenguer was put in charge of forming a new government, and the people of Madrid—poor, ignorant, and more agitated than ever—demanded a radical change from their leaders.

Marcelino also accompanied Andres on his first visit to the Cardinal Cisneros Institute, where, according to Doña Manolita's instructions, he would obtain the high school diploma that would in turn open the door to the university. His shortcomings in matters of education were still overwhelming at the time. Whatever he had stored in his head came from a few short years of rudimentary schooling, from reading books that his godmother had furnished capriciously, and from the *Treasure of Youth* encyclopedia that he'd passionately devoured in the previous few months. Thanks to the latter, he had amassed a little knowledge in a diverse and somewhat picturesque number of fields: world geography, applied technology, a little international folklore. He lacked, however, a systematic education in basic subjects such as mathematics, grammar, Latin, or French; he was ignorant of the most fundamental ethical and social concepts, and didn't have the slightest notion about good study habits. Nonetheless, his situation was significantly better than average considering Spain's dire educational predicament during the first decades of the twentieth century, when more than sixty percent of the population was illiterate, and teachers—scarce and often lacking proper training—received miserly salaries.

The system's shortcomings didn't bother Andres in the least on that cold morning when he walked down Calle de los Reyes in the company of Marcelino to cross the threshold of the Cardinal Cisneros Institute for the very first time. With the letter that Doña Manolita had left upon her death addressed to the director as a safe-conduct pass, they followed the school clerk with reverential silence as she led them down a wide corridor filled with winter light. Advancing with their laborers' caps in hand, trying not to make noise with their footsteps, they became increasingly aware of the incongruity of their humble appearance in that erudite place.

They didn't have to wait for long. A bony bald man came to fetch them from the bench where the school clerk had contemptuously directed them. They both rose as if triggered by a spring; the gentleman barely smiled in greeting. It was Don Eladio de la Mata himself.

He had them step into his office, which was littered with books, framed degrees, and portraits of other men, equally prominent, who had preceded him in the position. After reading the letter addressed to him by Doña Manolita, he listened attentively to the youth's statement and with brief but cutting gestures prevented the talkative Marcelino from interrupting him several times to contribute his irrelevant observations. Next he asked Andres a few questions, which in his opinion the young man answered with a maturity and seriousness not in accordance with his origins and age.

In conclusion, with modulated diction and perfect clarity, Don Eladio explained the principles that Andres needed to follow if indeed he was inclined to complete his studies and enter the university. He spoke of trigonometry, declensions, and commitment; of poets, chemical formulas, and persistence; of equations, syntax, and integrity. The young man listened in rapture, absorbing the words one by one and mentally noting all the names and concepts. When he departed from that office half an hour later, both the director and he himself felt that the goal was attainable. Poor Marcelino, meanwhile, suspected that something fundamental eluded him in life.

They left the school in silence and wandered the nearby streets. Marcelino, in front, unusually quiet, advanced with long strides, his hands in his pockets, and Andres followed, picking up the pace, trying not to lose him while still savoring Don Eladio's words. They entered a tavern next to the Mostenses market. Elbowing the crowd, they made their way up to the bar and Marcelino ordered two tumblers of cheap wine. As they drank wordlessly, enveloped by the din, Andres couldn't figure out what was the matter with Marcelino, what the reason was for his uncharacteristic quietness. He soon found out. The anarchist bricklayer took the last gulp of his drink, set it down with a bang on the counter, wiped his mouth with his jacket sleeve, and, eyes fixed intently on the kid, asked him to teach him to read and write.

From that day onwards, a phase began in Andres's life in which weeks and months melted into a confused mass of nonstop study locked up in his room. He slept the minimum and ate only when Señora Antonia forced him to, sharing the family's stew or fried eggs. He made an effort to participate in their conversations, pay attention to the news that Marcelino brought back from the street, and laugh at the boys' funny remarks. He'd try, but his mind was far away, ruminating on the Pythagorean theorem, considering the periodic table, reciting fragments of the *Aeneid*: *At regina gravi iamdudum saucia cura* . . .

His godmother's monthly allowance enabled him to live without too many hardships. Besides providing him with the indispensable tools—pencils, pens, ink—it allowed him to treat himself to certain luxuries on his quest to further his newfound knowledge: an atlas of Spain and its provinces, a laminated set of diagrams of the human body, a small blackboard. He even made a present to his landlady, invited Marcelino to a tavern, and handed some spare change to the kids for them to buy a cone of roasted chickpeas or a lollypop from La Habana.

During the time it took him to complete high school, things happened around him that would change the history of his country for good—things that he, with his thirst for knowledge, would have hardly understood had it not been for Marcelino's overflowing verbosity. Still eager in his resolve, the bricklayer was slowly learning to read and write near the brazier each night, immersed in his primer.

They celebrated their first Christmas together toasting with soda water and cheap wine to a happy and peaceful 1931. And although the year was not a calm one, they did regard as fortunate the changes that took place barely a few months later with the king's exile and the arrival of the Second Republic.

On the twenty-third of May 1932 the son of the humble maid and the illiterate miner, neatly combed, wearing a tie and showing no apparent signs of nervousness, passed his pre-university entry exam with ease and before a foreboding tribunal. Doña Manolita would have been proud to see that her pupil had satisfactorily carried out her plan. From the house of Señora Consuelo, the sturdy Asturian who lived in the second-floor apartment on the right, a long-distance call was put through to give Simona the news. She took the call in Don Ramon Otero's house: she was soaked with sweat from busily ironing her master's shirts. Deeply moved and unable to utter a coherent word in the unfathomable distance of the telephone lines, the poor woman was only able to repeat again and again, "My son, my son, my son."

Chapter 6

As stipulated in the will, the next step in Andres Fontana's life was the university. In the early 1930s, the University of Madrid still lacked a common nucleus and had numerous buildings scattered throughout the capital, most of them quite old if not downright obsolete. The University City was still in its construction phase, immersed in a long process that had begun in 1927, driven by King Alfonso XIII's goal of endowing it with a space similar to American ones, where integrated planning, functional architecture, and extensive areas devoted to sports and recreation would be a priority.

The birth of the Second Republic and Alfonso XIII's sudden exile did not slow down the project—quite the contrary: it gathered momentum but was now forced to eliminate any inclination toward grandiosity and excess. When Andres began his first course, the humanities were taught in an old, ramshackle building on Calle San Bernardo.

The same perseverance with which he managed to succeed at his baccalaureate exam guided the young man in his university studies. He excelled to such an extent that in his third year, Professor Enrique Fernandez de la Hoz, lecturer in historical grammar, proposed that he be granted a fellowship to help teach the Spanish courses for foreigners that would take place the following semester. He accepted the offer without even weighing the full consequences of the commitment.

Spreading the Spanish language was one of the activities of the Board for the Expansion of Studies, with lecturers sent year after year to universities in a number of countries and courses organized for foreign students and professors. Andres's affiliation with that program began in January 1935 and lasted until the end of March. He participated in conversation sessions, acted as a companion on visits and excursions, and attempted to solve any problems that arose among the group of American professors, from addressing language misunderstandings to finding a doctor at an ungodly hour to simply making the rounds of the most picturesque taverns in Madrid.

Andres was impressed by everything about those strangers. Their unflagging energy in capturing the simplest scenes with their modern cameras, be it a cat on a roof, a stone coat of arms, or an old woman in mourning selling eggs from a wicker basket hanging from her arm; the ease with which they spent money; the bright, almost thunderous colors of their clothes; those white-toothed smiles. Through them he learned to smoke his first filtered American cigarette and dance to the rhythm of swing with a Valkyrie from Detroit in the Hotel Palace's ballroom. He was moved, along with them, by the Roman aqueduct in Segovia and Velazquez's painting *Las Meninas*; he tasted the thick chocolate of La Mallorquina for the very first time; he taught the visitors typical expressions as well as how to drink wine out of an earthenware jug. Far from simply being a faithful guide for those three months, he also turned out to be of great help to those insatiable foreigners in practicing their Spanish once classes were concluded. He corrected their pronunciation of the letters *j* and *z*, clarified their subjunctives, proofread their essays, and, in short, made sure their stay turned out to be pleasant and fruitful.

Several weeks before they returned to the States, one of the professors—Sarah Bulton, the slender blonde who always wore pants and smoked nonstop, leaving a perpetual rim of scarlet on the filters—informed him that her university had set up a yearly program for bringing in foreign conversation assistants. If he was interested, she could recommend him. In the event that he were to accept, besides teaching his own language, he would have the opportunity to take advantage of his year in America to learn English and continue with his education by enrolling in courses relevant to his major: linguistics, American history, comparative literature. At the end of the course he could return to his career in Madrid having seen a bit of the world and having acquired new experiences and acquaintances.

The Americans returned to their country toward the end of March loaded with beautiful fans, typical pottery, and espadrilles, unaware that they left behind an Andres Fontana whose perspective on the world had been altered for good. He would go to bed turning over the proposal in his mind and would wake up the following morning the same way. Leaving his mining village to move to the capital had been a big step, but accessible; crossing the ocean to stay at an American university seemed more like leaping over a chasm. Immense, but fascinating.

The spring of 1935 settled in calmly over Madrid as Andres prepared for the last stretch of his course work and impatiently awaited news from the program in Michigan. Four weeks after the Americans left, he received an envelope in the mail that Señora Antonia handed him on his return from the university. Despite the great anxiousness he felt on seeing it, he took it to his room, opened it, and pulled out the letter, sitting down to read it unhurriedly at the foot of his bed. It had been sent by the head of the Department of Classical and Romance Languages, who informed him that, given the highly favorable report that he had received from Professor Bulton, he had the pleasure of extending a formal invitation to take advantage of a grant within the Hispanic studies program at the university. Andres's responsibilities would include teaching fifteen hours of classes weekly and participating in something called the Spanish Club on Friday afternoons. In exchange, Andres would live on campus, receiving a small stipend for his expenses, and could enroll in as many courses as he wished, tuition free. If need be, the university could pay fifty percent of the trip's costs. His engagement would last for one academic year, beginning on September 1, 1935, and ending on May 31, 1936. The letter was written in perfect Spanish, neatly typewritten on ivory bond, and signed with an emphatic stroke by Richard J. Taylor, PhD, Chairman. They needed to have Andres's answer by the end of the month.

Andres refolded the letter and slipped it back into the envelope, placing it in his inside jacket pocket before sitting down to lunch with the family, trying to hide his nervousness amid the conversation. As soon as he finished eating, he left the house and walked around aimlessly. When he returned at dusk he'd resolved his dilemma, but didn't tell anyone, and went straight to bed without dinner. The following morning he solemnly informed Señora Antonia of his decision while she hung the freshly washed sheets on the patio wire. He wrote a letter to his mother for Don Ramon to read to her.

On July 14, 1935, Andres embarked from the port of Cadiz on the *Christopher Columbus,* where his berth was located on the lowest deck for that journey to an immense unknown country. He initially planned to return to Spain in the summer of the following year once his classes had concluded, but an invitation to collaborate on a summer course for high school teachers made him change plans and postpone his return until the beginning of August 1936. He thought that with the extra money from that course he would be able to buy some clothing and modern appliances to take home as gifts.

That small change of plans irremediably altered his destiny, for in one of history's cruel tricks, he never returned. He remained in America with a shrunken soul and a suitcase full of new clothes, half a dozen cartons of American cigarettes, and four portentous GE electric irons. Señora Antonia, his mother, and his sisters would have to continue to spend long years ironing the old-fashioned way.

The civil war changed his country forever. Madrid prepared itself for a hard resistance and its physiognomy was radically transformed. The statue of Don Agustin de Argüelles that had greeted him each morning on leaving his caretaker's apartment on Calle Princesa was removed so as not to hinder the movement of troops and vehicles. The Hotel Palace ballroom where he had danced, led by a blond knockout, became a field hospital. At the beginning of the conflict, all University City facilities were in an advanced stage of construction, with some already finished and operational. However, the fresh paint, shiny windows, and recently varnished writing desks wouldn't last long. The bloody war would reduce a proud university to rubble, crushing as well a large part of its scientific, artistic, and bibliographic heritage, and forcing numerous members of its faculty toward the abyss of exile. As soon as Madrid fell, that ambitious monarchic dream of a magnificent American-style campus was brutally wiped out and its buildings reduced to frightful skeletons. Of the forty thousand trees that had been planted, only the roots remained. The area containing classrooms was occupied by trenches; the laboratories, by parapets. Barricades were erected using encyclopedias, dictionaries, and sandbags; rifles and bodies were scattered throughout the lecture halls and libraries.

Thousands perished, among them Marcelino, who had fallen in the Hospital Clinico with a shattered skull, lying facedown on the floor and carrying in the left-hand pocket of his combat jacket a crumpled half-written letter. In his childish scrawl he'd begun formulating a greeting intended for a destination far across the ocean: "Dear Friend Andres, I hope this letter finds you in good health . . ."

Chapter 7

————————

With the help of several graduate students, I had transferred the first batch of Andres Fontana's legacy from the storeroom to my office, heaping the boxes and piles against the wall. I had the feeling that I was finally beginning to rescue him from darkness.

From then on, his profile began to take shape before me as I directed a more human focus on his life. Everything made more sense now: his letters, his movements, his correspondence. Thus the days rolled by as I proceeded on a firm footing—or so I thought—on the straight path toward reconstructing my life. Until an unexpected call at the beginning of October made me stumble. It was Alberto, once more shattering the harmony.

We hadn't spoken to each other since the summer, before I had learned through David of his imminent paternity. In fact, as soon as I found out, it was I who dug in my heels and refused any type of contact whatsoever. I chose to avoid him, knowing that it would be painful to be confronted with the crudeness of the circumstances, like throwing acid on an open wound. Most likely Alberto had also understood and decided not to continue calling in order to spare me further suffering. Or perhaps he didn't understand and simply forgot about me, immersed as he was in his vital new project in a refurbished loft with that young workmate who now was also his life mate.

It seemed a lifetime ago that Alberto and I had struggled so that he could take the examination to join the higher ranks of the civil service. For three grueling years we had made a coordinated effort with the aim of obtaining our objective. When we got married, neither of us had finished college. I was a semester and a half away, and he only had a couple of months to go. At the time we thought it wisest to concentrate our efforts on his professional career. Besides being a year ahead of me in the university, Alberto had a perfectly clear idea of what he wanted to do with his life: prepare for the public service exam as his father and brothers had. My future plans, on the other hand, were vaguer. In fact, they hardly existed. I liked languages, I liked books, I liked traveling. Undefined banalities, in short, with little hope of them soon materializing into some type of productive job that was moderately well paid. So Alberto, whose résumé was inferior to mine, devoted himself to studying. And I, meanwhile, put my humble aspirations aside and made sure our little family got ahead.

The success, naturally, was all his: he had prepared manically for the exam, obtaining his objective on the second round. Meanwhile, I neither took an exam, nor got any congratulations on passing, nor substituted professional garb for my old jeans and the thick wool sweaters that I knitted for myself on the run. But I did do other things that might have contributed, in at least a tangential way, to the triumph of my young and promising husband. While he memorized his laws and statutes locked in a room and wearing earplugs, isolated from everyday routines, I gestated, delivered, and brought up his two kids, and devoted myself night and day to making sure they didn't interrupt his much-needed quiet with their crying and childish protests. My life wore on, glued to a stroller carrying one baby while another baby was forming inside of me, through endless miles and hours seated on cold stone park benches. Later it was two boys that I led by the hand with their minute steps, picking them up from the ground when they fell, wiping their tears and noses, dealing with their cuts and bruises.

While my husband remained isolated in his legal bubble, ignorant of domestic trivialities such as paying the rent and gas bill or buying eggs, chicken, and laundry detergent, I worked. Tutoring students while the kids had their naps or crawled on the floor in between my students' legs; translating medical texts with one hand while with the other I bottle-fed David; typing up indecipherable manuscripts with Pablo stuck to my breast. So that Alberto could study as I would have liked to be able to study myself.

In spite of it all, and with great difficulty, I managed to establish a career. I had no choice, however, other than to put aside my desire of pursuing my PhD and instead find a respectable job in order to help Alberto in his noble effort to become a high-ranking state servant like his father—the father who, like my own, had thought it a dishonor to the family that we married so young and with a more-than-noticeable pregnancy rounding out my silhouette. The father who had never cared about his son, or his son's wife, until the *Official State Gazette* finally published his offspring's appointment. Only then did he seem to have forgotten our dishonor and once again opened the doors to his world. A little too late. But Alberto willingly returned to the fold with the same astonishing ease with which he later left me to start a new life with Eva. As if nothing had happened; as if there had never been a before.

When he passed his public examination, I was finally able to look for a steady full-time job. My experiences giving so many private classes to dozens of teenagers made me dismiss the idea of devoting myself to teaching high school. I was not cut out to explain the passive voice and relative clauses while struggling with the hormonal explosions of my students' awkward stage. So I pinned my hopes on a position at one of the new universities that had begun to flourish at the time, a spot in the lowest echelon of teaching. That is how I started out.

Eventually I finished my dissertation and found a stable job. We changed residences: from a small, poorly laid-out apartment in an old neighborhood, we moved to a much larger apartment, recently built and with two terraces. The kids grew up and started coming and going, and life went on. Until one day someone crossed paths with my husband and suddenly his wife and domestic world must have seemed terribly boring. Toward the beginning of the summer, when the heat began to beat down ferociously, Alberto finally announced that he was leaving home.

For the first time in my life I was aware of how fragile the things we believe to be permanent really are. When Alberto left that night, he took more than simply a suitcase with summer clothes. My confidence also left with him, my innocent belief that existence is something that can be planned and that my life would follow a unidirectional and preestablished path through the years. When he closed the door behind him, he left not only a woman with a broken heart but a woman irrevocably changed: a being who had thought herself strong had been turned into someone vulnerable, disbelieving, suspicious of the rest of the world.

And now his call once again caught me unawares. I realized that one of my children must have given him my number. His voice seemed alien in the distance. It sounded the same, but no longer transmitted that complicity we'd shared for almost twenty-five years living together. Now it was the voice of a thoughtful, distant man who spoke to me about lawyers, checking accounts, mortgages, and powers of attorney. I accepted his proposals unconditionally like an automaton, raising no objections and offering no alternatives. Deep down, I didn't care.

We'd never established boundaries in our property and our common life beyond those that the force of habit had imposed: which side of the bed we slept on, where we sat at the table, how we ordered the closet and our bathroom shelves. We'd started our life together with so few possessions that everything that came afterwards we ended up sharing: the two cars we'd drive to work, the apartment we lived in, and a little cottage on the beach. Alberto was now offering to put the apartment and cottage up for sale, pay off our outstanding mortgage, and divide the money between us. I wasn't against it or for it. As far as I was concerned, he could torch them.

After hanging up I remained motionless, my right hand still clutching the receiver as I tried to rewind and digest the conversation. A couple of seconds later the phone rang once again, abruptly breaking my solitude. I figured it must be him again; perhaps he'd forgotten to tell me something. The voice on the other end, however, wasn't his.

"Blanca, it's Luis Zarate. Are you free for lunch? I want to propose something to you. Or rather, two things."

. . .

I met the chairman at the entrance of Guevara Hall and together we headed toward the campus cafeteria. Although I tried to feign absolute normalcy, I still had Alberto's words buzzing in my ears. His voice had hit me with such unexpected intensity that, while the chairman spoke I only pretended to be listening, nodding every now and then as we served ourselves, when really my mind was lost in other directions. After we carried our trays over to a table, he brought up his reason for seeing me. I had no other choice than to return to reality and pay attention.

"The department has been invited to participate in a new program of continuing education courses," he said, attacking his salad conscientiously. "They've proposed that we offer a course that could be of general interest. I thought that your stay here could provide a good opportunity to prepare something related to contemporary Spain. Little is known of your country in these parts: practically all Hispanic influence comes from Mexico. That's why it might be interesting to design a course that shows a different aspect of Spanish, a course aimed at those interested in improving their command of the language while learning about present-day Spain. What do you think?"

In fact, I had no thoughts on the matter, neither that one nor any other he might have proposed. But I tried not to show it too blatantly. "It seems interesting," I lied while poking at a sad-looking mushroom on my plate.

"It wouldn't be like an academic seminar; it'd be something more informal," he resumed. "You could use newspaper articles, fragments of novels, any kind of material that you think might be useful. Even movies: I've got a good collection of videos. It would only take up a couple of afternoons a week and it doesn't pay badly."

"Who would the students be?"

"Professional adults; graduate students from other departments, perhaps; people connected to the university; Santa Cecilia residents interested in learning more."

Despite my lack of interest, the offer was tempting. I liked class-room work and to be able to design my own material. Besides, I had nothing special to do in the afternoons and the money would always come in handy. Still, I was unable to commit.

"Can I think about it?"

He looked at me with curious eyes, as if trying to figure out if I really did need time to make a decision or if in fact I didn't quite accept his proposal for some other reason.

"By all means, take your time. In any case, Rebecca has the exact details regarding the course requirements, if you wish further information. Well, and now here comes my second proposition, shorter and simpler."

I was convinced that no matter what he said, it wasn't going to elicit enthusiasm in me. But I pretended.

"Tell me about it."

"I don't know if you're aware that in this country between the fifteenth of September and the fifteenth of October we celebrate National Hispanic Heritage Month. I think it's something that goes back to the sixties, a tribute to the richness of the Hispanic contribution to our culture."

"What does it involve?"

"A bunch of different projects, from folklore festivities to political rallies. The university's committee on international relations, for its part, hosts a debate in which our department usually participates by contributing a representative to the panel. And it occurred to me that this year you could be that panel member."

"To speak on what?"

"Usually on anything and everything. It's quite a large panel, with seven or eight participants from different areas and fields related to the Hispanic world. Professors of Latin American history, international relations, political science; some visiting professor, a doctoral student—"

I didn't even let him finish.

"Would I put you in a tight spot if I said no?"

"Not at all; it was only an idea. I can propose it to some other colleague. Or even I could participate."

"I'm sorry, but I'm not at my best right now, if you know what I mean."

"Don't worry, it happens to all of us once in a while . . ."

We began to gather up our trays and left them on the trolleys, since it was time to get back. Luis kept talking the whole way, monopolizing the conversation without asking me anything or waiting for me to speak, aware that I had little desire for conversation.

"So you're in Rebecca's hands now; she'll give you all the details regarding the continuing-education course if in the end you're up for it. Do let me know, okay?" he said as we exited the elevator.

I forced a smile, muttered another okay in response to his, and turned to head back to my office. A hand on my wrist, however, stopped me before I began to walk. "If at some point you feel like talking, you know where to find me."

He turned down the hall toward the conference room and I went in search of Rebecca, still a little confused by that unexpected gesture. Perhaps I wasn't as alone as I thought. Perhaps the solution lay in filling my life with new affections instead of continuing to lament the lost ones.

I found her door closed, with a yellow Post-it reading: *I'm off to lunch,* so I returned to my office to continue working. Mulling over the course proposal, I still felt the unexpected hand of Luis Zarate on my skin. Then I remembered Alberto's call.

But I resisted once more. I forbade myself to think about his settlement proposal, forbade myself to ask how this could be happening to us.

Fontana's papers became my refuge once again. I plunged into them for a long time, using them as a painkiller, until the rapping on the door brought me out of my absorption. On looking up, I found Rebecca's ever-pleasing face.

"I know you wanted to see me, and I know what it's about. Here's all the information."

I asked her to sit down while I removed a bunch of documents from the only other seat in the small office apart from my old armchair.

"Have you ever been to Spain, Rebecca?" I asked without even knowing why. Perhaps because, despite our current friendliness, I'd never considered how much she actually knew of my country, or perhaps because at that moment I needed to have recourse to something that would give me a sense of warmth.

She was slow to answer my simple question, taking off her glasses first and then wiping the lens with the end of her shirttail.

"Once I was about to go, many years ago. I had a Spanish friend, you know? A great friend. She lived here in Santa Cecilia and we'd organized a trip to spend the entire summer in Spain. But something unexpected happened that spring and we were never able to go." She raised her eyes. "One of these days I just might try again."

We returned to the subject of the course project. I was practically convinced that I was going to accept, and we spoke of dates, time slots, and possible participants until we realized that it was almost five: time to start wrapping up the day. Rebecca gathered her papers and began to leave. Standing at the doorway, she paused, regarding me with a half smile, her eyes tinged with nostalgia.

"She was a wonderful woman. Her memory still lingers here."

Chapter 8

The following week the department was covered with signs announcing the National Hispanic Heritage Month debate, so we all saved the date.

"You'll be there, right?" Rebecca asked on the day of the event, popping her head briefly into my office at noon.

"I suppose so. And you?"

"Of course, I never miss it. I'll come pick you up."

The lecture hall was practically full, and everyone was still settling in. The stage, however, remained empty except for a couple of technicians busy installing microphones in front of nine empty chairs. I was relieved that none of them would be mine.

We bumped into Luis Zarate, who was chatting in the hall with colleagues and students. On seeing us, he broke away from the group and came over.

"I trust you'll find it interesting, maybe even fun. I would have loved you to participate, Blanca. Perhaps some other time."

"Some other time, for sure," I said, knowing full well that such a time would never come. "Are you on the panel?"

"I'm afraid so; I have no other option. I hope I won't bore you . . ."

I was convinced that he wouldn't. He had the gift of gab, was quick and clever in his conversations, and had a considerable amount of knowledge. I had growing proof of this because we saw each other often: meeting in offices and hallways, or at lunch in the cafeteria.

Rebecca and I sat at the end of one of the first few rows. Soon the lights dimmed and the panelists took the stage while the room slowly fell silent.

Luis Zarate, dressed in black as usual, sat in the third chair from the right, where I would have no doubt been sitting had I accepted his invitation. The last panelist to cross the stage in a few long strides was Daniel Carter, the university's former professor whom I'd met in Meli's Market. Wearing a jacket but no tie, he looked self-assured, with that contagious energy of someone recently arrived. Before taking a seat he went around giving the other speakers handshakes, affectionate gestures, and a quick hug or two. But he was unable to exchange a word with our chairman: when he passed by Luis Zarate, the latter seemed absorbed with writing something in his agenda.

"Why is your friend there?" I asked Rebecca in a murmur as Daniel finally sat down next to the moderator.

"They always invite a visiting professor who has something to do with the Hispanic world, just like Zarate invited you."

"Wasn't he only passing through?"

Although it was impossible for him to have heard me, just then he spotted us and gave us a quick wave.

"He's thinking of staying longer than he initially intended," Rebecca explained in a quick whisper.

There were no more explanations: the moderator had started introducing the various participants. A Guatemalan painter, a professor from the Art Department, dressed in a huipil covered with embroidered flowers and birds. A young, skinny Argentinian professor with a blond goatee, a specialist in international economic relations. A mature journalist, just back from Ecuador, where her daughter worked for the Peace Corps. A graduate student about to finish her dissertation regarding relations between the United States and Chile during the Allende period. Along with my two acquaintances, plus two other participants whose affiliations I didn't catch.

The debate flowed smoothly. In deference to the majority of the audience, English was for the most part the language used, although everyone peppered it with Spanish when references or evocations so required.

They spoke of domestic and international issues related to the Spanish-speaking world, and offered opinions and forecasts regarding the twenty-first century. The subjects were wide-ranging: Hugo Chavez's rise to power in Venezuela, Pastrana's dialogues in Colombia with the FARC guerrillas, Clinton's increasingly flexible policies toward Cuba, the Latin invasion of pop music, and finally the chances of an Oscar nomination for Pedro Almodovar's film *All About My Mother*. That was when the sparks flew.

"Mention of that prize gives me great satisfaction," Zarate said as soon as the subject was raised. "And not only because of the recognition it would confer on the wonderful creative quality of the filmmaker himself but, fundamentally, because it finally confirms what some of my colleagues have refused or have been unable to appreciate in recent Spanish cinema."

No one replied; all the speakers waited for him to continue, not quite understanding his meaning.

"I'm referring to," he went on, "the reactionary position taken by a specific sector of our Hispanic studies academic community."

His panel colleagues remained silent. Until, unexpectedly, Daniel Carter slowly unglued his back from his chair, leaned forward, and, instead of speaking to the public, turned to him.

"Out of mere curiosity, Professor Zarate, might that assertion have something to do with myself?"

"I don't think that Professor Zarate's intention was to—" the moderator tried to intervene.

"Because if that were the case—and forgive me, Raymond, please," he continued, interrupting the moderator while raising his hand so that he'd be allowed to continue, "—if that were the case, perhaps you could be more direct and explicit instead of hiding behind what must be for the audience some confusing rhetorical posturing."

"You're totally free to interpret my words as you please, Professor Carter," Luis Zarate answered with a trace of haughtiness.

"Then explain yourself more clearly so that you'll be free from subjective interpretations."

"All I've tried to say is that perhaps such a nomination would encourage some academic researchers to reconsider their assessment of Almodovar's output—"

"I don't think anyone in our profession has ever questioned the quality and originality of Pedro Almodovar's movies."

"—assessment of Almodovar's output as well as other productions of equal interest, I repeat, as a cultural product worthy of the most thorough scientific study," Zarate continued, completely ignoring his interlocutor.

The far-ranging debate had suddenly devolved into a sort of corrosive ping-pong match between two lone players. The public, meanwhile, kept up with the nimble exchange of opinions without a clear idea of where it was all leading.

Despite the sophisticated dialogue, I began to sense something more. Something personal, carnal, human. It slithered beneath each of their interruptions, although neither one of them mentioned it outright. Something must have happened at some point in the past to give rise to the palpable hostility between the veteran visiting professor and the chairman of the Modern Languages Department.

The dispute amplified. Luis Zarate attacked with an incessant sputter of words and very little body language: static, backed only by the movement of a pen that he occasionally jabbed against the table to stress his point. Daniel Carter, for his part, accompanied his words with more generous gesticulations as he leaned back in his chair with the apparent ease of someone with a good number of battles under his belt.

"What I'm trying to say is there are lots of academics who are still stuck in old social criticism," Luis Zarate insisted, "as if no advances have been made in either research methodology or Spanish culture since Carlos Saura or the publication of *Time of Silence* by Martin-Santos. As if the Marxist compromise was still alive and Spain was still a country of brass bands, castanets, and bullfights."

"Good God, Zarate, don't tell me we're discussing bullfights today . . ."

Perhaps it was the tone more than the comment itself that brought a peal of laughter from the audience. I looked around and noticed that, far from being annoyed, most of the audience was enjoying the heated discussion.

"You'd defend yourself much better in that domain than I would, no doubt about it," Zarate replied. "Your peculiar fondness for that gory spectacle is well known, as I understand. Perhaps it's another example of the stagnant stereotyping to which I'm referring."

"And you no doubt see it as my clear support of stale Francoism? Because it's the only piece of nonsense left for you to say."

"Don't trivialize the matter, Professor Carter, please. We're carrying on an intellectual debate."

"I'm not trivializing at all, my friend. You're the one who brought up the old clichés of Spanish culture. Although you've missed a few to complete the perfect postmodern Hispanist's catalog of demons. How about the Guardia Civil's three-cornered hat?"

This last comment came out of his mouth in Spanish, and while ninety-nine percent of the audience didn't understand it, I had to make an effort not to laugh out loud. Daniel Carter must have noticed something in my face from the distance because, raising an eyebrow almost imperceptibly, he shot me a knowing wink.

"I'd appreciate it if you resorted to arguments of weight, Professor Carter."

"I don't need for you to lecture me as to what type of arguments I should resort to, thank you," Carter replied, resuming a calmness devoid of any trace of banter. "You are the only one who from the very beginning perverted this discussion, manipulating it to turn a simple personal situation that is beside the point into an alleged disagreement of intellectual proportions."

The chairman was ready to counterattack, but Daniel Carter, in whose patience a certain boredom could be discerned, decided to unilaterally consider the issue closed.

"Well, my friend, I think we'd better leave it off here." And adding emphasis to his words with a sonorous slap on the table, he concluded, "I think we've bored the audience plenty with our little dialectic dispute. Let's allow our moderator to wind down the debate, because if we don't, we'll be wallowing in it until next year's Oscar nominations, when the favorite candidate will be a movie on the sorrows of an orphan in Uzbekistan and we will have forgotten the reason why we were arguing on this long-ago day."

Perceiving a slight flash of irritation on Luis Zarate's face, I intuited that he would have liked the skirmish to continue until he had thrashed his opponent. But he was unable to do so, and with no prospect of a clear winner or a harmonious conclusion the debate was simply closed.

The moderator thanked everyone for attending and the hall once again filled with noise, movement, and light. While we all got up, the panelists began descending from the stage. Daniel, in the distance, signaled for Rebecca and me to wait for him as he headed toward us, making his way through the crowd.

However, he had to pass Luis Zarate, who at that moment was exchanging a few words with two professors from the Department of Linguistics. I thought they'd avoid each other or that at most they'd greet each other coldly. But to my surprise, Daniel stopped beside him and gave his arm a light squeeze.

If the two phrases that he spoke had been in English, they most likely would have been indistinguishable among the dozens of voices around me. But perhaps because he chose my native tongue, his words reached my ears with perfect clarity.

"Don't take things so seriously, kid. Get your head out from all those papers and get a fucking life."

Chapter 9

While Daniel Carter said good-bye to several colleagues who didn't want to let him go, we exchanged a few words with our chairman on our way out of the event. If the debate had irritated him in any way, he didn't show it. Neither did the last remark his opponent had thrown at him in private seem to have annoyed him. Or at least that was the impression he gave.

"That's what the university is for, right? To stimulate debate and critical thinking," he joked before leaving. "By the way, Blanca, have you decided yet if you'll take on the course?"

"I was going to tell you tomorrow that I have. It seems interesting; I think I'll like it."

"Then I count you in. Rebecca will take care of the formalities."

We watched him leave, apparently alone. From the corner of my eye, however, I saw that farther off, in the semidarkness, one of the young professors from the department, whose name at that moment I was unable to recall, was waiting for him. Together they headed toward his Toyota with license plates from Massachusetts and disappeared into the night.

"I thought I'd never get away," Daniel announced as he finally approached us. "I'm very happy to see you again, Blanca: you're the only truly authentic one in this convoluted debate regarding the Spanish essence, which the rest of us only know secondhand. What's in your fridge, Rebecca?" he then asked, rubbing his hands vigorously. "Something tasty so that you can invite Professor Perea and myself over for dinner?"

I was surprised by his comment as well as by his spontaneous self-invite—because of the evident regard he seemed to have for me despite our hardly knowing each other; and because his self-invite, not merely glib, included me without even consulting me. I raised no objections, however, for his proposition was infinitely more stimulating than what awaited me that night: a bland omelet accompanied by a couple of isolated episodes of some outdated television series.

"A wonderful piece of Alaskan salmon," Rebecca answered. "And I think there are still two or three bottles left in that case of merlot you brought from Napa."

"That settles it. Shall we walk there now?"

As we made our way to Rebecca's house nearby, we spoke of the event that had just taken place. Without taking sides with either him or Luis Zarate, I confessed to Daniel that his unexpected comments on the stereotypical Spain almost had me in stitches.

"You probably served as my inspiration."

I didn't react, not knowing what to say.

"Seeing you in the audience from up there," he then clarified, "suddenly brought a thousand images of your native country to mind, and not only the stale ones that your chairman and I mentioned."

"As long as you didn't picture me playing the castanets in a long-tailed gown in the shadow of an Osborne bull," I retorted in Spanish, unable to hold back.

He laughed heartily and then translated for Rebecca what I'd just said.

"That Spain that your chairman pretends to anchor me in, and that I myself discovered in depth at the time, with its lights and shadows, has been buried for decades," he went on.

"Fortunately," I pointed out.

"Yes, fortunately. What we cannot do is deny that it existed and that, like it or not, it has contributed to shape the country you've got today."

"Perhaps Professor Zarate ignores that essence," Rebecca intervened, ever loyal to her boss. "Even though his father is Spanish, perhaps he has not lived there long enough to know the country in depth. Besides, he shares his Hispanic roots with Chile, his mother's land; maybe he leans more toward that culture—"

"That doesn't justify his behavior," Daniel interrupted. "Our professional worth is not measured in proportion to the passion we may feel toward one country or another but rather in terms of the works we publish, the conferences we attend, the dissertations we supervise, and the courses we teach. Affection is not quantifiable but rather a totally personal matter."

"But I suppose that affection helps somewhat," I said.

"You bet it helps," he confirmed sarcastically. "But some have not realized it yet."

. . .

I'd never before crossed the campus at night. It was the first time I saw its classrooms and offices almost in complete darkness and its dorms totally lit; the first time I didn't see students hurrying from one class to the next but rather sitting indolently on their doorsteps, smoking, talking, laughing, as the day drained away; the first time I saw the basketball courts with their lights humming loudly as the balls rebounded on the boards and lingering smells from the evening meal emanated from vents in the cafeteria kitchen.

We left the campus behind as we headed toward Santa Cecilia Plaza, the most urban area of the small city. Hardly a month had gone by since my arrival, but it seemed more like a century had elapsed since that first morning I'd sat down at the café in the plaza, lost and disoriented, making an effort to accept my new place in the world.

On hearing Daniel mention Andres Fontana, I quickly came back to the present.

"He loved to sit in this square, you know, Blanca? He always said that it had the air of a run-down Spanish town."

"In a way it does," I admitted.

"It's only logical, right?" Rebecca said. "The city founders were old California natives, Mexicans of pure Spanish descent, when not outright Spaniards."

"Maybe that's why this plaza and Los Pinitos were his favorite spots. He'd stroll around ruminating about things; he said that's how he oxygenated his brain."

By then I was aware that Los Pinitos was where I had walked on that earlier afternoon when the vision of the photographs of the dead professor altered my approach to my work on Fontana.

"There seem to be problems with that area now; they intend to build a shopping mall, right?"

They answered yes almost in unison.

"In fact," Rebecca went on, "a shopping mall may bring economic benefits to Santa Cecilia, but it would level a lovely spot that those of us who live here have always felt to be our own. A place which is very dear to our heart and our families, a place for leisure, for picnics with kids . . ."

"A place for students to horse around . . ." Daniel added.

"Or to simply take a stroll . . ."

"In any case, the battle is not altogether lost: there are solid doubts regarding the project's viability," Daniel continued, "because the legitimate ownership of the land seems to have been tangled up for more than a century."

"I thought it was a public space that belonged to the town," I said.

"The municipality manages it and can negotiate its concession because there is no irrefutable proof of its historical ownership. It's a very confusing affair."

"That's why there's a citizens' platform trying to find some kind of legal glitch to stop it, but they've been at it for months and have yet to find a way," Rebecca interjected. "And the deadline to appeal the project is by December, so we all fear the worst."

We were caught up in conversation when, hardly a few feet away from us, a door opened and someone came out onto the sidewalk, momentarily blocking our path and halting our conversation.

The door was to a small clinic that seemed to be closing. The lights inside were practically out, and whoever was now leaving must have been among the last employees to go. The door, held by a young nurse in scrubs and clogs, remained open for an instant without anyone coming out and prevented us from continuing along in a straight path. As we began taking a detour into the street, a wheelchair emerged.

Its occupant was wearing an old sweatsuit and had light hair that fell below her shoulders, a pale face full of wrinkles, and lips painted vermilion. A shocking sight, or at least far from that of a conventional elderly woman. Despite the fact that night had fallen long before, she was wearing a large pair of sunglasses. Behind them, covering her right eye, was a gauze bandage.

"Well, well, well . . ." I heard Daniel whisper in a hoarse, almost inaudible voice.

"Mrs. Cullen, Professor Perea, what a surprise to see you here! Professor Carter, I remember we met in the library the other day; I'm pleased to see you again. Look, Mother, look at all three of them!"

The person to greet us so enthusiastically while pushing the wheelchair was none other than Fanny. She came to a stop, placing herself smack in the middle of the sidewalk while the nurse slipped back into the clinic.

"Good evening, Fanny. Nice to see you again, Darla," Rebecca greeted them cordially. "Any problem? I trust it's nothing serious this time around."

The old lady didn't pay any attention whatsoever to her words. She didn't reply, didn't even look at her, as if she hadn't heard her. I thought that perhaps her mental faculties were somewhat diminished; judging from her aesthetics, it was certainly a possibility. But as if to confirm how mistaken I was in my judgment, she spoke up.

"Now, now . . . Look who we have here . . ."

I immediately knew she was referring to Daniel. Perhaps they were also old friends, I thought. Everyone around here seemed to receive the university's prodigal son with great affection.

"It's been a long time, Darla," he said somewhat indifferently. "How is it going? How are you doing?"

They greeted each other from the distance of a few yards. Daniel, with his hands in his trouser pockets, made no movement to come any closer.

"Wonderful: you can see how I'm doing, dear," the old lady answered cynically. "And how are you doing, Professor?"

"I can't complain. Working, as usual . . ."

Both their sentences conformed to the norms of courtesy, but one didn't need to be too sharp to recognize the chill. Before I was able to conjecture any further, Rebecca decided to intervene.

"What happened to your eye, Darla?"

"Mother bumped into the door of the bathroom closet, was badly hurt, and bled a great deal. Today we came to have it checked."

"Shut up, Fanny, shut up, don't exaggerate so much . . ." Darla growled. "It was only a small domestic accident, that's all—nothing serious."

"This is Professor Perea, Mother," the daughter went on. "I've spoken to you about her several times; you finally get to meet her."

"Delighted," I said. For some unknown reason I imitated Daniel in his behavior and did not move closer to her.

"Another little Spaniard in Santa Cecilia; isn't that just wonderful. My daughter has already told me what you're up to here."

"Also working, Darla. Like everyone else at the university," Daniel burst in without giving me time to answer.

"I've been told that you're involved with the papers that our old friend Andres Fontana left behind," she said, addressing me as if she hadn't heard him. "And? Have you found anything interesting? Bank checks? Anonymous messages? Love letters?"

"Among Professor Fontana's papers there are only professional documents, Darla," Rebecca clarified. "Professor Perea simply—"

To my good fortune the clinic door opened again, interrupting the uncomfortable conversation. A grim-faced man in his fifties emerged, carrying a briefcase, and I surmised it was the doctor who had treated Darla. Behind him, this time wearing jeans, his nurse proceeded to lock the door with a large bundle of keys.

"Remember, Mrs. Stern, don't remove the bandage until next week's visit. And make an appointment beforehand, please."

There was not the least trace of sympathy in his tone. Most likely mother and daughter had showed up without notice at the end of the day, forcing him to stay behind a good while longer than normal.

Fanny had begun apologizing with hasty excuses, citing various obligations between work, her spiritual meetings, and caring for her mother, but no one was really listening. Taking advantage of the doctor's presence and his final words of advice, Daniel had already moved on and Rebecca and I followed, muttering a brief farewell.

"Why don't you come pay me a visit one of these days, Carter!" the old woman screamed from a distance.

"See you, Darla, I wish you all the best," he answered without turning back.

"What a pair!" I said as we passed over the pedestrian crossing.

"Yes, what a pair . . ." Rebecca repeated with a short laugh, as if trying to downplay the situation.

Daniel kept walking in silence. I noticed that Rebecca grabbed his left arm affectionately with both hands. He, thankful but somewhat absent, finally took his right hand out of his trouser pocket, placed it on top of hers, and patted it.

"No one ever said the past was devoid of shadows."

Chapter 10

Only ten minutes before my new course was to begin, the telephone in my office started ringing with a loud din. I didn't answer; I had no time. A half hour earlier, after mulling over the syllabus for the thousandth time, I'd decided to change the sequencing of certain topics; but when I tried to print out the new syllabus, the printer jammed. I then turned to the photocopying machine, which bore a sign that read: TEMPORARILY OUT OF SERVICE. Neither Fanny, Rebecca, the chairman, nor any professors were at hand; the conference room's closed door signaled a long departmental meeting. Once more I turned desperately to the printer, opening and closing it repeatedly, taking the ink cartridge out, then replacing it. In the middle of my hand-to-hand combat with technology, the telephone rang again insistently. I finally picked up the receiver reluctantly and hurled a cutting "Hello."

"Are you out of your fucking mind? I bumped into Alberto and his pregnant Barbie in a restaurant and he told me that you've decided to sell all of your things and start signing papers. But do you know what you're doing, dear sister? You've never behaved like this, Blanca; you've always grabbed the bull by the horns . . . What's the matter with you: have you gone nuts all of a sudden or what?"

Just as she had done so many other times, my sister barged into my life unannounced and at the worst possible time. Ana, thirteen months my elder and so radically different from me that we didn't even seem to have the same blood. An emergency physician and mother of four kids, she was outspoken, biting, and prone to meddling. A bundle of pure energy capable of taking on the world by storm, she would call in the middle of her night shift, perhaps between treating a renal colic case and a motorcycle accident victim.

"I know what I'm doing, Ana; of course I know what I'm doing," I answered swiftly, with little conviction.

"You've really lost it, sister!" she went on, undeterred. "This business of your husband's cheating has affected you more than you think. Where is that spunk of yours? The son of a bitch fools you for months, then suddenly informs you that he's going to live with that bitch, and then shortly afterwards you learn that she's pregnant, probably before he walked out on you. So, as a prize for his remarkable behavior, you let him off scot-free to do whatever he wants with your things. He can sell your house and leave you on the damned street while you conveniently take off to California on holiday to celebrate . . . Wake up, Blanca! Get back to your old self, dammit!"

"We'll talk it over calmly, I promise. This is not a good moment: I'm working."

"What you need to do is to make life for that son of a bitch Alberto as hard as possible."

"Come on!"

My outburst was actually directed at the printer. Since it refused to heed to reason, I decided to try hitting it with a clean blow. But my sister, in the distance, did not pick up on it.

"What are you saying?" she yelled. "You're not going to defend him on top of it!"

"There's nothing to accuse or defend him against, Ana. What has happened has happened: he's found another woman he loves more than me. And he's left. And that's that," I said, smacking the machine on its left side. "I don't see any reason to make things more complicated than they already are. As long as I don't have any contact with him, that's enough. In any case, don't worry, I'll think about everything you've told me."

In truth, I had no intention of thinking about everything she'd told me; all that I wished was for her to calm down, hang up, and forget about me. To add emphasis to my words, I gave the machine another whack, this time going for the right-hand side. It was of little use.

"You'll *think* about it!" she roared. "If you think about it the way you've done so far, I fear the worst, sister. What you need to do is return home and continue being your old self. Continue with your life. Without your husband, but with your life. With your work, your kids nearby, with your old friends and the rest of your family."

"We'll talk about it, Ana. I've got to go now."

Right then Fanny's round face popped in the door.

"Your new students are waiting for you in room 215," she announced.

"I'll call you some other day. Kisses to everyone. Good-bye! Good-bye!"

I hung up the receiver with one hand while my other delivered one last whack to the printer. And, miraculously, the machine began making a raspy noise and spitting out paper.

"Help me, Fanny, for God's sake," I begged her in an agitated voice. "Staple these pages in twos, please, like this, you see?"

She enthusiastically rushed to my rescue, so much so that in the process she knocked over a pile of Fontana material at one corner of the table that was still awaiting my attention.

"I'm so sorry, Professor Perea, I'm really sorry," she muttered, flustered, as she bent over to restack the papers.

"Don't worry; you finish with this, I'll pick it up."

I put my jacket on in a split second, then began gathering what had just fallen to the floor: a couple of typed pages, a handful of old letters, and a pile of postcards. I tried to put it all back on the table, but Fanny, with her particular way of doing things, had covered its entire surface with the copies of the syllabus. Instead, I hastily left it all on my armchair and swung my purse onto my shoulder, causing a few postcards to slip to the floor. I picked them up again while Fanny, triumphant, handed me the ready copies.

"You're a sweetheart, Fanny, a sweetheart," I said to her, sticking the syllabuses into my folder distractedly along with Fontana's postcards.

I walked into class winded, relieved to have gotten rid of Ana and to finally have the programs ready, apologizing for the five-minute delay.

The course had been advertised as Advanced Spanish Through Contemporary Spain, a mixture of culture and conversation class. After I introduced myself, the students introduced themselves, revealing a broad range of interests: passion for travel, professional needs, curiosity about history. There was also a diversity of ages and backgrounds, from a professor emeritus in history to a thirty-something sculptress in love with Gaudi's work.

From the very first moment, out of intuition hard-won after practically twenty years of slogging it out in classrooms, I knew the course was going to work out.

I'd decided to start the class on a light note, knowing how it could help everyone adjust to the new setting and group dynamic. Although thanks to my sister's call I was in no mood for jokes and witticisms, having only a great urge to lock myself up in the toilet to cry, I applied a golden rule for any good professor and left all personal issues in the hallway. Like an actor who steps onstage, I simply got going.

"During the seventies there was a very popular television program in Spain called *One, Two, Three . . . Respond Again*. Would you like to play?"

My goal, obviously, went beyond mere entertainment. My intention was to tie their world to mine in a totally informal manner. The answer was a resounding yes.

"Okay, then, for an imaginary twenty-five pesetas, I want cities in California that are named after a Spanish saint. For example, Santa Cecilia: one, two, three, respond again . . ."

I was unable to warn them that one of the rules of that old show was to start the string of answers with the example given, because before I was able to open my mouth they were already off and running with saints' names: San Francisco, Santa Rosa, San Rafael, San Marco, San

Gabriela, Santa Cruz, Santa Clara, Santa Ines, Santa Barbara, San Luis Obispo, San Jose . . .

When they'd reached two dozen saints and were still going strong, I asked them to come up with places in California containing Spanish words or phrases.

Alameda, Palo Alto, Los Gatos, El Cerrito del Norte, Diablo Range, Contra Costa, Paso Robles, Atascadero, Fresno, Salinas, Manteca, Madera, Goleta, Monterey, Corona, Encinitas, Arroyo, Burro, La Jolla . . . With a pronunciation often far from the original and at times distorted to the point of incomprehension, their unending list covered ports, mountains, counties, and bays.

With an emphatic gesture I indicated they could stop.

"And Chula Vista, next to San Diego," one of the students added, unable to resist including one more name.

"How about Mariposa County?" another blurted out.

"Okay, okay . . ." I said.

"Let's not forget Los Padres and the Camino Real: they're the origin of it all."

The one who spoke was the emeritus history professor, whose name I now knew was Joe Super. All eyes turned to him, toward his Hawaiian shirt and wise blue eyes. He then asked me permission to add something else.

"Of course, as long as it's in Spanish."

"I'm going to try my best," he said with a charming gesture that brought a general peal of laughter. "Los Padres National Forest refers to the Spanish Franciscan monks who began the exploration and colonization of California in the second half of the eighteenth century. They were driven on by a force that, wrong or right, enabled them to accomplish their objectives. And El Camino Real is the result: the string of missions that these fathers founded throughout California."

"Twenty missions, right?" Lucas, a graduate student in foreign relations, asked.

"Twenty-one," Joe corrected. "They begin in Southern California, with San Diego de Alcala, and end in the north, very close to here, in Sonoma, with San Francisco Solano. Very little is known in Spain about this, right?"

"It's true," I acknowledged with a sense of collective shame.

"That's sad, because all this is part of your inheritance, both historical and cultural."

Having finished with *One, Two, Three,* I resumed the class and we had a pleasant, fruitful session for another hour or so. But in some recess of my subconscious those references to fathers, missions, and trails must have taken hold, because at one point I suddenly remembered that among Fontana's papers, I'd seen in passing some mention of the Franciscans and their buildings. Those documents remained in a couple of boxes set aside in a corner of my office, needing further attention. Once I gave it, perhaps I'd be able to fill in the gaps.

I left the campus as soon as the class was over, satisfied by the results and exhausted after an entire day of nonstop work. I finally took a deep breath, inhaling the smell of eucalyptus in the late afternoon.

"How did your new course go?"

I had been walking along the sidewalk, distracted, when the voice came from a car that had halted beside me. Like me, Luis Zarate was about to go home, and instead of his customary work clothes, he was wearing a pair of shorts and a deep-red sweatshirt with the logo of some university other than Santa Cecilia. Next to him, a sports bag occupied the passenger seat.

"Extremely well. It's an excellent group, very motivated. I'm lucky."

"I'm glad. Would you like me to give you a lift home?"

"Well . . . I appreciate it, but I think it'll do me good to walk awhile and get some air. I've been locked up since nine o'clock this morning, I didn't even go out for lunch."

"Whatever you like. Enjoy your stroll, then. I'll see you tomorrow."

I was about to return the farewell, but he had already rolled the window up, so I didn't make an effort. I simply raised my hand in a good-bye gesture. And suddenly, unexpectedly, the window rolled back down.

"Perhaps we could go for dinner one of these days."

"Whenever you like."

I was not taken aback by the invitation. In fact, I was quite tempted, and even if the invitation had been for that very same evening, I would have said yes. Why not?

"Do you know Los Olivos?"

One more in the long list of words from my native tongue in this foreign land, I thought, recalling the recently finished class.

"No, I don't know it. I've heard it mentioned several times, but I've never been there."

"They serve wonderful pasta and excellent wines. Let's talk about it, okay?"

The car disappeared into the distance and I resumed my walk home, rapidly reviewing the different parts of that intense day. I made an effort to put the memory of Ana's phone call aside, categorically refusing to stop and think if behind the impetus of my sister's words there was an undeniable piece of truth. Instead, I turned my attention to more pleasant things, like Luis Zarate's invitation. Then to Fontana's papers, which had absorbed me, enticing me to make sense of them all, to the point of leaving off all other obligations to the last minute, even forcing me to satisfy my hunger with a miserable sandwich spat out from a vending machine. It was a job that was becoming increasingly gratifying and simultaneously made for good therapy. The more I was engrossed by the dead professor's legacy—the more conscious I became of his charisma and worth—the less I thought about my own predicament.

By then I had already realized that, after a spell as a lecturer, his intention was to return to Spain and continue with his projects there: to sit for a public entrance examination in the then prestigious positions for secondary-education teachers, perhaps even return to university and maybe in the meantime find a job at some private school or academy. The Spanish Civil War in the distance, however, froze his will and soul. Overwhelmed, dismayed, devastated, he decided not to go back.

Among his papers I hadn't found any desire to return after the war to that motherland, irremediably different from the one he'd left behind, although one could intuit the occasional shadow of nostalgia in his writings. But he remained resolute: he packed up his feelings along with the emotions and impressions of his youth and stored them in the back room of his mind. From then on, he settled in his host country with a definite sense of permanence, devoting himself to teaching his country's language and literature, to transferring his feelings, his knowledge, and the memory of his lost world to hundreds, perhaps thousands of students who sometimes understood how much this meant to him and sometimes did not.

There were many testimonials from students who had at some time or other over the decades attended his classes. I suddenly remembered the postcards that I'd hastily placed in my folder that very afternoon.

I pulled them out while I kept walking. It'd grown dark, but the streetlamps provided plenty of light to skim over them. There must have been about a dozen: short missives that greeted the old professor, sending regards from remote cities or in a few lines narrating how life was treating them. At first glance they didn't seem to be organized according to any specific criteria, so that the most disparate places were paired with dates that danced haphazardly in time: Mexico City, July 1947; St. Louis, Missouri, March 1953; Seville, April 1961; Buenos Aires, October 1955; Madrid, December 1958. Postcards of the Teotihuacan pyramids, the Mississippi River, Maria Luisa Park, Recoleta Cemetery, the Puerta del Sol.

I smiled on seeing such a familiar picture of the Puerta del Sol during that period. There was the bright Tio Pepe billboard, the clock announcing the New Year, the perpetual crowd at the heart of the capital. I stopped beneath a lamppost to take a good look at it, while beside me a constant stream of students hurried along with their backpacks.

I looked for the postmark date: January 2, 1959. The postcard's succinct contents appeared to have been hastily written with a fountain pen:

> Dear Professor,
> Spain continues to be fascinating.
> My work is coming along well.
> After the grapes, I'll go in search of Mister Witt.

The text was further confirmation of the close relationship Fontana had with his students.

But what shocked me was the closing:

Wishing you a happy new year,

Your friend,
Daniel Carter

I had begun my research project thinking that it concerned the legacy of one man. But this innocuous postcard from Madrid now opened up an intriguing glimpse of a far greater puzzle. What I was to discover in the following weeks about Daniel Carter—both from himself and from others—would enable me to begin piecing together that larger enigma. And although I had no way of knowing it at the time, these discoveries would in turn leave an indelible mark on my own life.

Chapter 11

The Spain that welcomed Daniel Carter the first time he crossed the Atlantic had already shaken off the brutal slumber of the postwar years. It was still a sluggish, backward nation, but amazingly picturesque to the eyes of an American student.

He brought with him twenty-two years and a handful of vague reasons for his trip: a certain fluency in the Spanish language, a growing passion for its literature, and a great desire to set foot in that distant land to which he was bound ever since he boldly decided to ignore his destiny.

The son of a dentist and a cultivated housewife, Daniel Carter had grown up in the comfortable conventionality of the small city of Morgantown, West Virginia, tucked away in the foothills of the Appalachian Mountains. His parents' dream was that their firstborn—an outstanding student and athlete—would become at the least a brilliant lawyer or surgeon. But as often happens in such cases, the parents' plans were moving along on one track while the son's followed another.

"I've been thinking about my future," he finally told them, dropping the phrase casually between bites of pot roast and boiled green peas. A dinner like any other, on an ordinary late Sunday afternoon.

"Law, finally?" his mother asked cheerfully with a forkful of mashed potatoes halfway between the plate and her mouth.

"No . . ."

"Medicine, then?" his father interjected, hardly hiding his satisfaction.

"Neither."

They looked at him in astonishment as he began explaining in a strong voice what not even in a hundred days of conjecture they would have guessed. Upon completing his undergraduate studies, he had no interest in specializing in law despite being admitted to Cornell Law School, nor was he in the least interested in medicine. He wouldn't remotely consider a future surrounded by judges, operating rooms, criminals, or scalpels; what he wanted to do with his life was to know other cultures and to devote himself to studying literature. Foreign literature, to be exact.

Daniel's father folded his napkin with extreme slowness, his eyes fixed on the tablecloth.

"Excuse me," he whispered.

The slamming front door resounded along the street. His mother was left speechless. Tears began to well up in her lovely green eyes as she wondered when and where they had gone wrong in rearing the son whom they thought they had provided with an exemplary education.

However, they knew Daniel was headstrong and had a fiercely passionate temperament, so they realized that this resolution, no matter how ridiculous and far-fetched it sounded, was firm. The younger brothers exchanged kicks beneath the table but didn't dare utter a word lest they be caught in the crossfire.

From that day on, silence spread through the house. Weeks went by in which Daniel's parents barely addressed him, naïvely hoping that perhaps exhaustion would end up instilling some sense in the wayward youngster. All they achieved was to heat up the atmosphere to such a disagreeable extent that, far from encouraging him to change his attitude, they accomplished the exact opposite, awakening in him an overwhelming desire to get away as quickly as possible.

His next step was to apply for graduate studies at the University of Pittsburgh. Past the deadline and by the skin of his teeth he managed to get accepted in the classical- and Romance-languages program, bolstered by the French and Spanish courses he'd taken previously. The family's stable income and the hastiness with which he'd applied, however, disqualified him from receiving a scholarship. His father maintained his unyielding refusal to finance such an absurdity, so Daniel abandoned the family home at the end of summer, carrying with him a canvas backpack, sixty-seven dollars, and the still-festering family rift.

His first objective once he landed in Pittsburgh was to find a part-time job. He figured that the paltry savings he'd accrued as a lifeguard that summer—his sole capital—wouldn't last long. He quickly found a night job at H. J. Heinz, the great manufacturer of ketchup, beans, and pickles.

The first semester flew by. He had strong yearnings and few needs, renting a room in a dilapidated house that he shared with seven other students, five cats, and a good number of broken windows. He didn't much care about its decaying state, using it only for sleeping. His remaining time was spent at the university and completing his shifts at Heinz. He would eat in any old corner, sometimes a cold can of beans as he sat on some step going over his grammar exercises, or a cheese sandwich downed in three bites as he hurried along the hallways between classes. In his scarce free time—whenever he had an unoccupied hour—he could be seen running around the university's athletic track like a being possessed. It didn't take long for that tall, extroverted kid, full of energy and always in a hurry, to become popular among his classmates. In the factory, though, they would tease him whenever they saw him with a book during breaks, seated amid piles of boxes in his work uniform. He did not cut himself off completely, however. In a feat of multitasking, he didn't miss out on anything that might be happening: from the latest honorable defeat of the Pittsburgh Steelers in the NFL to the jokes about the bosses, women, and the lives of his fellow laborers, who came from all kinds of backgrounds.

Among his second-semester courses was Twentieth-Century Spanish Literature, which took place in the Cathedral of Learning, Pitt's emblematic landmark.

Daniel arrived at the first class early, just after lunch, hurried as usual. He stretched out his legs and relaxed as he waited for the professor's arrival, risky behavior for someone exhausted from the nightly effort of loading trucks. In a few minutes his chin was resting against his chest, his hair was covering his eyes, and his mind was plagued by those strange presences that swarm in the first moments of sleep.

A quick, sharp kick to his left foot jolted him awake. He immediately muttered an embarrassed "I'm sorry" while swiftly recovering his composure. Before him stood a dark-complexioned man with a corsair's thick beard, dark combed-back hair, and emphatic eyes like two pieces of coal.

"Siestas, at home and in summer. And, if at all possible, in the shade of a grapevine, with an earthenware jug of cold water by your side."

"I beg your pardon, sir . . ."

"We come here to work, young man. There are better places for napping. Your name, please?"

With a still somewhat shaky command of Spanish, Daniel was debating between specializing in this language or French, not knowing for sure which of the two cultures he would end up marking as his territory. But he grasped the meaning of the message immediately, just as he grasped that its speaker didn't seem in a mood to tolerate any kind of nonsense in his classroom.

Before shattering the family's expectations for good, his contact with the Spanish-speaking world had been confined to basic grammar and an arsenal of somewhat unrelated facts regarding painters, monuments, museums, and certain gastronomic curiosities such as octopus, oxtail, and those marzipan rolls with the sinister name of "saints' bones." Added to that, at most, would be reading Hemingway's *For Whom the Bell Tolls* one long summer night, and a handful of stray expressions mumbled by mustachioed Mexicans in Westerns on Saturday afternoons in the Warner Theatre of his native Morgantown.

But it was not long before that man's classes tipped the balance for Daniel. The poets of the Generation of '27 along with a fascination with the Spanish Civil War ultimately persuaded him that his studies in Spanish language and literature, despite his family's opposition, had been worthwhile. His relationship with his parents, however, never quite sorted itself out. They still couldn't understand why their son wasted his outstanding intellect in pursuit of an absurd academic specialty that in their eyes augured an uncertain professional future and a hardly promising social position.

Perhaps his decision was merely due to a rebellious impulse, to an unconscious urge to lash out against the established order of things.

Whatever was the spark, it soon burst into a flame that torched his elders' plans and left a clean slate upon which to establish his career. And hovering above it all, intangible but powerful, was Andres Fontana's push.

In the end it all came down to a verse—a simple handwritten verse found in the folds of a dead poet's pocket. Words of apparent simplicity that Daniel would have never fully understood had his professor not opened the young student's eyes. Andres Fontana wrote them in white chalk on the blackboard: *These blue days and this sun of childhood.*

"What was the sun of Antonio Machado's childhood like, Professor?"

The question came from a bright-looking female student with the face of a mouse and large horn-rimmed glasses who always sat in the front row.

"Yellow and luminous, like all others," blurted out a smart aleck.

A few laughed timorously.

Not Fontana.

Nor Daniel.

"One only appreciates the sun of childhood when one loses it," the professor said, leaning against the edge of his desk with the chalk between his fingers.

"When one loses the sun or loses one's childhood?" Daniel asked, raising a pencil in the air.

"When he no longer has the ground he has always walked upon, the hands that have held him, the house he grew up in. When one leaves for good, pushed by an external force, never to return."

Then the professor, who had scrupulously adhered to the syllabus until that day, dropped all academic formalities and spoke to them. Of loss and exile, of letters stored away and memory's umbilical cord; of something that, despite mountains and oceans separating souls from the sun of childhood, is never severed.

By the time the classroom bell rang, Daniel was absolutely certain where his future lay.

A few weeks later, having finished reading "Lullaby of the Onion" by Miguel Hernandez, Fontana caught them by surprise with a proposition.

"I need a volunteer for . . ."

Before Fontana even finished the sentence, Daniel had already raised his arm toward the ceiling in all its noticeable length.

"Don't you think, Carter, that before volunteering you should know what it entails?"

"It doesn't matter, Professor. You can count on me."

As the days went by, the young man's attitude did not cease to amaze Fontana. Throughout the many years that he'd been laboring away in American classrooms, he'd come across students from all types of background and of all natures. In very few, however, had he seen the enthusiasm exhibited by that tall, lanky kid.

"I'll need you for three days. We're going to hold a gathering of Hispanists, sort of a conference. As of Thursday we'll be assembling here; you must be available at all times until Saturday afternoon, for whatever we may require of you, from accompanying the visitors to their hotels to serving us coffee. Can I still count on you, or are you already regretting that you volunteered?"

Despite the fact that Fontana had spoken to them about what exile meant in connection to Machado's verse, Daniel back then hardly knew a thing about the numerous professors and Spanish university assistants who two decades earlier were forced to undertake that long and bitter road. Some had left during the civil war and others had done so when it came to an end and they were dismissed from their posts. The great majority underwent a long journey through Central and South America, wandering from one country to the next until they found a permanent place; a handful of them ended up establishing themselves in the United States. There were those who returned to Spain and settled as best they could amid the Franco regime's intransigent rules. Others returned and stood firm in their beliefs despite the harshness of reprisals. And then there were those who never left, living an internal exile, bitter and silent. The list of the intellectual diaspora was considerable, and Andres Fontana was to meet some of them a few days later.

"By all means, sir, you may count on me; I'm at your service."

He tried to sound convincing, but was lying. He had to work at the Heinz factory five hours on each of those nights. By means of some complicated swaps and a bunch of generous promises of double shifts during the following days he was finally able to convince a couple of colleagues to cover for him. He knew that to return the favor would entail a major effort and that he'd have to be totally reliable. But, out of pure intuition, he anticipated that those three days in the company of Hispanists would well be worth his while.

Driving Fontana's Oldsmobile, he picked them up from the airport, train station, and bus depot. Some of the newly arrived were fluent in English but had heavy accents; others were more limited. He taxied them back and forth, seeing to their every need with skill and grace; was courteous to them all; and memorized their various names, titles, and specialties. They discussed their country's literature in a foreign land, constantly taking the words out of each other's mouths, always eager to talk. Daniel made an effort not only to get to know them but to understand them and find out what was behind the strange labels of *galdosiano, lorquiano,* Cervantist, or *valleinclanesco* that they applied to one another regarding their areas of specialization.

In the process he also sought out in them the nostalgia of the childhood sun that Fontana had spoken to him about, but found only stray traces here and there, as if there was an implicit agreement among them not to bare their souls or touch upon deeper matters. They stuck to the surface of the banal, tossing barely a few crumbs of memory to the birds. One cursed the damned cold of those parts and recalled the warmth of his native Almeria. Another longed for Rioja wine during one of the lunches at the abstemious university cafeteria. A third one hummed a ballad at a well-endowed passing waitress: *"A good stew instead of so much corn, now, that would be quite the treat!"* They hardly spoke of politics, touching upon it at times but refusing to be drawn in. No one wanted a black cloud looming over such a cordial conference.

Daniel went out of his way for them and learned a thousand new things. Rich-sounding words and titles of books, certain phrases, names of authors and towns, and even a swear word or two such as that blunt *"Coño!"* that many of them peppered their conversation with.

When Saturday afternoon rolled by, he and the department secretary dropped them off one by one at their trains, planes, and buses. After several successful trips throughout the afternoon, they thought they were done. Daniel stood in the practically empty hotel lobby, waiting for Fontana so he could return his car keys and get to the factory.

And then he saw them walk out of the bar.

"What's the plan for this evening, kid?" one of them asked from a distance. "There are still three of us left and your boss told us that you'd take care of everything until the end."

A cold sweat ran down his spine. He had a double shift that evening, and he'd already arranged it with one of his factory colleagues: a quiet Pole, father of five, who didn't put up with jokes.

"I didn't know anything about it, sir," he said, searching with urgent eyes for Fontana.

"Don't tell me that, young man! We decided to change our tickets at the last minute so as not to take the red-eye flight. We've just had a bite to eat, and you don't expect us to stay cooped up in our hotel till tomorrow morning."

"I must speak to Professor Fontana; please forgive me."

He tried not to show panic as he sought out the professor. He found him by the hotel entrance, seeing a couple off on their way to Buffalo.

"Well, now we're done," Fontana said in satisfaction, patting his student on the shoulder. "Good job, Carter. I owe you a couple of beers."

"I don't think so, Professor . . ."

"You don't want to go for a couple of beers with me some day next week? Well, then, we'll have coffee. Or better yet, let me invite you to a fine restaurant: you deserve it."

"I'm not saying I don't want to go out for a couple of beers, sir. What I'm saying is that this isn't over yet."

He pointed discreetly to the three professors inside the lobby with their hats in hand, waiting for someone to take them out on the town.

"I've already got plans," Fontana mumbled below his breath, coming to a dead stop. "No one told me these three intended to stay an extra night."

Daniel knew already that there was a woman in Fontana's life. He didn't know her name and hadn't seen her face, but he had heard her voice. Accented, but in good English. He knew because he'd taken her call in Fontana's office some days earlier, when he'd gone there to receive instructions for the conference. "Answer, Carter," Fontana told him on the third ring while he quickly slipped on his jacket. "And say I'm on my way." He only heard her pronounce his name: "Andres?" And afterwards a "Very well, thank you" when he relayed his professor's message. Enough for him to realize that it was a relatively young woman. After that, nothing else.

"But we'd agreed that my duties with you would be over by Saturday afternoon," Daniel insisted. "I have to work at the factory today; I've got to make up to my coworkers for the days that they've stood in for me."

"Don't piss me off, Carter, for God's sake."

"Professor, you know I'd be delighted to, but I can't, really . . ." he insisted, handing over the keys to his car.

The loud honk of a horn on the other side of the street interrupted their conversation. They both turned their heads toward a white Chevy with a woman seated at the wheel, her hair covered with a floral silk scarf and her face hidden behind sunglasses. Fontana raised his hand, motioning for her to wait.

"Think of something, Carter, think of something," he mumbled, hardly parting his lips and not grabbing the keys his student handed him. "You can see there is nothing I can do."

"If I don't show up at the factory tonight, I'll be fired on Monday."

Fontana lit a cigarette with an anxious puff. On the other side of the lobby window, the three professors seemed to be getting restless.

"You know that if I were able to, I wouldn't hesitate, Professor, but—"

"The department will soon have to evaluate the scholarship applications for the following semester," Fontana said, cutting him short, emitting a puff of smoke.

"And you think that this activity could be considered an academic merit?" Daniel asked, immediately catching the hint.

"Even outside normal hours, no doubt about it."

The horn honked again and the three professors were about to emerge from the revolving door.

"I'll keep your car another night, then."

Fontana's large hand gave him a squeeze on the neck.

"Take good care of them, kid."

He took one last deep puff, flung the cigarette to the pavement, and crossed the street, headed toward the Chevy.

Chapter 12

—————————

They drove around Pittsburgh aimlessly, Daniel behind the wheel of Fontana's car, throwing fleeting glances at his watch. He had to find a way to keep the three Hispanists entertained in the Steel City no matter what, and there were only forty minutes left before his shift began. It started to snow.

For a copilot he had a Mexican professor, an expert on San Juan de la Cruz, with whom he chatted in English once in a while. Behind, wearing their coats and smoking like the possessed, were an elderly, unobtrusive Spaniard and another, younger one who got by in a confused linguistic hodgepodge that Daniel was barely able to decipher. It was too late to visit the Carnegie Museums, so Daniel passed by Pitt Stadium on the campus and crossed his fingers, but no luck: the Pittsburgh Panthers weren't practicing that evening. He kept driving to the vicinity of Forbes Field, but the Steelers' stadium was deserted too. He had thirty minutes left by the time they reached Loew's Penn Theater and he suggested they go inside to see Elvis Presley in *Love Me Tender*. None of the three showed any interest. How about a visit to the Atlantic Grill on Liberty Avenue, local temple of German food? The silent elderly professor roared with laughter and proceeded to have a coughing fit. A drink at the bar of the Roosevelt Hotel? No response.

Twenty minutes until clock-in, Daniel figured, looking at his watch again. It kept snowing. That damn scholarship.

"Listen, young man," the Mexican finally said as they crossed one of the bridges over the Monongahela River for the third time. "We humble professors, whom you have the kindness to accompany this evening, come from New York. I teach at the Hispanic Institute at Columbia University, Professor Montero is professor emeritus at Brooklyn College, and young Professor Godoy has just begun teaching at Wagner College on Staten Island. We are all accustomed to restaurants, movie theaters, and sporting events. What we'd like this evening is something unique, something that can only be done in Pittsburgh, do you understand?"

"Perfectly," Daniel said, taking a sharp turn.

Finally he had an idea. Perhaps it was madness, but he had no other card to play.

The factory reduced its activity during the night, but didn't stop it altogether. The first hurdle was the guard.

"Wait for me here, please."

He left them smoking in the car with the heater running full blast. Confused and intrigued, they watched through the windows while he headed toward the security booth. What he said next did not reach the ears of the three professors. Fortunately.

"Good evening, Bill," he greeted the guard, reading the tag that was pinned to his chest. He didn't know them all by name but remembered seeing this one before and knew he wasn't too bright.

"Good evening, kid," Bill answered back without quite ungluing his eyes from the sports section of the *Pittsburgh Post-Gazette*.

"My shift begins now," Daniel said, showing his card, "but you wouldn't believe what happened to me as I drove here."

"A flat tire?"

"Far from it. I saved three lives."

"You saved three lives?" Bill asked, setting his paper aside.

"Yes, sir, three lives. And perhaps even the future of this company."

He pointed to the car, where the three Hispanists sat perplexed, puffing their Lucky Strikes. Daniel continued in a confidential tone.

"I have here with me three European representatives of the food and agriculture industry. They were coming on a business visit to the famous Heinz Company, but their rental car broke down shortly after leaving the airport and had to be left in a ditch. Their motor caught fire; they could have died."

"My goodness . . ."

"But I happened to come across them by pure chance. And, thank goodness, even after the long delay, I've been able to drive them all the way here."

The guard scratched his head apprehensively behind his left ear.

"I'm afraid they can't come through now. At this time only employees have access."

"I know, but they have to see the factory right now."

"Why don't they come tomorrow?"

"Because tomorrow is Sunday."

"They can come Monday."

"Impossible: they're expected in Atlanta to see the Coca-Cola Company."

Daniel himself was astonished by the ease with which the lies were flowing out of his mouth. All because of that damn scholarship.

"Well, I don't know what to tell you, my friend . . ."

"Well, I wonder how you're going to explain to the manager next week that these sales representatives returned to Europe ready to sell millions of gallons of Coca-Cola there and not one single product of ours."

Once again the guard scratched his head.

"I may get myself into some trouble, right?"

"That's what I think."

Two minutes later they were all inside.

"Welcome to the heart of America, gentlemen," Daniel then declared in a screeching Spanish, trying to sound triumphant.

"Excuse me?" the professor emeritus asked.

"What is the essence of the American way of life?" Daniel asked.

He'd gone back to his native language: he needed it for the operetta that he was about to enact. Hardly giving them time to weigh in with a reply, he automatically answered himself: "The hamburger, naturally!"

They walked along the corridors as Daniel continued talking non-sense, all the while wondering what the hell he was going to say next.

"And what is the key to a good hamburger? You think the meat, perhaps? No way. The roll? Nope. Not the lettuce or onion either. The key is the ketchup! And the ketchup's secret lies right here. In Heinz!"

They'd reached the area where the bottles were filled, dark and deserted at that hour with all the machinery shrouded in a cemetery of silence. He searched for the light switches, flipping them all on until the fluorescent lights revealed the factory room's immensity. Luckily the night manager was elsewhere. Pacing back and forth, he improvised explanations for each of those gigantic machines, since he was largely ignorant of their purpose, having been in that area of the factory only a couple of times. But in a desperate flight of imagination, on coming upon what he vaguely recalled as the labeling machine, he dramatized its task. Afterwards, when they'd reached the area of closing and seal-ing, he insisted that each of them put a handful of screw tops in their pockets. Working their way backward, they finally reached the vat that initiated the process of filling. Daniel, with a leap, climbed onto the platform and stuck a finger inside. Seconds later, it emerged red.

"Ketchup, gentlemen, the company's prized product! Come and try it for yourselves!"

He held his hand out to the youngest of the professors who, still somewhat disconcerted, didn't dare refuse.

"Go ahead, Professor!" he insisted, forcing him to stick his hand into the tank.

He then helped up the Mexican, who was a little more reticent. His right hand also went straight into the tank. The mature Professor Montero, in spite of their insistence, refused.

While they descended the platform, Daniel again checked his watch. Time was running out and he had no idea as to what to do next. He then took them to the locker room and asked them to wait outside while he put on his sand-colored overalls, which all employees were required to wear. At the back could be heard the noise of the conveyor belts and the mechanical forklifts used to stack boxes on the trucks. Men's voices were shouting out orders and there was an occasional loud laugh. Meanwhile the professors, incongruous in their long dark coats, ties, and hats, were still wondering what on earth they were doing there.

As Daniel was leaving the men's locker room, three women were coming out of the women's locker room.

"Hello, student," two of them said in unison in a mocking tone. The third one slightly blushed on seeing him.

They were dressed in casual clothes and had makeup on, having just changed from their uniforms. The first was a tall brunette, the second a plump blonde, and the third, who had blushed, had chestnut-brown hair. The Mexican and young Spanish professor finally showed a spark of interest. The older gentleman coughed.

"What's up, girls? Are you already going home?" Daniel greeted them.

"What else?" the blonde said, feigning annoyance. "Prince Charming's not going to take us out dancing."

He seized the opportunity at once.

"Gentlemen, let me introduce you to my friends Ruth-Ann, Gina, and Mary-Lou. The prettiest women on the entire North Side, and the manufacturing industry's quickest canned-soup packers of all time. Girls, you have before you three wise men."

He spoke at top speed, realizing that he had barely a few minutes left before he had to press the Stop button on the mechanical forklift stacking boxes. While they shook hands and exchanged names, he moved close to the blonde's ear.

"Five bucks to each one of you if you show them the town for three hours," he said in a whisper, surreptitiously handing Gina the keys to Fontana's car. "And Thursday afternoon I'll invite you to the movies."

"Six bucks apiece," the one called Mary-Lou quickly corrected him. "And after the movies, dinner."

"Sirs, these lovely ladies are anxious to continue to show you around the premises of our great company. And afterwards they've offered to take you dancing. You won't find better company in the entire city, I can assure you. Although I'm afraid I'd be a nuisance, so if you'll allow me, now I'll leave you for the night."

The Hispanists were dumbfounded to see him dash out of there immediately. But before long those three young women, with all their charm and self-confidence—not to mention cocktails and cha-cha steps—made sure the Hispanists soon forgot him. Those three professors would forever remember that visit to Pittsburgh as an academic get-together like no other.

. . .

It was a significantly altered Daniel Carter who, nearly two years later and with an impressive number of classes and lectures under his belt, visited Professor Fontana one afternoon. He was now a seasoned young man, both physically and morally. He poked his head through the open door of the professor's office on one of the top floors of the imposing Cathedral of Learning.

"Come on, Carter, come on in," Fontana's robust voice greeted him in Spanish. "I was waiting for you. I see you are short of breath as usual. Sit down quietly for a while, please."

Daniel was more than used to the reigning chaos of crammed shelves, piles of essays and exams, and that office desk always littered with papers. With the passage of time, Andres Fontana had gone from being his academic supervisor to his respected mentor and even his friend who unfolded for the American some of the mysteries and idiosyncrasies of a country that had not yet healed from the wounds and horrors of its long civil war.

The professor maintained his austere Spanish formality in dealings with both colleagues and students. He was quick, resolute, solid in body and spirit, with a broad torso and large hands that seemed to have been created for some purpose less sophisticated than teaching. Although approaching fifty, apart from a few white hairs at his temples and in his beard, he still had a dense head of dark hair, always combed back, and a raspy voice that never spouted gratuitous praise. Despite his years of living in the United States and speaking flawless English, he had not rid himself of his native accent. Nor, after teaching for half a lifetime, did he hide his disapproval of a certain relaxed behavior among the students: untimely laughter, the occasional dash down the hallways, and that involuntary fondness of some for dozing off in his afternoon classes. He had little patience for frivolity and was stubbornly intolerant of laziness and procrastination. Nonetheless, he was generous and open to dialogue: always ready to talk to students, always capable of listening and debating without prejudice. Always ready to lend a hand.

Using his pen like a rapier, he made a few more energetic cross-outs without raising his eyes from the page, handwritten by some mediocre student whom he was tearing to pieces.

"I take it we're still interested in spending a good period of time in Spain," he said, holding his cigarette between his lips while his gaze remained fixed on his merciless corrections.

"Yes, sir, that's certainly the case."

Despite the trust they'd established with the passing of time, in academic settings they maintained an exquisite conventionality.

"Well, there's something I need to tell you. Start by taking a look at this."

A packet of several pages attached by a paper clip came gliding over the table and Daniel caught it on the fly. "Fulbright Program," he read aloud.

"It's finally going to make it to Spain, praise be to God."

As if to underscore his ironic comment, Fontana forcefully made one last horizontal line on the massacred text. Then he screwed the top of his fountain pen back on and concentrated on the issue at hand.

"It's an international academic exchange program financed by the United States Congress. Spain, however, had been kept on the margin until now, as in so many other things. But since our countries seem to be enjoying a sweet understanding at the moment, they've finally decided to open the door and a joint commission will soon be created."

"What exactly does the program consist of?" Daniel inquired, avidly glancing over the papers.

"Scholarships for graduate studies or research at a university in the chosen country."

"I just hope you don't ask me to entertain a few professors like last time in order to get it."

Fontana laughed heartily.

"Don't worry, I guarantee that this time around everything will be done by the book," he said, putting out his cigarette in an ashtray full of butts.

He still had a hard time recognizing in that young man the impetuous kid who not too long ago had arrived in his classroom with faltering Spanish and an overwhelming desire to learn. He'd toned down, smoothed out his rough edges, increased his command of the language tenfold, and, in spite of this, had not lost an iota of enthusiasm or the intellectual curiosity he'd arrived with on the first day. He'd obtained the scholarship that had finally freed him from his night work at the factory and allowed him to concentrate on his studies with even greater determination. But he still had a long way to go in order to achieve what he had been headed toward from the very start, Fontana thought. He still needed to be guided.

"Do you think I have a chance?"

"You tell me," the professor answered with a touch of sarcasm.

"Maybe I'll be lucky."

He folded the papers, stuck them in the back pocket of his pants, and began picking up his books, folders, and jacket from the floor with the haste of someone who is constantly short on time and overwhelmed with things to do.

"Just a minute, Carter, wait. I wonder when you'll be able to see me without having to dash off after five minutes."

"You know that I'm taking six classes this semester, Professor, and—"

"Don't burden me with your troubles, kid. Concentrate on what I've just finished telling you. These people need to be presented with a serious, well-thought-out project. Please sit down again."

Daniel obeyed, intrigued.

"I've thought of someone. Ramon J. Sender."

"Who is he?"

"A very good writer to start considering as a possible subject for a doctoral dissertation. And, moreover, a friend."

He flung a book across the large working table.

"Alive?" Daniel asked, skillfully catching the book with his left hand.

"Alive and well. He teaches modern literature in Albuquerque, New Mexico, and continues to write. I've just spent some time with him at an Amherst conference on narrative."

"Didn't he come to the Hispanist get-together?"

"He was unable to. And you can't imagine how I missed him."

"Visiting professor?"

"Full-time. Exiled."

"*Requiem for a Spanish Peasant*," Daniel read on the cover, then flipped through the pages of the slender book. "Quite short," he added as his only opinion.

"And very good. Definitive. It was published in Mexico four or five years ago. He's got a long list of titles to his name."

"Has there been anything previously written on him?"

"Hardly anything at all. He is persona non grata in Spain and also abroad in many places. This is why, if you finally agree, you'll have to tread with care."

He left the office with *Requiem for a Spanish Peasant* added to his already heavy load and with the conviction that he'd fight tooth and nail for that scholarship, which would also mean one more step in the reconciliation between his country and the Spain he was so eager to discover. He needed, first, to calmly ponder the idea of Sender. He had already spoken with Fontana about his intention of focusing a future PhD dissertation on some contemporary author. But he did not know the proposed author and preferred to have a clear idea of who he was before blindly rushing into an arduous two-year period poring over his work. Still, Daniel found the idea of his being condemned both inside and outside of Spain morbidly seductive.

Once in the hallway, ready to run off so as not to be late for his next class, he heard Fontana's voice in the distance like thunder, delivering one last sentence that he was not too sure he understood.

"Let's see if we can stick it to them all without their realizing it!"

Chapter 13

A TWA Lockheed L-1049 Super Constellation carrying Daniel Carter touched down on the Barajas runway one morning at the end of the scorching hot summer of 1958. The young man brought with him two suitcases, a portable typewriter, and a freight of bound-less optimism. His subsistence would be governed by the Fulbright scholarship that had been awarded to him, and at an exchange rate of forty-two pesetas to the dollar, he was hoping to be able to stretch it to live comfortably for the entire school year.

At that time Spain was still one of the poorest countries in Europe. Only four out of every hundred homes had a refrigerator, and women were not allowed to open a bank account or travel abroad without their parents' or husbands' consent. Although Spain had slowly begun to modernize after the 1953 Pact of Madrid between Franco and the United States, under which Spain received economic and military assistance in return for allowing the U.S. to build military bases, the country remained in many ways relatively primitive at the time of Daniel's arrival.

At the airport, a skinny young man approached him swiftly. Without removing the partially chewed-at cigarette dangling from his mouth, he offered to carry Daniel's luggage in a half-rusted wheelbarrow. Once outside the terminal and after a little tug-of-war with a colleague, the driver of a black taxi opened the rear door obligingly. "Where would the gentleman like me to take him?" the taxi driver said with a toothpick between his teeth.

"Calle Luisa Fernanda, number 26," Daniel replied. It was his first effort at communicating on Spanish soil.

He soaked up Madrid through the windows. Everything seemed fascinating, from the desolate arid area along the road from the airport into the suburbs to the increasing density of buildings and people as they entered the capital. The taxi driver, meanwhile, ready to extract a generous tip, offered to be his guide. Speaking at the top of his voice, to make sure Daniel understood correctly, he said, "If you wish to ask me anything, mister, I'm at your disposal."

"Thank you very much, señor," Daniel replied courteously, though preferring to continue absorbing everything silently.

Without being completely sure, he began to suspect that they were taking more turns than necessary. At times he even thought they were passing through the same place twice. He took in everything: workers in overalls and berets standing in front of a ditch, maids rushing by, and a pair of policemen dressed in gray uniforms. Blind lottery mongers yelling, "Twenty lucky same-number coupons for today's drawing!" Mothers with baskets on their way to the market; three priests dressed in cassocks crossing the street simultaneously. All extras, basically, on that great stage he'd been imagining for months.

"And this is the Puerta de Alcala: what a beauty," the taxi driver explained after zigzagging awhile. "And there is the Cibeles Fountain— look: like a queen. And now we're heading toward the Gran Via. Look, look, what a diva: Sarita Montiel in *The Last Torch Song*. The poster has been there for almost a year and each time I go by the Teatro Rialto my heart begins to race. You better not return to your country without seeing her sing 'Smoking While I Wait.'"

Daniel's eyes darted from advertisements for liquor and detergent to the names of subway entrances to municipal police blowing their whistles energetically as they directed traffic; from billboards announcing local and foreign films, to young ladies in dresses with tight-fitting waists and high heels that clicked gracefully along the sidewalks, to skinny, well-groomed men, smoking compulsively while hurling flirtatious remarks and obscenities without the least trace of decorum. Everything seemed captivating under the relentless September sun.

"And now we come to the Plaza de España. Take a look: the Torre de Madrid, just completed, is said to be almost five hundred feet high. What do you think?"

"Magnificent," Daniel lied. He didn't bother to explain that he had just stopped over in New York for a couple of days on his way to Spain.

"Thirty-seven floors and a fleet of fancy elevators," he added proudly. "The tallest skyscraper in Europe. And still people go around saying we don't do things properly here."

"Magnificent," Daniel repeated while his gaze rested on a woman in mourning who, seated on the ground with a child in tatters at her bosom, extended her hand, begging a few feet away from its main entrance.

"And now we're reaching your destination, coming into the neighborhood of Argüelles. This is Calle Princesa, and that over there, which is hardly visible, is the Liria Palace, the Duke of Alba's cottage; you should see how the fellow lives. And now we turn down Calle Luisa Fernanda, like the title of the zarzuela. At the end of the street we reach number 26, just as you requested. So here we are, my friend. Thirty-three fifty for the ride, plus ten pesetas for the luggage and for volunteering the information. You're not going to claim the tour was no good, eh, mister?"

Daniel knew full well that he could have done that same journey for half the price with a less sly and more honest taxi driver, but he paid the amount without complaining. An affordable extra, he thought, for the course that he'd just received—Spanish Picaresque of the Twentieth Century. Live.

The tip was another matter.

"What's this you've given me, my friend?" the taxi driver asked on seeing the strange coins the American had just handed him. His half-chewed-up toothpick, propelled perhaps by his shock, ended up on the ground.

"Fifteen cents, sir. So that you start learning a little about my country too."

He left his guide behind grumbling something unintelligible about his ancestors and carried his luggage into the building. The lobby was wide, that of a respectable bourgeois apartment building, with two polished lamps hanging from the ceiling, an ample stairway, and an elevator. To his right was a glass cubicle, presently empty, and next to it the open door of an apartment with a sign labeled CONCIERGE.

He rapped on the door but no one answered. He then found a bell, but got no response either. Finally he poked his head in and saw a plain room containing a round table covered with a crocheted tablecloth and with four chairs around it. "Hello," he said out loud. "Hello . . . hello . . ." he repeated still louder. No one appeared. Convinced that there was no one there, he decided to drag his luggage into the room and take off to explore the city, unwilling to waste a single minute of that first morning.

He wandered about aimlessly, once again absorbing everything with all five senses. He tried to decipher ads and conversations while savoring the unfamiliar aromas that emanated from various shops. Salted meats and fish, pickled products, dry goods, fritter stalls. Then he came upon a kiosk and his attention turned to the headlines that blared out the day's events. He read the front pages and chose several publications almost at random, hoping to get a deeper picture of the country he'd just landed in: *Ya, Pueblo* and *ABC*, because the salesperson declared they were the most widely sold. He then added *El Caso,* which promised juicy details regarding the murders perpetrated that summer by a criminal with the surname of Jarabo. And a color magazine whose name was paradoxically *Blanco y Negro (Black and White)*, which bore a photo of a puny dark kid on its cover whom they introduced as Joselito, "the little nightingale." At the last moment he noticed two young brats, practically glued to his legs, who were eyeing the children's publications rapturously while one eagerly scratched his head and the other dug intently at his nose. Daniel asked for three copies and was asked in turn, "Does *Tiovivo* suit the gentleman?" He gave two to the kids and added the other to his pile of publications.

After paying with a one-hundred-peseta bill and receiving a few coins for change, he realized that life in Madrid was going to be surprisingly cheap. So much the better, he thought as he pushed open the door to a nearby café. He could do more things, visit more places, buy more books. But for the time being, his priority was to figure out how he was going to fill his hungry stomach at eleven thirty in the morning. He found a place that announced in red letters its specialty was sandwiches and appetizers.

He spread out the newspapers he'd just bought on the table and tasted what the waiter had chosen for him, since he was unable to decipher the blackboard listing the house specialties: half a loaf of bread, stuffed fried calamari, and a glass of white, somewhat muddy wine served directly from a barrel. He devoured the newspapers as well as his order, and discovered between bites that Franco's boat was named *Azor* and learned the location of the port of Vigo. He also found out that a bullfighter by the name of El Litri would return to the rings the following season and that, as the paper went to press, a railway worker had been run over by a locomotive in the Estacion del Norte.

It was almost two o'clock in the afternoon when he returned to his initial destination. Through the still-ajar door of the concierge's apartment, noise and movement could be heard. A humming, an open faucet, the scream of "I'm coming, I'm coming, I'm coming" on hearing the bell ring. Small hurried steps coming closer and closer.

"Our Lady, Mother of Fairest Love, what a handsome lad you are, Mr. Daniel!" was the greeting from the plump lady, Señora Antonia, who appeared at the door drying her hands with a cloth.

He was unable to hold back a peal of laughter before such a compliment. Immediately afterwards, at her behest, he leaned down almost at a straight angle so that the concierge could place two wet, noisy kisses on his cheeks. She had been reserving them for two and a half months, ever since she'd received the letter from Andres Fontana informing her of the young American's arrival.

"Come on in, my son, come on in; the stew on the fire is practically ready. Imagine my going to the drugstore just the moment that you showed up!"

Daniel wanted to tell her that he'd already eaten something earlier and not to worry about him, that perhaps it was best that he lie down for a while. But he lost the battle even before he began it and had no choice but to sit at the table, which was already set, and place the checkered napkin on his shirtfront, just as she instructed. Who could have told him that that stew, the first of many that he'd consume in his life, with its soup, its meats, and its chickpeas, would—like so many other things in the coming months—have a flavor that was indefinable? Not even with the aid of the bilingual dictionary that he carried in his suitcase could he describe it.

Sleeping was a very different matter. The country that welcomed him no longer distributed ration cards or had a welfare service for the needy. Its proud autocracy had begun to crack, ingratiating itself with the Vatican and the United States government, and elevating to the top echelons of economic and political power a team of technocrats who, with an even greater ability than their predecessors, had the same interest in democratizing the country. That is, none. And the stagnation also seemed to permeate other spheres of life: in the average height of Spaniards, for instance, which was barely five foot seven for men and a few inches less for women; and correspondingly in furniture and household goods, still made for that small stature, like the insufficient bed that awaited Daniel in the bedroom that had belonged formerly to the concierge's sons.

"Oh, blessed Lord! What bed am I going to put you in with that height of yours?"

She began to clear the table: to her satisfaction, the American had had a second serving of stew, devoured half a platter of rice pudding, and topped it all off with half a pot of coffee. As soon as he saw her piling plates, he stood up, ready to help.

"Out of the question, my son, out of the question!" the concierge protested energetically. "You go ahead and start putting the suitcases in the room; I'll be there right away."

Sure enough, the bed was too small—but just how small, Daniel would have to find out.

"Lie down, kid, lie down . . ."

With great difficulty they contained their laughter. Daniel's legs stuck out of the bed from the middle of his calves on down.

"Mauricio the carpenter will fix this for us; you'll see," she said, tapping him lightly on the arm as if to reassure him. "What is your height, Mr. Daniel, so that I can tell him?"

"Six foot two," he answered automatically, adjusting to the language but not to the country's measurement units.

"And how much is that in plain Spanish, if I may ask?"

"Excuse me?"

"In meters, kid: how tall are you in meters?"

"Well . . . I don't know."

"We'll take care of that in no time at all," Señora Antonia mumbled under her breath as she left the room in search of her sewing kit. She was back a few seconds later. "Lean back against the wall," she said, unwinding the tape measure. Daniel obeyed, amused. "Wait, I can't reach," she said, bringing close the only chair in the room and hopping on it without a second thought. "Let's see, lift your head; don't move, there. A meter eighty-seven: there, now you know your height, in case you're called for the draft, God forbid."

Daniel was unable to understand the meaning of many of the widow's words and turns of phrase, but nonetheless he sensed perfectly her affectionate, generous disposition. Between them both, the young American student and the widowed Spanish matron, the bed problem was soon solved with a little ingenuity and the combined help from Mauricio, a neighborhood carpenter, and the mattress maker next door. The former used a few boards to construct an extension of the bed; the latter made a mattress specifically tailored to the addition; and Señora Antonia sewed some additional pieces of cotton onto the sheets to lengthen them.

After a few days' adaptation to Madrid in the concierge's humble dwelling, Daniel should have ventured to find more spacious quarters: a nice pension for young provincial gentlemen, a centrally situated hostel with lots of natural light, or perhaps a room in the infamous Students Residency. But he chose to continue living in the dark room that opened onto a patio in which there was always linen hanging and the smell of bleach, his only light coming from a bare bulb as he read, seated on a bulrush chair in the absence of a good, comfortable armchair. None of this seemed to bother him; in fact, quite the contrary. He found it to be vital, authentic, down-to-earth.

There might have also been in his choice not to move an unconscious desire to perpetuate something that had been abruptly interrupted more than two decades earlier. For it was at Señora Antonia's former quarters on Calle Princesa, before she had become a widow and her sons had flown the nest, that Professor Andres Fontana had lived during his student years in Madrid. He suggested those accommodations to Daniel as an initial option during his first days in Spain, after writing Señora Antonia from Pittsburgh to request that she receive his American student at a weekly rate of two hundred pesetas.

There were many reasons that, added together, left little room for doubt that Daniel would remain there. The stews with their tasty broth with bread to dunk; the freshly brewed coffee with which he opened his eyes in the morning; his hand-washed shirts that were starched and ironed with such care . . . Señora Antonia's anecdotes and her sharp memory of former times that, in uninterrupted sessions by the brazier table, would help him discover the substance of the country he was in; the wellspring of popular speech that he heard on a daily basis; the turns of phrase and funny anecdotes—all of these he began to jot down copiously in a small notebook that he thereafter always carried in his pocket.

And, perhaps without his realizing it, there was another reason why he remained: something intangible that he perceived the very first moment he crossed the threshold of that dwelling and encountered the crocheted tablecloth and the aged print of a village wedding. The smell of food on the fire; the framed print of the Sacred Heart; the almanac of dark-haired women with Cordovan hats and sad eyes; the constant sound of the radio, at times almost inaudible, with its stream of game shows, serials, and ballads. The enveloping warmth and tenderness. The fact that, after the abandonment he'd felt ever since he'd renounced a future in medicine or law, he was finally certain that someone truly cared about him.

Chapter 14

—————

B ut domestic life wasn't meant for Daniel. Right from the start he also took to the streets, wandering across a Madrid that constantly unfolded before his eyes, offering up its secrets at every corner. He invested his initial days in that erratic rambling through various neighborhoods, taking in the plazas and parks, churches and taverns, wine cellars, shops, schools, and department stores—and quickly showing his identification each time a hardheaded keeper of the peace and national security would, in the unlikeliest spot, plant himself before him.

Once that initial thirst was satisfied, Daniel finally decided to set a more definitive course and pursue his future. His objective was an area to the west of Madrid, close to his neighborhood of Argüelles, a place that, despite being the formal justification for his stay, he had yet to set foot in.

On a cloudy day in early October, the Facultad de Filosofia y Letras in University City awaited him just as it had Andres Fontana over two decades earlier. In the interim, a civil war had taken place, with a thorough sweep of undesirable professors and students and a program of reconstruction at all levels that would radically alter the institution's essence.

Minutes before Daniel was to head there, the widow came up

to him holding a pot in her hand with a rag wrapped around its hot handle. Having scrubbed the stairway on her knees, she was now about to serve him breakfast. The ordeal of having to go from one concierge job to another after her husband's death, dragging her sons along with hardly anything to eat and the constant struggle to get ahead, ended up making her stronger. After hiding her tears so that they wouldn't see her pain, loading furnaces, taking out the garbage, and swallowing countless miseries, she had become a resolute woman with no room for discouragement in her squat, compact body.

"Where are we off to today so elegantly dressed, my son?" she asked him while she poured the hot milk into his coffee.

She'd noticed Daniel's tie, full of stripes and colors, so different from the dark, sober ones the common Spaniard wore. It was the first time she'd seen him wearing it since his arrival.

"I'm afraid it's time for me to get down to work," he said while dunking one of the fritters she'd just bought fresh from the stall.

"So the good life is over, then."

In a few bites he polished off the fritters. He then answered:

"Or maybe it's just about to start. We'll see . . ."

On his way there, he once more pondered how he was going to present his project proposal to the Fulbright Commission. Fontana and he had sometimes spoken at length about it on their way from one class to another as they walked the neo-Gothic halls of the Cathedral of Learning, and on other occasions as well, such as while sharing a couple of beers after class on the long warm days at the end of spring, when the relationship between them had matured sufficiently so that their conversations extended beyond teaching hours.

"Caution, kid," Fontana would repeat. "Caution and a level head."

"Why do you insist so much on caution, Professor?"

"Because Ramon J. Sender is not liked by many, and it's best we don't cause any misgivings."

Fontana knew all too well what he was talking about. The writer from Aragon was then, in the late 1950s, a figure with a peculiar reputation among Spanish writers exiled after the civil war. A prolific novelist, essayist, and journalist even before the conflict, his life as a man of letters and arms on the Republican side was, however, full of ups and downs. A dissident of the Communist Party, accused by its leaders of dark episodes of cowardice and treason, afterwards he was subjected to a long campaign to discredit and unceremoniously exclude him from the circles of expatriate solidarity.

Sender himself had always refuted those accusations, although he openly recognized episodes of lack of discipline and even negligence in carrying out his military duties during the war. But where the Communist Party saw disloyalty and vileness, Sender and his few defenders saw it as a simple disagreement with the politics and military conduct of the party: a personal form of rebellion before the arbitrary authority and a heroic defense of his integrity as an individual. In any case, the reality was that the writer, faithful to his political compromise, had, like many others, gone into exile. Far from being considered one more among the group of exiles, he was instead treated like an enemy on numerous occasions, an awkward traveling companion during the diaspora's long journey.

He remained, however, loyal to his position. With his family destroyed forever—his wife executed in the cemetery of Zamora and his children taken in by a multimillionaire American woman—and after sojourns in France and Mexico, he ended up settling in the United States, where he continued to write and teach, remarried, and made new friends, many American, some Spanish, Andres Fontana among them.

Those talks with Fontana came to mind as Daniel made his way to the University City in search of his destiny. Once he arrived there, a concierge uniformed with the elegance of a colonel gave him directions.

"Dr. Don Domingo Cabeza de Vaca de Ramirez de Arellano, in Office 19, at the end of the corridor to your right."

He walked the corridors with a reverential attitude, hearing only his steps on the burnished floor. It was nine thirty in the morning, classes had already begun, and not a soul could be seen outside. He finally rapped on the door of the office indicated, whereupon a well-tuned voice told him to come in.

Not even if he'd purposely gone looking for it would he have found a room or a man so different from what he had expected. Cabeza de

Vaca had been a colleague of Fontana's in their prewar student days, and Daniel had naïvely expected to find on that first visit a certain similarity to his professor's personality and habitat.

Neatness, tradition, elegance. Three new concepts to write down in his vocabulary notebook. Three characteristics applicable to both the individual and his surroundings. A large walnut desk with turned legs, a silver inkstand, a calendar block, and an ivory crucifix. A lectern with an antique tome lying open, dark green velvet drapes, an enamel tray with a heraldic coat of arms, a glass bookcase full of leather-bound books. Behind the desk, a slim man of exquisite appearance, with pale skin, an impeccable suit, gray hair combed back, cuff links on his shirtsleeves, and a golden clip across his tie. He did not rise to greet Daniel but simply stretched his hand over the table. A light, thin hand, but not without a certain energy.

"A pleasure to meet you, Mr. Carter. Please sit down."

Daniel obeyed, fully aware of how out of place he was in that office and in such a presence. Hastily he adjusted his tie knot, straightened his lapels, and smoothed back his hair, which always had a disobedient tendency to fall over his face. He suddenly felt his attire to be too intense and too bright.

"What an honor that my dear colleague Andres Fontana has shown his faith in me by entrusting me with your tutorial. What a great honor."

Cabeza de Vaca's voice was modulated; his esteem for the Pittsburgh professor seemed genuine.

"Fontanita, Fontanita . . ." he murmured to himself. "How well things worked out for you in the end, you rascal. How glad I am, how . . . Good, Mr. Carter," he continued, changing tone, "so you are interested in specializing in our contemporary narrative."

"That is correct, sir."

"Excellent, young man, excellent. A wonderful academic objective. A fantastic idea."

Daniel did not need to be perfectly bilingual to read between the lines and notice that both adjectives, "wonderful" and "fantastic," had been uttered with something close to irony.

"And would you be so kind as to briefly explain the underlying reason for such a choice?"

It took Daniel seven and a half minutes to thrash out his reasoning; he had prepared the speech beforehand. The great Spanish literature and its noble authors, the strength of its prose, tradition, and heritage, the true representation of a people's spirit. An intense blah blah blah delivered in decent Spanish with a strong foreign accent, in which there was no room for the words "silenced," "exiled," or "dissident." Much less the name of Ramon J. Sender.

Cabeza de Vaca listened to him with the stillness of a marble statue, his silver fountain pen poised between his fingers.

"And would you be kind enough to give me some hints regarding your work methodology?"

Close monitoring, rigorous research, straightforward interpretations. Five long minutes of verbal acrobatics to avoid openly saying that he intended his work in Spain to center mainly on visiting the settings where the life and novels of an exiled writer took place.

"If I understand correctly, then, your intention is not to lock yourself up inside lecture halls and libraries."

Daniel attempted to camouflage his growing unease with Cabeza de Vaca's somewhat incisive professorial tone.

"Well, the truth is that my main intention is to find influenzas, points of departure, sources, and inspirations."

"Influences."

"Excuse me?"

"It's influences, not influenzas. Carry on, please."

"Influences. I'm sorry, sir. I mean to say . . . I meant to say . . . that my intention is to follow in the authors' vital footsteps to better understand their subsequent production."

The sentence came out just perfect; he'd studied it well. His satisfaction, however, was short-lived.

"To tread the same paths, feel the landscape's throb, before commencing your intellectual task—is that your intention?"

It had been many years since Daniel had felt that sensation: an excessive heat in his face and the realization that he was blushing.

"I'm afraid I don't understand, sir."

"What is it you don't understand?"

"Some of those words, Professor, I don't know their meanings."

"You'll learn them in due time, young man. Let us continue. And now tell me, do you have a particular author in mind?"

Before requesting Cabeza de Vaca as Daniel's advisor, Fontana had considered various options and thought of a handful of classmates who were now part of his old university's faculty. Through contacts with colleagues at other American universities, he'd obtained information on their careers and status, on their relations with the political regime and their level of involvement with the authorities. He didn't want his student to face problems in a Spain loaded with controls and rules: he was looking for someone who would officially accept Daniel within the institution, sign the necessary documents, and let him work at his own pace. Someone to whom that dislocated foreigner would barely matter. A mere bureaucratic link, a simple official procedure. Nothing else. Fontana himself would take care of the academic guidelines that would give shape to Daniel's future dissertation upon his return to the States.

He finally decided on Domingo Cabeza de Vaca despite the fact that his colleague's field of specialty was far from contemporary narrative and, even more so, from those writers exiled by the civil war. Knowing full well that he belonged to the winners' camp and that in his world there was not even a remote shadow of a link with those who for three atrocious years were on the other side, Fontana nonetheless intuited that Cabeza de Vaca could be trusted. However, he preferred not to be too explicit just in case, hoping that his colleague, who was absorbed in a seven-century-old universe of manuscripts, would accept a bureaucratically appropriate operation but remain altogether aloof. Nevertheless, for Cabeza de Vaca, that wasn't enough apparently; it wouldn't do. He needed to know more.

As for Cabeza de Vaca's question regarding his personal interest in some particular author, Daniel knew he could not lie. He was aware that it was not in his interest to speak openly about Sender; that he would be better off sticking to generic writers and abstract themes. But Fontana and he had considered this scenario and agreed that, in the event that Daniel was corralled, deception was too dangerous an option.

"I must admit that there are some authors in whom I have a particular interest, although they are all worthy of . . ."

Cabeza de Vaca raised an eyebrow, and Daniel knew there was no way out.

"Ramon J. Sender, sir."

"Frankly interesting . . . In other words, what you intend to do is to follow Sender's footsteps in Spain so as to afterwards research his literary production."

"That is so, more or less," Daniel acknowledged in a somewhat quieter tone.

"Then, and correct me if I'm mistaken: you don't contemplate reading the author's works while in Spain?"

He stirred in his chair, crossed his legs, then immediately uncrossed them. This was going further than he and Fontana had foreseen at Pitt.

"It's not possible, sir."

"Would you be kind enough to explain the reason?"

Daniel again changed posture and readjusted the knot of his tie, which was choking him.

"It's hard to come by his books in Spain," he finally admitted.

"Hard?"

"Impossible, rather."

"For some reason in particular?"

Daniel cleared his throat and swallowed hard.

"Censorship, sir. Ramon J. Sender's books are forbidden."

"And do you think that is correct?"

Daniel noticed that his mouth was dry. His head, however, was boiling.

"Do you find this to be correct or not, Mr. Carter?" the professor repeated.

Daniel knew that he was taking a gamble and that this could be the end of it all: of his stay in Spain, of his scholarship, of his still-incipient professional career. But he took a risk because he felt he had no other alternative.

"No, Professor. I don't think it's correct."

"Why?"

"Because I don't think voices should be silent."

"Silenced."

"Excuse me?"

"We are not talking of personal decisions but rather of external impositions, right or wrong?"

"Yes, sir," he whispered.

He did not want to show that at that moment the only thing that really mattered to him was not being kicked out of there.

The professor's reaction took a couple of seconds to surface, and in the interim, while they held each other's gaze, Daniel's mind passed in hasty sequence through the worst scenarios. Fontana had been mistaken: trusting this colleague of his had been a terrible decision; he would never work on Sender's oeuvre; the Fulbright Commission would be informed and his scholarship rescinded, and he would have to return to Pittsburgh shortly thereafter. Good-bye to Madrid and his dream of traveling throughout Spain. Perhaps he should have listened to his parents and given up on his absurd dream of specializing in a foreign language. Perhaps his professional destiny was really in law school or in the emergency ward of some hospital. Or in the Heinz factory, loading trucks with ketchup and cans of beans until his weary body gave out.

"Very well, Mr. Carter, very well . . ." the professor finally declared, a faint mocking smile lingering in the corner of his mouth. "In spite of the uncomfortable moment that I have made you go through, I have no doubt that you will end up being a good Hispanist once you've consolidated your command of the language and moved forward with your research. For the time being you seem to be well on track, with firm opinions and an evident determination."

Daniel was about to gasp in relief, to loosen up and finally feel safe.

"But you still have an arduous road ahead of you," the professor added. "And for this reason, as a first step and before you embark on your mission, we must fulfill some formal requirements."

Once again he felt somewhat alarmed but was sure that the worst was behind him. The professor, meanwhile, continued to elaborate in his well-measured speech.

"So that we cover all the academic requirements, we're going to enroll you in two courses. The first will be Visigothic Paleography, with a special emphasis on *Commentary on the Apocalypse* by Beatus of Liebana. I teach it on Mondays, Tuesdays, and Wednesdays at eight o'clock in the morning. The second, Comparative Analysis of the Silos Glosses and Saint Emilianus Glosses, Thursdays and Fridays from seven thirty to nine in the evening."

The young American began searching for phrases in his half-baked Spanish that would exempt him from having to study something so absurdly alien to his interests.

"Excuse me, sir, but I . . . well, my intention—"

"Although, you will be exempt from attending the courses of either of these subject matters without being prevented from obtaining an A if I have you back here next month to inform me how your sojourn in Upper Aragon went, following in Sender's footsteps."

Daniel's face must have shown something like stupor. Cabeza de Vaca, breaking with his exquisite iciness, burst out laughing.

He continued. "Your words are convincing, as well as the letters of recommendation that I have received from the University of Pittsburgh and the report from the Fulbright Foundation. Although, naturally, I was not ready to accept a student from my dear Andres Fontana without first reestablishing contact with him. Not out of distrust. Please understand me: I would have accepted any request of his without any hesitation whatsoever. But I didn't want to pass up the opportunity to learn how my old colleague was doing and to find out how he has fared all these years."

Despite being overcome by a wave of relief, Daniel suddenly realized that he didn't know much about his professor's past either. Their conversations had almost always centered on the present and, especially, the future: plans, projects, and objectives. The little he knew about Fontana was confined to classrooms and lectures, to the historic and literary past of his country.

"It was moving, believe me. I never learned of his whereabouts since we finished our studies in 1935. I knew that he intended to spend a semester as a lecturer at some American university, but I was unaware if he'd ever returned, if he'd fought in the war or not, if he'd been killed, or if he'd survived."

"He never returned to Spain," Daniel stated.

"I know, I know. Now I know everything. I've found out what that miner's son's perseverance and drive ended up forging. He was never intimidated by us, all the young gentlemen teeming about the place. I always admired that in him: the self-confidence, his ability to adapt to everything without ever losing the perspective of who he was or where he came from. It's been a great pleasure to be in touch with him again. And he's sent me a message for you. Here, transcribed word for word."

He handed Daniel a folded sheet of paper containing a handful of simple words in English. *Let him have his way*, Daniel read to himself. So that was what his teacher advised.

"Contrary to what you two schemed in the very beginning, I pledged to Andres Fontana not only to act as your nominal supervisor to fulfill the formal requirements of your scholarship, Mr. Carter, but to truly help you in any way within my power."

"I'm most grateful, sir."

Cabeza de Vaca continued talking as if he hadn't heard him.

"Unlike what you thought at the beginning, deep down your project pleases me. Or I'm going to make an effort for it to please me, to be more precise. You will soon find out why."

He then leaned sideways, grabbing something that was not visible from behind the walnut desk. It turned out to be a crutch that the professor skillfully adjusted beneath his right arm while making an energetic effort to stand up. Only then was Daniel able to see his injured body.

"The war took my girlfriend, two brothers, and a leg. One needs to be very strong to overcome something like that and look at the future without anxiety. I wasn't able. I lacked the courage and, because of this, took refuge in the past. I withdrew all the way back to the Middle Ages," he said, collapsing into the chair once more and dropping the crutch on the floor. The resounding noise of the wood against the tiles didn't seem to faze him. "Between codices, the chronicles, and cantigas I found the peace that memories and nightmares deprived me of."

"I understand . . ." Daniel whispered, although he didn't understand at all.

"But my coping mechanism is by no means the most sensible. That is why I think I must make an effort to understand and help whoever insists on moving forward. You know, I've been considering this matter since I reestablished contact with Fontana. And although I never pictured myself defending this position, I've reached the conclusion that this country would be heading in the wrong direction if all intellectuals hid as I did in the distant past. I think we need to move toward the future and to listen to the voices of those who survived the atrocity of our civil war: those who stayed and those who left; those who are still here and those who are in exile."

"Are you referring to exiles like Sender, sir?" Daniel asked doubtfully.

"Exactly. The only ones who have been silenced forever are the dead. The rest, even in the distance, still remain sons of the fatherland, keeping its memory alive and ennobling our language with their words. To ignore them and to perpetuate the painful division that separates those outside from those inside will only stunt our country's intellectual development even more."

"That is also how Dr. Fontana sees it, Professor," Daniel ventured to say.

"And that is how I believe we should all start thinking around here. To consider those who can't or don't want to come back as an essential part of our culture is, like it or not, a moral responsibility. So count on me in your efforts. I've got a feeling there won't be much I can do for you, but here I am, just in case. I only ask you in exchange to keep me abreast of your progress."

"I will do as you ask. Thank you very much, Professor" was all Daniel managed to reply.

"I'll be waiting for you," Cabeza de Vaca concluded, extending his hand but not getting up again. "You have before you a heroic monarchist soldier and a 'Knight Wounded in the Noble Service of God, the

Fatherland and the Charters.' A dreamer who didn't have the luck of his mentor, swallowed a tall tale of the great crusade, and didn't know how to get out of the way at the right moment."

Daniel firmly shook his hand, transmitting a mixture of admiration and bewilderment.

"I will return in a month's time, sir, I promise."

"I hope so. And one last thing before you leave. You probably don't know the film *Welcome, Mr. Marshall!*, right?"

"No, I don't know it."

"It was released several years back, in 1953, if I'm not mistaken. It is both amusing and distressing. See it if you get the chance, and then you can reflect upon it. Try not to do the same thing your compatriots do in the film. Respect this nation, young man. Don't pass before us without stopping to try and understand who we are. Don't rely on the anecdotal; don't judge us simplistically. We trust you, Daniel Carter. Don't let us down."

Chapter 15

———————

The calendar moved through autumn; Halloween went by with its witches, scarecrows, and pumpkins. Then came a period of rain, and in tandem my mood also clouded over.

The cause was no longer a continent and an ocean away, but much closer: in my immediate surroundings and my daily work; in the morass that Professor Fontana's output had become with the passage of time. The texts I was working on dated from the sixties; some were typed, but the majority of them were still in longhand. My problem, however, was not with the writing itself but rather its content: the lack of coherence between the texts; the gaps and absence of a core. As if large chunks of information were missing, as if someone had ripped entire sections right out.

Moreover, the subject matter of the texts was quite different from that of previous decades. Spanish authors, the literature of exile, and so many other recurring themes appeared to have been gradually dropped after Fontana settled in California in the early sixties. Where there once were novelists, poets, and playwrights, I now found the names of explorers and Franciscan monks whose lives and actions I didn't know anything about; old chronicles about the Spaniards in that northern fringe of New Spain; along with the names of prisons and missions.

Trying to find any coherence in all that information had been driving me crazy all week long. Doubts kept piling up until Thursday afternoon, when I finally decided to turn to someone whom I perhaps should have sought out from the start. Before doing so, I stopped at Rebecca's office to be pointed in the right direction.

"Try in Selma's Café, next to the plaza. He usually goes there every afternoon if he's in town."

On leaving Guevara Hall I found the weather unsettled and the surrounding area agitated. People were revving up, according to what some students told me, to start a demonstration against the construction of the mall in the area of Los Pinitos, that spot of peace and green that I'd discovered weeks earlier after seeing the photos of Andres Fontana in the conference room.

The *Santa Cecilia Chronicle* and the university paper devoted increasing coverage to the issue: feature articles, op-eds both for and against, letters to the editor. The major opposition to the project evidently had originated in the university, and among its visible leaders was my student Joe Super, the professor emeritus from the History Department who on the first day of class had mentioned the Franciscans and their missions. The reasons were convincing: it would be an environmental disaster and possibly even an illegal use of that land, since the legitimacy of its ownership, according to what Rebecca and Daniel had told me, was not altogether clear. It was not private property, nor was it public, despite the fact that the local authorities were in charge of its upkeep. As a result, a medley of interests had created a platform against the project.

I noticed that some of the students were carrying signs or megaphones, and farther afield there was a youth with Rastafarian dreadlocks and an enormous drum. The event had not started yet, but there was already quite a bustle. I came across cars sporting flags and honking their horns as a sign of support. I made my way through a group of elderly ladies, one of whom tried to sell me a bright-orange T-shirt with protest messages emblazoned on it, while another handed me a sticker with simply the word NO!

I managed to cut through the crowd and reached my destination zigzagging between the demonstrators; in fact, I wasn't going too far. My objective was a café that looked as if it had been open for a few decades, a place I'd passed by a dozen times but had never entered. And there, next to the window facing the street, I found him.

"I've come looking for you."

"What a great honor," he said, standing up to greet me. "I was watching you wend your way through all those nuts but didn't imagine you were coming to see me. Have a seat. What's up?"

On the table, in front of an old leather armchair, he had a laptop, a few books, and a pad full of notes and doodles. I wasn't too sure it was the most appropriate moment; perhaps my invasion had been somewhat abrupt. It was he, though, who'd offered to give me a hand with Fontana the evening we shared an improvised dinner at Rebecca's place.

"Are you sure I'm not interrupting you, Daniel?" I said as I removed my raincoat. "We can talk some other time if this is not a good moment."

"Of course you're interrupting me. And you have no idea how grateful I am at this hour, after a full day's work, for a good, long interruption."

The place was comfortable, cozy: wooden floors and walls, armchairs strewn about, and a couple of pool tables. Behind the long empty bar, a waiter dried glasses unhurriedly while he watched a football game on a large silent screen. Almost inaudibly through the loudspeakers came Crosby, Stills, Nash & Young's legendary "Teach Your Children."

"Rebecca told me that you come here almost every afternoon," I said while attempting to smooth my hair after the windy walk.

"During the morning I usually work out of my apartment and in the afternoons I prefer a change of scenery, to get a breath of fresh air. This is a good place; there's practically no one here at this time of day. And the coffee isn't too bad. Of course, it doesn't compare to a good *café con leche* at a Spanish bar, but it's better than nothing."

He raised his mug as if to catch the waiter's attention and motioned without words that he bring another one for me.

Among his books I discovered some I'd read by fits and starts when my sons were small. Back then I used to carry large tote bags in which the most unexpected things would accumulate: Playmobil toys mixed in with packs of Ducados cigarettes, a couple of bananas, pens without their caps, half-eaten ham and cheese sandwiches. And some book or other. Always a book that I'd dip into as best I could while David came down the slide or Pablo kicked his first ball around or we sat in the pediatrician's waiting room. In time I quit smoking and improved my purchasing power, and my kids forgot about firefighters and cowboys, asking instead for video games and the freedom to come and go as they pleased. And those tote bags turned into authentic leather bags, fashionable, the real thing. I was unable, however, to rid myself of the desire that they be large and almost always contain a novel.

The waiter appeared with my coffee and refilled Daniel's mug.

"Spanish writers from the end of the century, that's what I'm up to: the last twenty-five years of your literature. Those who came before and those who appeared during that period. Although I imagine you haven't come to see me to talk about the whole gang, which I'm sure you know as well as I do."

"That's correct," I said as I tore open a sugar packet. "I wanted to talk to you about something else."

He looked at me with eyes that had read and lived a great deal before that gray afternoon.

"About Andres Fontana, I imagine."

"You imagine correctly."

"Is his legacy getting a bit complicated?"

"You can't imagine how much."

I answered with my eyes concentrated on the coffee's blackness. Unaware I was speaking in a hush. As if I were discussing the intimate problems of someone close instead of discussing a work-related matter. As if my entire assignment had suddenly turned into something personal.

"I'm here to help you with whatever you may need, Blanca, as I said."

"This is why I've come. By the way, do you know that I found a postcard of yours the other day among his things?"

"I can't believe it!" he said, laughing out loud.

"New Year's Eve, 1958. You were announcing your departure from Madrid to someplace or other in search of Mr. Witt."

"Oh my God . . ." he whispered while smiling with a trace of nostalgia. "That was my first Christmas in Spain, when I was still researching my dissertation. It was he who suggested that I work on Sender. Who would have guessed: that changed my life for good. Anyhow, I don't wish to entertain you with melancholy stories from way back when. Tell me, what kind of difficulties is my dear old professor getting you into now?"

I demurred before choosing the appropriate words, taking my time while stirring in the sugar. It wasn't altogether clear to me how best to express what I wanted from him.

"I'm done classifying by decades until the fifties and now I'm beginning with the texts of the California period, the sixties," I finally said. "They're interesting but very different from the previous."

"Less literary, I take it."

"That's right. They no longer focus mainly on authors or on literary criticism, as had been the case up to then, although there are always notes on the subject. In general they're more historical, more Californian, less familiar; that's why I'm having a harder time classifying them. Besides, the dates are mixed up, and occasionally I'm at a loss because I have the feeling that information is missing."

"And what you want to know is if I know whether something is actually missing."

"That's correct. And since we're at it, out of mere personal curiosity, I'd also like you to explain, if you have any idea, that sudden turn in his career. Why did literature all but cease to interest him, and why did he instead plunge into the history of California, something that was basically alien to him and his academic interests?"

He took his time to reply, pondering the question with his big hands wrapped around the mug.

"Question number one, whether there is information missing or if I know what could have happened to whatever you believe to be missing, has a simple answer: I haven't got the foggiest clue. I left Santa

Cecilia shortly after his death, and as far as I'm aware, all his documents remained in the university without anyone touching them until your arrival. In fact, even I didn't get to see them outside his office."

"How long did you live here?" I asked point-blank, perhaps a little indiscreetly. Daniel Carter's private life had nothing to do with my work on Fontana or his affairs, but I suddenly felt an urge to know.

"About two and half years: less than six semesters."

"How long ago?"

"I left in '69, so that . . ." He performed a quick mental operation and added, "God, thirty years ago! Unbelievable!"

Reclining in his leather chair in his navy-blue sweater, with his long legs crossed and his left elbow on the armrest, he seemed completely comfortable, like someone who after so much coming and going in life is capable of being at ease anywhere.

"As for your second question, regarding the sudden turn in his research interests, the truth is that my answer is only a tentative one, because after so long my memories are somewhat vague. But I think he fell in love with the history of California from the very moment he settled here and that's probably why you noticed a change in his output. He discovered a connection between this land and Spain, and that—don't ask me why—fascinated him."

"And why did he come here? Why did he leave Pittsburgh?"

I too had made myself comfortable, thanks to the coziness of the café or the revitalizing coffee. Or Daniel's natural ability to make me feel at ease around him.

"All of us who knew him were surprised that, after spending so many years in a big urban campus such as Pitt's, he would decide to move to this small city at the other end of the country. But he had his reasons. First, he was offered the quite tempting position of department chairman. Secondly, he'd just gotten divorced, ending a relationship that had left a bitter taste in his mouth, so I imagine he wanted to get away from there."

I was surprised, not having seen any reference to marriage or divorce among his papers. And I told him so.

"It was a short marriage to a Hungarian biology professor. I hardly met her, but I know they were together on and off for a few years, mutually torturing each other, until they decided to get married. By then I was no longer at Pitt, but according to what he told me sometime later and without going into detail, a few months into the marriage they both realized it had been a mistake."

I would have liked to learn a little more about that, but he didn't seem to have any additional information.

"And although he didn't tell anyone," Daniel continued, "perhaps the main reason he decided on a change of scenery was because his health was starting to decline. In appearance he was strong and robust; his students often called him the Spanish bull. But his lungs were damaged. He was a chain-smoker, and the relentless winters and smoke from the Pittsburgh factories further ruined his health. So he decided to move, settle somewhere quiet with a moderate climate and less pollution. That's how he ended up in Santa Cecilia."

"And you followed him . . ."

Once again I realized my indiscretion too late, although it didn't seem to bother him in the least.

"No, no, not at all," he said, changing his posture. "I came years later; before that I was in a few other places. In time an interesting position opened in this department, he offered it to me, and that's how I landed here—although where I really wanted to go was to Berkeley. I thought this would only be a nearby, transitory stop."

"Did you manage to make it to Berkeley in the end?"

"Well, as a matter of fact, everything took a turn that no one had anticipated . . . To make a long story short, the result is that I never did become a professor at Berkeley, and Andres Fontana died a little over two years after my arrival in Santa Cecilia."

"Was he that sick?"

"Not at all. In fact, he felt much better here."

"Then . . ."

"He died in an accident." He took a sip of coffee before resuming his narrative. "Driving his own car, the old Oldsmobile that he had had for the longest time."

That end had never crossed my mind; unconsciously, I'd thought his life had extinguished itself from natural causes, the wear and tear of age.

I wanted to continue asking Daniel questions: he seemed open to answering without reserve. What he was offering me were broad brushstrokes of Fontana's life, but I found them valuable. I regretted not having come to him earlier: I would have saved myself hours of doubt and a headache or two.

The noise coming from the street suddenly diverted our attention and we both focused on what was happening on the other side of the coffee shop window. The young man with the Rastafarian hair and the large drum, like an alternative Pied Piper of Hamelin, started the demonstration. Behind him was a crowd made up of students holding signs and megaphones, young couples with baby carriages, professors and middle-aged citizens, schoolkids with colored balloons, and the energetic old ladies selling T-shirts and yelling like truck drivers.

"Should we get going?" he said, starting to pick up his books.

I put my raincoat back on as he finished gathering his things, leaving several dollars on the table without waiting for the waiter to bring the bill. Then he jotted down something quickly on a napkin.

"In case you still need me," he said, and handed it to me.

While I was putting the two phone numbers—cell and home, I figured—in a pocket, he slung his heavy backpack over his shoulder and I did the same with my bag.

"Thanks a million for clarifying a few things," I said as we left.

"On the contrary, Blanca, you're doing me a favor. I like to reminisce about my old friend, to talk about him again. It's healthy to unburden oneself of memories and make peace with all that has been left behind."

The afternoon's weather was getting bleaker; no sooner had we set foot on the street than I closed my raincoat, crossing my arms firmly against my chest, and Daniel pulled up the collar of his overcoat. The wind stirred our hair.

"You know," he added, a half smile visible amid his light-colored beard, "had he lived, Andres Fontana would no doubt have been at this protest. He was always against any meddling. I told you that he often took long walks in Los Pinitos, right? Especially in the last couple of months, when he still had no idea how little time he had left."

He then passed an arm around my shoulders, partly protecting me from the tumult and partly pulling me toward him. A couple of seconds later we were in the midst of the protest. In between yells, songs, slogans, and the booming of the drum, Daniel had to shout for me to hear him.

"He was fond of saying, half-serious, half-joking, that he walked there in search of the truth."

Chapter 16

Toward the middle of November my birthday approached and with it a handful of electronic greetings from family and friends. Along with their best wishes, most asked in passing when was I planning on coming back, but I was not forthcoming with dates because I didn't even know myself. My fellowship did not stipulate a precise end date, stating instead that I had three to four months to complete the assigned task. I still had work ahead of me, and for the time being had no intention whatsoever of returning.

Being a year older is not the most encouraging thing that can happen to someone whose husband has just left her for a younger woman. Nor did it raise my spirits that I lived far from my sons or that I received insistent calls from my sister every four or five days furiously goading me on to sabotage my ex-husband on his road to happiness. Nevertheless, I decided to celebrate the date, perhaps to prove to myself that life, in spite of it all, went on.

No one in Santa Cecilia knew it was my birthday. Perhaps because of this, and in an attempt to make the day special and add some color to my life, I decided to throw a party—a Spanish party for my recently made American friends, who had opened the doors to their homes and offered me their time and affection. A party in which none of the typical travel-guide Spanish ingredients would be missing; a wink perhaps to the long-past National Hispanic Heritage Month debate. I'd serve potato omelets, gazpacho, sangria, olives. I decided, however, to keep the reason for the gathering secret.

I ran off some invitations on the old office printer, which most of the time functioned capriciously. I distributed them among the department's mailboxes and handed out another batch to my students. I hadn't given everyone much notice, but that's just how it had worked out. Unexpectedly, unforeseen. Just like everything else lately.

Once people had confirmed, I calculated that there would be more than thirty of us, between those invited and their respective partners. Luis Zarate accepted from the very start, as did several other colleagues. Rebecca would be there, of course. Daniel Carter would come by if he managed to make it on time: the night of the party, he'd be returning from a conference in Phoenix, he'd told me over the phone. And most of my students wouldn't let me down either.

After initially hesitating, I finally decided to invite Fanny as well, but she refused, claiming that she always dined with her church members on Saturdays. I'd gotten used to her strange personality and we managed to get along well, even with affection. I was no longer taken aback by her small eccentricities and her messy way of doing things; time had turned her into a close presence, almost dear. Not exactly into a friend, but someone special.

"Is there anything I can help you with or lend you?" Rebecca offered when I told her of my plans.

Before I could reply, she assumed the answer was yes and started to reel off the essential supplies to convert my 450-square-foot apartment into a decent place for a party.

"Let me think . . . I've got a collapsible table and folding chairs for when I have a crowd at my place. I can also lend you cooking utensils if you need them and, if you want, a large tablecloth, glasses, and cutlery . . ."

I had no other choice than to cut short her overwhelming generosity, otherwise my tiny space would be so packed with stuff that the guests wouldn't fit. I accepted the table, a few chairs, and a couple of other odds and ends. The rest would be disposable.

"When I'm done Friday afternoon, I'll wait for you and we can stop at my place first, load the car, and take it all to your apartment. I have to go to Oakland on Saturday morning and most likely will only return just in time for the party, so it's better if we get it all ready the day before."

. . .

At a little after five, we pulled up in front of Rebecca's house. There was a lush garden and pool at the back, and a big hairy gray-and-white dog of dubious pedigree and with a preference for pizza crusts, she told me. His name was Macan and he was as genial as his owner. He just showed up one day ten years ago; Rebecca said her daughters found him tied to the rear wheel of one of their bikes. They put up posters in the area, but no one ever claimed him.

There were still indelible marks of the inhabitants who had passed through the house: skates and bicycles in the garage, raincoats on the clothes rack behind the door. Rebecca had three children and five grandchildren, none of whom lived nearby. However, the house didn't look like that of a mature, independent woman but more like one whose family members had just gone out to the movies or on a brief errand. Not a typical empty nest but rather a refuge to which they could all return at any moment and feel as if they'd never left.

"Let's begin in the kitchen," she proposed.

The room had a large window overlooking the garden and a wooden island with burners at its center, above which, suspended from an iron frame, hung pots, pans, and clusters of dried herbs. Rebecca's efficiency evidently went beyond the office: everything was in its place, the jars labeled, the calendar on the wall with neatly written annotations, and some recently cut flowers in a vase on the counter.

"This is for the gazpacho," she said, taking out an enormous electric contraption with a glass jar attached to it.

I said that a simple blender would do just fine, but apparently she didn't have one.

"And this is for the sangria. Pablo Gonzalez, the Colombian professor, brought it back for me from Spain some years ago," she announced, raising a large earthenware pitcher with a spout at the bottom. "Now let's go to the basement to fetch the chairs."

We descended to a large open room where household goods and odds and ends were neatly stacked. In the center was a ping-pong table, and along the walls were cardboard boxes labeled with the names of their owners and their contents; posters of bygone singers; hundreds of vinyl records; and loads of photographs, pennants, and diplomas affixed to an enormous corkboard. A junk dealer's paradise, with the order of a military parade.

While Rebecca located the folding chairs, I was unable to resist the temptation to take a look at the photos. Picnics on the beach, kids' parties, prom dances, toddlers who were now parents, and grandparents who were only alive in the memories of their descendants.

"Well, we're done," Rebecca announced as soon as she'd finished stacking a few chairs next to the stairs. She came over to where I was looking at the photos. "They're ancient," she said, smiling.

Just as she'd shown me the picture of Andres Fontana in the department's conference room shortly after my arrival, now she pointed out who was who in her large family. For each image she had a reminiscence, an anecdote.

"This was a Fourth of July on the beach; in the end we got caught in a huge storm that ruined our fireworks. Here we are on an excursion to Angel Island, in the bay. That day my son, Jimmy, ended up falling off his skateboard and wound up with a gash in his head. He had to have seven stitches."

She continued traveling in time as she went through the photos, until she came to one with a group of young adults.

"My God, what a sight! So many years ago! It's been a while since I've looked at this one. Let's see if you can recognize anyone," she challenged me.

I looked at the snapshot carefully. Four people in the open air, two men at the sides, two women in the middle. All leaning against a large red car covered in dust. In the background, a desert landscape and what looked like Mexican houses. In the distance, the sea. The first one on the left was a dark-haired man with a wide band around his head. Very skinny, with a flowered shirt and a beer in an extended hand, as if toasting the photographer. Next to him, a short girl, all smiles, with her hands stuffed in her shorts pockets, two braids, and a yellow shirt with the word PEACE emblazoned across it. The third figure was a young woman, slender and pretty. Her large mouth seemed to have been captured just as she burst out laughing. She was wearing countless colored necklaces and a long white dress that reached almost to her bare feet. Next to her, a tall man wearing a faded shirt and ragged jeans completed the group. One could hardly make out his face, which was hidden behind a mane of blond hair that reached his shoulders, a thick beard, and sunglasses. It looked like summer, and they were tanned, oozing happiness.

"No idea."

Although I didn't know who they were, I wouldn't have minded being one of them. So radiant and carefree.

"This is me," she explained, pointing to the girl with the braids.

"No!" I said with a loud laugh.

It was really hard to imagine that the elegant and mature Rebecca Cullen I knew was that girl with scanty shorts whose bosom proclaimed world peace.

"And there is someone else you know. Take a good look . . ."

I did, but unsuccessfully. Then she placed her finger on the last figure, the tall man with long hair and beard.

"Take a good look . . ."

Suddenly I thought I could recognize him. Although I could barely see his face, there was something in his figure that made me intuit who it might be.

"Daniel Carter?" I ventured to ask.

"Exactly," she confirmed with a nostalgic smile. "My God, how much time has gone by! Look, how young we were, the clothes we wore—the hair." She pointed again to the photo, moving her finger over the remaining figures. "This was his wife, and this is my ex-husband, Paul."

I stopped myself from asking what had become of them. There was no need, however, because as Rebecca moved away from the photos and got ready to pick up the chairs, she began to elaborate.

"That photo was taken in Cabo San Lucas, in Baja California. Although I look very young, my three kids were already born. Paul, my husband, was a philosophy professor here in Santa Cecilia. We'd moved to California from Wisconsin three years earlier. The Carters arrived a little later and we became good friends."

We were going up the stairs, Rebecca carrying the folding chairs, me dragging a table behind.

"At the time, I was centered exclusively on my family. I didn't work. The kids were still small and had come one after the other. We'd just finished buying this house; it was in ruins and we were still fixing it up. My parents came from Chicago that summer and stayed with our kids for a week so that we could finally have a vacation."

We'd reached the kitchen, and the efficient Rebecca of the present returned to reality. "Well, now let's go and load all this into the car. I think it's best if we put the table in first, because it takes up more space. Then we'll put the chairs in and the rest of the things on top, okay?"

I assented, although I really wanted her to keep telling me things about her life, about that summer when they were young and drove down the Pacific Coast in a dusty old car.

To my good fortune, Rebecca, like the efficient woman she always was, managed to do both things at the same time.

"Paul left us four years later. He took off with a doctoral student. My daughter Annie was nine at the time, Jimmy seven, and Laura five. He told me it was an animal passion, a force beyond him that he was unable to control."

We'd reached the front garden, next to the car. It was already dark.

"He came and went for a time, confusing the children and making me crazy," she continued. "He'd disappear for a week and then return begging for forgiveness, promising that his affair was over, swearing he'd be faithful for the rest of his life. This went on for four or five months."

She put down the chairs and opened the trunk while continuing to speak naturally and without drama, and at the same time without an excess of frivolity, with the right amount of aloofness that comes to us over time. Macan, the dog, had followed us from inside the house and observed the scene phlegmatically while lying on the grass.

"Annie, who up to then had been a sweet and diligent girl, became surly and quit making an effort at school. Jimmy began to wet his bed. Laura was only able to fall asleep if I would lie beside her. When I was no longer able to stand the situation, I filled a couple of suitcases and we left for Chicago, to my parents' house . . . Put the table in the back first, please."

I obeyed without a word and then she began putting the chairs in one by one.

"I settled there with the kids, but Paul would constantly call," she said. "He'd realized everything had been a mistake, that he'd behaved like a real idiot. He insisted that his romance had ended, that he'd never see that girl again. Natasha was her name; she was half Russian. He begged me to return to Santa Cecilia, saying that he couldn't live without the kids and me. He yelled like a madman that I was his only love. Finally he showed up in Chicago. He spoke to my parents and to us. He apologized for all the suffering that he'd made us go through; he promised everything would go back to normal. Now pass me the processor."

She spoke without pain, with her usual voice, concentrated and working methodically at her task.

"Until he convinced me. We came back home together and for several months all was perfect. The best of fathers, the most loving husband. He'd spend hours playing with the kids; he bought them a puppy. He'd cook in the evenings and place candles on the table; he'd bring me flowers all the time. Until one morning after breakfast, which he'd prepared for us all, he went off to the university and did not return. Not that night, nor the next, nor the following one. On the fourth day he came back. Is that all, Blanca?"

"So what did you do then?" I asked as I handed her the sangria pitcher, the last of the items.

She closed the trunk with a dry thump.

"I didn't let him back in. I told him to go to hell and I started looking for a job." She turned around and regarded me, her clear eyes framed in a handful of harmonious tiny wrinkles beneath the garden lights. And despite the sad story she had narrated, with a gesture not lacking sweetness, she smiled.

"I wish that summer in Cabo San Lucas had been eternal. None of us imagined back then how hard life would end up treating us."

Chapter 17

Daniel Carter left for Ramon J. Sender's native Aragon toward the end of October 1958. In the province of Huesca he visited Chalamera, the village that had seen the author into the world, and those places in which he'd lived during childhood, which would endure in the writer's memory. Alcolea de Cinca, beneath the mountain that, as he himself said, seemed to have been carved with a knife. Tauste, which would be the setting of his *Cronica del alba* (*An Account of Dawn*), revisiting his childhood love for Valentina.

Daniel trod many paths, sheltering from the rain in ruined chapels, sleeping in cheap inns, and speaking to the common folk, from whom he learned a never-ending string of words. He drank from the wineskins handed to him and ate what the generosity of others put on his plate. From Aragon he went on to Navarre, from Navarre to both Old and New Castile. Taking trains and buses when he was able to and hopping onto as many carts, vans, and pickup trucks as there were well-disposed drivers before him, the American student wandered through the old world, captivated by all that appeared before his eyes. In villages and fields he came upon recurring scenes of grimy children, women with large baskets balanced magically on their heads, pigs and chickens along the muddy streets, and toothless men in berets seated atop old mules. The geography changed as he traveled south, but the differences were never substantial. Backwardness and misery abounded in a Spain that five years earlier had reached only the same miserable per capita income as prior to the war.

Nothing could have been more different from what he'd left behind: a prosperous and dynamic nation with a young baby-boom generation and citizens who were increasingly living in modern homes in tree-lined suburbs; a country of Ford Fairlanes and Chevy Impalas, in which household appliances were no longer luxury goods but rather basic gadgets for the most mundane homes. A contradictory America, where prosperity and leisure pursuits lived side by side with anticommunist paranoia, the last throes of segregation, and the threat of nuclear war.

Regardless of the immense contrasts he kept stumbling upon during his Spanish journey, he enjoyed every moment in that hard land of stale crusts of bread, porridge and bacon, chicory, hand-rolled tobacco, church bells, imperial songs, and the Guardia Civil. The cold was biting when he got back to Madrid toward the end of November with calluses on his feet. He had five notepads full of his jottings, several rolls of film to be developed, and the feeling that he'd squeezed the utmost out of that initiatory trip.

Back again under the wing of Señora Antonia, he spent a few days savoring her stews before returning to his obligations and visiting Cabeza de Vaca.

He handed the professor the report that he'd spent two days typing in his room at the concierge's. In it he detailed his adventure step-by-step: his perceptions of that land of Sender's, his conversations with country folk, his visits to cities and villages. What he'd seen, lived, felt, and learned.

"Excellent, Mr. Carter, excellent," the professor said, putting the pages away in a drawer. "And now it's time to tap Madrid. I'll be waiting for you at the Prado Museum tomorrow morning at ten o'clock."

"Thank you for your interest, Professor, but I already know the Prado. I was there for an entire afternoon, I saw *Las Meninas, The Surrender of Breda,* and *The Third of May,* and also . . ."

Cabeza de Vaca's arching eyebrow suggested that it was best he keep quiet.

"Consider it my contribution to your comprehensive education, young man. Two intensive weeks of introduction to Spanish painting. Under my tutelage."

This is how the American spent the last stretch of the year, admiring famous paintings and absorbing lessons from his new mentor while they both slowly roamed the halls so removed in time. Through the professor's mediation Daniel also attended a few classes related to his interests and met some students who invited him to a couple of parties and an excursion to La Granja. And thus he passed the remaining days of autumn in Madrid, with its street vendors selling chestnuts and lottery tickets, promising an opulent future to a people still lacking in so many aspects of their life.

Without Señora Antonia having to insist too much, he accepted her invitation to spend Christmas Eve with the rest of her family at the home of her son Joaquin, who at the time lived in the Calle Santa Engracia. He had a wife by the name of Teresa and three girls who were captivated by that giant who spoke Spanish with a strange accent, ate *polvorones,* Christmas cookies, two at a time, and sang Christmas carols with them at the top of his lungs. He was so absorbed by it all that he didn't notice the pair of furtive tears that slipped out of the old widow's eyes as she remembered her Marcelino and those lost times, both atrocious and endearing, that remained frozen forever in her memory.

"You'll spend New Year's Eve with us, right, kid?" she asked him a couple of days later.

"Well . . . You know how grateful I am for your hospitality, but I was thinking . . . I am thinking . . . that perhaps I'd like to spend that night out on the town, if it's all right with you."

He had other plans. Or, to be more exact, he had another plan: to go to the Puerta del Sol in search of the roaring crowd. Nothing else. He tried to be faithful to Cabeza de Vaca's advice: "Don't just stay in the anecdotal; don't simply scratch the surface." And yet, knowing that this would fall into the category of the most banal and commonplace, he could not resist the temptation of eating his first twelve grapes at the chiming of the midnight bells, surrounded by a boisterous crowd complete with cider and noisemakers, overflowing with soldiers on leave and revelers of every sort, all dressed up for a party.

"Why don't you dine with us and then take off? I've already told my daughter-in-law that I'm going over to her place early in the afternoon to roast a piglet that comes from my village and which will turn out quite tasty, at least as tasty as those in Casa Botin."

"Do you think I'll have time?" Daniel asked, savoring it already. The widow knew that the young man's belly was a surefire avenue of attack.

"Don't worry, I'll make sure we're done by eleven."

And so it was: at eleven thirty he was in the Puerta del Sol. He even had time to buy a few postcards, scribble a few words on them, and drop them into an overseas mailbox.

On waking up on New Year's Day, he saw a kitschy new 1959 calendar on the wall near the dining table. Recently brewed coffee and warm fritters had been set out for him, just as on every other day.

"Well, kid, so it seems we have another year on our shoulders. What are your plans now: to stay in Madrid or take off like last time, to tread those godforsaken roads?"

"To leave, to leave. That's what I've got planned. I must get down to work."

"And where are you off to this time, if I may ask?"

"To the Canton de Cartagena, if I can find out how to get there."

Since *Mister Witt en el Canton* was the novel that won Ramon J. Sender the 1935 National Prize for Literature, Daniel had made up his mind that his second trip would be to that significant place in the author's body of work. The widow, ignorant in geography, was unable to help out, so he had no other choice than to study his worn-out map of Spain after breakfast.

Moving the empty cup of coffee to one side, he spread the map over the table. Taking the capital as a reference, he traced with his forefinger the outskirts of Madrid and continued outward to the nearby provinces, but what he was looking for didn't appear there either. He extended his search to the periphery, finally tackling the coastal areas. It took him a while to locate that corner of the peninsula and find the name of Cartagena: the Canton part was nowhere to be found. But there it was, tucked away in the southeast. He pulled out a red pencil and marked it with an *X*, thereby confirming his next destination.

Chapter 18

Crossing the peninsula by train from the capital was, toward the end of the 1950s, a heroic adventure that Daniel Carter experienced from the seat of his third-class coach like a privileged spectator in a royal box. On purchasing his ticket at the Atocha train station, he hesitated briefly about which class to travel in. Although back in his country he wouldn't have been able to choose between classes so lightly, the cheap prices of his host nation allowed him to consider all available options without making much of a dent in his pocket. First class, he thought, promised a comfortable journey but lacking in flavor. Second, neither great comfort nor new experiences. He finally decided on third class, a further step in his eagerness to discover the true essence of the Spanish people. He was not disappointed.

Coal locomotives were still the backbone of the *ferrocarriles nacionales*, the state-owned railway company, a crippled backbone for which maintaining schedules was a mere illusion, dependent on the crisscrossed traffic of dozens of mail and freight trains. In the coaches with wooden-slatted seats, people endured winter as well as they could with the warmth generated by the bodies lumped together. The chugging of the engine died down in the stations only to be replaced by the hammering of wheels, the hiss of boilers, and the relentless screech of brakes. Through the windows loads of wooden suitcases went in and out, along with cardboard boxes tied with strings, military backpacks, and bundles wrapped in cloth that concealed God knew what. He even saw a couple of chickens and a rolled mattress being passed from a father to his son in the town of La Roda.

Daniel marveled at how the platforms turned into provisional markets in which, depending on the locality, cakes from La Mancha, Albacete knives, or raffle tickets for a ham were being hawked. He was even more fascinated, in the absence of restaurant service, by the constant traffic of baskets of loaves of bread and lunch boxes brimming with slices of thick bacon accompanied by an encouraging "Would you care to try?" The wineskins passed from hand to hand while with ferocious bites the travelers devoured newspaper-wrapped sardine sandwiches the size of torpedoes. "Take a swig, my friend," they would tell the American, or "Try this sausage; have a piece of this black pudding, it's from our own slaughterhouse, you'll see how tasty it is." To nothing and to no one did Daniel ever say no.

The dense smoke of the cheap, unfiltered Celtas Cortos cigarettes and the thick smell of feet hovered over the endless kilometers. Mothers breast-fed babies, old ladies in eternal mourning sighed, and strangers exchanged comments about the coming crops, Antoñete's last corrida, and relatives who had immigrated to Barcelona the previous year.

At times, and with a great effort, he was able to concentrate on *Mister Witt en el Canton,* its cover discreetly wrapped in newspaper, as its author remained in exile. He'd read it in Pittsburgh the previous winter but now needed to cull some information. Despite the surrounding distractions, he proceeded to underline in pencil passages and names associated with the revolutionary fervor of the city to which he was now headed. Twenty-three days, according to what Fontana had told him, was what it took Sender to write in his agile prose the adventures and misadventures of the insurgent Cartagena during the First Spanish Republic of 1873.

Two plainclothes policemen walked up and down the aisle asking for identification with unfriendly faces. The volume of conversation dropped sharply and the eyes of travelers were fixed silently on the floor. Once the procedure was over, the lively conversations quickly resumed, with some passengers throwing fleeting glances or hiding a sigh of relief. Eventually sleep began to take over: some lay on the floor to snore soundly; others began to nod off with jerking motions on their neighbor's shoulder.

In Chinchilla, Daniel got out to stretch his legs and breathe some fresh air, which turned out to be cold. Taking refuge in the canteen, he ordered the same thing the two soldiers who were propped up against the bar were having: a glass of chicory with milk and a cup of anisette Machaquito.

Finally he reached his destination. To his surprise, the city he found at the end of that perpetual trip didn't initially seem at all like the ones he'd come across in Spain's interior.

It was Sunday, and people were dressed for the occasion, immersed in the routines of the week's most important day. Leaving church, having an aperitif, choosing cakes at La Royal. He followed the suggestions of two ladies he accosted in the middle of the street. "A place to sleep?" "Right here, in the pension on Calle Duque. Central and clean; why would you look any further?" He took a room initially for three days at the modest price of seventy-five pesetas per day. On carrying his luggage up the stairs, he noticed sharp pangs of pain in his head and a somewhat thick drowsiness, but blamed his indisposition on the cold that was still clinging to his bones. All of a sudden the room's small bed appeared pleasantly tempting, but he did not succumb to its siren song. Instead of lying down as his body was demanding, he mustered all the energy he possibly could and went back out. He didn't feel well and was aware of it, but his obstinate drive not to miss anything impelled him to explore the streets.

It didn't take him long to find himself in a pedestrian street. Long, narrow, and flanked by outdoor cafés, it gave onto a square that, like all others he'd come across in the city centers he'd visited, was named Del Caudillo in honor of the dictator Franco. Farther ahead the port could be discerned, but he was unable to reach it. His strength slowly dwindled and his mouth was becoming dry; the street noise and people's voices boomed in his temples. He decided to retrace his steps, to return to the busy thoroughfare, and he walked into a café, not realizing that the establishment he'd randomly chosen seemed predestined to receive him with generous hospitality: Bar Americano.

"A glass of water, please."

"Come again?"

The bald-headed bow-tied waiter had understood immediately but chose to think it over twice before serving him. The presence of that uncombed giant with wrinkled clothes created quite a stir in the premises. Among the vermouths and little plates of almonds, the Sunday clientele received him with disapproving glances, murmuring suspiciously without a shred of sympathy.

"A glass of water, please," he repeated. "Or of seltz—"

Without noticing the stares and comments and with his ability to react seriously hampered, Daniel stood motionless for a couple of seconds, waiting to have any type of liquid placed before him that would quench the dryness in his throat. But all he received was a tap on his shoulder, as if someone were trying to draw his attention.

"I think you've chosen the wrong place, my friend."

"Excuse me?"

On turning around he was faced with an individual with a thin, neatly trimmed mustache.

"This is a decent people's establishment. Please leave."

"All I want is to drink a glass of water," he explained. And turning his eyes on the waiter, he insisted for the third time in his effort to be served: "Or a Coca-Cola if possible . . ."

"Water is for frogs. And Coca-Cola you can drink in your own country. Get out immediately! Come on . . ." said this protector of the civilized world.

Daniel made another effort to explain his simple intentions to that man, whose face, voice, and mustache were becoming blurrier by the minute before his eyes and ears. His mumbled attempt, far from clearing things up, only served to reaffirm the initial assumption of practically everyone present: the disheveled foreigner was dead drunk. And it was hardly noon.

The next thing was to grab him by the arm.

"Get the hell out of here, dammit! This is no place for clowns like you!"

Daniel thought his Spanish must have come across as awkward and hard to comprehend; perhaps he'd mixed it up with English without realizing it.

"Leave me alone, please . . ."

Seeing that the bartender wasn't giving up, Daniel, bewildered as he was, jerked his arm away suddenly in his attempt to break loose. So much so that he almost knocked the man over.

By way of reinforcement before the foreigner's apparently brash reaction, a couple of volunteers hastily took off their jackets, ready to neutralize him. The altercation was quick, and in less than a couple of minutes the young man, befuddled and staggering, was once again on the street, exposed to the indiscreet stares of the passersby, with the ends of his shirt hanging out of his pants, his hair disheveled, and his sleeve half torn.

On seeing the guest's arrival, the desk clerk at the pension didn't even bother to lift his eyes from the dime novel *The Last Outlaw* that he was absorbed in. Without looking at Daniel, he simply handed him the key to his room and clicked his tongue in resignation; then, wetting his thumb with saliva, he turned the page. As if we're supposed to stop reading just because another weird traveler has come in, he must have thought. And certainly not at that moment, when the county sheriff was about to shoot a round of lead into the bodies of the two outlaws preparing to make trouble in the saloon.

Daniel spent thirty hours in his austere room, lying on crumpled sheets. At times he felt shattering cold, at others as if he were in the middle of a desert. Sporadically he would regain consciousness, rise from the bed, and with a faltering step make his way to the sink in his room for water. That was his only intake until the afternoon of the second day, when someone knocked on his door. First hesitantly, then insistently. With an effort, Daniel uttered a weak "Come in!" and a feminine head appeared with worry written all over her face. He didn't know who it was: the pension's owner, or perhaps an employee, or an angel with an apron who was sent from heaven. The fact was that this kind soul, alarmed by the absence of sounds from the guest, proceeded to change his bed, gave him an extra blanket, and brought him a couple of Okal pills, a glass of hot milk, and a hearty omelet sandwich that tasted divine.

That night he was able to sleep more peacefully, without shivering or having nightmares. The following day, well into the morning, he was able to gather enough strength to get up and slowly shower, shave, dress, and go out onto the street. From sweating and lack of food he'd lost several pounds and most of his memory of the quarrel at the Bar Americano.

The city welcomed him with a friendly sun. The modernist façades had fanciful wrought-iron balconies and the streets were packed with people. He was seduced by the light and the smell of the sea, but he chose not to be distracted in order to concentrate on his objective of finding a pharmacy. He knew that it had only been an inopportune flu and that it didn't require a doctor, but he still felt weak and wanted to avoid a relapse.

The Carranza Pharmacy was about to close for the prolonged midday break. The owner had left a good while earlier to stop by his club to read the paper and have an aperitif before continuing on home for lunch, as was his habit. When Daniel pushed the door open, the middle-aged assistant was already unbuttoning his white smock, eager to sit down to the rice and rabbit stew his mother had prepared for him the night before. He tried to dissuade the young man from coming in, saying, "We're closing, sir. Come back later this afternoon if it's not too much trouble." But Daniel remained firm. No way was he ready to leave the place without an arsenal of medicine. The give-and-take that ensued only came to an end when a woman's voice was heard from the back room.

"You can leave, Gregorio. Don't worry, I'll close up!"

Although he was ravenous, the assistant was reluctant to take the woman up on her offer.

He thought it best not to leave the pharmacy with a stranger inside. However, after taking a few more seconds to make up his mind, he let his hunger override any other consideration. After eyeing the newcomer from head to toe as if trying to gauge his degree of decency, Gregorio bid good-bye to his coworker with a hasty "See you later, then."

The pharmacy emanated a soothing serenity, with its marble counter near the door presided over by an antiquated cash register, the wide arch leading to the back room, the black-and-white-tiled floor resembling a chessboard. Waiting to be served, Daniel killed time by contemplating the ceramic jars lining the glass cabinets, trying to decipher their Latin labels.

"Please excuse me: I was busy unpacking an order . . ."

He quickly extricated his attention from the Latin and turned his head. Hardly ten feet away, there she was, her cheeks flushed from her previous effort while, with quick agile movements, she tried to smooth back the loose curls of her straw-colored mane. Unlike any conventional pharmacist, unlike any of his former classmates. Unlike any other woman he'd ever come across in his life.

"If you tell me what I can help you with . . ."

She spoke with her arms still up in the air, endeavoring to tame the unruly locks while she waited for him to speak. Her large mouth, meanwhile, smiled with a mixture of charm and surprise at the idea of finishing off the morning serving someone so different from the usual clientele.

"I think I've got the flu," he finally was able to say.

He listened to her in silence while she recommended different remedies to relieve the last symptoms of his general malaise. Then he heard her speak about the treacherous manner in which that climate constantly fooled strangers who tended to believe that the weather was always fair by the Mediterranean. Silent, engrossed, baffled, he listened to the advice with the faith of a convert, unable to take his eyes off her while her hands searched adeptly in cabinets and drawers and placed the medicines on the white marble counter.

When she finished doling out instructions regarding dosage and use, he had no choice but to conclude the transaction. As he counted out the money, he frantically searched for an excuse to prolong his stay and not lose sight of the untidy mane of hair, or the gray eyes or the long fingers, of this unexpected provider of his well-being. But his dulled brain seemed to deny him any success, instead slowing down his movements and allowing him to take all the time in the world to put away his change.

"You've been most kind. Thank you very much" was his courteous but somewhat formal good-bye.

"You're most welcome," the woman said, handing him the parcel. It seemed to him that, for a split second, their fingers grazed each other's. "Take care. And bundle up."

He assented, with the medicines wrapped in thin paper in one hand and a strange sensation somewhere deep within. As black and white tiles directed his steps toward the exit, he sensed her gaze fixed on his back. When he pulled the polished brass door handle, the glass rattled slightly. A step away was the street, where there were people. Anonymous people in crowds in which most likely he'd never again find the face he was about to leave behind.

But then her voice stopped him in his tracks.

"Are you a military man from the American base?"

The door swung closed and the glass stopped rattling.

"I'm American, but not military," he said without turning, without looking at her, without letting go of the handle.

Finally he turned around, and fleetingly, with a vertiginous spark of lucidity, he sensed that somehow he would never altogether leave.

The young lady had anticipated a negative answer before asking the question, since the foreigner didn't look like a military man despite his spotless appearance. His hair was longer than usual for such a profession, and his posture and gestures, although correct, had a more relaxed manner that didn't seem in any way military.

He wanted to offer her something beyond a few clues about his identity; his anxious desire was for her to see him for who he really was, and not simply as a passing client in search of medicine. He told her he was specializing in Spanish literature, that he aspired to be a professor, that he'd come to this port city on the trail of a novel . . .

Suddenly the door opened behind him, preventing him from continuing. Three little whirlwinds full of coughs and mucus stormed into the pharmacy, followed by an overwhelmed mother.

"By a hairbreadth! I thought we weren't going to make it!"

The room all at once filled with voices as the boys began chasing one another while the poor mother alternated between trying to control them and frantically searching for the prescription in her bag. One of them pushed another against a cabinet full of bottles, and the piece of furniture wobbled precariously, threatening to tip over. The culprit received a rap on the head by his mother while the victim ostentatiously exaggerated the effect of the collision, half hiding his face, screaming and stomping furiously on the floor.

Behind the counter, the girl, aware of her inability to recapture the bond between them, shrugged her shoulders and cast Daniel a look of apology and helplessness.

"Don't worry," he mumbled, forcing a smile that barely showed.

They were oblivious to the family quarrel as they exchanged their last words, looking at each other above the three small rascals and their long-suffering mother.

"Good-bye," her mouth read, since her voice was lost amid the kids' wails and the mother's angry rebukes.

"Good-bye," he replied almost silently.

Finally he mustered the courage to take his eyes off that beautiful mouth and those large gray eyes, and left the pharmacy.

Never had the street seemed so cold.

Chapter 19

———————

She wasn't out of his sight for a second as he walked behind her, following at a distance with no idea where her springy steps or his impetuous foolishness would take him. He knew that the reasonable thing to do would be to return to the pension, take his medications, and rest quietly. But he couldn't. Instead, he positioned himself at the corner to lie in wait, making an effort to hide behind a delivery truck parked nearby. Until he saw her emerge.

Earlier, the mother and the three brats had left, followed by an ailing old man who had managed to slip into the pharmacy at the last minute like a worm. At last she herself came out while putting on a blue coat, removing from her face another subversive lock, half closing her eyes against the noonday glare. Without the counter between them, Daniel was able to contemplate the full length of her body as she buttoned her coat and put her keys in her pocket. Once again he felt something he was unable to define, not even in his own language.

Adjusting his pace to the young lady's graceful stride as she crossed streets and made her way among other pedestrians, he saw her greet one and all, stopping occasionally to chat with someone for a minute or two. Meanwhile, to pass unnoticed, he'd pretend to stop and tie his shoelace, light a cigarette with his face half-hidden in the hollow of his hands, or read an ad posted on the street. Several times he thought it was total folly: perhaps he should have approached her openly, asking her name, offering to accompany her, proposing to meet for a coffee. But he did not feel strong enough. He had difficulty thinking; he noticed his fever was still raging. Any other time he would have been up to it, but now he hesitated.

He continued behind her until they reached a short street that rose sharply. There was hardly anyone else in sight, and only rarely did a car drive by. He slowed down and retreated a few yards and again proceeded to follow her. Finally she turned onto a street that didn't quite seem like one: one side had a row of buildings of varying sizes and opposite was some sort of promenade with a hanging balustrade. Farther below was the port and, in the distance, the sea. The spell cast by the light, salt water, and peace hardly lasted the few seconds it took her to step into the doorway of what he imagined was her house.

A couple of seagulls shrieked above Daniel's head and the sun suddenly disappeared. As the wind picked up, he pulled up his jacket collar and buried his hands in his pockets. He'd return to the pharmacy in the afternoon; perhaps by then he'd feel better.

Before leaving the street, he saw that it was aptly named Paseo de la Muralla, or Rampart Promenade. He felt a pang in his stomach and realized two things in quick succession: the first was that sooner or later he would have ended up visiting this same spot, for this was where the fictional Mr. Witt, the protagonist of the novel that had brought him to this city, had lived; and the second was that, except for the sandwich given to him by the anonymous lady, he hadn't eaten in more than two days. Fortunately, this last matter was soon resolved at a local restaurant, and with a plate of stew before him he began to ponder his situation. By the time the sardines reached the table, the scales had tipped. The custard brought with it certainty: for the time being his research efforts would take a backseat. At the most unexpected moment—magically, almost—something had crossed his path that was much more urgent.

He returned to the pension to lie down for a while until the remedies that she'd prescribed took effect. It would do him good: again he was cold, his legs felt weak, and he noticed that, although it lacked the virulence of the previous days, the fever still hadn't left him. He lay down dressed, thinking of her, determined to try and reestablish contact as soon as he'd rested a little. But he fell into such a deep slumber that when he woke up, disoriented and dulled, it was already nine fifteen in the evening. He left his room in a rush, putting on his jacket as he descended the steps three at a time, cursing his blunder with a loud "Fuck!" and combing his hair with his fingers as he ran outside. The few passersby were hurrying home to family dinners; the streets were practically empty and all the shops closed. He soon confirmed what he dreaded: the Carranza Pharmacy was too.

The next morning he set out with the firm intention of finding the nameless young lady. However, only the assistant was serving the crowded customers when Daniel entered the pharmacy. He patiently waited his turn while from the back room could be heard the radio broadcast of the Epiphany lottery. He listened to various customers speculating on how they'd spend the prize if they ever won.

"How can I help you, sir?"

"Aspirins, please."

Although he didn't need them, he was hoping that, along with the painkiller, Gregorio would provide him with some clue regarding his young colleague. To Daniel's disappointment, however, all he got was the small medicine parcel skillfully wrapped in paper.

"Eight-fifty, just for you."

"Excuse me?"

Daniel thought he was missing something. Perhaps the assistant was alluding in some way to seeing him the previous day. Or maybe making a joke about Daniel being a foreigner. Or, better yet, offering a cryptic message that might have to do with the absent girl. But he was mistaken. The assistant wasn't dispensing any type of personal treatment but rather repeating for the umpteenth time what he thought was a witty remark. "Eight-fifty, sir. Very cheap. And for you, Doña Esperanza, the usual, right? Two boxes of laxative suppositories and Carabaña seltzer water."

While Daniel again discreetly slowed down the payment process, just as he'd done with the girl, he realized that the opportunity to ask for her whereabouts was slipping away from him. Now or never, he thought.

"Is the young lady not in today?" he finally dared to ask, pointing to the back room.

Loudly, as if Daniel were not only a foreigner but also deaf, the assistant declared to the four winds:

"No! No! The young lady isn't in today! She's off shopping! The Three Wise Men: tonight the Kings come!"

Intoning at the top of his lungs, *"Here come the Three Wise Men, here come the Three Wise Men, on their way to Bethlehem . . ."* He rang up the next sale while the radio in the background was announcing the third-prize number, which had just been pulled out of the lottery drum.

For the rest of the morning Daniel wandered the streets in her pursuit, constantly changing course, sweeping his eyes past corners and over groups of friends, toward entrances to shops and café terraces. But the area of commercial activity was limited, and after making a couple of rounds Daniel realized it was already one thirty and the shops were preparing to close for the afternoon break.

And then, finally, he saw her, as graceful as a reed, with her rebellious curls once more eluding the bobby pin that tried to hold them down at her nape, wrapped in a beige raincoat firmly belted around her narrow waist. She walked sheltered by two elegant-looking women who appeared to be twice her age and who seemed to be deep in conversation. Then she spotted him as well: the handsome American with the flu whom she'd attended on the previous day; the student who aspired to the extravagant profession of teaching Spanish literature at some university in his distant country.

For the second time in his life the resolute Daniel Carter was at a loss about what to do. Fiercely independent from an early age, he had seen more of the world than many others in their entire existences; had been able to earn his keep working shoulder to shoulder with rough industrial workmen; had read all the Spanish classics; and had traversed countless dusty roads of that strange country, all on his own. Yet he was left totally disarmed as she approached.

"I hope the medicines took effect."

He was never able to recall what he answered: perhaps some triviality plagued with grammatical and pronunciation mistakes. He realized that the encounter had come to an end only when he saw her back vanish in the crowd. He hadn't learned anything about her, again losing her without even finding out her name. But the memory of her face and voice accompanied him throughout lunch, and not for a moment was he able to dispel her from his mind as he distractedly tried to read in the first hours of the afternoon, lying like a prisoner on his narrow pension bed, feeling fragile as never before, with nothing to do, nowhere to go, nor anyone to share what was burning within him.

When he sensed that life once again filled the streets after the long break that Spanish families devote to the midday meal, he got ready to go out. He was still unaware that on that afternoon Melchior, Caspar, and Balthasar, in their annual miracle, were about to arrive simultaneously in hundreds of villages and cities throughout the country.

The unexpected merrymaking that Daniel encountered on the street astonished him—so much so that, for a few minutes, he was able to rid his mind of the young lady from the pharmacy and concentrate on the spectacle of the parade. He was fascinated by the children's reactions and the sumptuous garb worn by the Three Wise Men and their retinue. His forgetfulness was short-lived, however, for chance willed her to emerge unexpectedly.

They were on opposite sidewalks, almost directly facing each other as the procession passed between them, amid screams and applause. She was wearing the same raincoat as in the morning, now with a green scarf around her long neck. She laughed and spoke to someone by her side, suddenly shattering Daniel's hopes. A young man with cropped hair and a tanned face, who smiled, nodding his head as she said something to him, holding on to his arm with familiarity. Possibly her boyfriend. Perhaps her husband. Probably military, a navy officer.

Daniel's interest in everything that surrounded him suddenly evaporated like a soap bubble. The kids applauding enthusiastically no longer seemed adorable creatures and changed into small yelling demons. The majestic attire of the Three Wise Men and their attendants suddenly seemed grotesquely ostentatious for that country in such need of other, more pressing things.

He felt a sudden wave of heat, and thought his fever was spiking. Suffocating, he decided to leave, to return to the pension, to flee from that roaring commotion, which now was unbearable. But he was unable to do so with the speed he wished, because he realized that he was immobilized by the crush of people, trapped within the crowd that, ignorant of his dashed hopes, was still delighting in the procession. As he made an effort to escape, she spotted him from the opposite sidewalk and waved. She seemed sure of herself, cordial, and he replied awkwardly, copying her gesture while beaming a forced smile, hiding an immense wish that he had never showed up in that diabolical city. He was finally able to jostle his way through the crowd, but before disappearing he was unable to avoid turning around one last time in their direction. They were speaking to each other, and he had no doubt it was about him.

Back in his room, the drums of the damn parade were still booming as he tried to read but was unable to concentrate. He remained lying there for what seemed an endless amount of time with his arms folded behind his head and his eyes fixed on a water stain on the ceiling. When he was finally able to analyze the situation calmly, he realized it had been absurd from the very start to think that she'd be accessible, and pure arrogance to have imagined that behind her friendliness, her smile, and her radiant eyes there was anything besides simple courtesy toward a lost foreigner.

Once he half convinced himself that there had never been a glimmer of hope, he was finally able to resume more mundane activities and realized he had a wolfish appetite. Although the procession had ended a while ago, he was in no mood to go out onto the deserted streets, in which there would still be a sad vestige of the extinguished racket. He went down to the reception desk hoping that the woman who had succored him the night he had a fever would prepare him a sandwich. As Señora Antonia would say, "Bread lessens all sorrows"—a piece of wisdom from her boundless catalog of popular sayings. He would see if it was so.

The clerk from the day of his arrival was there, again absorbed by his reading. This time he was riding across the Arizona desert, still not knowing if the judge would end up sentencing the cattle rustlers or not. *Born for the Gallows*, Daniel was able to read from the corner of his eye.

"Interesting?" he asked for the hell of it, although deep down he couldn't care less.

"Bah. I liked *Lead in the Chest* much better. And *The Coward's Trail*—no comparison. I have them here somewhere . . ." he said, momentarily disappearing beneath the counter. He presently resurfaced with a couple of well-worn little books in his hand. "If you want me to lend you one to pass the time, they're not due back at the kiosk until tomorrow."

Daniel had seen many Westerns at the movies but had never read any in book form, not even those of his legendary countryman Zane Grey. It seemed silly to start with one written by a Spaniard; who knew what nonsense that could be?

"So, are you going to take any, my friend?" the clerk insisted. "If you want the truth, they're both worthwhile. And if you don't like these, tomorrow I can bring you others, like *The Coyote*, since I've got a bunch that I've had for years. Those are about California, and the characters seem Spanish. I'm not sure if you—"

"Thanks very much, but I've got my own books in my suitcase."

He was not lying—he had reading to do—but more serious stuff, more essential to his career: Spanish contemporary authors with whom he was beginning to get acquainted.

"Well, it's up to you, but as far as I'm concerned, you're not going to find anything better than this. Come on, take one, man . . ."

The conversation was interrupted by the arrival of the anonymous angel who had come to his rescue during his fever. In slippers, in her fifties, and wearing a checkered apron.

"Modesto, are you going to do the night shift today, or is your cousin Fulgencio finally going to show up?"

"Well, I don't know, Catalina; he hasn't said anything to me yet."

"I need to know if I should start preparing dinner or wait a little longer. I've got noodle soup and marinated mackerel. Would you like me to bring you a plate up to your room, son?" she said, addressing Daniel, who was still leaning on the counter. "The evening is getting ugly; this way you won't have to go out on the street again. And it'll do you good: you look awfully skinny. Even with that fever you've had, you don't stay still for a minute, and you may end up having a relapse. I'll set some of ours aside for you, because where two eat, three can eat as well."

"Wait, Catalina, he still has to choose a novel. Which one will it be, my friend?"

Lead in the Chest was the price he had to pay for dinner.

He had thought he'd spend the following day in search of information that would open his eyes to Sender's sources when writing his novel. Before going to bed he'd gone over his notes regarding places and characters. But suddenly all of that no longer seemed to interest him, and although he had made a firm commitment to his work, he also decided that, if things remained this gloomy, he would return to Madrid the following day.

About to fall asleep, he added one more resolution to his list: not to evoke the memory of the young lady at the pharmacy. Thinking it over carefully, she was not worth all the fuss. Her strides seemed overly energetic, her very presence somewhat overwhelming for a medium-size woman of her age. And that hair of hers, so wild, seemed a bit too flashy in comparison with the well-combed dark hair that Spanish women usually had. Prettier women had crossed his path and would in the future, he told himself; women who were more accessible, less distant. It was settled, and he fell asleep. But half an hour later, he was dreaming that he was sinking his fingers into the curls at her neck and, drawing her close to him, kissing her wide sweet mouth.

. . .

The next day dawned with pouring rain and it didn't let up until evening. A dark, sad day, with a leaden sky, empty streets, and shut-down shops. Far from being discouraged, he took to the street carrying an umbrella with two missing ribs that Catalina had lent him and a well-worn copy of *Mister Witt en el Canton* still covered in newspaper to avoid parading the name of the exiled author in plain sight. His vague objective was to discover some clue to what could have inspired Sender to create the character of the old English engineer that the writer placed in the revolutionary Cartagena of the First Spanish Republic. But there was no one around who could give him any reliable information on that day of gift giving and family gatherings. Moreover, the public library was closed.

The only one who seemed to shed any light on the subject was an elderly customer who looked like he'd had a few too many. In a tavern on the Calle Cuatro Santos, he explained to Daniel that Sender was a rotten Red and that his name was not mentioned in that country of peace and order that the Caudillo had brought about. To round off his discourse, he stood up unsteadily and delivered a resounding "Long live Spain!" The clicking of heels that accompanied so patriotic a salute would have sent him falling backward had Daniel not caught him.

He returned to the pension drenched and in a mood as black as the day itself. He let the afternoon roll by absorbed in another brainy contemplation of the spots on the ceiling and then started to write a letter to Professor Fontana that didn't go beyond the salutation. Toward seven o'clock he went down to the reception desk to take a look at the local paper. A notice announced that that evening *The Prince and the Showgirl* was being released in the Central Cinema in CinemaScope and Technicolor. If he hurried, he'd make it to the seven-thirty showing. It might distract him a little, even if it meant listening to Marilyn Monroe and Laurence Olivier flirting in Spanish.

He started packing as soon as he got back to the hotel, deciding to head back to Madrid the following day even though he hadn't found one single interesting piece of information for his work and still had the image of the pharmacy girl fresh in his mind despite his effort to purge his mind of her. To compensate for the former, he'd have a chance to consult other resources at the National Library. The latter he'd dispel in time.

In order to avoid contingencies similar to those encountered on the outbound trip, at the station he purchased a first-class return ticket. There would be plenty of time to mingle with the true essence of Spain;

as of now, all that mattered to him was getting out of there, the sooner the better.

He chose not to board the train before the appointed time, devoting himself to watching the hustle and bustle of people and belongings as he sat on a platform bench. There was not a trace of the previous day's rain, and he found himself savoring the last feel of the Mediterranean sun on his skin, as he had no intention of returning to that place.

He liked train stations and their routines; it amused him to speculate on the lives of travelers and their destinations, the reasons for their comings and goings. Some of the Spanish customs he found a bit excessive, like that tendency to take several family generations along to say good-bye to or greet some of their members.

He watched with rising spirits before his imminent departure while behind him, from the canteen's open door, amid the early-morning clinking of plates and glasses, the radio was playing. The lilting rhythm penetrated his bones, and without his realizing it his foot was soon tapping out the beat. He realized how in no time this city would be pushed to the far reaches of his memory and the only thing remaining would be the faint images of a literary figure whose face he had never found and a woman whose name he was unable to learn. An elegant middle-aged couple, a distinguished-looking old lady, and three young people hurried onto the platform, loaded with luggage. Instinctively, he opened one of the newspapers he'd just bought and took refuge behind it while beyond its right edge he continued to watch them.

They were all accompanying a young lady with straw-colored hair who was evidently traveling to Madrid after the Christmas holiday. Later he would find out that it was to finish the last year of her pharmaceutical studies. He saw them exchange kisses and hugs, which intensified when it came to the brother, a young air force lieutenant with cropped hair and a tanned face.

He waited until the last second to hop onto the coach. Through the window he could see how the family—huddled together and already feeling her absence as they continued to wave at the train—diminished in the distance.

The girl, meanwhile, made an effort to contain a stubborn tear that was threatening to fall and concentrated on organizing her luggage. A large suitcase, a traveling bag, her blue coat . . .

"May I help you?" she heard behind her back.

Once more she received him with a glorious smile and those gray eyes that sparkled like the sea before her balcony on winter mornings. He finally learned the six letters of her name.

Chapter 20

I had always enjoyed experimenting in the kitchen, putting new twists on traditional recipes. Any excuse or minor event had been a good reason to sit family and friends around the table to celebrate. The end of the school year, an anniversary, my sons' smallest successes, or simply a Friday night. Sometimes these were noisy meals with crisscrossing conversations and eternal after-dinner talk. Other times they were small gatherings with wine and candles until the wee hours, bringing the feeling that the world had come to a standstill beneath one's feet.

But everything was different now that my age-old friends were at the other end of the world and my family had disintegrated. The only event I could celebrate was that the calendar had just certified I was a year older.

A sad perspective that, properly looked at, might be a good incentive to settle into my new life, one that I had not chosen, full of absences and uncertainties. Suddenly, from one day to the next, I had had to reinvent myself and begin feebly muddling through, like a child learning to walk, except that I already had four and a half decades behind me. At an age when I should have reached a serene maturity, safe and secure in what I had achieved, I instead felt vulnerable, disillusioned, without expectations, and with my self-esteem in tatters.

Toward noon I went in search of food supplies. I needed eggs, potatoes, garlic, tomatoes for the gazpacho, and peaches for the sangria. The Cantabrian anchovies, a few wedges of aged Manchego cheese, and some other delicacies I'd purchased a few days earlier at the price of gold. What I still lacked were the basics, for which I chose the G&G behind the square rather than the more exclusive Meli's Market.

I went with a clear objective and finished quickly, since I was in a hurry to get back and start cooking. When I was on line waiting my turn, I suddenly remembered that I didn't have any paper napkins. Cursing under my breath, I made a U-turn, wondering where the damn napkins would be. In the middle of the paper goods aisle I saw her. She seemed to be scrutinizing a box of Kleenex, turning it over and over while supporting herself on an orthopedic walker. Her hair was dyed an outrageous shade of blond for her age, and even with her enormous sunglasses her identity was unmistakable: Fanny's mother, Darla Stern, the former department secretary who was unable to elicit in Daniel Carter the same sympathy he always displayed toward other people.

I subtly turned around in case she recognized me or in case Fanny, who no doubt was close by, suddenly appeared by her side, forcing me to stop and chat. To avoid running into them, I grabbed my napkins stealthily and disappeared.

The day went by amid the smell of Spanish omelets and the noise of pureeing tomatoes. As I worked in the kitchen I chased away the errant ghosts that accosted me, wielding the magic that smells have to conjure our pasts and kindle our emotions. Everything was ready at half past seven. Rebecca's folding table looked like an immigrant's dream, and the nostalgic specters peacefully rested in their cages. I wore black, played a new flamenco CD by Ketama, and, to give it the ultimate Spanish touch, placed in my hair a couple of bright red carnations that I'd bought on my way out of G&G.

I had just finished applying a second coat of mascara when the phone rang. I figured it was Rebecca calling to ask if there was any last-minute item I needed, or perhaps someone apologizing at the eleventh hour for not being able to make it to the party. But I was mistaken. The voice at the other end, so many miles away, belonged to someone who more than twenty years earlier had been literally a part of me. Someone several inches taller than I and out loose in the world despite the fact that I would have liked him to be by my side eternally, never growing beyond the height of my shoulder.

"Heyyyyy! Where the hell have you been hiding, Mom?"

My son Pablo, most likely out on the town in the wee hours. He'd been on the beaches of Cadiz since summer, lured by the surf, his latest great passion until some other obsession took its place. Despite all predictions, he had finished his BA in business administration in June, something unexpected given the fact that he'd had to retake three classes. He was impulsive and unpredictable, and so was his decision to take a year off before thinking of anything useful in terms of his professional future. Unlike his brother, who a year earlier had gotten a scholarship for a master's at the London School of Economics, after graduation Pablo had decided to surf the waves in southern Spain. This weekend, however, he had returned to Madrid and was calling from there in the middle of a night of partying.

"Boy, you're old, Mom, forty-five . . . No . . . I'm just joking . . . you're still a kid . . . The prettiest!"

I couldn't avoid smiling as a pang of melancholy shot through me. Paralyzed inside the bathroom's small perimeter, I sat on the edge of the bathtub to listen to him. My kid. How quickly he'd grown up.

"Hello . . . can you hear me?" He kept talking at the top of his voice, a hard-to-identify din in the background. "We're here . . . and we're talking about you. We've gone out for dinner and then for a couple of drinks, and we've slowly gotten carried away, and . . . and . . . and this one is going to be in a hell of a lot of trouble when he gets—"

A ferocious peal of laughter completed the phrase. I didn't know who he was referring to by "this one"; probably one of his friends. He didn't even give me time to figure it out; he only said, "Wait, let me pass him on to you."

"Hello, Blancurria. It's me."

I could feel the smile that Pablo's voice had drawn on my face freeze into a grimace. It was Alberto, my ex-husband, with a nasal voice.

Using my former affectionate nickname, the one that showed concern, companionship, complicity.

"Here I am with Pablito, who's got me a little trashed . . ." he continued without waiting for me to say anything. "The kid has turned into a man, with such long hair that I'm wondering when he'll cut it . . . but he won't listen to me, as usual. Maybe you can tell him something and convince him; you know he ignores everything I say. Well, so . . . so happy birthday. I've got no present for you, since you're so far away. The other day I saw a painting, nothing much, a piece of nonsense, a marina with some boats, not much of anything, but I thought: For Blanca, who always misses the sea in winter. But then I remembered that you were no longer around, that you'd left . . . well, that . . . that I'd left . . ."

Then he fell silent and I was unable to utter a single word. The background noise was still deafening and made the silence between us all the more tense. We remained like this for a couple of seconds that seemed never-ending, both of us speechless, him at his bar and me in my bathroom, each conscious of the presence of the other in the distance. Despite the physical distance and the open abyss between us, for the first time in a long while Alberto and I felt some kind of closeness. He was the first to speak up again.

"I'm not sure if this has been total madness . . ."

A knot ran down my throat and tears welled up in my eyes. I struggled to contain them and with an effort managed not to shed a single one. The pain was intense, however. Alberto. Like a lightning bolt his face came back to mind, his all-encompassing presence. His noisy step on descending the stairs, his warm back next to mine as he slept. His brown hair, his laughter, his fingers, his skin. For a moment I yearned for him to be right, for it all to be a bad dream. For that child of his growing within another woman's body to be nothing but a figment of my imagination. I thought that maybe we could still reassemble our lives, start all over again, forgive and forget. And I wanted to tell him.

But due to some strange lack of neural coordination between the faculties of thinking and speaking, or perhaps to the crucial lifeline that lucidity once in a while tosses to us when we are at the edge of a precipice, the words that came out of my mouth were altogether different.

"Good-bye, Alberto. Don't call me again."

With hardly any time to process what had just occurred, I hung up just as my doorbell rang. Glancing at my watch, I saw it was past eight: time to begin. Before coming out, I took a fleeting look at my image in the mirror. The Gypsy ornamentation over my left ear came across as somewhat outlandish, so I tore the flowers out of my hair, tossed them into the toilet, and flushed. With a smile as false as Judas's, I then went out to greet my guests.

The first to arrive, of course, was Rebecca. With a large spinach dip and a gigantic bowl of guacamole, ready as usual to help. Then a Portuguese professor and her Canadian boyfriend and, hardly two minutes later, three students of mine with several bottles of wine. Luis Zarate, the chairman, was next with a bottle of tequila *reposado* and wearing a pair of jeans. It wasn't long before the apartment filled with voices, music, and smoke. The plates and food platters emptied at a vertiginous speed while I made an effort to drown, at least superficially, my sorrow. Some were coming in while others left; it got hot and someone opened a window. There were those who did not introduce themselves and those who brought friends along. Another pupil of mine came a while later bringing a guitar and a Uruguayan couple whom I didn't know. While I greeted them, I felt someone touching my arm to draw my attention.

"I'm off to get some limes and more ice. I'll be right back."

It was Luis Zarate, who had spontaneously taken charge of the bar on his arrival. Contrary to what I'd expected, he'd come alone, without the young German professor with whom I'd seen him on some occasion or other and with whom, according to the departmental gossip, he'd been going out for a while. I'd never imagined him as a party man and night owl, but, to my surprise, he was quite skillful at preparing margaritas and caipirinhas as he spoke to everyone good-humoredly.

"Perfect, but don't disappear. We need you to continue preparing drinks: the night's still young. By the way, where did you pick up that skill?"

"There's a trick," he said, coming close to my ear. "Low-impact academic training. I took a cocktail course a couple of years back, but don't mention it to anyone."

"Okay, but treat me well, so that I never have to use it against you."

"As well as you'll allow me . . ."

He again shortened the distance between us. Judging by his attitude, half the cocktails that he'd prepared since his arrival he'd drunk himself. But he was relaxed and fun, so I played along.

"When you change the printer in my office, we'll talk," I answered with a laugh. I had had a couple myself. "For the time being it's enough that you be in charge of the ice."

"And how about . . ." and he again came close.

I didn't let him continue; grabbing him by the arm, I walked him to the door.

"You know there is a 7-Eleven on the corner. Don't even think of driving."

"At your orders, my *doctorsita*," he said, putting on a Mexican accent. I couldn't help smiling as I closed the door behind him.

Amid the laughter and mingling of languages, someone began strumming a guitar, which gave way to clapping hands and out-of-tune renditions of old Spanish and English songs sung at the top of the lungs without an ounce of embarrassment.

At some point in the evening, between the verses of a popular Mexican song, I heard knocking at the door. I thought it was finally Luis, who'd gone a good while ago and not yet returned. But instead it was Daniel Carter, wearing a black leather jacket, with a traveling bag in one hand and a plastic bag in the other.

"I almost thought you were going to let me down."

"Not for the life of me," he said while removing his jacket and depositing his luggage on the floor. "My plane was delayed; I was on the verge of wringing the pilot's neck."

Without giving me time to reply, he took my hand, grabbed me by the waist, and, adding his loud voice to the off-key choir singing a popular Mexican song—"*because I'll be brave enough not to deny it and scream that I'm dying out of love for you . . .*"—he dragged me across the room with four artful steps in search of some omelet leftovers, not very likely at that late hour.

The party ended just before dawn without a single piece of my culinary effort left and without hearing from Luis Zarate again. With the departure of my last guests, my responsibilities as a good hostess disappeared as well, so I decided to leave everything as it was and go straight to bed. I had no energy to start straightening up. My fatigue and the drinks allowed me to fall asleep immediately without devoting a single further thought to either the party or my sad telephone encounter with Alberto.

The next day, after a restorative shower, I got down to business. In between balls of napkins, empty glasses, and dozens of bottles without any traces of what they had once contained, I found two items left behind from the previous night. One was a red sweater lying on the floor behind the armchair; I remembered one of my students was wearing it. The other was a plastic bag from Barnes & Noble. Looking inside in an effort to identify its owner, I found a book and an envelope with my name on it. I suddenly remembered the bag that Daniel Carter had been carrying along with his luggage.

The envelope contained a simple card with two sentences written in firm black letters—

**May the light of the years let you see your path more clearly.
Happy Birthday**

—and a medium-size book with a yellow dust jacket: *A History of California*. Leafing through it, I did not understand the meaning of that unexpected present, figuring it was a sudden choice of a gift made out of mere courtesy. Nor did I know how Daniel had found out about my birthday, although I figured Rebecca must have told him. After one last look, I put it aside and continued cleaning.

I aired out the apartment, filled three enormous garbage bags, conscientiously mopped the floor, and threw a load of bottles into the recycling bin. I realized I was famished and, having an empty fridge, I went out for lunch. I took the opportunity to buy some newspapers, then went for a short stroll and returned home. A Sunday afternoon in autumn, a difficult time to keep melancholy in check, all the more so after the previous evening's call.

I turned on the television in search of something to distract myself. CNN spoke of an air traffic accident in Mexico with a death toll of eighteen, the explosion at an old people's home in Michigan, and the arrival of the new *Pokémon* movie in theaters. Flipping through the channels, I came upon a repeat of *Rambo III,* two home shopping programs, a report on dog groomers, and an umpteenth stale episode of *Miami Vice.* Santa Cecilia's local channel was again airing a follow-up program on the Los Pinitos project. I watched it for a few minutes as the cameras filmed the grounds and a few passersby were interviewed. With varying degrees of fervor, they were for the most part against the mall. Afterwards they spoke to my student Joe Super, the professor emeritus of history whom I already knew to be an energetic activist in the pro-preservation platform. He hadn't been able to come to my party, having told me ahead of time that he'd be out of town. He spoke convincingly regarding the disastrous consequences of the mall they intended to build. Four other members of the platform then spoke and I began to lose interest, falling asleep as one of them detailed the uncertain legal ownership of the place.

When I woke up night had fallen. Disoriented, I looked at my watch and realized that I'd had a three-hour nap. Perhaps it was due to the exhaustion of having cleaned the apartment, or the alcohol and the late night's toll. In any case, regardless of the reason, the crude reality was that I was there, alone, sleepless before a long night. I'd just finished a novel on Friday and hadn't had time to buy another book or go to the library. After flipping once more through the channels, I ate a yogurt and went through the papers, which in a few hours seemed to have lost their newsworthiness. I read an article on intelligent design and an interview with Oprah Winfrey, then ate a banana, cursing my decision not to take home my laptop that weekend because of the party. When my eye caught Daniel Carter's book, *The History of California,* I opened it and began to read.

It soon became clear that his present had not been a mere hurried purchase. During the afternoon we spent together drinking coffee, I'd mentioned the difficulties that Fontana's papers were giving me lately. As I read further, I began to understand that, in the constant headlong flight forward that seemed to dominate every aspect of my life over the past couple of months, I'd been too impatient in assessing Fontana's legacy, leaping over barriers and holes, urgently dodging the fissures and obstacles that constantly appeared in his writings.

Fontana's ex-student was now suggesting another approach, one that made all the sense in the world and that, in spite of being so obvious, I hadn't stopped to consider. Peace and quiet, along with thorough documentation, would be essential in plotting out the route of the old professor's writings within the real map of the time and the facts.

I read several chapters in one sitting and already began appreciating with greater clarity the latter years of his work. But the part pertaining to the Spanish presence in California didn't go beyond the first three chapters and I realized I needed to know more.

Toward four o'clock in the morning I was finally about to fall asleep, when I decided not to leave something important for the next day. I got out my cell phone and texted:

LESSON LEARNED. I'LL TRY TO BE UP TO THE TASK.

Even though I realized that Daniel probably would not read the message until the following day, some impulse had driven me to thank him right away. I had hardly turned off the light when I heard a *beep-beep*. Half-asleep, I clicked on the envelope icon.

AS ALWAYS.

Chapter 21

It wasn't brand-new but, compared to my old piece of junk from the Pleistocene period, it was a technological marvel. I didn't even stop to plug it in. Instead I went in search of the person responsible.

"Your getaway is forgiven," I announced from the door. Behind the desk sat Luis Zarate as he usually was, restrained and professional. Apparently.

"Are you sure?" he asked, raising his eyes from his computer screen.

"We missed your margaritas, but I've gotten a decent printer. Not bad."

"I even managed to buy the ice, you know? But in the end I chose to go home. I was pretty loaded and one more step would have been disastrous."

"For your hangover or your reputation?"

"Both, I guess. How did it end?"

"Well . . . a little too long, but it was a fun night."

"Do you think I'll be able to recoup some of what I missed out on?" he asked as he got up from his chair.

I was still standing by the door, with no intention of stepping inside. The week had just begun and we all had a lot of work. It wasn't the moment for a laid-back conversation; I'd just stopped by his office to thank him for his gesture, with the intention of taking up no more than a couple of minutes of his day.

"I'm afraid that, as hostess, I've fulfilled my share of celebrations for the time being."

"Then it's my turn now," he said, leaning against the front edge of his desk. Closer to me, more at my level.

"Are you going to organize a party at your place?"

"I'd like to, but I'm afraid that, unlike you, I'm a hopeless host. But we have a dinner pending at Los Olivos, remember?"

It was true. Ever since the afternoon on campus when he'd stopped his car beside me to chat at the end of the workday.

"As I said, whenever you want to."

My answer was sincere: I wasn't averse to the idea of going out to dinner with him. There were always a lot of things to talk about, and after displaying his more human and less formal side at my party, he'd scored some points on my likability scale.

"Thanksgiving is coming up; would you prefer before or after?"

"I've got no plans. Whenever it suits you best."

"My mother summons me to Concord to celebrate family holidays, a duty of being an only child. Before that I have a couple of pending engagements. Perhaps it would be best to leave it to my return."

I was going to answer that it really didn't seem that complicated, but I held back. Or perhaps it would be more accurate to say that I was interrupted, for three women arrived at that moment, professors from the Modern Languages Department, whose offices were on another floor and with whom I'd hardly had any contact. One was Lisa Gersen, who was commonly thought to be Zarate's girlfriend, a thirty-something with ivory skin who always had her hair back in a tight bun and wore heels to work. The other ones were colleagues who, like Lisa, taught German.

I moved aside, imagining they had an appointment with the chairman.

"We'll be in touch," I said to Luis in parting.

As I motioned to leave, they protested, insisting, "There's no need for you to go; we can wait."

Luis stood and looked at his watch.

"Perfect. So we can settle on a date for our meeting."

Although he was speaking in Spanish, Luis clearly preferred not to mention the word "dinner." "Our meeting" was what he said. Perhaps casually or perhaps to deflect the attention of someone who had been or still was emotionally close to him. The last thing I needed was to interfere in a relationship, I thought, when I was still recovering from my own romantic debacle.

I didn't even stop to check on the functioning of my new printer or to mull over why Luis Zarate had preferred not to call a dinner by its name. I had something urgent to do: return to the book on California that Daniel Carter had brought me in an innocent bag as if it were simply another piece of reading material. The book that had awakened my need to know.

Half an hour later I had decamped to the library. There, in a remote corner of the fourth floor, alone and isolated from noise, I began delving through various sources to find the geographic and historical underpinnings of what had happened in that territory called California, which nowadays spreads across two nations.

I spent the following day as well buried in the library. I found moving passages and hundreds of facts that enabled me to begin piecing together a vast picture of my countrymen's involvement in the creation of California and to envision how the writings of Andres Fontana fit within this larger scope. I hardly spoke to anyone during the two days that I remained sequestered. I simply advised Rebecca of my whereabouts and dove into my research like someone looking for scattered treasure at the bottom of the sea. Around one o'clock on the second day, I paused in my work to get something quick to eat.

Entering the campus cafeteria alive with the commotion of students, professors, rattling plates and cutlery, and the smell of not-too-tempting food, I spotted Daniel Carter from a distance. With his light-colored hair, his height, and his relaxed appearance, it was always easy to spot him in a crowd. He was having a lively conversation with a couple of professors, and they seemed to have finished their lunch. I could hear a couple of guffaws in the distance. I figured he hadn't noticed me.

I chose a chicken burrito and a Coke, waited on line to pay, and ensconced myself in a corner with the university's paper for company. Upon my third bite of the burrito, the chair opposite me suddenly ceased to be empty.

"What a great surprise to find you here, Professor Perea. I'd already given you up for missing."

"It's your own fault."

He gave me a quizzical look.

"Your book made me want to know more about California. By the way, I should have tracked you down earlier to thank you: forgive me."

"You already did so the other day at ten to four in the morning. Or am I starting to dream about you?"

As I slowly got to know him, I also began to get used to his natural way of going about life, the affectionate way in which he treated everyone and everyone who knew him treated him. He flirted with the waitresses, the uglier and fatter the better. He'd hug his friends without reserve, would look at things through the lens of irony, and made everything around him seem easy.

I'd only seen him tense with a couple of people, coincidentally the same day. With Zarate, at the National Hispanic Heritage Month debate. And with Fanny's mother a little while later. I never knew the reasons for those lapses in understanding, and in truth I didn't care. I was more interested in being able to continue to count on him to help me see the light in his old professor's accomplishments.

"You didn't dream it, but you did manage to deprive me of sleep. And force me to lock myself up like a recluse in the library."

"You can't imagine how happy I am," he said, pinching off a bit of my burrito.

"But you just had lunch . . ." I protested.

"You made a better choice than I did today; my goulash was lousy. Tell me more: what have you been up to?"

"Everything is much clearer now. I'm starting to realize how he gradually became fascinated by the story of the Spaniards in this country, how he became personally drawn into it all, and that's why he made an about-turn in his line of research and grew increasingly passionate about the old California. And I'm beginning to have a clearer idea about what that world was like."

"So where exactly are you, then?"

"I am working with documents pertaining to the last Franciscan missions toward the end of the Hispanic California period. A few years before it briefly became independent and then became part of the United States."

"The story of the missions is quite fascinating, although it has taken me years to admit it. I remember that when Fontana was busy investigating them I found it a boring subject."

"Why?"

"Because back then I was a complete ignoramus, even though I thought I was brilliant. I didn't understand how some simple adobe constructions, a handful of shabby priests, and a bunch of Indians whose names, languages, and principles had been altered could have aroused the interest of a scholar of his standing. And even though he'd often try to, he was unable to convince me." He broke off another piece of my burrito. "The last, I promise."

The cafeteria had slowly emptied; there were only three or four tables still occupied. The background noise had diminished and there was only a casual good-bye here and there and the distant clatter of plates.

"Perhaps he got tired of doing the same thing for decades," I suggested. "Perhaps he needed new perspectives in his lines of research. And in these missions, so distant in their geography while at the same time so near to his own culture, he may have found something vital."

"You're probably right. But tell me something, just out of curiosity: Have you found any reference to a so-called Mission Olvido?"

"In the material I'm studying in the library now?"

He shook his head.

"In Fontana's papers."

"No, but I still have a lot to sift through. Why do you ask?"

"Because I remember that he mentioned that name several times toward the end of his life. I imagine you'll come across it if indeed there is something."

We left the cafeteria still talking, and after saying good-bye we each went back to our duties. I returned to the library wondering about the mission he had mentioned and how it related to the twenty-one missions erected by the Spanish Franciscans along that extensive route in western California known as the Camino Real. I'd become familiar with many of them over the past couple of days—San Diego de Alcala, San Luis Rey de Francia, San Buenaventura, La Purisima Concepcion, Santa Ines, Nuestra Señora de la Soledad—and their stories of courageous friars, violent soldiers, rebellious and devout Indians, ambitious kings commissioning expeditions to unknown territory, and an old Spain anxious to extend its boundaries ad infinitum, without foreseeing the fleeting nature of its conquests. But I had never come across any reference to a Mission Olvido, of that I was sure. I filed that piece of information in the *Missions* folder of my memory for future investigation. I eagerly pushed open the door to the library and walked into my very own carpeted paradise, where all the available knowledge that I needed awaited me.

Midmorning the following day I received an unexpected visit from Fanny, who was agitated and nervous. Small drops of sweat rolled down her temples, and she sighed with relief on seeing me.

"I finally found you, Professor."

It really wasn't easy to find me in that remote corner of the fourth floor of the library, an area almost always deserted. The great majority of students would congregate on the main floor, in the most accessible areas and in front of the computers.

"Is something the matter?" I asked, somewhat alarmed.

"Nothing, thank God. It's just that I've been looking around for a while and couldn't find you. Mrs. Cullen sent me. This is for you."

She handed me a cream-colored envelope with my name on it. Inside was a handwritten note from Rebecca in which she invited me to share Thanksgiving dinner with her and her family. An elegant move done with particular tact so as not to propose something unexpectedly in person that I might not feel like participating in.

Thanksgiving Day didn't really mean much to me, given that it was a celebration alien to my culture and to my personal inventory of nostalgic holidays. I could have just as well passed the day alone in my apartment, reading a book or seeing a movie without feeling alone or missing my children, the turkey, or the pumpkin pie. But I knew that for Americans it was an important day, so I was comforted to know that Rebecca had invited me.

"Give my thanks to Mrs. Cullen, please, Fanny. Tell her I'm delighted to accept and I'll stop by to see her as soon as I can."

"Okay," she whispered in a soft voice.

She had begun to move to and fro like a rocking chair, with her feet glued to the floor, her hands held together behind her back, and her gaze lowered in concentration. Her attention was no longer focused on my words; the "Okay" that she'd just finished uttering would have served to answer anything. Her eyes, meanwhile, wandered across the table, which was covered with books, maps, and various documents I was working with.

Finally her gaze sought mine.

"Aren't you working on Professor Fontana's legacy anymore, Professor Perea?"

She asked the question timidly, almost embarrassed, as though she might be invading my privacy.

"Yes, Fanny, of course I'm still working on that, although I'm coming closer to finishing with the processing part. But before continuing, I needed to do research on some things, which is why I'm here. It won't take me too long, I'm almost done. In a couple of days I'll be back at my office and will continue working there. We'll get to see each other often."

She nodded while continuing to rock back and forth. Her straight hair, held to one side with a child's clip in the shape of a pink cloud, moved rhythmically as she once again focused her fishlike gaze on my research material. Three open books and a few that were closed. A bunch of photocopies. Two extended maps. Several sheets of paper covered with notes.

"He also worked like this," she finally said, pointing to it all with her finger. "Like you, with lots of papers and maps on top of the table, always writing a lot. He used his fountain pen and a typewriter. He didn't really like to type much, so Mother did it for him sometimes. Mother could type fast. Very fast. But she didn't like transcribing the papers in Spanish, because she could not understand them. Only in English. But he preferred to write in Spanish. And to speak in Spanish. Uncle Andres was a good man. Very good. He always gave me presents. Shoes, clothes. And dolls. He would take us in his car. And he would buy me ice cream and shakes. Especially strawberry."

It took me a moment for her words to sink in, to be able to accept that the Fontana of my sleepless nights and that Uncle Andres, whose name she pronounced so differently, were one and the same. I was surprised to hear that Fanny and the professor had had such a close relationship. She kept talking without looking at me, and although her eyes still seemed fixed on the table, in fact they were wandering through the past.

I didn't interrupt her; I don't think she would have heard me.

"He once took us to the Santa Cruz Beach Boardwalk, next to the sea. It's very old, the oldest amusement park in California. Some of the rides were lots of fun. *Lots* of fun. And other ones were dangerous. *Very* dangerous. I rode in practically all of them. The one I liked best was the roller coaster. He got on with me and held my hand tight so I wouldn't be scared. Mother stayed on the ground. It was a wonderful day."

The half smile on her wistful face suddenly disappeared.

"I was very sad when he died. I was asleep. Mrs. Walker, the neighbor, woke me up. Mother was no longer in the house; she'd left in the middle of the night. I didn't like being with Mrs. Walker: she called me stupid and other nasty things. Uncle Andres never bawled me out; he always said to me 'Very good, Fanny!' or 'Well done, Fanny!' *He's* also like that with me. He never says anything mean to me, or disagreeable. Only nice things."

I blinked, surprised. I'd lost the thread and I didn't know who she was referring to now. I could see she was making an effort to scrutinize her mind, chipping away at memories and sensations while she rocked to and fro. Her gaze remained vacant and the words kept flowing out of her mouth artlessly, but with a certain delicacy.

"He's like Uncle Andres but different. I don't see either one of them, but I know they're there. They're both good with me. He also says to me, 'Come on, Fanny! You can do it, Fanny. Good girl, Fanny.'"

Then it all made sense. I remembered the stickers on her car, the messages on her office wall. I knew who *He* was, that other being who treated her with the same love that Andres Fontana had. She was speaking of God, that personal God that she had molded to her specifications to shine into the dark corners of her life.

"Mother doesn't like that I speak so much of Him," she carried on in her monotone. "I think it's because she knows that He is not going to give her anything of what she wants. Of what Uncle Andres gave her when I was little—not afterwards. Presents, car rides. Sometimes he even lent the car to her so that she could drive it without him. I'd sit by her side and she would speed, speed, speed. She liked driving a lot, but we didn't have a car because father took it when he left us and we could not afford to buy another one; that's why Mother would sometimes drive Uncle Andres's car. I like driving too. After the accident his car was totaled. Mother wanted to keep it, but it couldn't be fixed. It was ruined."

Her monologue was interrupted by the arrival of a couple of female students in sweatsuits. Carefree and tanned. They chatted and laughed, ignoring us, their blond ponytails bobbing. The fact that they were unable to find the book they were looking for seemed extremely funny to them. Their frivolous talk brought Fanny back to reality.

"I think I have to go; it's late now," she announced, bringing her watch up close to her eyes. "I'll tell Mrs. Cullen that you'll go see her as soon as you can."

I watched her walk away with her clumsy gait while I grabbed a felt pen to continue with my work. But I wasn't even able to uncap it because Fontana and Fanny still hovered in my mind. Fontana and Fanny, Fontana and Darla Stern—unexpected connections that suddenly came to me. I was unaware that mother and daughter had had a close relationship with him, but it didn't seem so far-fetched. Fontana had been the department chairman and Darla his secretary; Fanny, then a somewhat clumsy fatherless girl, had likely elicited tenderness from those around her.

Time had reassembled things. He was absent now; they were still here. He was dead, but they were alive and with him in memory—at least, Fanny was. But perhaps Darla was too.

I forced myself to resume my task and once again pored over the map of the old missions. From Santa Barbara to Santa Ines, from Santa Ines to La Purisima Concepcion. The afternoon advanced into evening, the setting sun visible behind the windowpane. The image of the Spanish professor and the girl Fanny on a roller coaster remained, hovering before me, keeping me company like a little spider hanging from a nearly invisible thread.

Chapter 22

The following morning I returned to Guevara Hall to see Rebecca, who received me warmly as usual, serving me some tea. She worked with soft background music and freshly cut flowers by the window, making me envious. Despite planning to do so at the beginning of each semester, I never managed to have a teapot or CD player in my office. Not even a simple bouquet of daisies or an old transistor radio. The furthest I'd gone was a couple of pots of plants that ended up drying out on me during the holidays.

"My kids and grandchildren will be there, as usual. I prepare the turkey according to my maternal grandmother's recipe, and after dinner the boys will watch the football game on TV and the girls will clean up, as tradition demands," she said with an ironic wink.

"I'd be delighted to spend such a special day with all of you."

She fell silent for a couple of seconds, as if hesitating about sharing something else.

"Daniel Carter will also be coming."

"Wonderful."

"And . . . and someone else."

She again fell silent for an instant and then she added:

"Paul will also be there."

"Paul . . . your ex-husband?"

She said yes with a simple nod. She hadn't spoken to me about him since the day we loaded her car with the chairs for my party; I had assumed Paul had disappeared out of her life for good. But everything indicated that I was mistaken.

"Perhaps because . . ."

"If you mean a reconciliation, the answer is no."

"Then?"

"Well . . . because life always ends up taking unexpected turns, Blanca. Because sometimes we believe that we've got it all clear and we suddenly realize that nothing is as firm as we'd thought. What I want now is for him to be able to see his kids again."

"But I thought you'd lost touch with him, that—"

"At the beginning he'd call us once in a while and tried seeing the kids twice a year. But they were never able to understand his shifting attitude: adoring them one minute, neglecting them the next."

"So they slowly distanced themselves," I suggested.

"Yes. The distance grew in every way and it got to a point that we preferred not having any news from him."

"I imagine he didn't live nearby."

"He never quite settled down permanently: he changed universities a bunch of times, and although he had a few relationships, as far as I know, none lasted. Meanwhile, the children grew up and set out on their own lives. But now I want to bring them all together again."

"But why, Rebecca, after such a long time?"

"So that they can say good-bye. It's very likely that it will be the last time they'll see each other."

She took off her glasses and closed her eyes, and with her fingers massaged the place at the top of her nose where the frames of her glasses had left two faint marks. I thought she must have a headache. Or perhaps she just wanted to protect herself before answering the question she knew I would ask.

"They still don't know that he's coming, right?"

She shook her head.

"Paul has been living in California for the past three years, confined to a nursing home in Oakland. I go see him once in a while. He's got Alzheimer's."

. . .

The day finally came, the fourth Thursday of November. Just as Zarate had forewarned me, the university became deserted as the majority of students flew back to their family nests, the dorms and shared apartments emptied out, caps, bicycles, and backpacks were no longer visible, laughter and voices fell silent in classrooms and corridors. And the solitary expatriates like me were fortunately welcomed by friends.

It took a while for me to decide what to wear that day. I had no idea about the degree of formality with which Rebecca's family celebrated the date, nor what the atmosphere would be like given Rebecca's decision to invite her ex-husband without letting her children know. Perhaps they would accept it readily, understanding their mother's feelings. Or perhaps they'd take it like a kick in the stomach and be incapable of understanding her desire to close the vital circle of a fractured family. Fractured but real.

I chose a burgundy velvet suit and a pair of long silver earrings that had captivated me the previous spring on a trip to Istanbul with Alberto and his brothers. The earrings I never got to wear, saving them for the summer, for those relaxed nights by the sea, for those dinners replete with the smell of salt and the sounds of friends and laughter. For those everyday evenings that never did come. In those months of heat and bile there had been no dinners beneath the stars nor laughter nor friends. Only anger and perplexity, which had driven me to change my life. But all that was part of the past. Now it was time to look forward, and in homage to that future unfolding before me I decided to put on my old yet new silver earrings.

At five o'clock in the afternoon, an odd dinner hour for a Spanish stomach, I knocked on the door of Rebecca's house with a bottle of Viña Tondonia purchased at the price of a ransom and a box of chocolates for the kids. The door was opened by a couple of lively blond girls no older than six who demanded that I answer a series of questions and conditions before letting me through. "What's your name? Where are you from? Who are those chocolates for? How many kids do you have? Show us your shoes. Bend down. Show us your earrings. Will you lend them to us later?" Then they sped away like bullets, headed for the garden. Only then did I perceive the presence of Daniel nearby. With his long body leaning again the doorframe, he had been watching the scene in amusement. He had on a gray jacket and a blue shirt and tie, and was holding a glass.

"Test passed," he said, smiling as he came up to greet me.

"Don't think it's easy: kids are unforgiving, and if you don't get on their good side from the start, you're lost. The tie looks good on you, but it's crooked."

"Those two little devils tried taking it off. They're very dangerous."

"Let me see." I handed him the wine and the box to free my hands and straightened his knot. "Now perfect."

The house seemed unusually quiet for the preamble to a great family dinner. However, behind the sliding doors that separated the entrance from the living room, the muffled sound of a conversation could be heard.

"How are things?" I asked while he led me to the kitchen.

"I have no idea; I arrived just ten minutes ago. Rebecca is talking to her children now, I imagine explaining the situation. Undoubtedly, they must be somewhat bewildered on seeing their father here. He was brought a while ago; he's in the garden with the nurse who accompanies him. The grandkids are also out there horsing around and looking at their grandfather as if he were an oddity."

"They hadn't met him before?"

"They didn't even know of his existence."

My eyes panned across the kitchen while he poured me a glass of wine. Everything was impeccably organized for the dinner. Platters and salad bowls, bread baskets, pumpkin pies. The oven gave off a mouthwatering smell as we sat on a couple of high stools beneath the hanging pans.

"Paul was a friend of yours, right?"

"A great friend, many years back." He took a sip while his gaze rested on an indefinite point beyond the window. "In a complicated period of my life, he was my greatest support. Later on, fate took us in different directions and we lost contact. He left his family—I think you already know that part of the story—and I roamed around different places until, in time, I ended up settling in Santa Barbara. Throughout the years, however, I kept up my friendship with Rebecca. And she's kept me abreast of what she learned about his life. His comings and goings, his squalid affairs, his wandering throughout the country from one university to the next, always with greater misfortune. That's how I learned about his mental instability and professional decline. And, finally, of his illness."

"And you hadn't seen him until today?"

My question made him shift his gaze back to me. He spoke calmly, without melancholy.

"When he was committed, a couple of years back, Rebecca told me about it and I went to see him in Oakland, close to here, in the Bay Area. I owed him at least a visit to his particular hell, just as he'd once acted so honorably in witnessing mine." He took another sip and again looked outside. "These are stories from long ago, old stories, practically forgotten. Of when I left Santa Cecilia, some . . . how many years did I tell you the other day had gone by? Thirty?"

The kitchen was still quiet. Rebecca and her children remained locked in the living room, where once in a while a voice could be heard above the others, and the children's laughter could be heard coming from the garden.

"When I saw him again after all that time, I did not find the person I was expecting," he went on. "The live wire that my friend had been was no longer there, that philosophy professor just a bit older than I, smart as a fox and incredibly fun, whom I'd met when I first arrived at this university. In Paul Cullen's place I found only a shadow. But since I know that shadows also appreciate company in their own way, once in a while, every two or three months, I go visit him."

"Does he talk to you? Or does he understand, at least?"

"He neither talks nor understands. At the beginning he was still able to get by, although he'd forget words and was easily disoriented. Little by little, however, his vocabulary became more limited, until his memory completely deteriorated. On the first visit he only recognized me for fleeting moments; it was painful but touching. The last time we had seen each other was under difficult circumstances, so that first meeting was particularly special. The second time, he treated me affectionately, but I think that he was never quite able to tell who I was or what I was doing there. From the third visit onward, we were unable to keep up even a simple conversation."

"But you continue to visit him . . ."

"I spend the afternoon with him and recount things, nonsense. I speak to him about books and movies, about trips, politics. About the NBA, about the nurses' butts. Whatever comes to mind." He drained his glass. "Come meet him. I've also spoken to him about you lately."

Almost without realizing it, I was dragged to the garden turned zoo, full of strange human creatures who were supposedly being watched over by a Japanese au pair. A five-year-old Terminator had just finished ripping his pants with a torn branch and a pair of twins were fighting like tigers over a yellow plastic truck while their keeper stubbornly defied a Game Boy. The two dangerous blondes who'd received me upon my arrival—Natalie and Nina—were subjecting their Uncle Jimmy's girlfriend to a cosmetics session. Lying in a hammock, the poor thing stoically bore the makeover as the two sisters wrung her hair into impossible buns and painted her nails a raging green. Out back, next to the pool, a pinkish chubby nurse turned the pages of *People* magazine and commented on the latest intimacies of Hollywood's celebrities to a man seated in a wheelchair.

"Betty, this is our friend Blanca," said Daniel. "She wants to meet Paul and you."

Daniel's presentation left no doubt of the importance of Betty in Paul's life: she was the conduit to him.

"It's a pleasure to meet you, dear," she said. "We're having a lovely afternoon. I was just telling Paul that I don't like JLo's new look, what do you guys think?"

"And this, Blanca, is Paul."

He'd gotten behind his friend's chair and placed his hands on his shoulders, massaging them. Paul didn't seem to notice.

My only image of Paul was from former times: that photo pinned on the bulletin board in the basement of that house that had been his, of the young man with wild dark hair, a ribbon across his forehead, and a beer in his hand. Nothing to do with the small being with thin hair and eyes lost in infinity to whom Daniel spoke as if his mind were there in the garden with us.

"Do you recall I recently spoke to you about Blanca, Paul? She is working on Fontana's legacy, you know. You remember Andres Fontana, right? Do you remember how much you both argued about Thomas Aquinas at my place? My Spanish friend was tough, eh?"

Rebecca's voice calling us from the kitchen door suddenly replaced Paul's eternal silence before his old friend's questions. The children flooded into the house and the rest of us followed. Daniel pushed Paul's chair while Betty resumed chattering about the latest gossip in the world of entertainment. Until Rebecca, bless her heart, rescued me.

"I love your earrings. Thanks for the wine and chocolates. I hope the kids have treated you well."

She smiled, but her eyes bore a residue of sadness.

The house had suddenly filled up with voices and noise. The little ones washed their hands in a nearby bathroom and slowly settled in the dining room. Sounds could be heard on the stairs: conversations among adults, children's laughter. Rebecca meanwhile spoke without looking at me, gliding across the kitchen from one place to another nonstop, organizing what was missing to take to the table.

"I'll introduce you to my children now. Forgive me for not being with you earlier: we've had a long conversation."

"Don't worry in the least. I've been with Daniel and have met Paul. Tell me, how can I help you?"

"Let's see . . . First, I think we should carve the turkey and set out the side dishes."

Before long we were all seated around a large rectangular table, outfitted with a russet tablecloth and white porcelain dishes. Five children and twelve adults. The family, their partners, and their children. Plus a friend from the old days, the female Japanese au pair, Paul's nurse, and myself. Sixteen active minds and one absent. Annie, Jimmy, and Laura,

Rebecca's children, friendly like their mother, had greeted me warmly before we took our seats. Paul sat between Betty and Daniel and the next spot had a card with my name. A centerpiece with autumn fruits rose in the middle of the table. One of the young blondes, Natalie, seated opposite me, didn't stop squinting while darting monstrous faces at me. I returned a few.

Daniel leaned toward me.

"Rebecca wants me to say a few words. Here I go, without a safety net."

He then asked for everyone's attention by tapping his fork against his glass.

"Dear Cullen family, dear friends. Rebecca has asked me to say a few words for this Thanksgiving dinner, and since I've never been able to deny anything to this woman, not even in a hundred lives, here I am, in the capacity of the family's oldest friend, ready to act as master of ceremonies. But before that, before giving thanks, I'd like to take the liberty of telling you a few things that have been on my mind for some time now—ever since Rebecca told me about her decision to bring us all together here today.

"When I exited your life, you, Annie, Jimmy, and Laura, were still very young, so most likely you hardly have any old memories left." He then turned his attention toward the children. "Did you know, Natalie and Nina, that when your mother was your age, she baked a cake in the kitchen of my house and we almost all caught fire?" A theatrical gesture simulating an explosion caused a burst of laughter from the kids and made Annie cover her face with her hands. "And you, Jimmy: when I carried you on my shoulders, you'd say that you could almost touch the clouds. And you, Laura, you were so little that you still fell sometimes when you tried to walk. And once, with your dad's help," he said, placing a hand on Paul's shoulder, "I built you a house out of wood and cardboard in the garden. It stood for nearly three days before it came crashing down on a stormy night.

"A long time has elapsed since then, but even though I haven't seen you in all these years, through your mother I've been able to follow your lives: your careers, your loves and progress, the birth of your kids, these handsome boys and girls who are seated among us at this table, eager to sink their teeth into the turkey. Rebecca and I don't get to see each other as much as we'd like to, but our late-night phone conversations can last for hours, so I am kept up-to-date. Did you know, kids," he said, addressing the youngest, "that your grandmother is like an owl and doesn't sleep at night? When the entire world goes to bed, she revives and starts doing things: she gets on the Internet, cooks strange recipes, swims in the pool, calls someone up. Until the wee hours. Sometimes, I receive those calls of hers.

"This is why, Annie, Jimmy, and Laura, I know about what you've lived through, what you've suffered, and the wonderful people you've turned out to be. I know that the three of you are conscious that all of this would have been impossible without the encouragement of this great woman who has prepared the dinner we are all about to share. And this is why I want to ask you that, for her, even if it is only for her, you accept things the way they are today. That we are all here this evening, gathered around this table.

"Getting older when you're a grown-up is not as much fun as when you're a kid. No one gives you interesting presents, only books, records, ties, and nonsense like that. But to reach a certain age has its positive side. You lose a few things along the way, but you also gain others. You learn to see the world from a different perspective, for instance, and you develop strange feelings, such as compassion. Which is nothing other than wanting to see others free of suffering, regardless of the previous suffering they might have caused us. Without holding anyone accountable or looking back. Today we don't know if Paul suffers or not: we are unable to probe his brain. Perhaps being here today may not make him any more or less happy, although it is thought that people like him don't lose affective memory or the feeling of pleasure and that, in their own way, they're grateful for a simple affectionate word, a spoonful of ice cream, or a caress.

"It is said that compassion is a sign of emotional maturity. It's not a moral obligation or a feeling that springs from reflection. It's simply something that, when it comes, it comes. Wanting to have Paul among us today is not a betrayal or a sign of weakness on the part of Rebecca.

It's simply, I think, an example of her enormous generosity. For me, Paul was a great friend, my best friend during a certain period. He did things for me that I wish no one would ever have to do. Did you know, kids, that he once had to cut my toenails? Clip, clip, clip, with an enormous pair of old scissors that someone lent him. He was a great friend to me, but that is only one aspect of him.

"I am aware that he was not always a good inspiration as a father or as a partner, and that it's hard to forgive and forget. His presence today won't overcome the past or compensate for the years of absence. But Rebecca has so wished it and I ask that we respect her decision. Paul may not have been a good father, but I know, because he told me so himself, that in spite of how disordered his life was and in his own way, he loved you all a lot, very much. Until the last minute that there was a spark of light in his mind.

"I don't want to go on any longer because that turkey is waiting for us to eat it. Today is Thanksgiving and I believe all of us present here, regardless of how the past has made us suffer, have lots of things to be thankful for. What I'm not quite sure about is to whom we must be thankful, because that is a matter of personal choice. But, thinking about whom we could all thank today, an old song has come to mind that Rebecca liked in the old days: a song that is on a big black record that I know she sometimes plays on that piece of junk she's got in the basement. Because in her strange nights, in case you didn't know, kids, your grandmother also sings and dances around the house, with the music at full blast and in her nightgown. Yes, yes, don't laugh: spy on her late at night, you'll see. That song I'm telling you about was sung ages ago by another grandmother also a bit crazy by the name of Joan Baez, who in turn borrowed it from another mad grandmother by the name of Violeta Parra. The song's lyrics are in Spanish and it's called 'Gracias a la vida.' It gives thanks to everything that helps us be happy on a daily basis. The eyes to see the stars, the alphabet to compose beautiful words, the feet to roam through cities and puddles, and all those daily activities that some no longer have, and those of us who do should feel immensely grateful for. Because sometimes, even if the going gets tough, in the end we always have those small things. So let's all give this Thanksgiving Day a loud, strong 'Here's to life' in Spanish and English: *¡Gracias a la vida!* Here's to life!"

There were very different reactions at the end of the speech. The younger, captivated by the rhetoric and the gestures of that bearded comedian who seemed to know all the family's past secrets, screamed "Here's to life!" at the top of their lungs while tossing their napkins in the air amid loud laughter. Annie ran upstairs, while Laura, clutching her husband's hand, continued to shed silent tears, which had begun a good while back. Daniel got up and hugged Rebecca, and Jimmy's girlfriend and I exchanged glances full of bewilderment and emotion. The Japanese au pair, not knowing what was happening, shot pictures with her digital camera right and left, while Betty the nurse, in view of the fact that no one seemed in a hurry to start eating, decided to begin serving the turkey herself. Only Paul was oblivious to it all, until his son, Jimmy, got up from his place and came over to occupy the chair that Daniel had vacated when he got up to hug Rebecca. With great tenderness, he held his father's hand and caressed his face. From the corner of my eye I thought I saw that—very slightly—Paul smiled.

. . .

A couple of Tupperware containers full of leftovers was not the only thing I brought back from the Cullens' house that Thanksgiving night. I also took a moderately sweet sensation hard to describe, a subtle whiff of optimism that I hadn't felt in a long time. A vague certainty that everything, at some point, can become better.

Besides food for a couple of days and uplifted spirits, that night I also secured two small invitations to keep my social life active. One came from Rebecca and her daughters: to go shopping, observing the tradition of the day after Thanksgiving.

"This way you can start buying presents for when you return to Spain before Christmas. Because that's when you're going back, right?"

Rebecca's unexpected question, while we were clearing up in the kitchen, caught me unawares. I focused on drying a saucer as if that trivial task required my five senses.

"I don't know, we'll see."

I was not deceiving her: I had no idea what I was going to do once I'd finished sorting out Fontana's legacy. And there was less and less left. With the end of my professional duties there would no longer be any excuse to stretch out my stay, although on a couple of occasions it had crossed my mind to contact SAPAM, the foundation that financed my work, to inquire about the possibility of obtaining another, similar fellowship. In fact, although it was unnecessary to my work's progress and not one of its requirements, I often thought that perhaps it would be wise to contact them to let them know that everything was going well. I sometimes thought about asking Rebecca for the telephone number and address, or to talk to Luis Zarate about it. But something always came up, and out of forgetfulness or simple neglect, or because I was in a hurry, I never got around to doing it.

On the other hand, however, I was aware that sooner rather than later I'd have to return. I wanted to see my kids, I had to go back to my university, and at some point, despite my reticence, I had to confront Alberto face-to-face and talk to him. My stay in California was a kind of balm, a sweet bandage for the wounds that he'd inflicted on me. But beneath that comfortable bandage was the crudeness of real life, and eventually I'd have to take it on.

The second invitation came from Daniel after he drove me back home that evening. On reaching my apartment, he asked me about my weekend plans.

"I'm going shopping tomorrow with the Cullen girls. I'm told it is the year's big shopping day, Black Friday, right? They insist that I can't miss out on it."

"Of course not. It will be an amazing cultural experience. Quintessential America."

"And on Saturday I'm off on a little excursion. Rebecca is going to lend me her car. I want to visit Sonoma."

"The city of Sonoma or Sonoma Valley?"

"The mission of Sonoma, San Francisco Solano, at the end of the Camino Real. You know that for the last couple of weeks I've been reading about the missions in Fontana's papers, and I'd like to see this one at least. And by the way, Mission Olvido, which you asked me about the other day, hasn't come up yet."

"I figured as much. And do you have to go this weekend?"

"No, I could do it some other time, but I had nothing better to do this weekend. Why do you ask?"

He'd gotten out of the car to accompany me to the door. We kept talking in front of my building, beneath the façade's faint light and surrounded by an uncommon silence.

"Because I'd like to accompany you, but I'm unable to this weekend. I return to Santa Barbara tomorrow: another dinner awaits me at my place, a somewhat unique Thanksgiving. This year I didn't want to miss out on Paul's reunion and his family, so that's why we've postponed it until tomorrow."

"You're going to eat turkey two days in a row?"

"In truth the turkey is just an excuse for a few old friends to get together and catch up on a load of things. We drink like fish, play poker, and fix the world among ourselves; that's what we basically do. A somewhat marginal and quite irreverent version of the traditional Thanksgiving, to put it mildly. If you wish to come, you are more than welcome: you'd be the first woman to have the honor of sharing that night with half a dozen troglodytes loaded on whiskey up to our ears."

"Thank you, but no thank you," I declined forcefully. "Terrible plan."

"I figured. Nonetheless, you could take advantage of the time to visit the Santa Barbara mission instead of the Sonoma one."

"The queen of missions," I clarified.

"That's what they call it. In fact, I live relatively close, we could . . ."

My nonverbal refusal made him desist.

"Very well, I take the proposition back. But I'll be back on Tuesday, so if you wait for me and don't go alone to Sonoma the day after tomorrow, we could go together next weekend. We could even try to visit some other mission if we have the time, although I'm not quite sure if there's another one in that area to the north of the bay."

"Yes, there is another: the twentieth, San Rafael Arcangel. Founded in 1817 by Father Vicente de Sarria."

"I'm impressed," he said with a laugh. "What have you been doing since I last saw you, getting a PhD in missions?"

"Basic research, what you suggested."

"Is that how you were taught to do research at the Complutense University of Madrid?"

"No," I answered categorically. "This way of working I've learned all on my own, chipping away at stone for years. Okay, then, call when you get back. And thanks for offering to come with me."

I climbed the stairs to my apartment feeling that something was a bit off, but I was unable to identify what it was. Something in the last part of our conversation. I already had the key in the lock when I realized it. I ran down the stairs and onto the street as he was driving away.

"Daniel!"

He jammed on the brakes after having gone a couple of yards and rolled down the window.

"How do you know I studied in the Complutense?" I yelled.

He answered from behind the wheel, in the same manner I had addressed him: at the top of his lungs.

"I guess I just imagined so. Fontana studied there. And so did I for a while, when it was still called Universidad Central. And other dear people that I met in Spain. I probably put you in the same boat without realizing it."

Chapter 23

P rofessor Cabeza de Vaca was seated at his walnut desk, waiting for Daniel as if nothing had happened between his last visit and this one. His appearance was, as always, meticulous. The thick curtains of his office kept out the morning light, and the inkstand and ivory crucifix occupied their customary places, in perfect harmony.

"Well, young man, I'm happy to finally have you back," he said, holding out his hand without moving from his armchair. "It's already mid-February and I've not heard from you since before Christmas. I imagine that your incursion into the old Canton must have been an intense experience."

Despite his effort to give an update, not one single image came into Daniel's mind of the literary settings that he'd gone in search of and never found. Instead there appeared a prolonged sequence of images and sensations: Aurora's face, Aurora's eyes, Aurora's smell. Her infinite tenderness, her hearty laughter, her voice.

"Intense, sir, indeed," he finally was able to mutter after clearing his throat. "A very intense experience."

"I imagine, then, that you've returned to Madrid with a profound knowledge of the geographic background of Sender's novel."

He assented without words. He lied, of course. He had hardly glanced at the settings of *Mister Witt en el Canton*. Instead, he'd ventured to explore the territory of the woman who'd captivated him there. The tiny scar on her cheekbone, the softness of her lips, and those four beauty marks right next to her hairline. The gentleness of her fingers as she caressed him and the taste of the sea in Madrid—hundreds of miles from any coast—eternally present on her skin.

"I also imagine that you must have familiarized yourself with the historical events that are mentioned in the book."

Again he assented; again he lied. The only events of relevance that had stuck in his memory were those that had to do with Aurora. That first encounter in her father's pharmacy while she tried to put her disheveled hair in order. His stealthy pursuit of her, feverishly refusing to lose her. The encounter in the middle of the street the next day, not knowing what to do or say. His bitterness over the feast of the Three Wise Men, when he rashly imagined what wasn't true. That long train journey in which they began to know each other, the beginning of all that was to come afterwards.

"And likewise I imagine," Cabeza de Vaca continued, oblivious to the thoughts that assailed the American's mind, "that you have already written a preliminary report regarding your thoughts and findings."

Daniel's response this time was to clear his throat. Unable to continue lying, Daniel murmured something unintelligible.

"I don't understand what you're saying, Carter. Speak clearly, please."

"That I've been unable to do it, sir."

"What is it you haven't been able to do? To find relevant information for your work or to write the pertinent report?"

"Neither of the two."

Cabeza de Vaca showed his surprise with a stern yet subtle puckering of one side of the mouth.

"Would you be so kind, if it isn't an inconvenience, to explain the reason?"

Daniel cleared his throat once more.

"Personal matters."

"How personal?"

"Extremely personal, sir."

His endless waits at the entrance to the school of pharmacy, craving to see her race down the steps in her half-buttoned coat, her arms loaded with books. The calls at ungodly hours to share trivial things. The long, hidden kisses in half-lit corners. The countless walks, hand in hand, along Madrid's streets as they tried to teach each other their respective languages. Aurora to him: science and laboratory terms, everyday expressions and words to describe family, childhood, the schoolyard. Daniel: simple nouns, verbs, and basic adjectives in her first steps toward English. Aurora is beautiful, Aurora is gorgeous. I love Aurora from morning until night.

How to explain all this to the scrupulous philologist? How could that helpless medievalist, lost in his world of codices and scrolls, understand the distressing cold he felt inside each time he walked alone kicking stones beneath the streetlamps after dropping Aurora off at her dorm at ten? How could he know the way he felt night after night locked up in the concierge's room, lying in his patched-up bed, imagining her long-boned body, her smoothness, her warmth?

Now it was the professor's turn to clear his throat, followed by a question.

"Might we be speaking of a lady, perhaps?"

Powerless before the inevitable, Daniel nodded.

"Homo sine amore vivere nequit . . ."

"Excuse me?"

"Man, Carter, cannot live without love. And less so in a foreign land."

"I . . . well, the truth is that—"

"Don't bother explaining, I have no intention of prying into your private life. But if you'll allow me, I'd like to give you a piece of advice."

Daniel did not expect a caustic admonishment; it wasn't Cabeza de Vaca's style. He expected something more along the lines of: Remember that you've incurred responsibilities and duties—that the purpose of the Fulbright grant that you are enjoying is to finance an academic project, not a love affair. Both Professor Fontana and I have placed our utmost trust in you, so you should devote yourself to your career. Forget about romance and concentrate on your work.

However, such words did not spring forth from the mouth of the old monarchist soldier.

"But first I have a few questions. With your hand on your heart, are you convinced that it's not a bird of passage?"

"Do you mean 'bird' as in 'fowl'?" Daniel asked, confused.

"I'm afraid your metaphoric sensibility is not too sharp today, young man. Allow me to reformulate the question in other words: are you sure that this is not a mere transitory rapture?"

"I'm afraid I don't understand, sir," he admitted, without being able to hide his embarrassment. "Rapture, did you say?"

"I'm inquiring whether there is truly on your part a willingness to commit, an unbending desire to jointly overcome the misfortunes that life throws your way, which, keeping your particular circumstances in mind—and if you'll allow me to be totally frank, I anticipate it will be quite a few . . ."

Daniel stirred uncomfortably in his chair, and the professor decided to cut straight to the chase.

"For you to understand once and for all, young man: are you sure that this is the love of your life?"

Finally Daniel understood, and did not hesitate.

"A hundred percent, sir."

"Well, then, my friend, don't let her escape."

Minutes later, leaning on his crutch by the window, Cabeza de Vaca saw them kiss and then go off with the carefree stride of those immune to anything beyond the periphery of their feelings. Her arm tightly around his waist, his around her shoulders, half-hidden by her disheveled mane, pulling her close to him. The old professor imagined that they were speaking nonstop, getting up to speed on what had just transpired in his office.

Cabeza de Vaca knew full well how fleeting happiness was, the brutal simplicity with which the claws of destiny are capable of wiping out everything we erroneously believe established. And still, he would give his only good leg to feel in his soul again that grandiose, confident sensation of falling in love.

Between classrooms and caresses, test tubes and libraries, spring finally bloomed before Daniel Carter and Aurora Carranza. At the same time, almost without his realizing it, he opened his eyes to that American passionate about Spain, its literary heritage, and a woman, and the helpless, melancholic medievalist poked his head out of his cave. And he saw there was light outside. That the world moved on, that wounds healed, that people loved each other.

The Holy Week holidays came around and Aurora, inevitably, had to return home. They said good-bye at the same Atocha station platform that had received them three months earlier. This time an eleven-day separation awaited them. "I'll miss you," "Me more," "No, me," "Think of me," "You too," "I'm already thinking of you . . ."

As a precautionary measure Daniel made the firm commitment to take full advantage of the coming days. Since his February meeting with Cabeza de Vaca, he had decided to focus once again on his studies. And he had managed, with Aurora always close by and his love for her intact; he'd been capable of resuming his work at a good pace. Until she left and his plans came crumbling down as soon as he felt her absence. On his third day without her, he lost all interest in everything. He hadn't anticipated how much he was going to miss her. He chose to stay home, longing for her painfully, as if short of air. Waiting for a call or a letter, altogether impossible given her recent departure. And contemplating the future.

"But what's the matter with you, dear boy, tormented like a lost, wandering soul, moving here and there all day long?"

The widow's question oozed with maternal anxiety. While she cooked she could hear Daniel coming in and out of his room constantly, incapable of reading more than ten minutes straight. While she ironed, she could see him sullenly pacing the room like a caged lion, grumbling, moving things about without rhyme or reason. First thing in the morning he'd take off to go for a run on the University City track, a practice from his Pittsburgh days that he'd taken up again once settled in Madrid. In the early afternoon, he'd head to the Café Viena to have a coffee with a drop of milk. The rest of the day he was unable to concentrate on anything beyond the thoughts that plagued his mind.

"It's because of that girl you've been buzzing about with since after the Christmas holidays, right? The long, skinny blonde with a blue coat who I finally saw you with last week on Calle Altamirano?" she asked as she sprinkled a few drops of water on one of his shirts.

"Do you think she'll come with me to America when it's time for me to leave?" he asked point-blank.

No, son, was what she was about to tell him: not even an idiot would think so. But before opening her mouth, she put down the iron and looked at him closely.

He had taken a tangerine from the earthenware fruit bowl that dominated the dining room's brazier table and was slowly peeling it, his eyes on the ground and his hair falling over his face, concentrating on stripping the rough skin as if beneath it he'd find relief for his suffering. Such a good handsome young man, a foreigner but yet close to her heart, the widow thought. With a stature that made everything in the place look too small for him. With that accent and that outlook on life that she found both strange and tender.

"Head over heels," the widow said, sitting in front of him.

"What?"

"You've fallen in love head over heels, child."

"I guess so."

"And you're busy calculating the time left for you to return to your country and the numbers don't add up."

"Less than three months, that is the time left."

The faded portrait of Antonia's wedding with the deceased Marcelino and the reproduction of a Julio Romero de Torres painting on the calendar month of March stared down at him from the wall as usual.

"Because I'm wondering, even if you'd wish, you couldn't just stick around for her," the widow said, measuring her words.

"And do what? How could I earn a living in this country? What kind of future would I have? At the most I could teach English, but no one here is interested in a foreign language unless it's French," he said without lifting his eyes from another tangerine. He'd already peeled four and hadn't eaten a single one. "But if she consented to come with me, then, perhaps . . ."

She shook her head slowly in a gesture of resignation, sighed, and then clutched his hand above the crocheted tablecloth.

"You haven't understood, Daniel. Son, you still don't get it."

"Get what?"

"That it doesn't matter if the girl wants to go with you or stay here," the widow said, pressing his wrist tightly. "Here she has no say about what she wants or doesn't want."

"But—"

"Either you get to the altar before you go, kid, or there's nothing to be done."

Chapter 24

Holy Tuesday, noon. Time to return home for the midday meal. Three bodies advanced toward the Paseo de la Muralla in Cartagena after having an aperitif in the Mastia Bar, talking among themselves about trifles with all the natural excitement of a family gathered for the holidays. Until she saw him. Leaning on the balustrade with his back to the sea, waiting for her. Confused, bewildered almost, she excused herself from her parents.

He was again moved to see her face and mane, watching her approach with her elastic gait, once again having her mouth close to his for which he would have sold his soul to the devil without hesitation. With great difficulty he fought his urge to kiss her.

"What are you doing here?" was all she was able to mutter. The tone of her voice gave away a mixture of nervousness and misgiving.

"I've come to ask you to marry me," he said, bringing his hand up to her face.

She stopped him. The caress and the marriage proposal were both left unfinished.

"Not here, Daniel, not like this . . ." she mumbled.

"I cannot return to my country without you: you must come with me."

His explanations could have dragged on forever, but there was no time. At her back, on the other side of the street, they heard a voice. Her mother's, specifically, calling her daughter with the sharpness of a combat knife.

"Don't even think of it, you nut . . ." Aurora whispered.

Too late. He'd already grabbed her by the hand and was dragging her with him to the opposite sidewalk.

"My name is Daniel Carter. I'm an American and want to ask for your daughter's hand."

He'd practiced it. Dozens of times. While the concierge was washing the dishes or hanging the clothes in the inside patio or checking the salt in the lentils by the stove; he, waiting to be corrected, had repeated his proposition over and over again to her like a litany. This was why the sentence came out perfectly, worthy of the highest mark: ten. What he wasn't ready for, however, was their reaction.

Carranza the pharmacist was left speechless, unable to utter anything coherent as he gazed incredulously at the accomplices in this absurdity. The mother, irate and with a frown, pure class and dignity behind the pearl brooch on her lapel, finally spoke up.

"I believe you are very confused, young man."

Afterwards she sized him up arrogantly from head to toe.

"Please leave us alone," she added.

"Señora Carranza, I—"

She didn't even deign to look at him again.

"Let's go home, Aurora," she commanded.

"No," Aurora answered stubbornly, clutching Daniel's arm with both hands.

"Let's go home right this minute, I said," the mother repeated with greater vigor.

"Señora, just one moment . . ."

She ignored him again haughtily. Some pedestrians approached, observing the scene with curiosity. She gave them a brief greeting and a fake smile. Then, as they moved away, she once more focused on the two.

"Don't make a scene in the middle of the street, Aurora," she snarled, trying to contain her ire. "Have we all gone crazy or what? Where on earth has this smart aleck come from? And what are you doing with him? Let's go home immediately; I'm not going to repeat myself."

"I will not leave until you listen to him."

"Aurora, I'm running out of patience . . ."

"Señora, I beg you . . ." Daniel insisted for a third time.

"Leave us alone, I said!" she screamed at the top of her voice, on the verge of hysteria. The heads of the passersby turned back in the distance and she, self-conscious, lowered her voice without tempering her acrimony one iota. "What the hell has come into you, for God's sake?"

Just then Aurora, unable to stand the strain any further, broke down in sobs. Unrestrained, grief-stricken, pouring out her tears in a mixture of frustration, anger, and sadness. Daniel attempted to hug her, to protect and shelter her, but now it was the father who finally stopped him.

"Do us a favor and please leave," he said with authority while he pulled Aurora toward him. "Come on, honey, let's go too."

Realizing that his boldness had cost him something that he hadn't quite foreseen, Daniel finally came around to reason.

"We'll talk . . ." he said to Aurora by way of a good-bye.

The mother's stern voice once again made itself heard.

"Everything has been said in this matter! By no means are we going to permit our daughter to have a relationship with some foreigner, do you hear me? Don't come near her again. Ever!"

"But you must listen to me even if it's at some other moment, please. I only want to . . ."

His words fell on deaf ears. Before he'd finished the sentence, all three of them had started walking the short distance to their house, the mother still furious, the father silent and thoughtful, and Aurora, his Aurora, awash in a desperate flood of tears.

Disconcerted, he watched them move away while above his head a few seagulls screeched. And for the first time he began to doubt.

In the six months that he'd been in Spain, he had always made an effort to find an explanation when faced with countless instances of irrational behavior. The servility of the people before everything that was imposed on them by the authorities, the lack of reaction and critical thinking, the stubborn pride. That recalcitrant stagnation before progress and that prudish and proverbial logic, incompatible with modernization. Faithful to Cabeza de Vaca's advice, however, he'd always tried to find a justification for everything, a reason that would support the untenable or would make the complex palatable. Daniel had often responded with more-than-gracious acceptance when the levels of absurdity were impossible to assume. "Respect these people; don't judge us simplistically," the old monarchist soldier had asked him on their first meeting in Madrid. And this was what Daniel Carter did—until that way of seeing the world through a special lens not only affected how he saw others but turned against him personally, going straight for the jugular. Then it hurt. And although he struggled not to, he had no choice but to admit that the soul of his adopted country could also be ungrateful and unfair.

There was no way of seeing Aurora again that afternoon. From an early hour he waited outside her place, but she did not come out. Neither did she poke her head out of any of the windows, nor could he make out her silhouette at any of the balconies. He phoned her from a noisy café with a telephone token that he'd gotten from a waiter behind the bar. A surly voice told him she was not in, but he knew it was a lie. He also went to look for her at the pharmacy without luck, anticipating that he would find only Gregorio and his clientele with all their ailments. He wandered around disoriented, not fully aware of where he was or where he was going. He came across men dressed in long tunics and pointed hats under their arms and ladies in black wearing mantillas, and he was reminded of the happy days in Madrid when Aurora had spoken to him with tenderness of her city's Holy Week celebration, which he expected to be captivating but now began to appear increasingly sinister. Typical of people stuck in the Stone Age, he thought, with the mind-set of an American coming from a large, industrialized city.

While he struggled to sleep at two in the morning, little did he suspect that Cartagena's upper crust already knew that a foreigner of an uncertain reputation had asked for the Carranzas' daughter's hand in marriage in the middle of the street. The buzz of conversation never reached his pension's inner room, but ever since the encounter with the parents on the Paseo de la Muralla, it flowed throughout the city: *I'm telling you, in the middle of the street, yes, yes, Marichu almost passed out and Enrique was left speechless, how could it be otherwise, a vagrant or God knows what, it's said the fellow doesn't have a penny to his name, what gall, the thing is he's not at all bad-looking, but you tell me, no one knows where he's come from, what nerve, a hustler, what are we coming to, he might even be a communist, I bet you he's even a Protestant, or an atheist, I don't know which is worse, and the girl has locked herself up in her room and refuses to come out, what insolence, what shamelessness, this is what happens when you send girls to the university, so what actor do you think he looks like?*

It wasn't yet nine o'clock on the following day when he was again at the Paseo de la Muralla, half-hidden in the distance behind a palm tree, alternating his gaze between the luminous sea and Aurora's doorway. At a quarter to ten he saw the pharmacist, Carranza, emerge alone. Half an hour later the mother did so with one of her small children, the kid enduring a severe reprimand.

The stage was beginning to clear, but he decided to wait a bit longer. After the previous day's wait he knew the windows and balconies of the Carranza home by heart, the peculiarities of its architecture and the bad-tempered face of the concierge, a puny-looking man who answered to the name of Abelardo and who, knowing the tension that boiled in the building and instructed by the pharmacist's wife, guarded the entryway with the zeal of a Cerberus.

Daniel stood for a long time hoping for a break in his luck, accompanied solely by his thoughts and the seagulls that flew over the port. A tense hour-and-a-half wait, until the simultaneous arrival of the mailman, a grocery store deliveryman, and a couple of sailors loaded down with a large package briefly blocked the section of street in front of the entrance as they spoke to Abelardo:

"We have to deliver this to the home of Colonel Del Castillo."

"This certificate is for Señora Conesa. Please sign here. Good afternoon."

"Abelardo, Osasuna lost three-to-nothing. Boy, your forecasts are really off—so much so that never in our fucking lives is the sports lottery ticket going to lift us out of our poverty."

"Come on, help me with this sack of potatoes, then I'll tell you who is going to win the Betis-Celta game."

"Let's see if you get it right for once . . ."

The lively exchange of soccer commentaries and other talk created the opportunity.

"Gento? Are saying Gento? Come on, man! Where is Kubala—"

It all happened in a flash. Before Abelardo was able to give his opinion regarding the Hungarian's soccer passes, the American, in four stealthy strides, was inside.

The building was fitted with an elevator but he chose not to use it. Impetuous, with urgency beating in his temples, he climbed the steps three at a time to the second floor. Once there, however, he was assailed by confusion. All morning long he'd been yearning for this moment and, once there, he hesitated. Two doors awaited him, identically bolted and barred while he deliberated. Would it be best to ring immediately? Wait for someone to come out and inquire with discretion, perhaps? Time was running against him; the sports-chatting voices could no longer be heard on the street. The elevator started up: someone was coming.

Fortunately for him, his bewilderment lasted only the time it took for the left door to open. A voice was then heard coming from inside the apartment, preceding its owner.

"Yes, yes, I won't forget, but boy, all of you are a pain in the neck . . . Okay, see you later. Good-bye . . ."

That bony and magnificent old lady with gleaming hair was going to add something else when she saw him. Daniel, in turn, didn't know what to do. It was too late to vanish into thin air, and he was too surprised to think clearly. He finally decided not to move and wait. Quickly combing his hair with his fingers, pulling the cuffs of his shirt beneath the sleeves of his jacket, adjusting the knot of the tie he'd worn to make himself presentable, he waited expectantly.

Surprised by the presence of the stranger on the landing, the lady gave a brief start and, with quick reflexes, brought her finger to her mouth and whispered a sonorous "Shhhhhhhhhh." Daniel recognized the woman wearing a sable stole and double-strand pearl necklace as Aurora's grandmother, the one he had fleetingly seen at the station. Basque by birth, somewhat peculiar, as Aurora had told him. Known to everyone as Nana.

"You are the American who has got my granddaughter all worked up, right?" she mumbled in rapture.

"Yes, Señora. I'm afraid I am."

There was no time for formal introductions or to correct misunderstandings.

"Well, you should know that the girl is a complete mess, my daughter is livid, and no Christian soul can live in this house another minute," she continued matter-of-factly. "I've told them I'm going for a little walk, that I have a lot of errands—though in truth I only wanted to get away from here. But I'd like to speak with you, young man, so if you want, you can meet me in half an hour at the Gran Bar."

And with an energetic and perfectly manicured aged hand, she showed him the stairs. The jangling gold coins on her bracelets added emphasis to her order to leave without delay.

. . .

"My daughter is old-fashioned and my son-in-law is a dunce" was the first thing she said after exhaling a long puff of smoke.

Daniel had seen her come in and stood up to receive her, pulling out the chair so that she could sit down and holding a lighter up close as she placed in an ivory holder the cigarette he'd offered her.

"They're stubborn as can be. It won't be easy to make them change their minds, so you're going to have to earn it if you want to take the girl to America."

The amazing coolness with which she related intimacies to an unknown foreigner, one who was supposedly a threat to the family's honor, confused him.

"You know, dear, I too had the opportunity to go overseas when I was young," she went on after a sip of vermouth. "I had a suitor who went to Argentina; what was his name? . . . Ay, ay, ay, what was his name? . . . Ro . . . Ro . . . Romualdo—that's it—and don't for a minute think he left because things were not looking up here; no, no, no, by no means. He was from a wonderful, fantastic, magnificent family, but he left because he was an adventurer, enterprising, a go-getter who created a fabulous business of . . . of . . ." The short lapse of memory seemed to annoy her for a split second, but she proceeded with her conversation. "Well, of whatever. What difference does it make? The thing is that he got rich, real rich. I was told that he had buildings in Calle Corrientes and a hacienda in La Pampa and I can't recall how many other things, but do you know what?" she asked impetuously.

"No, I don't know," Daniel answered truthfully.

"Well, many years later I found out that he'd never married, so I sometimes think that maybe he did not do so because he spent his life thinking of me. The truth is that I didn't miss him much when he left, because it didn't even cross my mind to go with him; where was I to go, living as comfortably as I did in Neguri at the time? So I said to him, See you later, and I was much relieved. But afterwards, as the years went by and I turned it over and over in my head, I sometimes thought to myself: What would my life have been like had I accepted that suitor and run away to Argentina with him? Of course I'd dance the tango wonderfully and speak the way they do, with that accent of theirs . . ." Her eyes suddenly sparkled dreamily, like those of an adolescent, despite her almost eighty years. Then she put out the cigarette with extreme elegance and remained contemplating the diamond solitaire that shone on her ring finger, a point of brilliance in a hand clotted with spots, veins, and wrinkles; a beacon illuminating the sad evidence of decrepitude. She then lowered her voice and leaned close to Daniel's ear, as if she were about to whisper to him her most intimate secret.

"Imagine the impressive jewels our Aurora would now inherit."

It didn't take long for Daniel to figure out that this coquettish and talkative matriarch was considered by her daughter and son-in-law to be little more than an old scatterbrain with no power whatsoever to influence the clan's decisions. Her long-winded chatter centered on her opulent youth and on her dozens of admirers who danced with her at dazzling parties. She gracefully skipped over the painful aspects of her life, those which—consciously or unconsciously—had disappeared from her beautifully coifed head. The bankruptcy into which her crackpot of a father had driven the family's industrial supplies business after frenzied nights in the Biarritz casino; her hellish marriage to a tyrannical man who never gave her a wisp of happiness; the forced and hasty move to that strange region in search of a future that would allow them to save the furniture, sheltered by the mines of La Union; the deaths of her two sons in the civil war before either one turned twenty-five; the unbearable pain in her bones that the Mediterranean's humidity produced in winter and some other obscure ailment that she chose not to air. After chain-smoking five cigarettes from Daniel's pack of Chesterfields and drinking the three vermouths she'd ordered and he'd paid for, the old lady—"Call me Nana, dear," she'd said—got ready to go. She adjusted the stole around her neck, put her cigarette holder away in her bag, closing it with a loud click, and rose majestically while he pulled the chair out for her. Resolute on her complicity and as a form of good-bye, she reformulated the idea she'd put forth upon her arrival.

"You're very cute, but my daughter and son-in-law are a pair of dolts and aren't going to consent that you take the girl just like that." And then she smiled, charming despite her wrinkles, her forgetfulness, and her swarm of selective memories. "You love her very much, don't you?" He returned the smile, shrugging his shoulders, unable to lay bare his feelings under the circumstances.

"If it's true—if you really want to have her by your side forever—I'd look for a good godfather," she said, and to stress the point, she patted his forearm affectionately while lowering the tone of her voice. "In this country of ours, darling, everything can be obtained with a good godfather, don't forget."

Noticing the consternation on Daniel's face, the old lady immediately caught on to his dilemma.

"Think about it . . . There must be someone who can lend you a hand."

Without giving him time to react, she air-kissed him on both cheeks and went off with a flourish as if she were still nineteen years old and a bold adventurer were waiting to take her across the seas in search of new fortunes.

Chapter 25

The encounter with Nana improved Daniel's spirits. Deep down, everything was pretty much the same: the conversation had not solved anything, nor had she offered any tangible solution. Nevertheless, the old lady had managed to transmit a glimmer of hope, a tiny spark of energy so that he did not lose heart.

On the way back to his pension he mulled over her parting advice to find a good godfather. Although he wasn't too familiar with the wheelings and dealings of the Spanish, he suspected the old lady's suggestion went beyond the meanings of the word "godfather" that he already knew. His dictionary gave him an additional definition: one who sponsors or protects someone in his aspirations, advancements, or plans. Having discovered this, but uncertain about what to do with it, he left it on the back burner.

He phoned Aurora again from the reception desk of the pension. The old lady had informed him that she was refusing to speak to anyone except Nana herself and Asuncion, the aged nanny, who brought her bowls of broth, croquettes, and French toast in an effort to make her see reason. No one answered, and on his third failed try he gave up. Meanwhile, Modesto, the desk clerk, had been keeping one eye on *The Avenger of Colorado* and another on Daniel. Between shoot-outs in the

Old West, he wondered who the American was calling so insistently and why he was in such a bad mood, always slamming the receiver down after failing to get through to anyone.

"It seems you're enjoying this city, isn't that so, my friend?" he dared to ask Daniel, momentarily putting aside the commotion of bullets and dust storms in order to find out once and for all what this guest was up to.

Daniel nodded politely, but Modesto insisted eagerly, "Although this may not be like America, one lives well here, don't you think, Mr. Daniel? Our streets aren't exactly paved with gold, but everyone seems to manage and raise their kids as best they can, and on Sundays there are soccer games everywhere, and we've got the best bullfighters in the world. What more can I say? Some people even own fridges, and boy, the beers are nice and cold . . . And although the law of 'grin and bear it' still very much rules, in no time, I'm telling you, the tourism industry will make us all rich, you'll see."

Daniel didn't refute the desk clerk's predictions; what was the point of bursting his bubble?

"But in your country one is even better off, isn't that true?" the clerk continued in a livelier tone. "With those big cars that appear in the movies, and those long-legged blondes with their slim waists, smoking nonstop and openly showing their cleavages; good God, what babes they must have there, right, Mr. Daniel? And that soap of yours, which smells of bliss and doesn't crumble like mud in one's hands, and the lighters that look as if they're made of silver and never go out even if the wind is blowing, and the shaving machines that leave one's face as smooth as a baby's ass, not like the Palmera razor blades we use here. Boy, you're lucky to be an American, that's what I'm telling you, Mr.—"

"It's not such a big deal," Daniel said, trying to halt the untimely gushing about his country's material wonders.

"Not such a big deal, you say . . . I learn all about it through my brother-in-law, you know?" Modesto babbled on insistently. "He works at the Algameca Naval Base and he says those Navy people are really something. Everything's magnificently organized: they even use a blue-print to put up a wall. Agustin, my brother-in-law, tells me that Spanish workers erected a wooden shed the other day using half the nails they were given. After a while the American sergeant shows up, looks it over carefully, and says no to the shed, that it needs to be torn down and rebuilt—that if the instructions specify five hundred nails, five hundred nails it'll be. What a pair of balls on the guy! So the shed came down and went up again, with the five hundred nails all in place, by God . . ." He clicked his tongue in admiration. "Damn! Those Americans, they're something else!"

Listening to the concierge deliver his long-winded speech, Daniel became curious.

"If your brother-in-law works with the Americans," he said, choosing his words carefully as he slid the pack of Chesterfields across the counter in Modesto's direction, "that means there is daily contact between the Americans and the Spaniards."

"You bet there is, mister, you better believe it," the clerk replied, taking out two filtered cigarettes. The first he put between his lips, the other behind his left ear. "They recently placed ads in newspapers for Spanish civilian staff, and even I filled out the papers, but they didn't take me, God knows why not. I would've solved a lot of problems standing in my sentry box in my uniform, like a general: You can come in, you can't, let's see your ID, sir, please . . . Boy, I would've been fucking great there with the Americans if they'd hired me."

Indifferent to the clerk's musings, Daniel pressed on.

"But tell me, Modesto, do those Americans come and go from the base, or do they just stay there?"

"As far as I can tell, some come into town. You can see them once in a while on the streets, with tremendous cars, sometimes in uniform and other times wearing loud shirts that they don't tuck in. Haven't you come across any yet?"

No, he hadn't come across any Americans yet; he'd hardly had time in his brief stays. Or perhaps he had and wasn't even aware of it, absorbed as he was with his worries. Then he remembered the day he'd met Aurora, when she herself asked him in the pharmacy if he was from the American base. Nearly three long months had gone by since. Perhaps the time had come for him to meet them.

"Do you think that I'd have any problems getting in there to see them?"

"At the base, you mean? Well, I think it's going to be tough," the clerk replied. "My brother-in-law has told me that they've got everything pretty much controlled. Permits, passes, you name it . . . You might show up at the gate and they won't let you in. Now, if I was a guard and saw you coming along . . ."

Daniel began to see a way those Americans could help him in the search for a godfather that Nana had suggested. As the clerk went on to detail the smattering of geographical knowledge he had extracted from his cowboy novels, Catalina, his wife, appeared in the lobby armed with a feather duster and joined in the chat, resolving the matter with her usual good sense.

"But how the hell would you know how those people operate, Modesto, if you've only seen them from a distance and only dropped off your papers after the deadline had expired? We're going to call my brother Agustin right now. He works afternoons in a garage not far from here. Go ahead, dial the number, and stop talking nonsense once and for all."

Agustin didn't take long to show up, dressed in blue overalls and a beret, and with grease still in his fingernails. He was more than willing to help.

"Tell me, my friend, what is it you want to know? I'll get you up to speed right away."

Daniel learned from him that the joint U.S.-Spanish naval base was located in a pine-covered mountainous area about a mile outside of Cartagena. Although the Spanish and Americans lived and worked independently, from the very beginning the Americans tried to cultivate friendly relations with the local population with the encouragement of the high command. Events were organized to foster international cooperation. The wives of the American sailors would give birth to their babies in local clinics assisted by Spanish midwives and interpreters. The Americans would give chewing gum to the local kids who would form noisy circles around them, and some of the younger servicemen would end up marrying local girls, while others would spend their free days letting off steam with the whores of El Molinete, afterwards gallantly giving them cans of condensed milk and a pack or two of Philip Morris cigarettes in addition to the fees for their services. Catalina's brother offered several intercultural anecdotes as examples, but Daniel was only interested in one thing: how he could get onto the base to speak to some Americans there.

"I'm telling you, my friend," the brother-in-law declared, taking one last drag on his frayed Ideales cigarette, "without formal papers they won't even bother to raise the barrier. Maybe you could bump into some of your fellow citizens on the street or in the bars."

The chat at the reception desk continued, interrupted only by the arrival of an occasional guest, to whom no one paid any attention. They were all too absorbed in the conversation, with Modesto behind his counter, Agustin and Daniel leaning on the opposite side, and Catalina dusting nearby, interjecting now and then.

"What if I tried to visit them at their homes? Do you think they'd receive me?" Daniel asked.

"Well, I'm not too sure," Modesto said while passing his hand through his thinning hair and not having, in truth, the remotest idea of how foreigners would react in that situation.

"Boy, what houses they've built for themselves in Tentegorra. With washing machines, central heating, and carpets glued to the floor in all the rooms, according to what I've been told," the brother-in-law added.

"Do the military live there alone or with their families?"

"I think they live with their wives," Modesto speculated with renewed zest. "Otherwise, who else could those knockouts be that I come across once in a while in tight pants that give me this urge to . . . to . . ."

"Cut the crap, Modesto, otherwise you get all carried away and your blood pressure will go through the roof," Catalina scolded, cutting short his daydream. Adjusting her feather duster beneath her arm, she addressed Daniel, trying to impose some order on their conversation, which was going nowhere. "But you, Mr. Daniel, if I'm not intruding: Why are you so interested in seeing your compatriots? For a work-related matter or something of that sort?"

Three pairs of eyes were left awaiting some juicy explanation while a newly arrived client, tired of being ignored by the desk clerk, rapped on the counter with his key.

"Well . . . it has to do with something else . . . more . . . of a family matter, you might say."

Although he wasn't quite telling them the whole truth, he wasn't exactly lying. After all, his intention in the long run was to create a family with Aurora.

"In that case, if I were you—if I can speak freely—you know what I'd do?"

They all looked at Catalina.

"I'd go in search of the women first thing tomorrow. You see, we women have a better understanding of family matters than men do. Then, if it's necessary, they'll know how their husbands can best resolve whatever needs to be resolved."

Once again Catalina was the light that chased away the darkness. Just as on the murky night of his fever, when she'd come with a French omelet sandwich like manna, she'd offered a possible solution to his problem.

"What time do they finish work at the base, Agustin?" Daniel asked in a hurry, glancing at his watch. It was 4:20.

"At five o'clock a siren goes off."

"Could you please get me a taxi, Modesto?" he asked.

"Consider it done, mister. You don't want me to accompany you, right?"

Chapter 26

―――――――

No sooner had he arrived than Daniel had the feeling of having been torn away from the reality of Holy Wednesday next to the Mediterranean and transported as if by magic to an anonymous spot in his own country. Before his eyes was what seemed to be a suburb of an average American city: modern houses surrounded by immaculate lawns, red hydrants on the sidewalks, and blond kids playing Frisbee on the grass.

He walked slowly, incredulous, immersed in that almost surrealistic experience, until a group of mothers with babies in their arms and kids running between their legs guessed his nationality from his looks and greeted him in their own language: "Hi!" "Hello!" "Are you an American? How're you doing?"

With a short distance still separating them, he made a decision: not a word of the truth for the time being. No mention of his true intentions. In any case, he had no clear idea how to explain the hazy concept of the godfather, in the Spanish sense, that he was seeking.

Those six young mothers fit the image of a girlfriend that he would have chosen had he wished to have a peaceful future devoid of complexities. Now, as a first step, he would attempt to win these American women over, not quite knowing yet how or to what end.

After the greetings and self-introductions, he began to recount his wanderings through a Spain they hardly knew: nights in medieval castles where ghosts were said to wander; visits to cellars full of gigantic casks; and basilicas that seemed as vast as baseball stadiums.

"Wow! Fascinating! Really?" Soon the husbands also started gathering to hear of his exploits, and then everything began to change. They greeted Daniel with cordial handshakes and exchanged some friendly words. "How do you do? What a surprise: an expert in literature. How interesting."

Until they started talking over each other and his novelty began to wear off. Each of the newcomers had something to tell, the wives' attention was directed elsewhere, and Daniel's star, like the end of a fireworks display, slowly vanished until it disappeared. His glory had lasted only briefly and the feeling that his opportunity was slipping away from him was confirmed as the group began to break up: "Well, good luck, buddy. See you later. Have a good one," the men said. "A pleasure meeting you, Dan. We hope you keep enjoying your adventures," the women said.

Each couple slowly retired to their homes, dragging their little ones, leaving behind the landscape of children's laughter and speech. As the group thinned out and peace and quiet settled over the previously bustling area, Daniel's despondency grew proportionately. Perhaps he had acted in the worst possible manner, he thought as one of the last families moved off, turning their backs to him. Perhaps it had been a mistake to pretend to be a mere wandering compatriot, a charming student devoid of worries. Perhaps he should have been more direct, to have spoken to them of Aurora's angry parents, of her dogged tenacity, of his determination to find a way of not losing her. He should have confessed that, for the first time since his arrival in Spain, the visceral attraction to that unfamiliar culture had turned into uncertainty. That the eternal honeymoon he'd lived until then had started to crack.

Only two women remained, the most mature, in spite of their evident youth. There was a tall one with a chestnut ponytail, green eyes, and a yellow checkered shirt with a slight Southern accent. Her name was Vivian. And then there was Rachel, a blonde with a turquoise bandanna tied in the manner of a headband.

"Well, it's time for us to start thinking of leaving too," Vivian said with a certain laziness.

Neither of them seemed to have babies or small children in their charge; most likely their kids were the wild devils nearby on bicycles.

Daniel had a feeling that his last chance would depart with them as each went home and shut their doors, and then he would be left on his own again, standing before a precipice, having played his last card in vain, and the damn godfather still nowhere to be found.

"Where are your husbands?" he asked suddenly. What did he care at this point about being discreet or not, since he had little to lose?

"They're at the military base in Rota. They'll be back tomorrow morning," Vivian explained.

Two U.S. Navy wives alone, and a few hours ahead of him.

"Rota, how interesting. That's in Andalusia, right?" he asked, offering them a cigarette to prolong the conversation.

Rachel shrugged while he lit a match for her. Vivian said she thought so. Neither of the two seemed very knowledgeable about the country's geography.

"It must be nice for them to get back to home and hearth," he said, blowing out the match with a fake air of nostalgia. "I wish I had someone close by to take care of me . . . baked potatoes with sour cream, chocolate ice cream, pot roast. The good taste of homemade food . . ."

Traitor, the voice of his conscience told him. Isn't Aurora's impassioned love enough? Isn't what Señora Antonia provides for you on a daily basis sufficient?

"For someone to roast a simple chicken for you, for instance," he went on, paying no attention to his scruples. He'd have plenty of time to make peace with them; for the time being he had to concentrate on not letting his opportunity slip away.

He had hardly missed any of that in the more than six months he'd been in Spain, eating at taverns and cafés in addition to the concierge's. Tripe and gizzard, liver, fried blood, pigs' ears—everything was to his liking. But now he wanted to make sure that Vivian or Rachel noticed. Whatever it took to be able to sit at either one of their tables that evening.

The howls of one of the boys on their bikes abruptly silenced the conversation. It turned out to be Rachel's son, a nine-year-old whirlwind bleeding through the nose. Behind him followed his younger brother, explaining the fall, and a redheaded girl with two braids giving her own version. A minute later two other rascals appeared trailing a dog.

"I'm starving. What's for dinner tonight, Mom?" one of them asked.

"Macaroni and cheese," Rachel said, pressing a handkerchief against her elder son's nose.

"And what about us?" another kid wanted to know while he picked his bike up off the ground.

"Roasted chicken," Vivian announced.

Daniel was unable to hold back.

"With potatoes?"

For some unfounded reason, he intuited that he'd find a way out of his predicament through them. He was aware that he was at a total loss for tools to accomplish his objective: they didn't speak Spanish; they knew no one of importance in the city and had no idea how social relations worked there. From all appearances they came across as young mothers with no other goal than to look after their loved ones. They might not even care much for the local culture, lacking all intellectual curiosity and the sensitivity to appreciate the historical and artistic richness of their surroundings. Perhaps it was all the same to them whether they were on the Iberian Peninsula or in Haifa or Corfu. But still, beneath their simple domestic appearance, he had the impression that they were strong women, determined and resolute, who had been capable of abandoning their homeland and were now taking care of their kids for long periods of time while their husbands were absent, always ready to pack their lives in boxes and suitcases to start a new stint wherever the U.S. Navy sent them. Positive, supportive women, used to finding solutions for everything, adapting to a thousand changes and to always having things left up in the air pending the next promotion or unpredictable transfer that would relocate them once more to some remote corner of the globe.

They exchanged a fleeting glance.

"Come on in. As soon as we've organized the troops, we'll have some dinner."

Chapter 27

In the span of time between Holy Wednesday night and Easter Sunday, two diverging lines were in full throttle. On the one hand, the entire city went out of its way to celebrate the Holy Days. The streets were overflowing with people ready to admire the size of the thrones, the colorful robes, the light of the candles, and the procession of penitents. On the other hand, simultaneously, completely oblivious to the religious fervor and solemnity, a certain group of foreigners driven by a common objective concocted a strategic plan so meticulously formulated that the high command of the Sixth Fleet would have been proud to claim it as their own.

The program was put into operation on Thursday morning, when Vivian and Rachel showed up unannounced at the house of Captain David Harris, knowing full well that the highest-ranking authority of the U.S. base was already on his way to his office. They were sure, however, that his wife was at home. The only thing they did not calculate correctly was the time, which was too early for a housewife without kids under her care.

Loretta Harris, her hair in disarray, wearing a long robe and still half-asleep, received the two ladies who rang her bell at ten past nine with a raspberry cake as an alibi. She smelled a rat.

"Morning, my darlings."

Her voice was raspy and she made no effort to hide her lack of enthusiasm. Nevertheless she invited them in.

The protocol was the usual one: offer them coffee, light a cigarette, and wait for them to fire away. She had traveled the world for the past twenty-five years as the spouse of a prominent naval officer and knew full well that when the wives of lieutenants showed up at that hour in search of the wife of their husbands' superior, it was because they were in need of something urgently.

Vivian and Rachel had made the decision to intervene the previous evening at dinner. As his plate slowly emptied, Daniel also began to strip away any imposture before them, dropping the globe-trotter mask he'd initially hidden behind and revealing his true intention.

"I'm starting to think I did not enter this city on the right foot," he confessed, once mutual trust was well established.

They continued talking after dinner, with the American Forces Network on the radio in the background and their kids in bed. Everything around seemed cozy and familiar: the door handles, the back issues of *Time* magazine, the tablecloth's color—all courtesy of the U.S. Navy for their people around the globe. Perhaps that was why he somehow felt at home and finally told them the truth.

"No sooner had I arrived than I caught the flu," he began, "and I was almost physically kicked out of a bar by force because they thought I was drunk."

"Well, that's understandable," Rachel said with an ironic face. "They must've thought you were just another souse, one of the many who overdo it and start a commotion almost on a daily basis."

"That's one of the main problems our husbands are faced with now," Vivian clarified. "Some of our men drink too much and raise a ruckus, then end up in fistfights with the locals or among themselves."

"I suppose that gives a bad image . . ." Daniel said.

"Very bad," both corroborated in unison. Rachel continued:

"There are orders not to harass the Spanish population; to come across as friendly, generous, cordial, and willing to help. That's part of our husbands' responsibilities and we try to help them out."

"How?"

They told him that on Christmas they'd taken a potbellied brag-gart, a certain Chief Petty Officer Smith, and dressed him in red, with a white wig and beard, loaded him with presents, and brought him to the House of Mercy.

"We're also trying to organize a softball tournament among our kids and the Spanish kids. And, for summer, a swimming champion-ship."

"And a cultural week."

The two friends began to take turns talking, clearly excited about their projects.

"And a sports clothes fashion show."

"For the Fourth of July we're thinking of organizing an enormous fireworks display."

"And we're constantly giving away food and medicine to the nurs-ing home for the elderly."

Daniel, ruminating as he listened to them, was unable to tell if behind that enthusiasm there really existed a true human interest in ingratiating themselves with the local population, a courageous desire to help their husbands carry out their professional commitments, or simply a barrage of vacuous entertainment with which to fill the te-diousness of their exile.

"But we'll need something with dramatic effect," Vivian pointed out.

"Something really spectacular that involves more people."

"Like what?" Daniel wanted to know.

"We don't know, we're still mulling it over. Something that ev-eryone will talk about, that brings together more influential people. Perhaps a dance with lots of guests."

"Or a festival . . ."

"How about a wedding?" Daniel interjected.

Rachel was left speechless with her glass half an inch from her lips. Vivian paused in mid-puff. They both looked at him in astonishment.

"I volunteer. Willing to contribute with fifty percent of the required quota."

As the caffeine kicked in, Loretta Harris finally understood what the two girls wanted: for her to convince her husband to mediate with someone in the area with clout so that a young American could get the necessary permission from certain obstinate parents to marry their daughter. It would be a win-win situation if it succeeded: the cream of the crop of the U.S. Navy contingent in Cartagena sharing church pews and meringue wedding cake with a who's who of the local community. They had nothing to lose and a lot to gain.

Captain Harris's wife didn't find it at all odd to be asked to intercede for a civilian. Wherever there was no embassy or consulate nearby, it was not uncommon for high-ranking military officers to act as informal diplomatic representatives of their country. Therefore she didn't find the request absurd but maintained a cautious silence. In her long, nomadic life caring for her five children in posts around the globe, she'd experienced much more complex situations between military personnel and the local citizens: inappropriate pregnancies, irresponsible paternities, fights, thefts, blackmail, and fraud. To mediate for the simple happiness of a pair of lovers seemed like a piece of cake. And if this enhanced the reputation of the U.S. Navy in the minds of the local population and offered a means of building bridges between the two nationalities, so much the better. Vivian and Rachel were not altogether mistaken: if they managed to pull this off in a satisfactory manner, the result would be most favorable. But first she would have to make some inquiries. And if she found nothing shady, they'd carefully plan the operation.

Naturally, she did not share this with her visitors. She simply refilled their cups, lit another cigarette, and proposed the first step. To personally meet the affected party, that was the initial condition. To obtain basic information and gauge the matter's complexity, she said. She was free that afternoon and her husband had an official engagement until evening. "Coffee is over, dears," she announced, putting out her cigarette. "I want this Carter here at five o'clock."

· · ·

Modesto the desk clerk thought he was in the middle of one of his most torrid dreams when a jeep made a sudden stop before the pension's entrance and ejected two stunning American women squeezed into blue jeans. Without articulating a half-decent word in Spanish, they were able, however, to make themselves understood well enough for him to know who they were asking for.

"Ah, you are looking for Mr. Daniel! Mr. Daniel Carter, right?"

"Exactly," Vivian confirmed, winking one of her green eyes at him.

"Mr. Daniel has gone out; he's already left," he announced, pointing toward the street. He automatically regretted what he'd said. Damn it, he thought. If I'm not careful they'll just leave. "Although he may have come back and I didn't notice," he immediately corrected himself. "Or maybe he'll come right back."

"Well . . . perhaps we can leave a note for him."

"Yes, ma'am, by all means. Whatever that little mouth of yours asks for, good-looking. To obey, that's what we're here for . . ." Modesto answered Rachel without taking his eyes from her cleavage, which was accentuated by a short lemon-colored sweater.

He provided them with a piece of paper whose reverse side was filled with household sums, and an old pencil with a chewed-up top. While they wrote a note summoning their new friend to the home of the base commander that very afternoon, Modesto's feverish eyes darted back and forth from one to the other. He broke into a sweat.

"Thank you very much," they said in unison once they were done.

Before the eyes of the clerk shone the whitest teeth and the fullest lips he'd ever seen in his life. "Mother of God," he whispered with a dry mouth.

He accompanied them out, surreptitiously trying to brush against them as he opened the door with purported gallantry. Then he watched them leave, cursing his rotten luck for lacking the communication ability to delay them for a little longer. "Fuck," he said before spitting with fury on the sidewalk. Half a life reading those Westerns, only to be able to say "whiskey," "sheriff," and "saloon."

The morning also turned out to be fruitful for Daniel. First he'd decided to position himself on the Paseo de la Muralla, close enough to observe the comings and goings of Aurora's house, but far enough away so that his presence would go unnoticed. Just as on the previous day, first he saw the father leave and, although he was unable to make out his face, from the cold greeting he gave the porter he gathered that he was not in the best of moods. A while later the mother and grandmother left the building, caught up in an irate discussion he was unable to overhear. The moment he made out the ladies' silhouettes at the doorway, he vanished swiftly behind a palm tree.

After they turned the corner, he came out of his hiding place and headed toward the doorway. When Abelardo the porter saw him, he tried to defend the fort with all the vigor expected of him, only too aware that the American had already sneaked through once. Abelardo could not afford to be reprimanded again.

"You cannot come in! You are forbidden to enter!"

A one-hundred-peseta bill—the most convincing of arguments, folded between two fingers like a safe-conduct pass—tore down the barricade. Abelardo didn't think it over twice: the bill went into his left pants pocket as quickly as the young man slipped into the building and again climbed the stairs three at a time. The porter sighed in relief. What difference did it make if he received another scolding by the stormy Señora Carranza if with that money he was practically able to buy his son's First Communion suit?

A kind-looking person of considerable age with a chignon at the nape of her neck opened the door, alarmed by the impetuous ringing that resounded all over the house. He didn't even greet her or announce the reason for his visit. Nor did he identify himself. As soon as the door opened and he realized he had free access to the apartment, he said only one word, repeated three times and shouted loudly: "Aurora!"

A fraction of a second was exactly what it took for a whirlwind in pajamas to appear from the end of the hallway. She hurled herself into Daniel's arms with a wildcat's leap, clutching his neck, his torso, and his legs, digging her nails into his back, caressing his neck, crying and laughing at the same time. He, for his part, was only able to whisper her name while holding her tightly with all his might, one hand on her shoulder, the other on her slender waist, feeling her laughter in his ears and her tears on his face.

Two witnesses watched agape, not quite knowing if that embrace oozed pure shamelessness and sinful scandal or an overflowing tenderness that there was no longer any human means of containing. The first was Asuncion, the woman who had opened the door, who for more than forty years had devoted herself to the family and who, in light of the scene, was only able to let loose a hasty litany of "Blessed Virgin" and "Good heavens" that seemed to have no end. The other was Adelaida, the young domestic servant. Hidden behind an antique desk, she was bowled over at the sight of the couple and wondered why her boyfriend was not this romantic with her when on leave from the barracks.

Then Asuncion reacted, and her insistence on pulling Aurora from Daniel's arms was the only thing that brought them back to reality: "Girl, girl! GIRL!" Only then was he aware of being, for the first time, in the house where she'd been born; of stepping on the floor where she'd taken her first steps; of seeing for a fleeting moment everything that had surrounded Aurora throughout her life: the family photos in silver frames, the library inherited from the father's side of the family, the balconies looking onto the port, the portrait of a very young Nana smiling coquettishly at some anonymous painter . . .

Aurora, meanwhile, begged for the momentary relief from her suffering to be extended a little longer.

"Just awhile, Asuncion, please let him stay awhile . . ."

However, Asuncion was a hard nut to crack. She'd brought up Aurora, adored her, and for days had been suffering on her behalf. But before that she'd brought up the girl's mother, and knew full well the uproar she would raise if she were to find out that Asuncion had authorized the American's presence in the house.

"Out of the question: he must leave right now. For God's sake, girl, for God's sake, this cannot be!" the good woman repeated while she held the door open for Daniel to leave.

Aurora's eyes, while she tenaciously hung on to his arm, again filled with tears.

"I beg you, Asuncion, I beseech you, only for a little while and then he goes; I promise."

In the middle of this give-and-take, Daniel made an effort to remain neutral. He longed to stay not only a while longer but an entire lifetime, but he was also aware that his boldness in sneaking into her house had already reached a feverish pitch and it was not in their best interest to strain matters further. Until he was no longer able to hold back.

"Will you allow me, please? We promise you, Asuncion, five minutes, no more. We give you our word of honor," he said, bringing his hand ostentatiously to his heart.

"No," the nanny reiterated.

"Wherever you please and, needless to say, with you present," he then offered in a profusion of goodwill.

"No."

"And if you agree, I promise we won't bother you anymore."

Youth's courage and the appeal of courtesy finally defeated the gray hair. But Asuncion, still unwilling to be seduced by the ways and words of this fellow—who, she had to admit, was far from being the devil incarnate that she had imagined—imposed conditions and marked the territory with the zeal of a faithful watchdog: with a clock ticking, in her presence, and hands off or that was the end of it. Amen was all there was left for them to say.

She settled them in the kitchen, spacious, white, and square, with a great marble table in the middle. Where the girl had had her breakfast and had enjoyed bread and chocolate on returning from school. Where she'd done homework, read comics, and heard tales. Where there had been fights and secrets between siblings, hot milk on winter afternoons, and clandestine nips at the loaf of bread just before dinner. This was the territory that Asuncion had chosen for an urgent meeting about sentimental matters for someone who up until then had been the girl of the house. Daniel and Aurora sat facing each other, just like a visit to an inmate in prison. Asuncion, meanwhile, standing two steps away with the sullen face of a Civil Guardsman, kept a constant eye on the proceedings.

"There is someone who might be able to help us," Daniel finally said.

He informed Aurora of his incursion at the naval base and of the firm pledge he'd received from his compatriots.

"But what can they do?" she asked, covering her face in despair. "My parents know no Americans; they have no relations with those people."

"Well, perhaps they may start having one now."

That, of course, was nothing but pie in the sky, mere wishful thinking to inject a dose of optimism by offering a potential solution of which he was not too convinced himself. They shared a cigarette, passing it back and forth from one mouth to the other, from one hand to the other, brushing it against their lips on the same place, touching each other's fingers, and transmitting through their fleeting sense of touch a thousandth of that which their bodies would do if some mysterious force were to magically disintegrate Asuncion.

They'd just finished lighting their second Chesterfield when, with a watchmaker's precision, Asuncion announced that the meeting had come to its end.

"Come on, young man, or you'll ruin my life," she said, pointing to the door. Then she sighed deeply. No matter how much Aurora and Daniel insisted, both knew they couldn't squeeze a minute more.

"When do you return to Madrid?" Aurora asked as they both rose from their chairs with the willingness of convicts on the way to their execution.

"I'm not going to go without you."

"Don't say that, Daniel . . ." she whispered, bringing a hand to his face.

Asuncion checked the impulse.

"I said it was over."

He had no other choice than to cross the threshold. Once outside, he turned around and looked at her one last time. There she was, in one of her brothers' blue-striped pajamas, with her straw-colored curls askew, her eyes shiny from the welling tears that gave way to inconsolable weeping the moment he started down the stairs. Then, in spite of his good intentions, in spite of having resisted till the last second, he was no longer able to hold back. Knowing full well that he was contravening Asuncion's orders and risking losing her trust forever, he rushed back in and said good-bye to Aurora with the most grandiose kiss imaginable.

Chapter 28

———

News that the wife of the naval base commander was willing to meet him at her house added another whiff of optimism to his day. He read the note over and over, memorizing the details. The desk clerk, meanwhile, didn't take his eye off him, curious to know what those two bombshells had written.

"Modesto, could you order another taxi for a quarter to five, please?"

"Consider it done, Mr. Daniel. Are you off to see your American friends?" he asked, unable to hold back any longer.

"Not for the time being. I've got other matters to take care of today."

A taxi was waiting at the agreed-upon time at the front door of the pension. And a familiar figure was waiting next to it.

"I've found out we had a little visit this morning at home."

"What are you doing here, Nana?"

This time she was dressed in gray, with a black veil covering her head.

"I came to see you, dear. So that you can invite me for a coffee before the Holy Week services, since my body is not yet ready for genuflections. Where do you want to take me?"

"Nowhere. I'm sorry. They're waiting for me."

"Well, then, what a terrible shame you won't have time to read what I was bringing you in my bag."

He looked at her without quite believing her.

"As a matter of fact, it's a very short letter, not like those we wrote in the past to our beloveds, with all those trifles we'd tell them. But I'm sure Aurora would be delighted if you'd read it."

"I have an idea," he said as soon as he realized the old lady might withhold the letter unless he complied. "You give me the letter now before I leave and afterwards, when I come back, we'll meet and have a coffee or whatever you prefer."

"No, my dear, because by then Marichu will have grabbed hold of me and we'll both be busy getting ready for the procession."

"Shall we get going, sir?" the taxi driver asked impatiently. "It's ten to five and I have to be at the station at a quarter after five because I've got some travelers arriving with a bunch of luggage."

Holding up one hand, Daniel gestured to the driver to wait a moment, summoned all his patience, and again addressed Aurora's grandmother.

"You see, Nana . . ." he began with great care, "the truth is that I'd love to spend the evening with you, but I'm unable to stay because I have a very, very important meeting—important for Aurora and important for me."

"Let me accompany you. After all, I'm of the same blood as one of the parties involved. I may even be able to help you."

"I appreciate it from the bottom of my heart, but this is something I must resolve on my own."

"Sir, it's already five to . . ." the taxi driver insisted.

"Then, sweetie, I'm afraid I won't be able to give you the letter."

"Nana, please."

"Sir, the travelers are weighed down. I'll lose them if I'm not there in time."

"And I don't even want to tell you how disappointed our Aurora is going to be."

"Sir, four minutes to—"

"Get in the car, quick. But first give me the letter. And you, sir, drive as fast as you can, please."

He unfolded the missive with such fury that he almost tore the paper. It contained only a few tender words that recalled the happiness of his unexpected visit. Even so, he read it four or five times without paying attention to the old lady's incessant conversation as she got rid of the veil, put it away unceremoniously in her bag, and smoothed her hair while glancing into the rearview mirror.

. . .

Loretta Harris came out to the front garden of her residence to receive her guest. If she was surprised to see him with a respectable old Spanish lady on his arm, she hid it wonderfully.

"*Je suis* the grandmother of Aurora," she said by way of introduction, so that there would be no doubt of the legitimacy of her presence. Before Daniel was able to open his mouth, she burst forth with a cascade of outdated greetings in otherwise more-than-passable French.

The American lady looked at her with a mixture of astonishment and amusement, while out of the corner of her eye she sized up Daniel, the newcomer on whose behalf she was to act. He, meanwhile, did the same.

"Thank you very much for receiving us, Mrs. Harris," he was able to insert in a break in Nana's monologue. He pronounced these words in Spanish in deference to the latter, although he quickly clarified in English that the grandmother had tagged along against his will.

Loretta downplayed the matter with a toothy smile.

"Come in, come in, please," she said as she stepped aside to let the old lady pass. "It's a pleasure to have you here."

The large house, recently built and furnished according to American trends of the 1950s, bore no resemblance to the homes of respectable people that Nana was used to frequenting. The interior design conveyed the growing optimism and consumerism in the United States following the Second World War, reflecting a country that felt increasingly modern and powerful. Whereas Spaniards treasured lace and velvet curtains, small charcoal brazier tables, and parchment-like portraits of their great-grandparents, the Americans favored three-legged stools and brilliantly colored ashtrays. Where the Spaniards valued tradition, moderation, and opacity, the Americans offered luminosity and a lightness of spirit unknown in those parts.

The moment Nana caught sight of that fascinating display, she stopped dead in her tracks and brought a hand to her mouth with a theatrical gesture in an effort to contain her admiration. Her eyes then traveled along the walls filled with abstract paintings to the somewhat outlandish bright blue cone-like lamps.

"I love all this—I love it! Such modern houses, and with this furniture so . . . so . . . I don't have words: I'm simply fascinated!" was her impassioned initial comment.

"Thank you very much, dear," Mrs. Harris replied.

"Let's see if you can become friends with my daughter Marichu, darling," Nana went on, patting her on the arm, "and convince her to have the scrap dealer take away all the horrible relics that we have at home and buy things like these: so modern, so fabulous."

Loretta and Daniel looked at each other with a sideways glance. He made a gesture of apology and she reassured him, indicating without words not to worry, that there was no problem whatsoever with the presence of that most peculiar woman. When Nana was done reviewing the room, Loretta was finally able to settle her visitors into large armchairs whose style and comfort the old lady lauded excessively.

"Coffee? Tea?" the hostess was finally able to ask.

Aurora's grandmother's imperious gesture of displeasure immediately impelled her to add:

"Or perhaps a martini?"

The conversation took off in a mixture of Spanish and English peppered with a few sentences in rusty French that Nana contributed at odd moments as a testament to her trips to Paris and her happy summers as a single woman in Biarritz before the family debacle in which her dissolute father gambled away everything but the shirts off their backs. They remained there talking for a couple of hours, until Mrs. Harris figured she had a pretty good idea of the situation, including the genealogy of both families in Spain and in the United States, the Carranzas' social position, and the weak points of Enrique and Marichu. Sufficient material to get down to work, she thought.

The visit should have come to an end; the reasonable moment for Loretta to say "Well, then, my dear friends . . ." had arrived. But it was almost eight p.m. and everything was turning out to be much more amusing than anyone had anticipated. Besides, Loretta's husband had a commitment, and she began to feel the first pangs of hunger as well as somewhat light-headed from the alcohol. With hardly a second thought she invited Daniel and Nana to stay for dinner.

Before Daniel could even weigh the appropriateness of accepting the invitation, Nana was already requesting a telephone to call her daughter to tell her a monumental whopper to account for her prolonged visit. They heard her string together a pack of outrageous lies about her friend Maria Angustias falling in the middle of the street, a possible wrist fracture, and the necessity of remaining by the injured woman's side until someone came to relieve her in her Good Samaritan role.

"Don't worry about me at all," she insisted before hanging up. "One has to do anything one can for a bosom friend. I'll be back as soon as I can, don't worry, please . . ."

The dinner dragged on in relaxed conversation. When they had finished the Sara Lee cheesecake and coffee, Nana put her elbows on the table and gave a loud clap.

"And how about a game of cards, dears."

That was enough for Daniel to realize that the time had come to get her out even if it meant dragging her. His relationship with the Carranzas was already damaged enough, but there was still room for it to worsen.

The first thing Loretta Harris did the following morning was call Vivian. She confirmed that the operation was under way but asked her to find Daniel and look after him. She justified herself by saying that a little entertainment would be a good thing for the kid, not letting them guess that her real reason was to keep him away from the events that were to unfold in the following hours on his behalf. While the previous evening had been fun and fruitful for gathering relevant information, she perceived that leaving Daniel to roam freely around the city could be somewhat risky and maybe even counterproductive: he might show up in the least opportune place, behave inappropriately, or say something inconvenient. Nor did she think it a good idea for him to continue seeing Nana: she was lively and had style, but the old lady might be a real time bomb and cause any number of unpredictable consequences if she were ever to explode.

That was why the base commander's wife suggested that, since it was a holiday and the weather was lovely, the girls take him camping with their families by the sea until Saturday afternoon: her innocuous proposal was a means of getting them all out of the way. They complied, of course. A couple of hours later, the two families were off in search of Daniel, traveling in jeeps from which emanated the laughter of kids, high spirits, and Elvis Presley's "Jailhouse Rock" at full blast, unaware that by crossing the city from one end to the other in the middle of Good Friday they were destroying the solemnity of the most mournful day of the year in the most fervently Catholic country in the world.

Loretta Harris watched them leave while discreetly standing behind a curtain, smoking her fourth cigarette of the morning. When she figured they were no longer in the range of activity, she grabbed the telephone and dialed a number she knew by heart.

"Master Chief Petty Officer Nieves, here," a voice answered at the other end of the line.

And then the ball started to roll.

Nieves had arrived in Cartagena two years earlier with the assignment of making the lives of American military personnel and their families as comfortable as possible. From his features and body shape he could have easily passed for a descendant of Pancho Villa, but it was his prodigious bilingualism and not his warrior-like appearance that opened the doors to his placement. It was no wonder that the worthy rancher's son was able to move comfortably between English and Spanish, as he'd spent his life straddling Laredo, Texas, and Nuevo Laredo, Mexico, two cities joined by a bridge and divided by a river whose name changed depending on which shore one stood. Twenty-four months after settling on the shore of the Mediterranean, the Hispanic master chief petty officer moved about the city where he'd been posted as if he'd been born there. He had no knowledge of naval strategy, precision instruments, or deep-sea weapons, but he was a wonder at procuring whatever might be needed, from a couple of bicycles, to an appendicitis operation, to a box of Alka-Seltzer, to three whores for a quartermaster's bachelor party.

Side by side, Loretta and he now distributed their work equally. True, the American kid determined to marry a young Spaniard seemed charming. But the commander's wife had met a lot of kids without apparent blemishes and exquisite manners who, at the end of the day, turned out to be unscrupulous, compulsive liars, or simple crazies on the verge of a mental disorder. Therefore, they'd have to start by doing a background check on the man whom they were planning to help, to make sure he met the personal requirements. There were no problems in doing so: the wife of the base commander had plenty of means. Nieves, in turn, would be in charge of things on the local level. In a black oilcloth-covered notebook, he wrote down all the details that Mrs. Harris gave him: the exact name of the Spanish family, where they lived, whom they associated with, what they lived off, how much they possessed—everything necessary to get started.

In the following hours, each one extended his or her reach. Loretta Harris did so from a distance. Because of her husband's position, she was able to tap into a number of resources, but only those which her instinct sensed were dependable at any given moment. Two out of the five calls she made yielded promising threads to pull. The rest came on its own.

Nieves, meanwhile, worked on his terrain, striking up multiple conversations with contractors, shipping agents, sailors from the Spanish navy, and hustlers and opportunists of the unlikeliest type. He did not use the telephone but the street, the café tables, and the bar counters, all half-deserted on the most sorrowful day of Holy Week.

They got together that very same night. By then, through her complex web of contacts, Loretta Harris was absolutely certain that Daniel Carter was who he said he was. Nieves, for his part, had accumulated a considerable number of reports that suggested that their mission would be successful. The next step was to execute their plan.

At midafternoon on Saturday the caravan of campers returned to the city with Daniel, having been blessed with wonderful weather for pitching tents on the beach. They had raced, sung songs, eaten rations heated on the fire, and built sand castles, and the more daring among them had even swum while the locals observed them from a distance as if they were a platoon of aliens. On arrival, a handwritten note under Rachel's door awaited them. Daniel Carter was required at the Harris's home. Urgently.

For the umpteenth time in the last couple of days, a kitchen table served as the base of operations. Daniel sat at one end, his face worried and his appearance untidy: wearing a pair of shorts and a khaki-colored shirt lent to him by one of the young Navy officers, his face burned from the sun, and his disheveled hair still full of salt and sand. At the other end sat Nieves in uniform with his black notebook before him, exhaling the first puffs of smoke from the cigar he'd just lit. Leaning on the counter equidistant from both of them, Loretta Harris smoked a cigarette in silence, alert and attentive.

Everything was organized and needed to be settled that very same evening, at the dinner which the base commander and his wife were going to throw for a select group of guests. The sooner the better: it was preferable to catch them off guard rather than wait any longer for the tremendously muddled matter to get even worse.

As if he were training a spy, Nieves, with the precision of a neurosurgeon and the Farias cigar between his fingers, detailed to Daniel Carter the exact manner in which he'd have to proceed if the situation required it. For starters, at no moment was he to mention that the person responsible for his stay in Spain was a professor who had decided never to return to the One, Great, and Free Fatherland of Franco, nor that Daniel had been staying in Madrid for six months at the house of an anarchist's widow, nor that he was preparing a PhD dissertation on a leftist writer, regardless of whether he had received the National Prize for Literature. Nor should he mention his time among union workers in Pittsburgh, or that he'd completed his education on the basis of loans, or that one of his first notions of that distant place called Spain was acquired from reading *For Whom the Bell Tolls* by Hemingway, that novel of dubious ideology whose main character was an American professor who ended up as a blaster in the ranks of the International Brigades, defending the Republic against Franco in the Sierra de Guadarrama.

It would, however, be a good idea to dwell on his father's dentistry practice and his mother's talent at the piano, her multiple charitable activities, and her blood relation to a conservative congressman from the state of Wyoming, even though it was a second cousin whom Daniel had last seen fourteen years ago at a funeral. Regarding his religion, if he were asked, it would be best for him to simply say that he was a Christian: no need to go into detail regarding his growing agnosticism or the Methodist church his family attended. As for his academic education, in the event he was asked, the best would be for him to openly show his admiration for Spanish literature before the twentieth century, concentrating if at all possible on heroes, saints, monks, and romantics. El Cid Campeador, Saint John of the Cross, and Fray Luis de Leon could be praised without trouble; liberals, Regenerationists, or those tending to favor foreign ways were better left on the sideline. Exiles: absolutely forbidden to mention them. And as for Ramon J. Sender: not a single word.

"And regarding Professor Don Domingo Cabeza de Vaca, Heroic Carlist Soldier and Wounded Knight," Nieves concluded after expelling the smoke from the last puff of his cigar, "you can talk all you wish, until the early hours of the morning."

After listening to that string of advice, which showed a thorough knowledge of all aspects of his life, Daniel Carter didn't know what to say. On the one hand, he felt uncomfortable and hurt on seeing his intimacy assaulted, his interests distorted, and the personal decisions that he'd agonized over annulled.

On the other hand, he was forced to admit that they had done impeccable work. After all, he was the one who'd asked for help, without putting restrictions on the methods. Either he accepted the hand he'd been dealt, or he could return to his homeland the same way he'd come—alone.

Chapter 29

Nieves and Loretta Harris decided to gather everyone together on the evening of Holy Saturday. FRIENDSHIP DINNER was the reason that was posted on the door of the residence of the base commander. They were both aware that this wasn't the most suitable date, but trusted that those concerned would interpret the hasty invitation as merely a case of intercultural clumsiness by foreigners who knew next to nothing of their host city's social customs.

That very same afternoon, a couple of soldiers hand-delivered the imposing invitations with the U.S. Navy's blue-and-gold seal. Approved by the wife of the base commander, the list of guests was meticulously drafted by Nieves. It included the powers that be, the Spanish military high command, and a good number of couples of a certain pedigree; no one with influence, money, or a good name could be left out. The invitations were received with a universal sense of bewilderment, but not for a second did any one of them consider not attending.

For the majority of those convened, it would be their first face-to-face with those intriguing foreigners. Thus, the hours before the event were a mad hubbub for a great many of the invitees, especially the ladies, who (ignorant of its scheming and underlying purpose) urgently summoned their hairdressers and became frantic trying on various outfits in succession, discarding some as too excessive, others as too prudish, wondering what the hell one had to wear in order to fit in at such a gathering.

The men, for their part, received the invitation with surprise—not without concealed relish, for they knew that only the local cream of the crop had been included. It would be an unbeatable opportunity to strengthen relationships, consolidate business matters, learn the latest gossip on the juiciest affairs. In short, to keep the always profitable machinery of social relations well greased.

In the Carranza home the situation was no different. Marichu, the mother, in hair curlers and petticoat, blowing the nails of her newly completed manicure, hesitated between wearing a dazzling peacock-blue cocktail dress or a more demure ensemble in coral tones. The pharmacist, unconcerned, killed time solving a crossword puzzle in the living room, knowing that all he had to do at the last moment was to have a quick shave and put on his tuxedo. Nana, meanwhile, paced about the house fuming while she pondered a way to trick her daughter into taking her with them. There was nothing she could do; however, no sooner had the couple walked out the door than a bouquet of flowers arrived bearing a card from Loretta in which she apologized and requested a rendezvous for lunch the following day with the promise that she would fill Nana in on all the details. In reality, she wanted to keep the old lady as far away as possible from the scene.

At eight o'clock the guests started arriving at the Harris residence. A magnificent buffet awaited them, something extremely chic and unusual in the Spain of 1959, where the annual income per capita was about three hundred dollars. The good relationship that Loretta enjoyed with the wife of the commander of the Rota base as well as Nieves's close contacts had helped to make up for the scarcity of American products in the area. Waldorf salad, wild salmon fillets, New England lobster with butter sauce, and other imported delicacies arrived in refrigerated boxes bouncing aboard a military vehicle. Next to the victuals were several stacks of white porcelain plates with blue-and-gold borders bearing the U.S. Navy seal. Nothing was lacking.

Although Commander Harris had found out only on the previous day what his wife and subordinate were plotting, he trusted their competence—and he never snubbed a good party. As the guests were welcomed, she, charming in an intense red dress, greeted everyone, while he, his great bulk ensconced in a uniform with four stripes on its cuffs, received them with a grin. Both made an effort to put their best Spanish to use while Louis Armstrong's trumpet played in the background. Nieves remained in the background as well, in accordance with his rank.

The ladies' clothes and jewelry shone sumptuously as they sized up one another's finery and threw looks like darts at each other, while from the corners of their eyes they observed the modern décor of the American base commander's residence. As for the men, the standard attire was military uniform or tuxedos, although some, either clueless or ignorant, had showed up in their everyday suits, a terrible blunder that would remain engraved in the memories of their embarrassed wives.

With a couple of imperceptible glances at the rest of the gathering, Nieves indicated to the Harris couple who the Carranzas were. The elegant woman in the blue dress who laughed amid a lively group was the mother; the father, that distracted man curiously inspecting those strange paintings in which lines and geometric shapes crossed without rhyme or reason. They would not lose sight of them, although for the time being they'd leave them alone, not wishing to overwhelm them from the very start.

They all went up to the buffet, serving themselves from the different platters with feigned naturalness, by and large ignorant of what on earth they would be eating. To the country of markets and grocery stores, inns and taverns, the serve-yourself fashion had not yet arrived, and the business of having to choose a little from here and a little from there and afterwards eat standing up turned out to be diabolically complicated for Spaniards. The inability of most to hold at the same time plate, fork, conversation, and drink was evident, and more than a few, after several tries, decided to throw in the towel and abandoned their meals after a few bites, preferring to go hungry rather than see one's food splattered on some lady's cleavage or spilled on the floor.

A while later, a new exchange of glances between Nieves, Harris, and his wife served as a sign to indicate that it was open season. With an ingenuous question regarding the chemical composition of the famed painkiller with vitamins known as Calmante Vitaminado, Loretta corralled the pharmacist into one corner of the room and plunged him into an intense and somewhat incomprehensible chat about Spanish and American medicines. Almost simultaneously, at another corner of the room, the base commander had positioned himself in such a way that when some clumsy oaf was about to spill his drink and ruin Marichu's peacock-blue dress, with an agile movement the commander practically caught the glass on the fly. In so doing, he not only saved the dress's integrity but also managed to generate a series of thank-yous from her that served as an excuse to initiate a conversation.

Neither the pharmacist nor his wife could later recall in detail how the two conversations developed, but the truth is that Aurora's father suddenly found himself with a dazzling proposal to supply his pharmacy with two hundred penicillin capsules, the most sought-after medicine in that backward and shortage-prone country. Practically at the very same moment, the mother was delighted to accept an invitation to attend the Seville Fair in the company of the U.S. military's top brass stationed in Spain. Nieves was draining his seventh tequila as he observed both scenes delightedly from the rear guard while calibrating the next step of his plan.

Once the acrobatics of the buffet were overcome, the alcohol and rock and roll loosened up the atmosphere, mixing laughter with the clinking of glasses, while the horse-trading and gossip continued and some couples made an effort to adjust their dance steps to the beat of that strange music that invited movement. Nearby, a local official was busily trying to grope the wife of a lieutenant commander who was already impressively drunk.

The Carranzas continued to be seduced by the personal charm of Commander and Mrs. Harris, who until then had remained on opposite flanks and now began a surreptitious attempt to converge in response to a signal from Nieves, who, after making sure all four were together, slipped into the kitchen and from there out into the garden. Bringing two fingers to his mouth, he ripped the night apart with a piercing whistle. Five shadows emerged on the spot from a nearby house, two bodies in formal dress uniforms, two in cocktail dresses, and one in a tuxedo.

The quintet's entry momentarily hushed all conversation.

"Good evening, my dears!" Loretta called out from some point in the living room.

The men, handsome and tanned from camping by the sea, were an imposing sight. Their wives looked spectacular in dresses that revealed a display of arms, shoulders, and deliciously golden cleavages. Daniel, with a toned face and his always unruly hair subjected to a good dose of mineral oil, looked impeccable in a tuxedo. He quickly swept the room with his eyes and spotted the Carranzas next to the Harrises. Initial step completed; let's keep moving forward and on to the attack, he thought, with a knot gripping his stomach.

The hosts received the party of five with an enthusiasm bordering on euphoria, in part because that was the plan, and in part because both spouses had been drinking for more than two hours straight without a trace of moderation.

"Danny, my dear, you look absolutely gorgeous!" Loretta exclaimed with one of her horsy laughs. She practically elbowed her way through the crowd until she reached him.

"Dear Loretta, you look stunning. Thank you very much for this spectacular party," Daniel said, greeting her in well-practiced Spanish.

Afterwards, he kissed her hand gallantly. As if the two had adored one another since the beginning of time.

So far, his participation was coming along perfectly. Step one, entrance, reconnaissance, and positioning. Step two, a warm greeting to the hostess to get himself noticed. Step three, Commander Harris. Let's go for it, he ordered himself.

Witnessing the bear hug that the commander of the American naval base himself bestowed upon Daniel, whom just a few days earlier Aurora's parents had snubbed, her father choked on an ice cube from the scotch he was drinking and his wife noticed a slight cold sweat on her back that almost ruined her silk dress. With his three initial objectives covered, Daniel finally felt more relaxed. A handful of Spanish ladies crowded around Loretta, intrigued by this handsome young man. Figuring that he was available, they rushed to sniff out the prey, since they all had a marriageable daughter, niece, or younger sister ready to make such a stunner happy. Not to mention his evident closeness with the charming American couple who were treating them to the best party they could recall in years. To Daniel's good fortune, no one recognized him as the tormented stranger who for days had been melting out of pure love for the daughter of the couple who were now standing in a corner of the room, whispering in dismay.

Everything was unfolding according to plan, but on perceiving the group of females hovering around Carter, captivated by what Mrs. Harris had said about him and trying to attract his attention with flattery and clever remarks, Nieves's alarm button went off. This hadn't been foreseen. He and his coconspirators had assumed that they'd only have to convince Aurora's parents that Daniel was worthy of their daughter—not that he wasn't some kind of libertine or amoral boor.

What Nieves was not counting on was that Commander Harris's hug and his wife's effusive show of affection would suffice to dispel any mistrust among those gathered. He also realized that all the instructions he'd given the young man about how to behave or what to say and not say regarding his life were non-issues. No one was interested. The simple fact that the kid appeared in society endorsed by the Harrises altered his status from outrageous upstart to object of desire.

Nieves spotted the Carranzas with a hurried glance. They'd moved to a corner, ill at ease, out of sorts, not knowing quite what to do. Daniel, meanwhile, remained in the middle of the hall, flanked by the hosts, holding the empty gin-and-tonic glass—the contents of which he'd just downed in three gulps—discreetly concealing his amazement at the excessive praise that Loretta, at the top of her voice and in exuberant Spanish, was heaping on him, his ancestors, and his formidable professional prospects.

Nieves knew then and there that it was time to act. The pharmacist and his wife were so disconcerted that they'd lost all power of reaction. He had to help them, but there was no time for subtleties or subterfuges. For this reason, he circled the room with swift steps and placed himself behind the couple without their noticing his presence. He then stealthily moved in closer to them, until his face was right next to Marichu's right ear and the pharmacist's left one. And after taking the seventh Farias cigar from between his teeth, he delivered his message.

"Either you go up to the Harris's group and stake your claim, or the commander's wife will be the one to nab the gringo for *her* daughter. Chop-chop."

Not even the jab of a knife would have spurred Marichu Carranza on more effectively.

The druggist was trying to figure out where on earth that fellow dressed in a U.S. Navy uniform had come from, when his wife grabbed him by the hand and dragged him toward the group surrounding Daniel.

Once more Loretta took care of the rest.

The party finally ended in the garden at four o'clock in the morning with everyone dancing La Conga de Jalisco around the residence. Nieves watched the scene, satisfied, while he took a final swig of Tequila Herradura straight from the bottle. Mrs. Harris led the conga line and a long, motley stream of bodies with the unlikeliest shapes followed behind: Daniel clutching his girlfriend's mother; the pharmacist Carranza raising his legs clumsily as he grabbed onto the tuxedo jacket of his future son-in-law; and a local politician sweating profusely with his bow tie undone and shirt half unbuttoned as he moved along, sandwiched between Vivian's prominent buttocks and Rachel's prodigious bosom. The commander of the joint U.S.-Spanish naval base closed the parade, not yet aware that he'd scored one more in the list of historic agreements between the governments of Spain and the United States after the Pact of Madrid.

. . .

Aurora Carranza and Daniel Carter were married three months later, at noon on a magnificent Sunday toward the end of June. The bride wore an heirloom white organza gown, and despite her mother's efforts to comb her hair into a showy bun in the style of Grace Kelly, Aurora categorically refused to have her hair swept upward. The groom, in morning dress, waited for his future wife at the altar of the Church of the Caridad as if that were the moment he'd been anticipating all his life. On Aurora's side were the most prominent members of local society, while on Daniel's side were Domingo Cabeza de Vaca (accompanied by a professor of Visigothic history whom he'd begun to court during the spring); Señora Antonia and her sons, who didn't stop handing handkerchiefs to their mother; and the top brass of the U.S. naval base in Cartagena. Daniel's parents were also present, having come from the United States—thanks once more to Loretta's maneuvering—and putting aside their bitter disagreements of the past. Andres Fontana sent them a telegram from Pittsburgh: "With my most heartfelt best wishes for the great adventure that you are embarking upon together."

The wedding luncheon took place at the Club de Regatas with the Mediterranean serving as backdrop, and the couple spent their wedding night in the Grand Hotel. To the bride's mother's shock and Nana's delight, they didn't emerge from the nuptial suite until six o'clock the following evening. They then left on a whirlwind honeymoon that would take them to Chalamera, Pamplona, Biarritz, and Paris. The visit to Chalamera was a desire of Daniel's in order to show Aurora the land of the writer who had indirectly been the cause of their meeting; the stay in Biarritz was an homage to Nana; and the trip to Paris was a present from Daniel's parents in an effort to compensate somewhat for all their years of estrangement.

They didn't make clear to anyone the reason that drove them to visit Pamplona, and both families were able to understand the couple's urge for that stopover only when, among some photos sent by mail a few months later, was one of Daniel dressed in white with a red neckerchief, running like someone possessed down Calle Estafeta, inches away from the tip of a bull's horn. In another picture the newlyweds appeared sitting at a terrace café next to a well-built man with a white beard who only a few were able to identify. It was Ernest Hemingway, and that would be the last time he'd attend the festival of the running of the bulls. He left a record of it in a book, *The Dangerous Summer*, published shortly afterward in three installments in *Life* magazine. There were those who said that the excesses committed by the writer during those months, traveling across Spain in a mad bullfighting-and-bacchanalian pilgrimage, altered him so much that they cost him his life. For the young couple that summer, on the other hand, it was a time of glorious happiness.

Aurora brought to the marriage a degree in pharmacy and a trousseau of table linens and Valenciennes lace bedding sets inherited from her grandmother, but she could hardly fry an egg and scarcely spoke a few broken sentences in the language of the country that would welcome her until the end of her days. Without realizing it, she made the biblical words from the book of Ruth her own: "And Ruth said, Entreat me not to leave thee, or to return from following after thee: for whither thou goest, I will go; and where thou lodgest, I will lodge: thy people shall be my people, and thy God my God. . ." Daniel, for his part, offered as his entire fortune a prodigious knowledge of the Spanish language and a modest job offer secured through Andres Fontana to teach Spanish literature at a university in the Midwest while he wrote his dissertation on Ramon J. Sender.

Toward the beginning of August 1959, on board a flight somewhere over the Atlantic, a young American whispered two lines of a poem by Pedro Salinas into the ear of a Spanish girl half-asleep, whose unruly straw-colored hair covered part of her face. *I know when I call you / among all people in the world / only you will be you.*

Together they were taking a step toward a future whose outcome, fortunately for them, they could not yet imagine.

Chapter 30

He waited for me on the street, leaning against his car, a blue Volvo neither too new nor too clean. Dark glasses covering his eyes, his light-colored beard seemed even lighter in the morning sun, and his hair as always somewhat longer than the usual. With his arms crossed idly, and wearing a pair of wrinkled chinos and an old denim jacket, he looked relaxed and attractive.

"It looks as if you'd just woken up, I bet you haven't even had breakfast," was his accurate greeting.

I'd only had time for half a cup of coffee. I'd woken up with just enough time to take a shower, fix myself up a little, and leave home the moment the horn honked for the second time.

He'd called me in the middle of the week to set a date for the plan we'd discussed on Thanksgiving night.

"On Saturday I am going out for dinner with Luis Zarate, so it's best we leave it for Sunday," I suggested. After the Thanksgiving break, the chairman and I had finally settled on a day.

"And if he kidnaps you and you don't come back?" he said sarcastically. "Why don't we move it forward to Friday?"

I agreed. His presence was always pleasant and I had a growing interest in visiting that mission so often mentioned in Fontana's papers. Why postpone it any longer?

Before, however, there had been some somewhat murky days. The start of the last month of the year had brought with it a barrage of e-mails from Spain asking again about my short-term plans, sometimes discreetly, other times bordering on impertinence. My university colleagues wanted to know if I'd join them for the traditional dinner before the Christmas holidays, and my sister Ana censured me permanently with her bellicose ideas as to how to torpedo my ex. Our mutual friends— those with whom we'd brought up our children and had lived through so much—inquired diplomatically about my plans in an effort, I assumed, to coordinate things so Alberto and I didn't run into each other at someone's home. I put everyone off. "I'll let you know, we'll see, let's keep in touch, I've got a lot of work, good-bye, see you soon, good-bye."

The campus, meanwhile, began to take on that end-of-semester atmosphere. Not to mention end-of-year, end-of-century, end-of-millennium. Big changes on the horizon. For the time being, however, what worried students were the impending exams and deadlines for handing in papers, essays, and projects. The anxiety was palpable; its noisy presence made itself felt in leisure areas, in the recreational center, on the sports grounds, and in the cafés. Dorms and apartments remained lit until the wee hours, and the library, housing what seemed like a great camp of refugees, remained open twenty-four hours a day.

There was a feeling of last-minute pressure among the professors as well. Briefer hallway conversations, a ton of exams to prepare, mountains of tests to correct, and a great desire to put the first half of the academic year to rest. It was similar to what I had felt year after year at my university, except that now, for the first time in my life, I had no desire for the holidays to arrive.

It was clearer by the day that my work with Andres Fontana's legacy was coming to an end. The stack of papers on top of my table had progressively diminished as their contents were poured into the computer's memory. The documents, once read and classified, accumulated in Cartesian order in cardboard boxes lined up on the floor. Everything that I managed to understand and retain regarding the history of California in the previous weeks had facilitated my task a great deal, but nonetheless I was aware that any reconstruction of the final stage of the professor's life would lack cohesion. I was missing information, documents, pieces of the great puzzle that was his last investigative work. To create some kind of clarity out of what remained was beyond my reach. Perhaps that was why I had been so eager for Friday to roll around.

"How about we eat something first?" was Daniel's proposal the moment I confirmed I was famished.

In no hurry to hit the road, we stopped at a café on the outskirts of Santa Cecilia where a handful of hippie night owls shared space with workmen and white-haired grandmothers. Seated by a large window, we ordered eggs, bacon, pancakes, orange juice, and two cups of coffee.

We chatted away while doing justice to the pair of plates that a robust waitress put before us. The portions were more than generous, perhaps due to Daniel's lighthearted flirting in Spanish, which seemed to have brightened her morning's boredom.

"I give up," I said eventually. "I'm full."

"Finish it," he joked, "so that your family doesn't go around thinking we don't take good care of you in California."

I focused my eyes on the yolky remains of a fried egg.

"What's left of my family, and the little I matter to them . . ."

I hadn't finished saying those words when I already regretted them. Perhaps my intention was to make a humorous remark, but what came out of my mouth was a crude point-blank gush of bitterness. I felt disconcerted, not knowing why suddenly, without justification, I'd lashed out against myself. All the more so after I had recently begun to notice that my spirits were picking up. Perhaps that was why I dropped my guard. Or it might have been because for too long I'd been putting up with so many things on my own that I was no longer able to hold back.

"Don't say that, Blanca, for God's sake. I know you've got your kids; I've heard you talk about them. And even if you always go around making sure not to say a word about yourself, I'm sure there are others who are concerned about you. Someone who wants to know that you're well, that you're working hard, that you're healthy and take care of yourself, that you're making friends who appreciate you in this corner of the world so far from home and your normal life. Siblings, parents, friends, ex-boyfriends, future boyfriends, what do I know? Or a husband, or an ex-husband, more likely. Perhaps this is a good moment for you to tell me once and for all something about yourself beyond your progress with Fontana's past."

"You want to know something about me?" I said, lifting my eyes from the remaining food. "Well, I'll tell you. My sons, the two of them, have each gone their separate ways. They finished school and have flown the nest. One is studying in London and the other alternates between Tarifa and Madrid, horsing around, and of course both are pretty much off doing their own thing and don't give a rat's ass about me. My parents, both gone: my father from prostate cancer fifteen years ago and my mother from a brain hemorrhage four years ago. I do have, I must admit, a sister by the name of Ana who calls me every other day to crush my morale while thinking she's helping to fix my life, but unfortunately never in a way I would like to see my life fixed. And until a few months back I had a man by my side whom I was married to for almost twenty-five years. I thought we made a stable, reasonably happy couple, but one fine day he stopped loving me and left. He fell in love with another woman, he's going to have a child with her, and I've refused to see him since; that's why I decided to leave and that's why I'm here now. Not because I was particularly interested in the academic life of this university at the other end of world, or because I had the slightest interest in digging up a dead man's dusty legacy: I simply came here fleeing the purest, bitterest grief. That's all—that's my life, Professor Carter. Fascinating, right? So as you can see, no one cares if I eat or don't eat."

I was suddenly assailed by a momentary weakness and turned my head so as not to look him in the eyes. But I didn't regret what I'd just told him. Nor was I satisfied. Deep down, I didn't care one way or the other. I gained or lost nothing by cluing him in to my reality.

I gazed out the window without paying attention to anything in particular: neither to the sickly couple that had just walked into the café, nor to an SUV that was parking, nor to a half-broken-down truck that was going into reverse, about to take off.

Then I noticed Daniel's arms cross the table in the direction of my plate. Two long arms with big bony hands at the ends. With them he grabbed my plate with my knife and fork and the rest of my breakfast and pulled it toward him. He cut, poked, put down the knife, and raised the fork toward my mouth. With a tone of professorial authority, which he most likely used when he had to bring his students in line, he said:

"*I* care. Eat."

His reaction, which almost made me laugh, was compassionate, but had a hint of sharpness to it.

"Come on, let's go," I said when I finally swallowed the piece of pancake that he offered me.

I went out while he paid. He didn't take long to catch up with me. As we headed to the car leisurely, immersed in our separate thoughts, I suddenly felt his fingers grazing the nape of my neck through my hair.

"Blanca, Blanca . . ."

He said nothing more.

• • •

Sonoma turned out to be a lot like Santa Cecilia, yet quieter without the noisy students. We parked on a downtown street, next to the large Sonoma Plaza containing the city hall and a good number of ancient trees. Scattered around it were low buildings in motley colors: the legendary Toscano Hotel and the Blue Wing Inn, the Sebastiani Theatre, the old Mexican army barracks, and La Casa Grande, the house of General Mariano Guadalupe Vallejo during the first years of independence.

"And here is our mission . . ."

At the far corner of the square, simple, white, and austere, with a veranda supported by old wooden beams that ran its entire length, was San Francisco Solano, commonly known as Mission Sonoma. The end of a chain established by the Spanish Franciscans in their heroic missionary zeal, it was the last outpost on the fabled Camino Real, that open road over which friars in coarse leather sandals rode on the backs of mules. Like its sister missions, it had a cast-iron bell outside hanging from a crossbeam, a recurring symbol that dotted California from south to north, calling to mind those austere men who had settled there in a not-too-distant past.

We contemplated the mission in silence, standing still before it. Nothing extraordinary lay hidden behind its clean lines and simplicity. But in a certain way, and perhaps because of this, I think we were both moved. The clay tiles, the sun beating against the whitewash. A couple of minutes flew by.

"I wasn't altogether honest with you before."

He didn't ask me to explain; he preferred that I just tell him. And I did so without looking at him, without taking my eyes off the mission's façade.

"It's true that at first I agreed to take on Fontana's legacy as a mere obligation to get away from my own problems, to distance myself from them physically and emotionally. But that doesn't mean that I've taken it lightly. What began as a simple duty has somehow become a personal interest."

He didn't offer an opinion or judge; he merely waited a few moments, pondering my words. Then he grabbed me by the elbow and said, "Come on, let's go inside."

As with the twenty other California missions, San Francisco Solano was not completely rebuilt and little of the original building was left standing. But the aesthetics were there, the soul and structure, with its humble wooden cross, rough on the top part. A metal plaque summarized its history, intimate and poignant in its sobriety.

There didn't seem to be any other visitors, and so, with no company other than the sound of our footsteps, we walked around the chapel with its whitewashed walls, clay-tiled floor, and modest altar. Afterwards, we visited the wing the priests had lived in, which had a tiny museum that showed a scale model of the original mission behind glass, a copper pot, cattle-branding irons, and a handful of black-and-white photos from different periods of the mission's existence.

In spite of the reduced size of the premises and the humility of its

contents, the place emanated charm and serenity. On the walls of what
was thought to have been the refectory we came upon an ancient collection of watercolors and stopped to examine them. We admired fifty
or so images of the missions, beautiful despite their varying states of
decay before undergoing reconstruction: collapsed walls, roofs about to
cave in or already in ruins, belfries propped up by scaffolding, partition
walls with fissures, other walls devoured by vines, and overall a pervad-
ing sense of abandonment and loneliness.

"Do you think he was right?" Daniel asked, his eyes still fixed on
the image of an arcade half in ruins, without taking his hands out of
his pockets, without turning toward me.

"Who and about what?"

"Fontana, in believing that perhaps another mission existed whose
traces aren't recorded anywhere."

He kept looking ahead, motionless, as if behind the watercolors'
brushstrokes he could find part of the answer.

"Among his papers, I haven't found any evidence," I said. "But
according to what you yourself told me, he believed there was. Mission
Olvido was its name, right?"

"That's the name I heard him mention. Perhaps it was the real
name, perhaps an imaginary one he chose to give it, to label something
of which he never had proof."

A pair of tourists came into the room. The woman had a camera at
the ready, and the man was wearing a brightly colored fanny pack and
a baseball cap facing backward. We moved aside to let them through,
since the prints didn't seem to interest them.

"In any case," I added when we were again left alone, "I'm afraid
that there's still no trace of that lost mission."

As we slowly left the watercolors behind and moved toward the
interior garden, we heard children's voices. On stepping outside we realized that it was a school trip led by a young teacher and an elderly guide
who asked for quiet with little success. We moved a safe distance away
beside a central brick fountain, stopping to listen to what the guide
finally managed to tell them: sanitized portions of history, digestible
for an audience of fourth graders. Mention of the year of its founding,

1823; its founder, Father Jose Altimira; and the methods of work and teaching used on the Indian converts that were welcomed there.

We exited the mission in silence: Daniel, probably remembering the Andres Fontana he had known and those intuitions he had hardly paid any attention to at the time; I, still trying to reconstruct the professor from the testimonies he'd left behind. Two different versions of the same person: the man in Daniel's memory, and the intellectual legacy that remained.

When we left the mission and passed before the entrance's iron bell once again, Daniel halted. With his large hands he felt the thick wooden beams that held it and caressed their roughness. Then we walked instinctively toward the square and sat on a bench to savor the day's last rays of sunlight. Before us, between enormous trees, rose a bronze sculpture of a soldier with the old bear flag fluttering above his shoulder, an homage to California's ephemeral independence. Beyond it was a playground in absolute peace, with motionless swings and not a trace of children.

Despite my outburst that morning during breakfast, in a certain way I felt better after having told Daniel about myself. Unburdened, lighter, more at peace. Contrary to what I'd thought up until then, exposing my life to a stranger had turned out to be somewhat liberating. Perhaps because, in any case, I was growing stronger; or perhaps because that stranger was becoming less so by the day.

"Did you know that of all the missions, this one is for some reason the one Fontana showed most interest in?" I pointed out. "And its founder as well: Father Jose Altimira, whom the guide mentioned before when she told the story of the mission to the schoolchildren. He was a young Catalan Franciscan, recently settled in Alta California. I've found a few documents about him among Fontana's papers."

"And what did he learn?" Daniel changed posture, turning toward me with interest.

"That Father Altimira managed to get authorization to build this last mission at the worst possible moment. Mission Dolores of San Francisco was then in a deplorable state and he proposed to move it here, but his superiors did not give him the go-ahead. Mexico had recently gained its independence from Spain and there was already a feeling that it wouldn't be long before the missions were secularized. Meanwhile, the Franciscans refused to recognize any government other than their Spanish king. The governor of California, however, did accept Altimira's proposal, and thanks to him Altimira began its construction."

"I imagine it wasn't because the governor was concerned with the souls of the infidels."

"Of course not. He did so for a much more practical reason: to guarantee a stable presence in this area before the advancing Russians, who, in exchange for a couple of blankets, a few pairs of riding pants, and a handful of hoes, had gained from the Indians a great tract of land farther north, next to the Pacific."

"Smart guys, those Russians from Fort Ross. Would you like to go see all that someday? Tomorrow, for instance?"

"Remember, I'm having dinner with Zarate."

"Make up any old excuse and come with me again. You'll be way more bored with him."

"Cut it out," I said, half laughing. "Don't you want to know what happened to Altimira?"

"Of course I do. It was only a slight interruption. Carry on, I'm all ears."

"Well, in spite of having civilian authorization, Altimira lacked his superiors' permission. Regardless, he did as he pleased; he chose this place, which at the time was totally inhospitable, and used several branches to fashion an altar, then stuck a wooden cross in the ground and established this mission."

"A bit wayward, this Altimira, wasn't he?"

"Yes, quite rebellious, although in the end his superiors had to go along with him and allowed him to keep the mission active. Fontana found him a very interesting character. Among his papers one perceives a great effort to piece together Altimira's past beyond Sonoma."

"Any luck?"

"So-so. Once he established his mission here in Sonoma against all odds, the newly converted Indians living in it rebelled. Apparently he was an efficient manager and a good administrator, but was unable to establish an affectionate relationship with the natives. In his zeal to civilize them, it seems he was harsh and demanding, applying constant physical punishments and never winning over their trust."

"So they revolted."

"Exactly. Two or three years later, the Indians sacked the mission and set it on fire. Altimira and some neophytes escaped by a hair-breadth and fled."

"And what became of him?"

"It's not too clear. Fontana seemed to be greatly interested in following in his footsteps, but I haven't come upon anything further on the matter."

"Life in this mission must have come to an end then."

"Quite the contrary. Shortly after the fire and Altimira's flight, another Franciscan took charge of it: Father Fortuni, an energetic old priest who quickly put things in order and fostered the necessary morale to rebuild the mission. However, he would eventually have to face something worse than fire or looting."

"The secularization of the missions."

"Exactly. A secularization that started out badly. At first, the new Mexican military representatives came all the way up here, to Alta California, with the intent of reconfiguring the social order. Then, overnight, conflicts began on various fronts: between the military and the Franciscans, the latter loyal unto death to the old Spanish order; and between the military and the local nonindigenous inhabitants, the old Californios, also of Spanish origin, who until then had lived peacefully, devoted to farming their lands and managing their haciendas."

"And riding horseback, saying the rosary, singing, dancing and playing the guitar for their fandangos, which is what they called their parties in these parts. I'm not surprised they didn't identify with the idea of a republic, considering the good life they led under the Spanish monarchy . . ." Daniel remarked sarcastically.

"But they didn't have any other choice. Mexico had decided that the system of missions was an anachronism and immediately ordered the secularization of all of them and the distribution of the lands among the Hispanicized Indians and the new settlers who chose to establish themselves there. This too brought disputes, because there were some sly people who tried to get hold of these properties for nothing, and others, more reasonable, who thought the lands should revert to their original, legitimate owners."

"Who I imagine were the Indians," he suggested, "the native population."

"Yes, in fact. Because, according to what I've read, the Franciscans never intended to become proprietors of the lands they settled, and even though to a large extent they failed in their attempt and often employed unfortunate practices, their sole objective was to bring the natives closer to their faith and try to transform them into citizens more or less integrated into their communities."

We were still seated amid the trees in the square as the sun was setting, and only a few passersby diverted our attention from time to time.

"But they never achieved that . . ."

"No, because the grand plan to make the transfer was ultimately ignored and only a small percentage of the lands ended up being handed over to their rightful owners."

"And the Indians, practically uprooted by force from their form of life and culture, ended up being, as is usually the case, the great losers of the story."

"Unfortunately, yes. And the rest of what happened around here you know better than I, because it's the story of this country of yours."

"The brief California Republic, and afterwards the Mexican-American War. And, at its end, the Treaty of Guadalupe Hidalgo, which reconfigured our map and gave us all of northern Mexico, including California."

"The missions, from then on, would fall into complete oblivion until the 1920s, when they started being physically rehabilitated, and from the fifties onwards the historical investigation takes off."

"Ensnaring a few romantics like Andres Fontana during the last years of his career," he added.

"That's why you and I are here today, at the end of the fabled Camino Real, at the last mission of this chain of relics of Spain's colonial past. But hardly anyone remembers much about this anymore."

"Especially in Spain."

"Certainly. Except for me," I joked, "who's saved from ignorance thanks to an unknown foundation that gave me a fellowship I'd applied for without even knowing what it was."

He changed posture again, now staring blankly at some diffused point in the square. Perhaps the bronze heroic figure of the soldier of the Bear Flag Republic, or the empty swings.

"I was very lucky I got the fellowship," I went on. "It's turning out to be very comfortable to work without deadlines or pressure. They send me a check every month and I work at my own pace until, on completion, everything is organized and I provide them with a final report."

He kept silent, listening to me with a mixture of aloofness and interest.

"Let's go, then," was all he ended up saying. "Should we return to Santa Cecilia or should we take a walk around here?"

We strolled in the surrounding area, coming across pedestrian side streets with shops, art galleries, and cafés. Finally we reached an Irish pub that looked altogether incongruous there. At the door a concert was announced and we felt like having something, so we decided to go in.

It was long past lunch hour and dinnertime hadn't yet begun, but the place seemed willing to offer us whatever we might want. We sat at the bar. A trio of veteran musicians, all on the far side of sixty, prepared their instruments in a corner. One of them had a gray ponytail halfway down his back; another had on a black T-shirt covering his prominent belly and emblazoned with a marijuana leaf; a third was riffling through the contents of a large bag on the floor.

We ordered a couple of beers and kept talking amid green clover decorations and Gaelic captions. We spoke of Fontana once again, an almost unconscious tribute to the mission we'd just visited, prompted by him.

"During that last period, when he began to be interested in the history of Spanish California and the missions," Daniel said after his first gulp of stout, "I remember that he also took to buying documents on colonial history. Chronicles, maps, and bundles belonging, I imagine, to the missions or other related institutions."

"There is very little of that among what was given to me; everything is much more documentary. Where did he come up with all this?"

He shrugged.

"He'd find things any old place and would pay just a couple of dollars for something. Apparently very few people appreciated those documents' worth, since they were written in Spanish."

"Perhaps he was looking for Mission Olvido."

A basket of french fries was placed before us and we started to nibble at them.

"Perhaps," he said. "I remember once he suggested that it could even have been situated near Santa Cecilia. Probably that's why he was interested in getting ahold of old documents from the area, in case he might come across any information. But are you sure there is nothing about that in the papers you're working on?"

"Nothing at all, as I told you. Although I still have the impression that there are things missing in his legacy, something more that would shed light on his last batch of work."

"It's strange," he added thoughtfully as he grabbed a few more fries. "Ever since you told me that you felt there were missing documents, I can't stop wondering what could have happened to them. Perhaps part of the material was misplaced in some move. Or perhaps he got rid of it himself, although I doubt it, because he wasn't in the habit of throwing anything out. You cannot imagine what his office looked like. The cave of Ali Baba."

The pub had slowly filled up and the atmosphere was becoming livelier by the minute as the elderly musicians got ready to play.

"I found lots of notes pertaining to a library at the University of California where most of the records regarding the missions are located. That is another visit I'd like to make."

"The Bancroft Library, in Berkeley. That's where he was returning from when he was killed. He'd been consulting documents and data. Night was falling; it was the seventeenth of May 1969. It was raining, one of those heavy spring showers. A truck crossed his path, he skidded . . ."

"How sad, right?" I sighed. "To dedicate so much time to rescuing what has been forgotten and end up dead, lying alone in a ditch on a rainy night."

Daniel took a few seconds to respond. The conversations of those around us filled the silence in ours. When he finally did speak, he did so with his eyes fixed on the glass he held in his hands. Turning it as if he were trying to find in it the inspiration to say what he intended.

"He was not alone in the car. Somebody else died in that accident."

"Who?"

The musicians broke into the first chords of Celtic music and the noise of the conversations died down.

"Who, Daniel?"

He looked up from his beer and finally answered.

"A woman."

"What woman?"

"What difference does her name make now, after so long? Are you still hungry? Should we order something else?"

Chapter 31

_____

We went on to talk about many other things, ordering more beers and some hamburgers, of which Daniel ate one and a half and I only half. Between the Celtic music and recollections of our visit to the mission, we let the rest of the evening roll by.

By the time we decided to start on our way back to Santa Cecilia, it was already pitch-dark. As we headed toward the parking lot, he saw something in a shopwindow, and after a simple "Wait a moment" he dashed inside the store, reemerging a minute later with a small iron bell, a replica of the missionary symbol. "A souvenir from this day," he said, handing it to me.

"You still have time to run away with me and forget about your chairman tomorrow," he warned me with his usual irony on pulling up in front of my apartment. "How about we go to Napa and visit a couple of cellars?"

"Negative."

"Okay, you win, even if afterwards you regret it. And what are you doing next week?"

"Work: tying up loose ends, settling matters pertaining to the legacy. Time has flown: we're already in December and, as I told you, I have less and less to do."

"And then you'll leave us," he added.

I delayed my answer a couple of seconds.

"I guess I have no other choice."

I could have not said anything else, keeping the rest of my thoughts to myself. But, since I'd revealed my feelings in the morning, I had the urge to continue. "I don't want to go, you know? I don't want to return to Spain."

"What you don't want to do is to come face-to-face with your reality."

"You're probably right."

"But you must."

"I know."

We were still sitting inside the parked car, in front of my place.

"Unless SAPAM could offer me another fellowship," I went on. "Perhaps, even though it's late, I should get in touch with them."

"I don't think it's a good idea."

"Why not?"

"Because things need their closure, Blanca, even though it may be painful. It's not wise to leave open wounds. Time cures everything, but before that, it's best to reconcile yourself with whatever you've left behind."

"We'll see . . ." I said, not too convinced.

"Take care, then."

He put his hand on top of mine and squeezed it. I didn't budge.

Suddenly my Taiwanese neighbor, a mathematics professor, appeared carrying an enormous box that, from its size, seemed to contain a television. His balancing act trying to get it inside the building distracted us.

I pulled my hand from under Daniel's, opened the door, and got out.

"See you soon," I said, bending down to speak to him through the open passenger's-side door.

"Whenever you want."

As soon as he saw me go in, he left.

• • •

The next day, Saturday, I took a walk past Rebecca's house around noon. I would have liked to talk to her about Daniel, Fontana, and the tangle of emotions they were weaving within me, as well as those earlier times when Rebecca herself had dealt with them, and perhaps even about the woman who died with the professor on that rainy night. Even though I knew Rebecca was in Portland celebrating one of her granddaughters' birthdays, I needed somehow to confirm it by seeing the closed windows, the garage door down, and not a trace of her good old dog, Macan.

Later that day, Luis Zarate showed up in his car in the very same spot where Daniel had dropped me off the previous night. How strange it was for me who'd been driving everywhere all my life to suddenly find myself without a car, waiting for someone to pick me up.

Los Olivos was our dinner destination; I was finally going to discover the city's most famous restaurant. Packed, with a good table reserved for us, it had class without fanfare, tall exposed-brick walls covered with large paintings, and bottle racks loaded with wines.

"Cabernet? Shiraz? Or would you prefer to try a petit verdot? I like your earrings; they look very good on you," Luis said.

They were the same I'd worn to Rebecca's Thanksgiving dinner. When I bought them at Istanbul's Grand Bazaar on that trip with my husband, I never could have imagined that less than a year later I'd be dining at the other end of the world with a different man, somewhat younger than me, who just happened to be my boss and promised, moreover, to be good company.

"Thanks, they're from Turkey. As for the wine, it's best you choose."

"There's something special you Spanish women have when it comes to dressing up. Spanish and Argentinians, and Italians too. Do you like pasta? I recommend the linguine *alle vongole*."

"I think I'm going to go for the mushroom risotto," I declared, closing the menu. "It's been ages since I've had rice."

"Excellent choice."

"I'll let you try it. Well, and how is everything going?"

"Good, good, good . . ."

The department, his classes, my classes, some books, some places, this or that colleague—a thousand different matters filled our conversation in the faint candlelight and over glasses of wine.

Without even being aware of it, as we moved from the hummus-and-tapenade appetizer to a salad and then to the main dish, we glided from the professional terrain into a more human sphere of things. Neither of us went into detail or openly expressed emotions or feelings as I had the previous day. But we did drop a few facts that until then we'd never talked about before. Nothing intimate: objective matters, general subjects, except that they nevertheless crossed the line of the purely professional. That he had a little daughter in Massachusetts, although he had never married the mother. That I'd just separated somewhat abruptly. That his transfer to California had resulted in their relationship cooling down. That my children hardly needed me anymore. He did not mention Lisa Gersen, the young German professor I'd seen him with the night of the debate and on one other occasion, whom everyone in the department thought was special to him. Nor did I ask.

Someone came up to our table unexpectedly in the middle of our dinner. One of my students, Joe Super, the adorable historian in my conversation course. I hadn't noticed him earlier because he was seated behind me.

I was happy to see him. So was Luis, with whom he shook hands.

"I only came to tell my dear and admired professor," he said with great charm in more than passable Spanish, "that I will be unable to attend your class next Tuesday."

"Well, we'll miss you, Joe."

And it was true. He was, without a doubt, one of the most participatory students, with a friendly manner and intelligent point of view.

"It's likely that others won't attend either," he added.

"Again because of the Los Pinitos matter, I take it," Luis stated before I had a chance to ask.

Joe Super was still actively involved in the platform opposed to the project. I remembered seeing him on television, and in our classes he occasionally alluded to the matter.

"That's right. Another meeting this Tuesday in the auditorium.

There's very little time left for the deadline to legally appeal against the mall project, and we're all a little nervous."

"In that case you're excused."

"And if you care to know how things are coming along, you can attend too."

"Thank you, Joe, but I think I'd better not. I'm only in Santa Cecilia in passing, as you are aware. In any case, you can tell me all about it afterwards."

"I presume our mutual friend Dan Carter will also be there," he said by way of good-bye. "I'm sure he'll chew me out for missing the pretty visiting Spanish professor's class."

With a friendly wink he returned to his table, again leaving Luis and me alone. The tone and content of our previous conversation, however, had been altered.

"Your mutual friend Dan Carter," he repeated, ironically raising his glass in the manner of a toast. "Once again the great intellectual rears his head."

Dan. That was how I'd heard his old Santa Cecilia friends refer to him. Rebecca often did so too. But Luis Zarate, as I knew full well, wasn't part of that circle.

"You won't be attending?" I asked, finishing off my risotto. I preferred to ignore his comment.

"No, thank you. I don't go in for that game," he said after his last bite of pasta. "Delicious," he concluded as he wiped his mouth. "In truth, all this business about Los Pinitos and its future is something I don't care about one way or the other."

I was shocked by his reaction but hid it as the young waitress took away our plates. My position was that of someone newly arrived in the community, totally ignorant of its matters. Nevertheless, I understood my colleagues' reaction toward the idea of razing a natural spot to build yet another shopping mall. "But you live here; it must matter somewhat. Almost everyone is against it. The reasons are clear: your colleagues are mobilizing nonstop—"

"You see?" he said with a half smile. "That old fox Carter has already lured you to his camp. Another glass of wine to accompany the dessert?"

I didn't refuse. Perhaps it was precisely that—the wine we were both drinking generously—that made me talk without beating around the bush.

"What bad vibes you two have, don't you?"

"It isn't as bad as that; it's only a misunderstanding. Do you know that the first ones to plant vineyards in this California country were your compatriots, the Franciscan monks? They brought some vines from Spain because they needed wine to consecrate—"

"Don't go off on a tangent, Luis. Tell me, once and for all: What's the matter between the two of you? What type of misunderstanding are you talking about?"

"Academic, of course. And personal, I may add. But nothing really too deep. Let's not dramatize. In fact, apart from the discussion in honor of National Hispanic Heritage Month, I've only spoken face-to-face with him once, although that first encounter was even less memorable."

"Aren't you going to tell me about it?"

We spoke with familiarity. He no longer made an effort, as he did in the beginning, to come across as the perfect gentleman, the perfect boss, or the perfect colleague, courteous and warm. But we got along just fine like that. We were different kinds of creatures but shared certain values, and that always made for smooth communication between us. Even though he was three or four years younger than I, we belonged to the same generation and had moved about similar terrain. That was why I got along with both Daniel and him, and I was bothered by the fact that they spent their time throwing poison darts at each other. Now I wanted to know the reason for the animosity that, no matter who it came from, always ended up affecting me.

"What do you care, Blanca? Your stance is the most intelligent: at peace with everyone regardless of the particular disagreements between them. One day you dine with me, another you have breakfast with him . . ."

"How do you know about that?"

"Someone mentioned to me yesterday that they'd seen you leave the Sonoma Road Café together, that's all. Santa Cecilia is a small town, what do you want me to say? In any case, it must be a great honor for you to have the great Daniel Carter eating out of your hand."

"Easy there, Zarate . . ." I said, finally trying my cheesecake. "In any case, I don't know what interest he could have in the Los Pinitos business beyond taking the side of his friends who oppose it."

I knew what it was. We had talked about it at some point and he had dragged me with him to that protest on that stormy afternoon we had coffee. But I was unaware that his involvement went beyond signing petitions.

"Well, don't doubt that he has enormous interest in the issue," he said. "Toward the end of last year's spring semester, Carter called me from his office in Santa Barbara to ask that I see him here in Santa Cecilia: he wanted to talk to me about something that he did not specify. I agreed to meet the following week. He walked in like he owned the place and, without even knowing me, came to tell me pretty much how I should run my department. Almost demanding that I act in a way that best served his interests."

I couldn't follow what he was saying. Perhaps it was the wine or the murkiness of the situation.

"It all had to do with the Los Pinitos project. He tried to convince me that the department should actively intervene with all its resources."

"What resources?" I asked without letting him finish.

"I don't know; I didn't give him the chance to explain. I don't know if he expected the entire faculty to sign a manifesto, or that we mobilize our student body, or that we make donations to the cause . . . I refused to keep on listening to him before he even went into details. I was as indifferent toward that whole affair as I am today. But I could not accept that someone no longer associated with this university, no matter how famous he was outside of it, would come to coerce me. To tell me what to do and what not to do, and the position we should take on issues that have nothing to do with us."

As Luis spoke, violent collisions began to occur in my head in a sequence I was unable to control:

Daniel and Fontana's legacy, Fontana and Los Pinitos, Daniel and me, Fontana and me. The thing that Luis Zarate never knew about I began to suspect at that very instant. In seconds my memory descended to the grimy basement of Guevara Hall. Could those be the resources Daniel had referred to? Palpable resources, documentary, quantifiable, belonging to a department that never took them into account. Had he intended to get from Luis Zarate a commitment for the department itself to unearth Fontana's legacy and put it at the disposal of the Los Pinitos cause? From the very beginning Daniel had had a hunch that there was some clue there that could derail the shopping mall project. What if, due to the chairman's refusal to get involved, he'd sought his own method to bring it to light?

"So I refused," Zarate went on. "Out of principle, *por cojones,* as you'd say in Spain, if you pardon my expression."

I did not react to the convincing nature of his words; my mind was still trying to piece it all together. Documentary resources, perhaps solid evidence among the thousands of papers I'd been working with for three months. Something that might have to do with Daniel's endless questions regarding my progress, my findings, regarding the elusive Mission Olvido that he often asked me about.

"That's where the battle ended. I don't think there's much more to it. Although it was interesting," he added ironically. "It's not every day that one stands up to a living legend."

Although my brain was still busy connecting the dots, my face must have betrayed my confusion. He noticed and did not miss the opportunity to enlighten me.

"Since you work in different fields, you may not be fully aware of the scope of the real Daniel Carter?"

"So tell me," I replied, wanting to know right that minute.

"In this country's academic Hispanic studies community—and

believe me we are a few thousand—he is a heavyweight. He's been the president of the powerful MLA, the Modern Language Association, and director of one of the most prestigious journals in our field, *Literature and Criticism*. Books of his, such as *Literature, Life, and Exile* and *Keys to Twentieth-Century Spanish Fiction,* are groundbreaking and have been used for years in Spanish departments all over the United States. His presence is valued like few others' in conferences and conventions in our field; to open or close an academic event with a plenary lecture of his is a guarantee of success. A positive referral or a letter of recommendation with his signature can fuel the professional career of anyone who receives it."

The profile of the man that started taking shape before my eyes began to annoy me as much as his attempt to use the resources of a department that for decades had been no longer his own.

"Your friend Daniel Carter, dear Blanca, is not a simple anonymous and charming professor with few responsibilities and lots of free time in the final stretch of his career. To this day he continues to be one of the figures with the greatest intellectual acuity and influence among the community of Hispanists."

Those revelations only increased my surprise. However, I didn't want Luis to notice it, and once more the cheesecake served as my cover.

"Besides," he continued, "he's got a reputation for being a charismatic fellow, with lots of friends and, according to what is said, with a somewhat peculiar past. It's a shame I've been unable to figure him out. Unlike you, my relationship with him has from the very start been marked by a total lack of understanding."

He finished off his tiramisu while I tried to piece together the puzzle before me. Then he spoke again.

"I don't believe in those sacred cows who think they can cast their shadow as far as they wish, you know what I mean?"

I was about to reply, when Joe Super came back to our table to say good-bye. We smiled at him; he smiled back. He hadn't altogether turned around when I finally began to speak.

"What is he really doing in Santa Cecilia, then?" I asked.

"Enjoying a sabbatical and writing a book. Or so he goes around saying."

"Spanish literature at the turn of the century, that much I know. But why is he here right now?"

His answer was swift. "That is exactly what I wonder each time I see him."

Chapter 32

I spent all day Sunday chewing on uncertainty. I did not see Daniel, nor did I call him, nor did anyone mention him to me because I hardly spoke to anyone the entire day. But he was still echoing uneasily in my mind ever since the conversation with Luis Zarate at Los Olivos.

I woke up early and wasn't able to get back to sleep. I went to the campus pool when it was still practically empty, swam without strength or enthusiasm. Afterwards I bought a newspaper next to the main square and had a coffee I couldn't finish. At noon I was unable to eat. My stomach seemed to have shrunk, but my mind kept churning away. What until then had seemed innocent and casual now came across as suspicious: the reason for his continued presence in a place he didn't belong, his persistent interest in my work, his knowing things about me that I couldn't recall sharing with him.

Rewinding the memory of the months that had elapsed since my arrival, I again pictured him in the extensive gallery of scenes and shared moments. I saw him walk leisurely down the campus pathways with a couple of books under his arm and his hands in his pockets, or jogging in the distance in sports clothes at dusk. I recalled the day we met at Meli's Market and the afternoon he dragged me in what seemed a spontaneous manner to the center of the demonstration.

266

That lunch when he kept nipping away at my chicken burrito in the cafeteria; the afternoon in which he spoke to me with affection about the Andres Fontana that he'd once known. His strong voice singing popular Mexican songs at my party; his arms pushing the wheelchair of his mentally absent friend and that speech of his that brought tears and laughter to those gathered, while he toasted to life and intoned a hymn to compassion. And even closer in time, his fingers on the nape of my neck after the unfinished breakfast, his intense attention to my stories about the Sonoma mission as we both sat on an old wooden bench. His mention of Fontana's death alongside a nameless woman, his advice inside the car to close my open wounds. His hand on mine before leaving. Always relaxed, warm, close. Perhaps too much so.

At midafternoon I went out again. I walked by Rebecca's house and again found everything closed and plunged in silence, since she had not yet returned. I then headed toward the library. Although it was Sunday, the library was packed with students. The heat was at full blast and most of the students were wearing short-sleeved shirts, some even in shorts and flip-flops.

I dug into a computer on the main floor in search of some references. How do you wish to make your search? the machine asked. I selected the option AUTHOR, then typed in the surname, followed by the name. The findings were immediately eye-popping: fourteen books of his, coauthorship of a bunch of others, dozens of articles in prestigious publications, a good handful of prefaces and annotated editions. Narrative, criticism, Ramon J. Sender, exile, voices, letters, analysis, nostalgia, views, identity, revision. All these words scattered in a nonrandom fashion among the titles of Daniel Carter's impressive output.

After that I headed for the third floor, where the Spanish literature section was located. I took several volumes from the shelf, skimming over some pages, while others I read thoroughly. Luis Zarate hadn't exaggerated. This was the work of a highly competent academic, not a simple bored professor with nothing better to do than accompany a recently arrived colleague on a visit to Franciscan missions and drink stout in an Irish pub.

I dropped everything toward seven. It made no sense to keep on reading; I'd more than confirmed what I wished to know.

There was a still a lot of bustle in the library's main central area when I made my way toward the exit: some students were just arriving, others were heading toward the computers, the majority looking for a table here or there to settle into. There were also those leaving, heading to the street, into the night, on their way back to their dorms or apartments, to normal life beyond the padded comfort of the carpets and the shelves crammed with books. Perhaps I should have left with them. Returned to my life, quit investigating.

But I didn't.

At the last minute and with my coat on, I decided to go in search of something my intuition advanced as a possible window to the truth. In search of one more puzzle piece to join to the bunch that I'd already accumulated.

I asked for instructions at the counter. "Press from 1969? The local newspaper? Everything is microfilmed. One moment, please." Minutes later I held in my hand the microfilm that I needed and seated myself before a powerful luminous screen that would enlarge the pages of a three-decades-old newspaper. Daniel had mentioned May 1969 in reference to Fontana's accident; I couldn't remember the exact date. Seven? Seventeen? Twenty-seven?

I began to go through the pages quickly. Until one particular front page of the *Santa Cecilia Chronicle* appeared.

USC PROFESSOR KILLED IN CAR ACCIDENT

Spanish Professor Andres Fontana, 56, chairman of the Modern Languages Department, was killed last night in a car crash . . . Aurora Carter, 32, wife of Associate Professor Daniel Carter, was killed as well . . .

I was unable to keep on reading. The library's heat became suddenly stifling. I noticed my dry throat, my stiff fingers holding on to the table's edge, and a profound sensation of weakness. Exhausted, I was finally able to rein in my attention and finish reading the three news columns on the screen: the rain, the night, a truck, the impact, firefighters, several hours, police, Spain, husband, death.

I refused to look for further information, lacking the courage. Had I done so, I would have come upon numerous details in the following days' newspapers. The funeral, who attended, where they were buried. But I didn't want to know, just as I didn't want my own imagination to pry into that painful and disconcerting triangle that had just been displayed before me. As soon as I got to the end of the article, I got up so abruptly that I knocked the chair over.

The woman in charge of the periodicals admonished me from the counter in an annoyed tone on seeing my hasty departure—that I should turn off the machine, I thought I heard her say; that I had to hand in the microfilm. I paid no attention, I didn't stop, didn't even turn my head. Picking up my pace, I left her there yelling after me.

The first thing I did on arriving back at my apartment was to send an e-mail:

Rosalia, I'm still in California. Please, try to find out as soon as possible all you can regarding SAPAM, the foundation that sponsored my fellowship. I need to know what is behind it, who runs it. I hope I'm mistaken, but I've got the feeling that someone has gotten me involved in the weirdest business.

The following morning, the department seemed the same as any other Monday. People, footsteps, the noise of some keyboard, the photocopy machine spewing out paper. I greeted whoever crossed my path, making an effort to sound natural, the visiting professor as always, the Spaniard fallen out of the sky who day by day locked herself up in the tiniest office on that floor before a bunch of old papers that no one cared about.

I opened my e-mail and found the answer I was waiting for.

A thousand meetings and just about to run off to another of the long ones. Madness, my dear!!! Regarding your fellowship all I can come up with is the terms and conditions, plus the documents and messages we exchanged with the University of Santa Cecilia, and you've got that yourself. But I've been able to rescue from the trash folder the message with the phone number of the person at SAPAM I was in touch with at the time, a very nice guy who spoke perfect Spanish. Here it goes, I hope it's helpful. Kisses, Ros.

P.S. Will you be back in time for the president's Christmas celebration drink?

I anxiously took a breath of air, lifted my old telephone receiver, and dialed the number with which Rosalia ended her message. Just as I feared, on the fifth ring the answering machine came on with his recorded voice. He first spoke in his own tongue. Afterwards in mine. Brief, quick, concise.

This is the answering machine of Daniel Carter, Spanish and Portuguese Department of the University of California, Santa Barbara. I'm presently out of my office. To leave a message, please contact the secretary.

I felt like flinging the phone against the window, shouting at the top of my lungs the worst insults hoarded in my memory, and then bursting into tears.

But I did none of this. Nothing. I simply crossed my arms on top of the table, hid my face in them, and, in the darkness and shelter of myself, thought. For a long while that is all I did. When I finally put order to my thoughts, I sent an e-mail to Rosalia asking her not to worry anymore. Afterwards, without opening any work document or putting a single finger on any of the remaining papers of the legacy, I grabbed the book on California that Daniel had given me, which was sitting on one of the shelves, then swung my bag over my shoulder and left.

"You already knew?" I asked from the door. Point-blank. Without even greeting her.

Rebecca lifted her eyes from the keyboard. Wearing an eggplant-colored shirt, surrounded by the usual harmony.

"Good morning, Blanca," she answered with her customary composure. "Do you mind clarifying what is it you are referring to, please?"

"You knew your friend Daniel Carter was behind SAPAM?"

She didn't seem surprised at my question. Before answering, she removed her glasses and calmly leaned back in her chair.

"I didn't at first."

"And afterwards?"

"Afterwards I began to suspect. But I've never confirmed it."

"Why?"

"Because I haven't asked him. Because it is none of my business. Because I can imagine the reasons that have led him to do what he's done, and therefore I've preferred to put aside any inquiry."

"Reasons that have to do with Andres Fontana and his wife. With your friend Aurora, right?"

"I guess. But I think it's best you speak to him."

"That is what I intend to do right now," I said, adjusting the bag on my shoulder. "As soon as you tell me where he lives."

"Aren't you going to call him first?" she asked while jotting down his address on a yellow Post-it.

"What for? He works from his house in the mornings, right? I prefer to see him."

I'd already stepped out into the hallway when I heard her voice at my back.

"Don't forget, Blanca, that, one way or other, we've all got accounts pending with our past."

On my way out I bumped into Fanny. She made as if she were about to stop, intending to show me something. I tried to feign a smile, but it didn't come out. "I'll see you later," I said without slowing down. I left her standing there, gazing at me, mute and disconcerted.

I soon realized that Rebecca was right. Not because of that last remark she made, which I didn't even give a second thought to, but because she implied that I should alert Daniel that I was coming over. No one opened the door when I rang the bell of apartment 4B of that large house subdivided into apartments. No one came out to meet me when I repeatedly pounded the white wooden door of his temporary home as hard as I could. So I sat down on the stairs and took out my cell phone.

I had two numbers for him, one for that transitory lodging and the other for his cell phone; he'd given them to me that afternoon I'd gone in search of him at Selma's Café. "In case you need me at some other time," he'd said. That time had come.

I called the first number anticipating what would happen. I wasn't mistaken: behind the nearby door I could hear the phone ringing and no one answered. Then I tried the second number. "The number you have dialed is unavailable," a lady said in a falsetto voice. And repeated it, until I finally hung up.

I took the book on California out of my bag. The one I believed had been a mere present, timely and clever, intended to facilitate my task. The one most likely for him to give me as a gift but was actually bait to motivate me to continue working, like the carrot one puts before the mule that pulls the waterwheel so that he never stops. A trick, a ruse. One more. I wrote on it: YOU'VE MANIPULATED ME AND YOU'VE BETRAYED ME. GET IN TOUCH WITH ME AS SOON AS YOU'RE BACK. The fury of my capital letters almost tore the paper. I didn't sign my name.

The book made a dry thump when I dropped it in his mailbox. Then I left immediately and decided not to call him again. Only to see him face-to-face, without subterfuges or excuses.

Thirty-four hours elapsed before he got back to me. Thirty-four sad, distressing hours until he found me at the most inappropriate moment.

I heard a quick rapping on the door, and it immediately opened. A head and half a body appeared. Light hair, light beard, a gray turtleneck sweater, and a jacket. And a tanned face that didn't conceal its worried look.

Barely two seconds were all he needed to evaluate the classroom situation. I stood next to the whiteboard, leaning slightly against the side of my desk, my arms folded across my chest and a felt-tip pen in my hand, fatigue written all over my face, and a clear effort to hide the annoyance that I carried within. Five students of my culture class scattered around, less than half the usual attendance.

He didn't say a word. He simply held something up for me to see, his expression serious. The book on California. Mine. His. The one he had left me as a present inside an anonymous bag on the night of the Spanish omelets, gazpacho, and laughter. The same book I'd dropped in his mailbox, wishing to convey that I wanted nothing that was associated with him. I imagined he understood. Then he made a gesture indicating that he was going to insert it somewhere. In my department mailbox, I gathered. I didn't say either yes or no and he didn't wait for my answer. He simply closed the half-open door and disappeared.

· · ·

It never was my intention.
I'll see you in the auditorium.
Come as soon as you can, please.

This is what I found at the end of my class in my department mailbox where messages were left, along with occasional letters from Spain. It was written on a white card without letterhead, squeezed between two pages of that book with a yellow cover that was all too familiar.

· · ·

There were five speakers onstage, among whom I recognized my student Joe Super and a couple of professors I knew by sight. Just as on the day of the demonstration, there was a diverse crowd: a bunch of students, the warrior grandmothers with a raised sign, respectable citizens by the dozen, and the kid with the dreadlocks. There wasn't, however, a trace of the almost festive mood of the day of the demonstration. Serious faces, scant smiles, and concentrated attention were all that was evident.

The meeting had started a good hour earlier. One of the speakers was commenting on some archeological digs on the grounds. On the stage, on a whiteboard, someone had written with a thick marker:

TEN DAYS TO THE DEC. 22 DEADLINE. If they didn't come up with something they could show the authorities by then, they'd lose the battle.

Daniel was waiting for me, sitting in the next-to-last row.

"We need to talk," I whispered without greeting him as soon as I
sat down next to him. "Let's go."

"Five minutes," he asked in a whisper. "I beg you, Blanca, just give
me five minutes."

"Either you're coming or you're staying; it's up to you."

The speaker whose turn it was mentioned his name, summoning
him to answer something.

"Wait for me," he insisted, grabbing my wrist while from the stand's
microphone his name and question were repeated.

I broke loose from his grip with a jerk. Then got up and left.

Chapter 33

Half an hour later he was at my door.

"I'm very sorry," he said, bursting in, upsetting my apartment's peacefulness with his large and disorderly presence. "I didn't think they were going to count on me: they called me at the very last minute; I'd just returned from L.A. When I saw your book in my mailbox, I came straight to you. I left yesterday early in the morning . . ."

I did not interrupt him. Had it been a day and a half earlier, I would have seized him by the throat upon confirming what I'd suspected. But so many hours had gone by that I simply let him talk. By then my rage had subsided and the anger that plagued me earlier had turned into something quite different. It was a sort of desolation, a dense bitterness that in the long run might even prove worse.

When he was done threshing out the list of excuses that I hadn't asked him for, it was finally my turn.

"Why did you lie to me?" I asked him coldly.

"I never meant to do it, Blanca. It was never my intention to deceive you."

He took a step forward, extended his arm to the back of my neck. As if by physical contact he sought to transmit an extra dose of sincerity.

"But you have," I said pulling away. "SAPAM doesn't exist and

275

the fellowship with which I've supported myself all these months is nothing but a ruse of yours that you've hidden from me this whole time. You concealed it from me and, by doing so, deceived me; you've disappointed me and hurt me."

"And from the bottom of my heart I'm telling you how sorry I am. But I want you to know that I never intended—"

I cut him off sharply. "I'm not looking for apologies, simply an explanation. The only thing I want you to tell me is what's behind this setup, and afterwards get out of my life for good."

He ran a hand over his head, then his beard, clearly uncomfortable.

"An explanation, Daniel," I insisted. "All I want is an explanation."

Unemotional, businesslike, icy. I made no effort to appear that way; it was simply how I felt.

"Okay, let me state from the outset that you are right, that the foundation for Scientific Assessment of Philological Academic Manuscripts—SAPAM—does not exist," he admitted. "You are not mistaken: it's a false name. But it does exist as an entity, let's say—not formally, but as something different."

"Like what? Like something you made up after the death of Fontana and your wife?"

He looked at me deliberately. Concentrated. Serious. But he wasn't surprised.

"I imagined that you'd end up investigating it."

The answer was so obvious that I didn't even bother to verbalize it.

He went on, "I established it in essence as the Aurora Carter Trust for the Memory of Andres Fontana. Aurora Carter or Aurora Carranza, which was her Spanish surname; it makes no difference. In short, it was a project to preserve my mentor's intellectual legacy through my wife's will."

"Don't give me all this linguistic crap. All I want to know is why, thirty years after both of their deaths, you've decided to come up with this sinister plot and get me involved."

He stuck his hands in his pockets and lowered his eyes, as if trying to find the means to focus on his answer, his gaze fixed on the horrible taupe wall-to-wall carpet that silenced my every step in that provisional lodging.

"Because it was the only viable option to bring to light Fontana's legacy," he finally said, raising his eyes. "The only solution that occurred to me when all the doors were closed."

"What doors?"

"The usual ones to go through the regular channels, that is, the Modern Languages Department."

"And who closed them to you? Luis Zarate?"

"Who else?"

I recalled the chairman's words during our dinner at Los Olivos, his rendering of the facts on the day he received Daniel in his office.

"I don't believe you. You tried to coerce him; you expected him to behave according to what best served your interests. And he didn't accept."

"I presume that's the version he's given you."

"A version neither more nor less convincing than yours."

"No doubt, but inaccurate. I never tried to coerce him. I simply suggested that perhaps the department should make operative use of its resources—"

"To intervene in the Los Pinitos matter, from what I gather," I interrupted him.

"Exactly."

"And although you didn't tell him explicitly, by mentioning those resources, you were referring to Fontana's papers."

"I see you're clued in on everything."

I chose not to answer; I just waited for him to continue.

"By then I had already begun to suspect that perhaps some interesting facts could be unearthed among the documents that were left behind in Fontana's office upon his death. Irrefutable documents that would show that Los Pinitos has historical importance, a solid reason to reject the plan to build an absurd and unnecessary mall in the area."

"Something as significant as a Franciscan mission."

"Exactly."

"Because if it could be proven that a mission had stood there, as Fontana had come to believe, everything could be brought to a halt."

"Or at least it could force a reevaluation. The Santa Cecilia town hall exerts its jurisdiction over the area, but lacks an ownership title; there is no evidence regarding whom it belonged to in the distant past. If we were able to explain that the place was once the site of a historic Franciscan mission, everything would have to undergo a revision. And the project, while this matter was being resolved, would have to come to a standstill."

"That's why you've always been so interested in knowing if the legacy contained some mention of the alleged Mission Olvido. Why you've constantly been trying to wheedle information out of me. Why you always made an effort to control my work: first you give me a book so that I can learn the history of California, then I take you to see a nearby mission . . ."

"No, Blanca," he denied forcefully. "I have never tried to control or interfere with your work. I've always had the utmost trust in you; the only thing I've tried to do at all times is to help you go forward. But you must believe me: it all came to a head as a result of Zarate's refusal. From then on, I had no other solution than to put the wheels of SAPAM in motion, maneuver it through the department without raising suspicions, and making the announcement public. And that's how you came onto the scene."

I was still angry and frustrated, but as we spoke I grew increasingly curious about the reasons behind that dark plot, about the complex relationship between the three of them that had led Daniel to behave in such a fashion.

"Besides, I still don't understand what the recovery of Fontana's legacy has to do with all of this. If you were only looking for specific information on a mission, why waste my time classifying his legacy down to the last detail? Why force me to put order to the thousands of tiniest pieces that make up the puzzle of his life? I've been giving it my all for the last three months, Daniel, doing a job nobody cares about," I said, raising my voice, unable to check my outrage.

"Wait, Blanca, wait . . ."

He spoke forcefully, gesticulating with hands that he'd finally taken out of his gray pants pockets. The clothes he was wearing were completely unlike those he usually had on when relaxing in Santa Cecilia. A good cut, good material, professional. Nothing like the wrinkled chinos and old denim jacket he had worn in Sonoma. His other face. His B side.

"Your work is of great interest—very much so. It's most valuable and fundamental, bringing sense to everything. But there are other matters."

"Well, then, spell them out once and for all."

"Let's see how I can explain this to you . . ." he said slowly, trying to come up with the right words. "The proposal to build a mall in Los Pinitos was the trigger—a very powerful trigger. But there was something else behind it. An outstanding debt."

"With Fontana?" I asked in disbelief.

"Yes, with Fontana; with his memory and his dignity."

"Are you telling me that thirty years after his death you still had to settle matters with your old professor?"

"That's right," he admitted with an emphatic gesture. "To my great regret, that is so. Even though three decades had gone by since his death, and Aurora's—and although I'd completely rebuilt my life and all of that was part of the past—there were still loose ends between us."

"I swear, this exceeds my power of comprehension," I murmured.

"Deep down, it's all quite simple. Sadly simple. To summarize what turned out to be the most dreadful years of my life, I want you to know that, after that horrendous accident, I hit rock bottom. Like Dante in his Inferno, in the midpoint of my life, I found myself in a dark forest after having gone astray. I descended to hell, and did a few stupid things."

"You still do."

My comment didn't seem to bother him.

"But back then, unfortunately, they were much more regrettable. And among them was to refuse to have anything to do with the memory of my old teacher. After the accident I fled, literally. In truth,

I did not know what I was running away from, but wanted to get away as soon as possible, far from anything related to my previous life."

"From your life with Aurora, I suppose."

"Especially. From my ten years of happiness with a wonderful woman whom I said good-bye to with a long kiss at our kitchen table at breakfast and who that very same night I saw for the last time muddied on the shoulder of the road, covered with a bloody blanket and with her skull crushed between crumpled metal."

I was moved by the harshness of his story; I was disconcerted by the naturalness of his account. I didn't say a word. I let him talk.

"But I overcame it. In time and with effort, after so much turmoil, little by little the despondency turned into a great grief, then into a bearable sadness, and in the end, a simple melancholy that in time slowly vanished."

I sat in an armchair and he sat on the couch in front of me, face-to-face, separated by a low table with a few outdated magazines on top, a firewall between us. He then leaned forward, resting his elbows on his knees.

"I'm not some kind of disturbed idiot clutching at a shadow of an absence, Blanca. It's been many years since I came out of the darkness," he declared. "It was a painful process but I learned to live without Aurora and was able to rebuild my life. But with Andres Fontana, unfortunately, it wasn't the same. I was so shattered by my wife's death, so lost and heartbroken, that I was never able to reconcile with his absence because I never shed a tear for him."

"And then, after the passage of years, you announced this alleged fellowship and hired me to dust off his legacy. Not only in search of documentary evidence against the shopping center, but also to clear your guilty conscience without even getting your hands dirty."

He did not answer me. He stared at me but didn't answer.

"I really trusted you, you know?" I went on, lowering my eyes toward the table that separated us. "Maybe you think my problems are insignificant compared to your own tragedy, but I also know what loss is," I said, raising my eyebrows at him.

"I know, Blanca, I know . . ."

"I arrived in Santa Cecilia disoriented and badly wounded, fleeing, struggling to rescue myself from the wreck my life had become."

"I know . . ." he repeated.

"And I clutched on to Fontana's legacy like a lifeline. Then you crossed my path, apparently always willing to help, to make my life easier, to make me laugh . . . to . . . to . . . And now . . ." I swallowed my feelings, trying not to fall apart. "I thought you were my friend."

He extended a hand toward me but I moved back, refusing to accept his contact.

"Blanca, let me finish telling you what from the very beginning was behind my actions. Before you judge me, you need to know about Fontana, Aurora, and myself. Afterwards, do whatever you deem fit: banish me from your house and life, hate me, forget me, forgive me, or do whatever you must do. But first you must listen."

The old photograph pinned with a thumbtack in Rebecca's basement came back to mind. The young, pretty woman with the broad laugh, white dress, and disheveled hair who was standing under the sun of Cabo San Lucas and whose life had come to an end one rainy night. Perhaps because of her I instinctively yielded.

"They hit it off from the start, from the moment Aurora and I settled in Santa Cecilia two years earlier. The three of us had a very close relationship, a relationship that far exceeded the boundaries of the purely professional. But between them, however, most likely because of their common condition as Spanish expatriates, they established a special bond with a mutual understanding that I myself sometimes didn't fully grasp. Invisible references and cultural codes, nuances that were beyond me and brought them closer together. A deep friendship ensued. And in time Aurora began to collaborate with him."

"Doing what?"

"She would often accompany him in his search for documentation; they'd compare facts and scrutinize papers together."

"She was a historian . . ." I ventured.

"Far from it: she was a pharmacist. In fact, when we arrived in Santa Cecilia she'd just finished her PhD in pharmacology in Indiana, where we'd lived the previous five years. Her field consisted of formulas and chemical compounds, but, I don't know why—perhaps because he instilled that passion in her—she began to feel a bond with those old Spaniards who wandered these lands centuries ago. Her Catholic faith in which she was brought up must have influenced her as well, by then channeled toward a much more active social commitment. She worked with immigrants and the elderly, participated in adult literacy programs, that sort of activity—something quite praiseworthy despite living with the wild agnostic I used to be. She was gradually captivated by the old Franciscan missions. When the accident occurred, they were returning from Berkeley, where they'd gone looking for documents on what they called Mission Olvido. With both of their deaths, that research was left unfinished and the chapter on the uncataloged mission was closed inconclusively."

"But—"

"Wait," he whispered. "Let me continue. I think you still need to know a few more things. Fontana, in his will, left four heirs. Half of his savings were to go to Aurora, which I ended up receiving. From that money, which I'd never touched, came all the monthly checks written out to you."

"And the other heirs?"

"The other half of the money went to Fanny Stern, still a child at the time. He felt a great fondness for her; her mother, Darla, whom you met that afternoon in the square, was the department secretary at the time. He had a special type of relationship with her."

"I know. Fanny herself told me," I said.

"He left it to Fanny formally, but for all practical purposes he left it to both of them. To the university he bequeathed his house, which was absorbed into what now are extensions to the campus. They tore it down years later and in its place built a laboratory, if I'm not mistaken. And I was named, let us say, his intellectual heir, and as such received the magnificent library that he'd slowly built over the decades. But his documents, his personal papers, his research . . . never reached me, and were left here, in Santa Cecilia, forgotten in a basement in Guevara Hall without anyone ever showing any interest in them whatsoever."

"But you should have been the one to reclaim them: they were your mentor's legacy and you were his beneficiary."

"I know. Legally, that was my responsibility. And morally too."

"But you never did so."

"No."

"Because you were never interested in their contents."

"Probably."

"And because you wanted to cut all ties connecting you with the past."

"Most likely."

"Nothing else?"

He gave me a dark, piercing look, pressing one hand against the other, weighing his words.

In the end it was I who suggested the answer that he refrained from uttering.

"Perhaps there was also a wish on your part," I said in a lower tone, "to distance yourself from Andres Fontana for good."

He nodded. Slowly at first, more forcefully afterwards.

"I was never able to forgive him altogether," he finally admitted with a heavy voice. "During my long mourning, in those dreadful months and years of pure grief, I cried only for Aurora. He, I only blamed. Not for having killed her: it was all an accident, that was always clear. But I did blame him in a certain way for having dragged her along with him, for having gotten her involved in something alien to her. For having, in a way, separated her from me, from my care, my protection . . ."

"So you decided to punish him. To keep his memory buried for more than thirty years in a basement full of dust, without a single human hand coming close to him to unearth him from oblivion."

He swallowed his emotions before continuing.

"It's a very crude way of expressing it, but perhaps you're right. I intentionally refused to assume responsibility for his legacy, and with this decision I also decided to push aside the memory of the man he was."

"Until some months ago, in light of this matter of Los Pinitos, you decided to pardon him. You thought that perhaps Fontana had been onto something after all, with his belated passion for those humble

Franciscans and his extravagant notion of the existence of a lost mission. So you decided to act."

A wistful smile became visible at the corner of his mouth. He leaned back on the sofa. Tense, sad, and tired. Like myself.

"Yes and no. When I found out through Rebecca about the urban aberration that was in the pipelines, I started to turn the matter over in my head. I recalled the walks that Aurora and he would take in the long afternoons of that last spring they were alive. All that fruitless effort came back to my mind, the work they never finished because death swept them away: their conjectures, their hopes, and especially their work's relevance to the present. Then I made some inquiries of my own and learned that Los Pinitos is presently under the town hall's custody, with no legitimate proprietor or recorded history."

"And you put two and two together."

"It didn't strike me as totally implausible that, among those lost documents, I might find some missing clue. But most important, I thought that the time had come to make peace with my past, and above all with that man who had meant so much in my life. To compensate for my unjust behavior and to try and pay some kind of tribute, half privately, half publicly, to the person and his work."

"So that's how it all began."

"Yes, Blanca. That is how my reconciliation got under way."

Chapter 34

The night advanced and there we were, facing each other, under the tenuous light of a corner lamp, without even a lousy glass of wine or some background music or a simple sip of water to attenuate the sorrow. There were no sounds to disturb us beyond those that occasionally slipped in from the street, muffled by the closed window.

The sadness was palpable. His feelings were no doubt true; in no way did I doubt his sincerity. But it wasn't enough. Beyond his words, which at times sounded both convincing and devastating, I felt once again the bitter sensation of having been betrayed by someone whom I had trusted blindly. As if history had repeated itself.

Coldly contemplated, hardly any of that had to do with the wound caused by my marriage's collapse. Alberto's disloyalty had been a devastating cyclone that turned my universe upside down. Daniel's manipulation was, by comparison, a simple summer storm. Even so, the emotional erosion that I was beginning to recover from had suddenly resumed. No matter how much he endeavored to string a clear and coherent speech regarding the genesis of that obscure plot, no matter how much he convinced me of his honesty, the fact was that I still felt deceived. I wanted to get to the bottom of the matter.

"So then, once you set up your foundation or whatever you wish to call it, why did you select me from among all the candidates?"

"They're your sons, right?" he suddenly asked, pointing to a picture on the shelf.

Next to the only spot of light left, sitting beside my keys, a Chinese restaurant flyer, and the replica of the missionary bell that he himself had given me, was the photograph that David and Pablo had sent me along with a pair of gloves and a Joaquin Sabina CD. *A belated happy birthday, Mother, as usual we're hopeless, forgive us,* they'd written on the enclosed card. The wet hair in their eyes, the laughter after an afternoon at the beach, the carefree breeze of the past.

"They're my sons, but that doesn't matter now."

As if he hadn't heard me, Daniel went up to the shelf where the photograph was.

"They look a lot like you," he said with a smile. The first halfway genuine smile that either of us had that night.

"Would you mind leaving it where it is?"

He returned my sons to their shelf and sat down again on the sofa.

"You never had any competition," he admitted, reclining against the back cushion. "You were the first to answer my call and I immediately knew that it was you I wanted here. I thought you amply fulfilled the requirements I was looking for. Just like that."

He spoke with earnestness now, his legs crossed and his tone natural.

"But my experience was hardly relevant to what was needed here," I countered. "My field of work, as you yourself know perfectly well, is applied linguistics."

"That was secondary. What I was looking for was an academic who was capable of doing the fieldwork methodically and accurately. Someone who spoke English and who had experience dealing with foreign universities. Besides, I was in a hurry. It was important to get started as soon as possible, the business of Los Pinitos was moving ahead quickly."

"Why did you insist on having someone from Spain? Why didn't you try to find someone within your own country?"

"Out of pure, absurd, and pathetic sentimentalism," he admitted.

"From the very start I felt that a compatriot could engage with Fontana more passionately. And to be completely honest, there was another criterion that to a large degree influenced the reason that I chose you: age. I assumed that someone with maturity would be able to approach the legacy from a wiser perspective."

He then unglued his back from the sofa and leaned forward, once more resting his elbows on his knees and again shortening the distance between us.

"I was looking for a professional and you for a new place in the world," he said, regarding me intently. "I needed something, you needed something, and both our paths crossed. Thanks to our contract, you achieved your objective, which I now know was to flee your surroundings as soon as possible. And mine, the urgent processing of my friend's legacy. Quid pro quo, Blanca, nothing else."

I turned my eyes away from his and focused on the window. Through it only a frame of black night could be discerned.

"Anyway," he added, "I want you to know that not a single day has gone by since I began to know you that I haven't thought of telling you everything."

"But you never did!" I yelled, venting the rage I thought I had under control. "That's the worst of it, Daniel! Had you been clear from the very beginning, we would have most likely reached the same place and you would have saved me a lot of pain."

"You're totally right, Blanca," he admitted. "I should have been clear with you from the start; this I know now, but I didn't before. Because I was not counting on you and me having any kind of relationship; I thought you'd simply be some employee who wouldn't know the whole story. And at first I didn't even intend to stay in Santa Cecilia. When Rebecca introduced us in Meli's Market, remember, I'd just come to meet you and make sure my project had gotten off the ground as I was hoping."

"Why didn't you leave afterwards? If you and I hadn't met, or if we'd let it rest at that first encounter, everything would have been so much easier."

"Because . . . sometimes things take an unexpected turn. Because . . . life is like this, Blanca. Sometimes plans are derailed . . ."

He got up and paced the room from one end to the other, which he accomplished in four or five strides, since the room was so small. Then he remained standing there as he went over the stages of our common journey from his point of view.

"I learned from you that the approach you were taking was not the one I had expected: you got much more deeply involved with Fontana and his world than I ever thought you would. I began to realize that I'd underestimated the extent of the task, the complexity of the legacy, and your attitude toward it. I decided not to leave. I rented an apartment, fetched from my home in Santa Barbara what I needed for the time being, and came back. For you to have me close whenever you needed me. Not to control you or manipulate you, but rather, simply, to be close to you and to accompany you on your path."

"Three months on my path is a long time. Three months in which you haven't told me one word—"

"Because I couldn't—because there was always something that held me back," he insisted. "Zarate was always nearby: I watched the growing closeness between you and him; I'd see you together on campus, in the cafeteria. I was sure that if I told you something . . . inconvenient about your fellowship, you'd feel obliged to inform him. An institutional duty, even a moral one, or am I mistaken?"

"Possibly," I admitted, much to my regret.

"Whether I like it or not, he's the department chairman; to deceive him is by extension to deceive the university. And that is something quite serious in my circumstances."

I stood up and massaged my skull, as if trying to relieve my brain or to pluck the murky ideas out of my head.

"You should have thought about that earlier, Professor Carter," I said, heading toward the door. "Much earlier. Now it's too late for everything. Even for you to stay here."

His face remained inscrutable as he observed me, as if wishing to transmit something through his clear, keen eyes. But he encountered the hardness of my shell, which I had been growing to protect myself from the rest of the world.

"There is one more reason," he added. "The last. The most fundamental, perhaps."

"What?"

"That I got to know you. That the next thing I knew, I was unable to
vanish as if nothing had occurred. I was too involved, too close to you."

An overwhelming weakness took hold of me.

"Please go, once and for all. It's no use for us to continue discussing
what could have been and never will be. I leave for Madrid next week;
there's nothing left for me to do here. I want to see my sons and return
to normalcy. It'll be hard to go back to my old life, but in it, at least,
I've got the coordinates clear and I know who's who."

He said nothing.

"You won't have to worry about my work," I added, my hand on
the doorknob. "Everything that was in the basement is practically
processed and organized; I've only got a few things to finish. What's
missing, if there really is something missing, I cannot answer for; that's
not in my contract. It's a shame that half of your project didn't reach
a satisfactory conclusion; I'm afraid it's too late now for any trace of
the mission you were looking for to turn up. You and your friends in
the coalition against the Los Pinitos project will have to swallow the
construction of the shopping mall or whatever other junk they choose
to build. The truth is, at this point I don't give a damn: as far as I'm
concerned, they could stick a nuclear waste dump there. But at least you
will have rescued your friend's soul from oblivion, which is no small
feat. After so many years of keeping him in limbo, you can finally ease
your conscience."

I opened the door, inviting him to leave. When he was already on
the landing, I remembered something and turned around.

"Wait."

From the shelf I grabbed the replica of the iron bell and gave it to him.

"I don't want to see it anymore. And I think the same goes for you."

Then I closed the door with a bang.

"Alone again, Blanca," I whispered to myself, slumping with my
back against the door. "More alone than ever."

Chapter 35

A combination of acetaminophen, coffee, and willpower made it possible for my world to get back on track the following day. After a night of restless sleep, I sat down to breakfast at dawn and as I ate my buttered toast I outlined my final tasks in that strange place. Then I set off to work, just as on every other day. Disillusioned and hurt, but back in the thick of things.

Throughout the day I tried to avoid everyone. I didn't even take a lunch break, so as not to bump into any of my colleagues or students in passing. I devoted myself only to the job at hand, shutting myself up and immersing myself in the last documents in the Fontana legacy to try to put them in some kind of order before I left Santa Cecilia. Regardless of who had devised my task—regardless of whether its sponsor was a solvent institution or a single human being with a turbulent past and emotional scores to settle—my responsibility was to carry it out with efficiency and thoroughness. Just as I'd agreed to do when I was hired.

My efforts at keeping isolated, however, failed: a few unforeseen interruptions spoiled everything.

The first was caused by Fanny. Past noon she showed up in my office with an amorphous sandwich in worn-out plastic wrap and a bottle of juice the color of cough medicine.

"I've noticed you haven't gone out for lunch; I imagine you must have lots of work. So I've brought you something," she announced, thrusting her arms toward me as if they were spring-loaded.

"Thank you very much, Fanny," I said, accepting her kind gesture.

Despite my feigned cordiality and her limited shrewdness, she must have perceived something in my face that unsettled her.

"Are you okay, Professor Perea? You don't look too good."

"I'm fine, Fanny, thank you very much," I lied. "Only a little bit busier than usual because I must finish this urgently. I return home very soon and must leave it all organized."

"When are you leaving?" she asked.

"Next Friday."

She stood staring at me without blinking, agape, her arms hanging limply at her sides. Then she turned around and stepped out into the hallway, talking to herself.

I hid the sandwich at the bottom of my bag so that she wouldn't suspect later that I'd never eaten it and continued with my work, but without any enthusiasm or energy.

Soon after, there was a rapping at the now open door and with it came the second interruption. I raised my head from one of the last texts regarding the secularization of the missions and, just a few yards away, was Luis Zarate.

I tried not to make it too plain that he was the last person in the world I wished to see; I'd even been coming in via the back stairs for the past couple of days instead of using the elevator to avoid having to pass by his office. At first it was due to my suspicions and later to my certainty regarding who was behind my fellowship; not sharing with him something so substantially linked to his own department felt like an overwhelming act of disloyalty on my part. But I still had to think, still needed time to clear my confused head and decide what to do, and so for the time being I'd avoided him. Seeing him at my door unsettled me.

"Did we have such a bad time on Saturday that you're running away from me?"

He spoke in jest, but I stammered before answering. No, we didn't have a bad time; quite the contrary, I could have said. Or: It was a lovely outing, a delicious dinner, and you're an attractive man. I feel at ease with you and we get along well. But I didn't say that either.

"I'm swamped, as you can see," I said instead, pointing to my desk covered with papers. I tried to sound credible, courteous, normal, but I was unable to convince him.

"Is that really all that's the matter?"

I noticed he was taking a couple of steps toward my desk and I immediately got up. As a defense, as a fake protection. I couldn't stand the idea of him seeing me fall apart.

"I haven't slept that well. Perhaps I had something for dinner that upset my stomach."

"You're sure there's no problem?" he insisted, taking a step closer.

"Sure, but I wanted to tell you that my work is coming to an end, and I've decided to go spend Christmas with my sons, so . . ."

"So you're leaving."

"Next week, along with the students. I was going to stop by your office later to tell you."

My lie clearly didn't convince him.

He took one last step. In the narrowness of my humble office, that meant he was already next to me.

"What's the matter, Blanca?" he whispered, extending a hand toward me.

I felt the heat of his fingers on my shoulder, but I didn't answer.

"You know you can count on me."

He came even closer, and I felt his breath. I remained silent: too confused, too tired, too fragile. His lips threatened to alight on mine, and I turned my face slightly, not allowing it yet not moving away from him. I heard his low voice next to my ear.

"Whatever it is, count on me," he whispered again, with his fingers still on my shoulder.

I could have screamed at the top of my lungs: Yes, I know, help me, get me out of this jam I've gotten myself into, make me forget everything and everyone, hold me tight, get me out of here! But I did not answer. Perhaps out of a sense of self-protection, perhaps not to further complicate matters. Afterwards, I just simply moved away from him, slowly.

At that very moment Fanny flew in like a whirlwind.

"Excuse me, Dr. Zarate! I didn't realize you were here!" she apologized hastily.

"Come on in, Fanny, come on in," he answered, resuming his cold department chairman's tone. "I've already finished talking to Professor Perea. I was just leaving. I insist, Blanca" was all he said in the way of a good-bye. "You know where I am."

"My mother wants to see you this evening, Professor Perea," Fanny announced the minute Luis was gone. Not giving me time to digest what had just happened between us; not allowing me a second to reflect. "As soon as I told her you were leaving soon," she went on in a rush, "she told me she wants to speak to you, that she might have something that interests you."

The idea of capping off that sad day with a courtesy visit to the elderly Darla Stern was about as tempting as taking a swig of turpentine. But it was true that Fanny spoke to me about her constantly, that on more than one occasion she told me how much she'd like for us to get together. And equally true was that I kept putting her off and making excuses, hoping that the encounter would never take place. I could imagine nothing less appealing than a face-to-face with an eccentric who most likely had nothing to offer beyond a rambling conversation and perhaps some dusty memory of Fontana that I no longer cared to hear. At that stage I was not in the least interested in the nature of their relationship, if it had been a strictly professional one or if at some point they took it a step further. But as a last goodwill gesture toward Fanny I felt obliged to accept the invitation.

"Okay, Fanny. Tell me where you live and when you want me to be there."

The third unexpected interruption, a further turn of the screw, came barely half an hour later. It was a call to my sturdy old office telephone, which unfortunately had no caller ID.

Daniel Carter. Again.

During the long hours of uncertainty after he had left my place the previous night and until I fell asleep, I'd resolved to get him out of my life for good, to avoid the slightest contact between us in the short period of time that was left before my departure. I wanted to forget that once upon a time I had crossed paths with an American colleague, tall and bearded, who spoke my language almost as well as I did; to rid myself of someone who had betrayed my trust and affection.

On hearing his voice, I thought of immediately hanging up, imagining that he was calling to reiterate his apologies and keep trying to peddle excuses. But I was mistaken. He sounded serious and firm. Not authoritative but almost.

"Don't hang up, Blanca, please. Listen to me just for a moment; this is important. I know Darla Stern wants to see you. She's also sent me a message, summoning me at eight. Just as she did you, I suppose. She says she wants to propose something to the two of us. Are you still there?"

"Yes."

"Good. Don't even dream of going to her house alone. Wait for me. I'll pick you up at your apartment and we'll go together."

"There's no need, thanks. I'll be able to get there on my own," I replied curtly.

A few seconds' pause, then:

"As you wish. But do not go before the appointed time, and don't go in without me. I'll be waiting at the door at eight."

. . .

The map Fanny had scribbled on half a piece of paper with almost childlike lines helped me find her house without any difficulty. From the end of the street I perceived a dark silhouette seated on the porch steps.

"Fanny won't be here," I announced coldly. "She told me she'd be at church but that she'd leave the door open. It seems her mother fell recently and can't walk."

At first, Daniel's reaction was evident not in his voice but in his hands. Standing up and facing me, he grabbed me by the shoulders with conviction and forced me to look him in the eye. Those eyes that, beneath the yellowish light of a streetlamp, didn't display the light-heartedness or irony that they had shown so many other times. Only sobriety and firmness. And perhaps a degree of concern.

Then he spoke without letting go of me.

"Listen well, Blanca. Although I stand by everything I said to you yesterday, I've been thinking hard about it and I understand your reaction perfectly well. I understand that you feel let down, that you no longer trust me and have decided to purge me from your life. If I had been in your shoes, I would have reacted the same way. Or worse. But what I now want to warn you about is something totally different. Something much more immediate."

I didn't answer. Or move.

"I'm completely ignorant of whatever it is we're going to encounter in there, but I have a feeling that it won't be good. I know how the woman we are going to see now used to be, and I very much doubt that the years have changed her. She always had a sharp tongue and I imagine still has. This is why I'm afraid that we haven't been invited here out of mere courtesy. I may be mistaken, and hope I am, but I have a suspicion that the only thing Darla wants to do is to stir up mischief and draw blood if the occasion presents itself. And if this is the case, I know beforehand that I won't be able to stand by and do nothing.

"What we're about to hear tonight perhaps will bring out the vilest side of me, the most despicable," he continued. "But I don't want you to misinterpret whatever happens in there. The fact that Darla and I may bring up certain affairs from the past doesn't mean that I'm anchored to them. I already told you yesterday that it's been a long time since I stopped clinging to what is lost; my boundaries between yesterday and today are clearly delineated. My dead have long been buried, and although I pour my soul into defending their memory, I am no longer with them. I am among the living. Here, now, with you. Do you understand, Blanca Perea? Do you understand me clearly?"

He waited for my reply without taking his gaze off mine. With his large hands clutching my shoulders firmly and his eyes staring straight at me, I finally assented with a slight nod. It was an impulsive movement, instinctive, one that I immediately regretted. I should have asked him to explain further. Or perhaps I should have left that very instant, fled from that dark past that had nothing to do with me.

But he gave me no choice. A strong squeeze of his hands on my shoulders conveyed his firm trust. And I was no longer able to turn back.

"Let's go. The sooner we're done, the better."

Chapter 36

With a couple of strides he climbed the four porch steps, knocked with his fist, and pushed open the door without waiting for a reply. I followed, going straight into a dark and gloomy living room crammed with furniture and junk.

A raspy voice emerged from the back amid the dense smell of decay and a lack of ventilation.

"For weeks I've been meaning to have you both over for dinner, but the news that Professor Perea is about to leave for good has caught me by surprise. I hope you can forgive me for not having had the time for preparations."

A lamp lit the room with a deathlike glow. In front of the old woman's armchair was a television with its volume turned off, projecting chaotic reflections on the nearby surroundings. Just as I remembered her, she had a thick mane of hair dyed a Nordic blond. Her face was creased by a thousand wrinkles and her lips were painted an intense red as if ready for a big party. However, her clothes, a tracksuit of uncertain color, indicated that she didn't expect to go anywhere.

"But if you're hungry, serve yourselves something; there must a leftover chicken leg from the other day, and I think there's also half a bag of bread and a cabbage salad from last week."

The mere thought of eating there was nauseating, but Daniel responded politely.

"We're fine like this, thanks, Darla."

"Take a seat at least. Make yourselves at home."

"We're in a bit of a hurry," he lied again. "So it's best you tell us why you have called us and then we'll let you watch TV in peace."

The old woman clicked her tongue.

"Ah, Carter, Carter, you're always in a rush . . . It's as if I were seeing you in the old days all over again . . . Either you were off to your classes or to one of those political assemblies or to demand something from the chairman; always hurrying like a madman."

He remained unperturbed. She clicked her tongue again.

"Those were good times, right, kid?"

Not a word for an answer.

"Oh, well," she added before his persistent silence. "I see you don't have time for a nostalgic romp. Too bad, because we could've had a wonderful evening, you and me, sharing reminiscences. Do you remember when—"

"Professor Perea and I would like to know once and for all why you have called us."

His tone was starting to shed the layer of false courtesy with which he'd started the conversation. Darla sighed theatrically.

"Well, if you insist on not wasting your valuable time on a chat between old friends, then let's move on to what's important."

"And what *is* so important? Can you please tell me?"

"Business, my friend. At the end of the day, no matter how intellectual or spiritual we pretend to be, we always wind up tangled up in money matters."

"You don't say . . ." Daniel said with obvious uninterest.

"Business, money: I sell, you buy—if you want what I have to offer, of course."

"I doubt it, but clue us in, just in case."

"Let me first greet our guest. How do you do, Professor Perea?"

"Fine, thank you," I answered sullenly.

I did not like the tone that the visit was taking on. I didn't like

Darla Stern, I didn't like the way she addressed Daniel, and above all I didn't like the way that I anticipated she'd treat me. She took a good look at me, squinting as she tilted her head to one side.

"Height-wise they're both the same size, wouldn't you say? And equally skinny, but this one looks a little more serious, right, Carter? The other one laughed more; she was more, more . . . And the hair color isn't—"

"Stop, Darla," he ordered sharply.

"Forgive me, dear, it was a mere observation," she replied, undaunted. "Well, let's get down to what brings us together. From what I understand, Professor Perea has been rummaging through the papers of our dear departed Andres Fontana."

Before I was able to answer, Daniel spoke on my behalf.

"Professor Perea, as we told you previously, has simply been working for the university, classifying his legacy."

"Pardon me while I laugh! The university doesn't give a shit about Fontana's legacy; his things had been living with the rats for years. Until suddenly—surprise, surprise!—a little Spaniard comes to stick her nose in them. And just then the illustrious professor shows up again, to stroll around the campus like in the good old days."

"You see," Daniel said without making an effort to hide his cynicism. "Mere coincidences."

We stood in the middle of the room; the atmosphere was becoming heavier by the minute, more surrealistic, with distorted shafts of light flickering from the silent movement of the images.

"Don't be a smart-ass with me, Carter. I've been told that you've turned into a real academic celebrity, but I know you for more years than either one of us could wish. And this story sounds fishy. *Awfully* fishy. You disappeared as if escaping from the plague; didn't stay to mourn the dead. You went missing, very much lost. And now, suddenly, here you are again and who knows with what intentions? But you can't fool me. Maybe I wasn't as erudite as you all, but I can still add two and two together."

"No one doubts that."

"This is why, even though I don't quite know what you're looking for in particular, I think I have something that might be of interest to you. Something that this one"—she jerked her chin contemptuously in my direction—"has been searching for. My little Fanny has told me. Ever since she was a child I instructed her to tell me everything that her brain registered. She's been my window to the world for years. She's told me that you need some papers of Fontana's that are not turning up. And I imagine that it's in your interest to find them as soon as possible if, as it seems, you're going to leave so soon . . ."

"You wouldn't have kept anything that didn't belong to you, right?"

There was a tinge of astonishment in Daniel's voice. The old woman answered swiftly.

"I took whatever I felt like: I was the one who buried him! Because you, his bosom friend, his adopted son, didn't even show up at the funeral."

"I had other things to take care of, unfortunately," he replied with bitter irony. "To bury my wife in her native country, for example."

"And how many times did you come back to visit your professor's grave? How many times did you worry about addressing what he left behind?"

"I don't visit graves; neither Fontana's, nor my wife's, nor anyone else's. They're in my memory and in my heart. I don't give a damn about what is left behind in cemeteries," he said, exasperated. "And now let's stop wasting time, if you don't mind. Tell us finally what it is you've got that could interest us."

He'd answered her first question about his lack of visits to Fontana's grave, but to the second, his unconcern for the legacy, he turned a deaf ear. She disregarded it and resumed her tirade.

"A bunch of boxes full of documents older than dirt, that's what I have. The last he worked on in his lifetime. In your obsession to flee from everything that happened here, it must have also slipped your mind that, in the weeks prior to the accident, Guevara Hall was being renovated and it was impossible to do anything normally," she went on. "That's why he took all the papers to his place: so he could study from there. I helped him carry everything. I can still recall how heavy the damn boxes were, I even broke a couple of nails hauling them. I was clueless as to what they contained; I don't understand that fucking language of yours and was never interested in academic matters. But he spent a good period of time absorbed with all that crap. He had it strewn all over the place until the very end."

Daniel half opened his mouth but was unable to say a thing.

"Where are they now?" I asked, unable to keep quiet any longer. The old lady guffawed.

"Do you two think I'm senile and am going to tell you just like that?"

"What do you want in exchange?" Daniel asked abruptly, coming back to reality.

"I've already told you: money, dear. What else would I want? I'm a destitute old woman who lives in a stinky house. Guarantee me a better future and you'll have the documents to do whatever you want with; you can wipe your ass with them as far as I'm concerned."

I figured he'd stop her from blackmailing him right then and there. I didn't think he'd give in to such a low form of coercion. Surely there was a way of getting possession of those boxes in a more conventional and less vile manner. But, as in so many other things lately, I was mistaken. It took only seconds for negotiations to begin, and to my surprise with me involved.

"First we'll have to check and see if they're documents that interest Professor Perea."

"Wonderful: you can see them, talk all you need between yourselves, and afterwards determine if the deal is to your liking or not. All I know is that I'm going to give the two of you only one opportunity. There will be a lawyer here tomorrow at ten. You'll have fifteen minutes to evaluate the contents of the boxes. If in the end you decide that they're of interest, you can take them. If not, I'll make sure that all those papers are destroyed in the afternoon, just in case you sophisticated intellects think you can trick this old lady into giving up this material by some other means. The price, by the way, won't be too high, something very, very symbolic."

"As symbolic as what?"

"A two-bedroom apartment in a residential care facility for people with special needs."

A hearty laugh emerged from her throat, cutting and bitter.

"You've lost your mind, lady," Daniel told her.

"Truth be told, I'm being more than generous with you, Carter. If you'd given me what belonged to me from the very beginning, I would have undoubtedly gained much more."

"I don't know what you're talking about."

The old lady took a while to answer. For the first time since we'd arrived, she seemed to be weighing her words to hit the bull's-eye dead on.

"You kept Fontana's money that should have gone to us," she finally uttered through gritted teeth. "The money he put in your wife's name in his will when she sweet-talked him into it."

"Be careful what you say, Darla," Daniel warned, pointing a finger threateningly.

"I know perfectly well what I'm talking about. Your wife seduced Fontana. And he ended up leaving her his money, which eventually fell into your hands. The money that should have been my daughter's and mine, if you two had never showed up around here and if he'd never fallen in love with her like an absolute idiot."

A shiver ran through me as I listened. Daniel answered, barely parting his lips.

"You don't know what you're talking about . . ."

"I know perfectly well what I mean. Andres Fontana was crazy about your wife and she played along. There she was, always by his side, with her long hair and permanent smile. Each time she showed up at the department, he'd be all giddy. You would hardly give her a few minutes of your time: you'd give her a kiss, joke around a little with her, and then go back to your work. Then she'd go off to see him and he'd devour her with his eyes; he'd turn into someone else, affectionate like a little lamb. During all the years I knew him, I never heard him laugh so much as when he was with her. He adored her, Carter, and you didn't even realize it."

"She's only trying to provoke you, Daniel," I told him in a whisper. "Let's get out of here. Don't let her continue."

"See? This one is bamboozling you the same way. Because this little friend of yours, just like the other one, also has a husband somewhere, right?"

I preferred not to say a thing. He, on the other hand, was unable to contain himself.

"What the hell difference does it make to *you?* Leave her alone!" he roared. Suddenly, perhaps to protect me, perhaps to restrain himself, he firmly grabbed one of my hands. "This is between you and me, Darla. Don't even think of attacking her!"

"In the end, history always repeats itself: that's how foolish and silly we humans are," she went on, unfazed. "The smart young woman seduces the mature man, and the mature man, who thought himself even smarter, ends up falling for her like a schoolboy. I don't know if you have someone waiting for you back in Santa Barbara or wherever it is you live when you're not monkeying around with this one here, but Fontana did have someone when your wife bewitched him. He had me."

Now it was a loud guffaw from Daniel that cut her off.

"Fontana didn't have anything with you. He was only a good man who felt sorry for you and your daughter."

"He was mine until you and your wife came along!" the old lady shrieked, furiously ungluing her back from her armchair. "He cared for Fanny and me, took us under his wing when my useless drunk of a husband left us. But then the wonderful Carters appeared on the scene to ruin it all. And when your wife dazzled him, he fell into her net and pushed us aside."

"He was tired of you, Darla," Daniel replied, trying to stay calm but barely able to. "Tired of your whims and demands, of your impertinent behavior toward him and the rest of us. I'm unaware of what there could have been between you two before my wife and I settled in Santa Cecilia; he chose not to tell me. Perhaps you had a little adventure—maybe so—but what I do know for sure is that, when we landed here, whatever affection he might have had for you at some point was over. Aurora and I were a means of liberation for him, a breath of fresh air. Our presence allowed him to distance himself further from you."

"You know what?" she went on as if she'd heard nothing he said.

"Everything that happened afterwards was your fault. You should have kept a closer eye on her. It was your responsibility: you're the one who took her from her country, separating her from her family and her world. You dragged her to a foreign land, but you were incapable of protecting her sufficiently. Perhaps all our sorrows could have been avoided if you'd been paying more attention."

What he had told me the night before in my apartment came to mind. His own thoughts on the matter, the long blame that for so many years he laid on Fontana . . .

"What the fuck do you know about my life with my wife?" he bellowed.

Then, with my hand still in his, he kicked a chair with such fury that it ended up crashing against the wall, littering the floor with fragments of fallen souvenirs and porcelain. The old lady ignored the damage and continued.

"I could see you both, I watched you, and was aware of everything. She came and went as she liked. And you, meanwhile, in your office, banging away at that typewriter all day long, which resounded throughout the entire floor of Guevara Hall. I can still hear you pounding at those keys: *click! click! click! click!* And then those blows you'd give the carriage return, like an animal: *boom! boom!* And once more the typing would start up: oh, God, what torture! But you were oblivious to it all; your professional aspirations came first. You wanted to get out of here, remember? Santa Cecilia was becoming too stifling; you wanted to go to Berkeley and make your career at a great university."

"Stop it, Darla . . ." He was trying to recover his composure, but his patience seemed to be running out.

"You were the most popular professor in the university, the most charismatic, the funniest, the handsomest," she hammered away. "And when you weren't locked up in your office or teaching to crowded classrooms or inviting your students to your home for parties that went on into the small hours, you'd spend your time rousing them on campus with your harangues against the Vietnam War and your fiery speeches against the system. Did you forget that too? You were reprimanded on several occasions, and proceedings were filed against you."

"Stop it, Darla. Drop it, please . . ." he insisted.

"Fontana and your wife died because of your selfishness," she hissed, "because you didn't want to know what there was between them, because you were too absorbed in your own world. You should've been more aware and not allowed them to become so friendly. You should've pulled them apart. If you'd done so, neither your wife nor my man would have ended up dead on the side of a highway."

A tense silence once again enveloped the gloomy room. I could perceive how Daniel was preparing to answer: how he was processing the information, ordering his thoughts, choosing his words. Then I realized that everything was going too far. Darla was dragging him to the abyss and he was following in her macabre game.

I let go of his hand and grabbed his arm.

"Let's go," I urged him, trying to pull him away. "Right now."

"One minute, Blanca. One more minute and I'll be done."

Changing his tone of voice, he once again turned to the old lady.

"Too much time has elapsed and there's no turning back, Darla. Nothing of what you told me today is going to bring the dead back to life. Your rants, true or not, can't make me suffer more than I already have, but that was the past and I made it through that terrible time. So, please, let's get this meeting over with."

"You just make sure you get me the money for an apartment for people like me, and everything will work out in the end."

"For people like you? So needy or so nasty?"

"Well, well," she said, feigning a smile, "I see that you haven't lost your way with words, Professor. I gather that it wasn't altogether corroded by all that junk you took. Has the great academic told you what he did when he fled Santa Cecilia? Did he tell you why he lost his post at this university? I only know part of the story, but I think it's very interesting. Tell her, Carter; tell her while you fuck your new Spanish bitch tonight, if you still get a hard-on."

"Now we're definitely leaving, Blanca," he said, not responding to Darla's obscenities. "And forgive me for this wretched spectacle; she's nothing but a pathetic old lady bearing a grudge for the last thirty years."

"Don't be so hard on me, dear," Darla said hypocritically, with feigned docility. "Tomorrow at ten. Don't forget."

"We'll think about it. Now, if you'll allow us, we're out of here. We've already heard enough crap this evening."

Leaving the old woman stewing in her armchair, we headed toward the door. I was hardly able to hold back my relief that we would finally breathe the fresh night's air, go out into the real world once more. However, as we were about to open the door, Darla's voice brought us to a halt.

"Carter!"

It was more of a rasping croak than a scream.

We both turned our heads, and in a flash I realized I'd been wrong when I thought Darla had nothing left to hurl at us and we could finally get away.

She was still slumped in her chair, her lipstick smeared and her cheap doll's hair disheveled as she prepared to hurl her last bomb.

"Maybe none of this would've happened had you been capable of giving your wife what she'd wanted more than anything."

A chilling silence preceded the explosion.

"A child, for example."

Chapter 37

———

Darla Stern burst out laughing one last time. A ghastly, biting laugh. I automatically looked at Daniel's face and saw how he half closed his eyes and slowly drew air through his nose. I anticipated his reaction and gripped his arm firmly, but he freed himself from my grasp and took a step forward, raising a clenched fist into the air. He was blindly going after her. I reacted quickly, knowing that I had to get him out of there right away no matter how. Get him away from Darla, from that skeletal body weighed down by age, arthritis, and sheer bitterness.

I planted myself before him, placing my hands firmly against his chest, halting his advance like a wall. With his fist still in the air and his hair disheveled, he barraged Darla with insults. Suddenly I was able to muster some degree of authority.

"Enough. She's sick and just provoking you. Don't fall for her game; don't let yourself be dragged into it."

With great difficulty I managed to keep him somewhat immobilized for a few moments that seemed an eternity, until I finally noticed his body relaxing slightly. Once again grabbing him by the arm, I pulled him with all my strength and was able to drag him away from that grotesque scene.

I did not ask him if he'd driven or not. I just listened to the sound of our footsteps on the wet pavement as we walked aimlessly for a long time. Countless questions assailed me, countless doubts. But I preferred not to talk or force him to do so. Then at one point in our erratic walk he halted and looked at me.

"Aurora was pregnant. She'd already had two miscarriages; this was our third hope, the most advanced of all her pregnancies. She had problems carrying them to term. Her yearning to be a mother was immense but, all in all, she faced adversity with admirable strength of character. She was magnificent, an extraordinary person."

He said nothing else and I, quite simply, assented, not knowing or judging. We moved on, once more walking in silence along deserted streets and squares. Everything was closed at that hour: the restaurants, the shops, the café. With the exception of a car now and then, we seemed to be the only ones wandering around in the area.

"You must have suspected too at some point, right?"

I surprised myself by asking a question like that, taken aback by my audacity, my insolent invasion of his privacy. But my subconscious knew that I needed to know. And he understood.

"At some point, no; I thought about it hundreds of times, Blanca. Thousands."

He let a few minutes go by, then cleared his throat with difficulty and continued.

"I spent three atrocious years detached from the world, absent, lost, disconnected from reality. Three years is plenty of time to do a few stupid things and also to think a lot."

"What conclusion did you reach?"

"That he silently, quietly fell in love with Aurora," he said in a troubled voice. "And she never realized it."

He again fell silent, pensive. Then went on:

"He was winding down, disenchanted after tumultuous relationships that never quite bore fruit, getting older and ready to spend his days wrapping up his career and his life without any more headaches."

"And then you appeared with her . . ."

"Then she appeared, full of life and enchantment. With her joie de vivre and tenderness, with the soul of the old country to which he had never returned. And he, who in spite of his bull-like body was a man with a fragile heart, was as we all are in the end: when he thought he'd seen it all, he simply fell in love."

I noticed a slight tremor in his voice and chose not to continue asking questions. I didn't need to know more; all the pieces were in place. Completing the puzzle, however, hadn't come free of charge, not for me and certainly not for him. His pain was visible in his drawn face, the tenseness of his body, and his long silences.

Our steps took us to his apartment. Perhaps I had instinctively directed them there. I accompanied him inside. Without even turning on the light, he took off his jacket, dropped it on the floor, and collapsed onto a couch.

With the lights turned off, I headed toward the kitchen area. It wasn't too hard: there was hardly any furniture or other obstacles to avoid; just like in my apartment, it was a temporary home without any evidence of the souls who had happened to pass through it year after year. I searched in the half-empty cabinets, the only light being that of a streetlamp coming through the window. Among half a dozen unmatched cups and several soup bowls, I found half a bottle of Four Roses bourbon. I poured two generous glasses and handed him one. He didn't thank me; he didn't even look at me. He just accepted it and took a long sip. I did the same. Our battered brains needed some help to digest the sinister memories dredged up that night and to placate the pain of desolation after the battle.

We didn't exchange a word until, after some time had passed, I got up. Daniel remained seated, ensconced in the darkness, with his legs apart and his hands together, holding the empty glass. I took it from him and put it on the table. I sat on his armrest and passed my hand over his hair, his beard, his still-contorted face.

"I'm going home."

Before I reached the door, he called me. In a husky voice, dark, as if it came from the bottomless well of the relived horror.

I turned around.

"Don't go. Stay with me tonight."

I returned to his side without a word and curled up next to him on the couch to keep him company while each of us wrestled with our own demons. Finally, without turning the light on and without taking his eyes off the wall, he began to talk.

"I've never been able to find a coherent explanation that justifies my senseless behavior during those years; I don't know if it was an act of rebellion or cowardice or a simple animal reaction to the desperation and pain, but after the accident I couldn't bear the idea of remaining alone in Santa Cecilia. I chose to leave without even finishing the semester, without telling anyone anything, and without the slightest clue where I'd end up. After wandering up and down the Pacific coast of Mexico, I ended up staying for almost three years in a fishing village next to Zihuatanejo. Three years in which I did nothing except torture my body and soul: I didn't read a single book, didn't open a single newspaper or write a single line. All I did was cram my body with all the shit I could lay my hands on, to isolate myself in my agony. I dressed like a beggar and hardly spoke to anyone. I'd stare at the ocean and take all kinds of crap; that's all I did."

"Until Paul Cullen went in search of you," I added, recalling our conversation on the day I met Rebecca's ex-husband. "On Thanksgiving night you told me that he'd been a witness to your own hell."

He smiled grimly in the darkness.

"Fortunately I must have had occasional moments of clarity, because after some time I called the Cullens. And then Paul came and, on seeing my state, stayed awhile. He cut my hair and nails, shaved me, and forced me to eat, as if I were a child. He dressed my wounds and the bites I had all over my body and hugged me the way he held his little children when they had fevers or nightmares."

"But he was unable to make you return . . ."

"I wasn't ready yet, and he understood it; I needed more time to grieve. I don't know why I allowed myself to hit rock bottom," he added, shrugging. "I swear to you that I haven't the slightest idea. But in the end I was able to snap out of it. For Aurora's sake and for my own: for her memory and for my sanity and dignity. When I finally recovered enough to realize what I'd become, I discovered that, at thirty-seven, I was nothing but a recovering addict, lonely as a mangy dog, poorer than a rat, and without any immediate prospects for work. Despite all that, I learned to live anew, standing upright, holding my head up high. Ready to fight to be happy again, but perhaps not altogether ready for someone to suddenly kick down the door that I thought had been locked for so long."

. . .

The sun's first rays were inundating the apartment when I woke up. It took me only a couple of seconds to get my bearings and remember the previous night in a flash. I was still lying on the sofa, but the spot Daniel had occupied was empty. From behind a closed door in the rear of the apartment, I could hear the sound of water running in the shower. On the floor there was a pair of running shoes that were not there before: evidence of an early-morning jog, I figured. I didn't know if he'd been able to rest at all, but I imagined not.

When I stood up my head was throbbing, my mouth felt furry, my joints were stiff and my neck sore. Barefoot and sleepy, I prepared a pot of coffee. The two glasses we'd been drinking from were in the sink, the bottle of bourbon in the garbage, empty.

He appeared a few minutes later. With wet hair, clean clothes, and glassy eyes, he walked into the kitchen area, rolling up the sleeves of the black shirt he was wearing. Black as his mood, dark as his soul. We didn't exchange a word; I simply handed him a cup of coffee. He brought his two hands toward mine. With his left he grabbed the cup, removed it from my fingers, and placed it on the counter. With his right hand he drew me toward him.

"Come here." He hugged me. "Thanks for staying. It's been an awfully long night. And very sad—a night of sharp knives. I never thought ghosts could come back with such force."

I leaned against him with my face on his chest and closed my eyes, still half-asleep. We remained like that for a long time.

Chapter 38

—————

When we finally returned to the present, Daniel shared with me the decisions he had made.

"Are you really going to give her the money for an apartment in exchange for some boxes full of papers that you don't even know the contents of?" I asked in disbelief.

"I'd rather run that risk than have her burn them or shred them. Besides, it's Fontana's own money that will pay for it, the inheritance he decided to leave Aurora, not imagining that their lives would both end together. I've never touched it except, as I told you, to pay for your work here. But there's plenty more; at first it was his savings and a not-inconsiderable insurance policy, and in time all of it has accrued into a considerable sum. I always believed that I'd end up donating it to the university or to some humanitarian cause. I never would have spent it on myself."

"I still don't understand."

"I've got no interest whatsoever in providing Darla with the slightest quality of life in her declining years; as far as I'm concerned, I couldn't care less if the worms eat her. But at least I'm comforted by the thought that in the long run this will benefit poor Fanny by getting her out of that house and providing her with a respectable home that someday will be hers. And from that perspective I don't think it's the worst solution. There's no doubt in my mind that he would have approved of my allocating his money for that purpose."

I did not insist, since it was none of my business, but I kept turning it over in my head while he spoke to his bank on the telephone and made arrangements.

At ten o'clock on the dot, we ended up back at Darla Stern's place. The morning light did not diminish the gut-wrenching atmosphere. Everything remained as sordid as on the previous night: scattered junk, the overturned chair, the mute television, and the nauseating deathlike smell floating in the air. The old lady was still seated in her chair, probably not having gone to bed the entire night. The only difference was that she remained silent, half-lethargic, with eyes closed. Perhaps sedated, perhaps exhausted. Or, quite simply, pretending.

A heavyset man with metal-framed glasses and a large gold ring on his pinky finger introduced himself as her legal representative, ready to take care of the transaction.

"Follow me, please."

Through a side door in the kitchen he led us to the garage that was dirty and in shambles. Then he opened another door using great effort, pushing it with his shoulder until it gave. Moving to one side, he invited us to step into a combination toolshed and garbage dump with hardly any space to move about inside, filled as it was with mountains of trash bags and piles of decades-old newspapers. Beneath the light of a weak bulb covered in grime and dead insects, the lawyer pointed to a bunch of boxes stacked against the wall.

While Daniel negotiated with him without bothering to hide his animosity, I opened one of the boxes to examine the object of the blackmail. In the midst of such squalid surroundings, I was unable to hold back a sigh of relief. I did not need to rummage too much to realize that it all seemed to match the rest of Fontana's papers. There, most likely, was what I'd been missing for weeks, almost months, in which the common thread of my compatriot's work had slipped through my hands like a slithery reptile. Yellowish, crumpled, and disorderly, those papers nonetheless would fill in some of the holes in the last period of the legacy.

Daniel's voice brought me out of my reverie; all he had to do was pronounce my name in an interrogative tone. I answered with a brief nod. He then took a checkbook out of his inside jacket pocket and signed several checks that went straight into the lawyer's ringed hand. Darla, seemingly ignorant of it all, continued to drowse back in the drawing room.

It took us several hours to get everything out of that creepy garage and into the trunk and backseat of Daniel's Volvo, and required two trips. We hardly spoke during the whole operation. It was he who finally broke the silence.

"And now what do we do?"

"I don't know, Daniel, I don't know . . ." I whispered. I took a deep breath. "I sense what you're thinking and I'm afraid the answer is no. It's too late: I'm already out of the story. And besides, I take off in no time, you know that."

I kept my eyes fixed on the boxes while I felt his on me.

"You can't or you won't?"

"I can't take care of this; it's too much material. And after everything that has happened over these past couple of days, I hardly have any strength left. I wouldn't be able to do it in so short a period of time: it's enormous, can't you see?" I said, pointing helplessly to the brimming boxes.

"You don't know if you want to."

I headed toward his bathroom without answering him or asking for his permission and washed my filthy hands. Around me were the meager toiletries of a man accustomed to living alone: toothpaste and a toothbrush, a razor, and a large towel hanging from a rack on the wall. The dirty exercise clothes from that morning were piled in a corner; on a shelf a radio. Not a trace of anything unnecessary.

"A lot of unexpected things have happened in the last couple of days . . ." I said, coming near him again while I finished drying my hands on my pants.

He hadn't moved; his attention was concentrated on the documents. Or so it seemed.

"Things that have changed us both—pulled us apart and brought us together—"

"But you keep thinking that I deceived you," he interrupted.

We raised our eyes at the same time. His light, mine dark. His tired, mine too.

"I haven't quite been able to convey to you how sorry I am," he went on. "I could repeat it from dawn to dusk, and I still wouldn't be able to forgive myself for having been such a boor with you. I've behaved like a fool and a coward. I understand how you feel and I'd give whatever it would take to be able to start over on a different footing. But unfortunately it's no longer possible, Blanca. Now we can only look straight ahead; there's no turning back. This is why I'm asking you to let me put the counter back to zero, so that we can start all over with no hard feelings."

We still stood before the boxes, motionless, our arms crossed.

"Everything would be over by next week," he added. "On the day of your departure, the deadline to lodge any appeal against the Los Pinitos project expires. You wouldn't even have to change your return ticket."

"But there's a much easier solution, Daniel: you take over. You can do this work as well as I can. Just as you told me, there's no need to be a specialist in any one field. Simply be accurate and methodical."

"There's not enough time. I could never move at your speed; I'd need to go back to the earlier material, familiarize myself with all of it to know exactly what I'm looking for. And I'm afraid it's too late. With so little time left, you're the only person right now who has a precise idea of what it's all about: the background, the specific gaps that need to be filled in, the connections between one set of documents and another, the pieces that need to match."

. . .

I left my apartment firm in my refusal and headed for my office. That very afternoon I would conduct my last Spanish culture class, and I still had work to do before it.

No matter how hard I tried to clear my mind and return to normal, the events and emotions of the last couple of days had been so intense that they affected my mood and turned my feelings upside down. I had difficulty concentrating on the last batches of papers and kept making mistakes at my computer keyboard. My mind was elsewhere.

After a period of total unproductiveness, I detached my gaze from the screen and directed it toward the piles of ordered and classified documents that had been Fontana's messy legacy three months earlier.

With no hope left of concentrating on my work, I leaned back in my chair to stop and think about him. I recalled his roundish figure in the old photos in the conference room; his dark beard, his lively, keen eyes. I mentally went over his writings, his letters, the countless notes written with his forceful strokes. I re-created the fifty-six-year path that fate had allowed him to follow. At first I had imagined that he'd died at a much more advanced age. "My old professor," Daniel often called him, and now Daniel was older than Andres Fontana had ever been.

Almost unwillingly, I began imagining Fontana and Aurora's final night and what their tragic end would have been like. Blinding headlights, sharp turns, brakes screeching. She, all contorted, her fingers like hooks grasping him when the countdown had already began. More glaring lights, broken glass, screams. The tapping of raindrops when everything came to a standstill, then silence.

I got up and approached the window. Leaning against the window frame, I contemplated the campus, practically deserted at that time of the afternoon. Students were wrapping up their last classes or preparing for exams as the autumn was coming to an end and winter approached. There were piles of leaves on the grass, and the branches of trees boldly displayed their nakedness.

The words of Darla Stern returned to my memory, dragging with them what was perhaps the last great certainty in the professor's existence. She was convinced that he'd been in love with Aurora. Daniel, from another perspective, thought the same. Were they both right? Was that the truth? The miner's son captivated by the wife of his friend and pupil, someone whom he'd never be able to have. Deeply attracted to that young and vivacious compatriot, separated by a barrier that he'd never be able to cross.

I turned away from the window and looked back at the pile that throughout the months had constituted the legacy, now in order. A vague yet nagging idea began to take shape, a premonition, a hunch that told me there was something among those papers that might corroborate what Daniel and Darla believed. Something that I had come across, that I'd read at some point without quite being able to grasp its meaning.

I glanced at my watch. Five minutes before my last class in Santa Cecilia. The first good-bye.

An hour later, when the session had lost any resemblance whatsoever to an academic encounter and we were busy exchanging e-mail addresses for that visit to Spain that all my students promised to make at some unspecified date, in the darkest corner of my brain a light went on. Tiny as a match in the middle of a pitch-dark clearing, almost imperceptible, but bright enough to shed light on my memory and guide me on my search.

As I quickly made my way back to my office, my conviction grew. I rushed in, knelt in front of one of the boxes of papers, and began to rummage in it with both hands. Then it appeared. A yellowing piece of paper on which Fontana, on an old-fashioned typewriter, had written out the first stanza of a poem by Luis Cernuda. One more fragment filed away like so many other of Fontana's writings.

Four lines from the poem "Where Oblivion Dwells," with four additional lines handwritten beneath them.

Wherein oblivion dwells,
In the vast gardens without aurora
Where I am but the memory of a stone buried amid nettles
Above which the wind flees its insomnia

Gardens without dawn
Without Aurora
Without
You

As soon as I'd read it, tears came to my eyes.

Removing the malicious stain that Darla Stern was eager to impose on Fontana, which had hounded Daniel in his gloomiest moments, Andres Fontana's true feelings surfaced between the verses. They expressed his silent love for the unexpected arrival from Spain who, without intending to, graced the last stretch of his life with a fullness he'd been longing for in his exile.

Echoes of his native tongue, of his country and his childhood. Evocations relegated to memory's back room, sayings and exclamations that he hadn't heard in more than three decades. Cooking pots by the firelight, quince jelly, Ave Maria Purisima. Her scent, the young laugh, the involuntary brush of her skin. Reason trying to rein in his feelings, which, wild, growing out of control, disobeyed.

A silent passion hidden from the world. Even from her, perhaps. But alive and real, powerful. Andres Fontana and Aurora Carter. The old professor long exiled and the Mediterranean woman who came by the hand of his pupil to that land that didn't belong to either one of them. So unlike in everything. So close at their end.

Suddenly, strangely, in a hasty connection, I grasped something else, and for a moment the dense fog that for months had settled over me cleared. In contemplating Fontana's passion for Aurora, I also realized something about Alberto. Through them I understood that what drove him away from me was the force of an unexpected love that crossed his path just as it could have crossed mine. It blindsided him.

In spite of Alberto's ineptitude with me, in spite of what was reproachable and reprehensible in his behavior and of all the pain that he'd caused me, the old professor's love helped me understand that, before the turns that destiny unexpectedly places before us, reason is sometimes useless.

. . .

There was not a soul left in Guevara Hall when I came out of my office, only closed doors and the sad echoes of the empty hallways.

On arriving back at Daniel's place, I found him seated before his working desk, in a total lack of concentration. "Come in!" he simply yelled when I rang. He didn't even get up to open the door for me.

He was slouched in the armchair, barefoot, his hands interlaced at the back of his neck, a chewed pencil between his teeth: the spitting image of a person with a mental block. Around him, strewn about the floor, were fragments of material extracted at random from the boxes he had received from Darla.

He didn't change posture on seeing me. Nor did he seem surprised or greet me. He simply moved his reading glasses to the tip of his nose and stared above them.

"You look terrible; let's go for a walk," I said from the door.

I waited for him on the street. It took him only a couple of seconds to appear.

"What this morning I said no to, now I say yes," I announced after we'd walked a dozen yards or so in silence. "I agree to process the contents of all the boxes that Darla has kept. I'm ready to tackle the task of trying to piece together the end of the legacy."

"You can't imagine—"

"But I want you to know the reason why I'll do it," I interrupted. "It's not because of the Los Pinitos issue, or out of professional ambition, or for you. I'll be doing it exclusively for Fontana. For the Andres Fontana whose life I have reconstructed for these past few months, for my commitment to him. To try and make sure his efforts don't fall into oblivion, like his old mission. I'll be doing it only for him. Keep that in mind, Daniel. Solely for him."

We kept walking without looking at each other, but out of the corner of my eye I noticed that his demeanor had changed.

"And don't count your chickens before they hatch," I warned him. "I've got conditions. The first is regarding my departure: I'm still leaving, no matter what, on the twenty-second. The second has to do with you. I didn't lie to you before: the amount of work involved is immense and I'm not going to be able to deal with it all in the short period of time I have left. That's why I need your help: I'll set the pace, but I need your eyes, your hands, and your head next to me one hundred percent for all the hours that are necessary, and without a guarantee of reaching any conclusion in time. So get ready to temporarily ditch your end-of-the-twentieth-century novelists, because you're going to have to cast your eyes much further back."

He came to an abrupt halt and turned to me. The worried frown of a while earlier had completely dissipated as if blown away by the evening wind.

"I'm in your hands, my dear Blanca."

Without taking his eyes off me, he moved aside a lock from my very long day's uncombed hair.

"Completely yours till the end."

Chapter 39

J ust as a field hospital is set up amid an earthquake's rubble, so too we went about our task, converting Daniel's apartment into some kind of documents laboratory. Both dressed in a comfort close to slovenliness, we placed in the middle of the room an enormous board supported by trestles and on top of it our computers, a scanner, and the printer I'd taken from my office. As a counterbalance to contemporary technology, there were a few relics that an old colleague of his had found for us in God knows what dump at the university: a prehistoric gadget to read microfilm, an old audiotape duplicator, and a pair of gigantic antediluvian magnifying glasses.

The place's sparse decorations made our job easier. We hung up some maps on the naked walls and arranged enormous piles of papers on the floor. There were all kinds of stuff: legal documents, sheets of paper scribbled in Fontana's unmistakable scrawl, and aging manuscripts with nineteenth-century handwriting. We even found a cross. A humble wooden cross, just two pieces of wood lashed together with a frayed cord.

"Where could he have gotten this?" I whispered.

Daniel took it out of my hands.

"God only knows . . ." he said, passing his fingers over its knots and rough edges, caressing its coarseness. "But if it helped him, it will help us too."

He propped it up against the old tape recorder just as the Franciscan monks planted their crosses in their missions. So that it would accompany us as it did them on the harshness of the road, to make the difficulties of our undertaking more bearable. Although neither of us was moved by religious feelings, just as they had not prompted him, that old cross brought us a little closer to the memory of Andres Fontana.

Death struck him before he could reach definite conclusions in his research, but it was obvious that the effort had been immense. He had visited almost all of California's archives and libraries that could shed any light on the Spanish presence in the area; he'd visited one by one the state's missions, as well as various dioceses and archdioceses. Where he didn't go with his own two feet he did so by mail in hundreds of letters that were answered by their recipients. His work had been thorough and painstaking to the utmost. Now it was our responsibility to rise to the occasion.

We began on Friday morning and completely forgot that in the calendar of normal people's lives there existed something called the weekend. At times we worked seated and at others standing, moving around the large table. Sometimes we kept apart, each concentrating on a specific piece of the legacy. Other times, however, we worked side by side, bent over the same document. Searching, finding, jotting. Shoulder to shoulder, heads touching, my fingers grazing his, his grazing my skin.

The verbal exchanges were scarce and almost telegraphic. By surprise, due to an unexpected setback, or out of admiration for something we had discovered, we'd sometimes let out an exclamation. In English or Spanish, indiscriminately. "Fuck. *Que tio.* Shit."

We compared information, we marked places, we identified patterns, until the first surprises started to appear.

"You told me in Sonoma that Father Altimira was the founder of that mission, right?" Daniel asked me at some point on Saturday afternoon from the other end of the table. "The unruly Franciscan who didn't have the permission from his superiors to build it."

"Have you found something on him?" I asked, surprised. "I've already come across him three times."

"And so have I, a bunch of times," he noted. "Here he shows up in a couple of written notes, listen:

December 1820: Father Jose Altimira announces to Colonel Pablo Vicente de Sola, last governor of Alta California, his new destination in these territories. 1821: Altimira thanks Sola for several favors. October 1821: Altimira notifies Sola of the delivery of a shipment of grain to a Russian ship...

The information was not truly significant, nor did it highlight any relevant fact, but it attested to the fluid relationship the recently landed Franciscan had with the higher civil authorities.

"In any case, there are more names that appear relatively frequently. I've come across Father Señan in four or five other references, and pretty much the same goes for Father Fortuni."

As we kept working, indeed, traces of the old Franciscan fathers started to surface regularly among the papers.

"Reserve Altimira just in case. Let's stack all his documents here," I said, pointing to one end of the table. "Make sure we don't lose sight of him."

And we didn't. Neither of him nor of anyone else, including Fortuni, Señan, and the dozens of monks, missions, jailhouses, laws, and governors who kept crossing our path.

Saturday came to an end, Sunday flew by, and Monday arrived. At the end of each day we'd go out onto the apartment's little terrace with our coats on and, letting the cold wind clear our minds, we'd stretch our legs against the balustrade and drink a glass of wine. Or two. Or three.

On Monday afternoon, however, we hadn't yet taken a break, when our peace was shattered.

"She's here!"

It was almost seven p.m. and we'd been scrutinizing papers and listening to a bunch of old tape recordings: interviews with priests, filing clerks, and fellow Spaniards, with Fontana's loud voice in the background. I was moved on hearing him; Daniel, even more so.

Then there was knocking on the door. Daniel called out his usual "Come in!" and, with hardly the time to say hello to her, we heard Fanny scream like someone possessed.

"She's here—I've found her!"

As soon as we realized who she was addressing with such boundless enthusiasm, we exchanged a perplexed glance.

"She's here, Professor Zarate! There's no need to keep on looking! Professor Perea is here, with Professor Carter!"

The slender figure of Luis Zarate appeared at the door without time for us to consider what to do. A loud rebuff flew across my mind. How could I have forgotten to inform the chairman, to disguise my absence with any old excuse?

Too late for regrets, we got up, greeted him, and stood motionless at one corner of the large table. He, meanwhile, stepped inside the apartment without waiting for Daniel to invite him in. Then he carefully let his eyes wander across all the material and equipment strewn about. Bundles, diagrams, maps. Our computers. The scanner. The prehistoric gadgets. And the printer. My printer. The one he'd given me.

The situation became extremely uncomfortable for all three of us and I again cursed myself for not anticipating that this moment might come to pass.

After the tense silence, Luis was the first to intervene.

"What an interesting encounter," he said ironically, without addressing either of us in particular. Then his gaze settled on me. "We're looking for you, Blanca, because it got into Fanny's head that something might have happened to you. She says that you didn't show up in your office either Friday or today. We've called your apartment several times but without luck. Your cell phone is out of service and Rebecca Cullen is at a seminar in San Francisco, so we were unable to learn of your whereabouts through her."

"You see, Luis, I—"

"Naturally it's not part of my duties as chairman to be searching the streets for someone who has not shown up for work," he interrupted me, "but Fanny was quite alarmed and at her insistence I had no other choice but to help find you."

"A thousand apologies, really. I should have told you that I'd be out temporarily," I said.

I was sincere. I regretted not having done so, but everything had happened so quickly that it didn't even cross my mind to clue in the department regarding my intentions—although my forgetfulness, it suddenly dawned on me, might have simply been an unconscious defense mechanism, an excuse to conceal a truth that would have been unacceptable to Luis.

I realized I hadn't seen him since the day he had shown up un-expectedly at my office. The day of that bitter visit to Darla Stern's house, after which I lay cuddled next to Daniel on his couch while he narrated in the darkness the saddest moments of his life. The same day in which Luis Zarate himself, within the fiefdom of his department, offered me his support with implications that were light-years from the merely professional. Any affinity between us, however, seemed to have been blown to smithereens by this new set of circumstances. I thought it safest for me to keep quiet for the moment. Daniel too remained silent.

"A very productive absence, from what I gather," he remarked while browsing through the material.

He lifted an antique map of California and pretended to examine it, then did the same with a letter from the Huntington Library in San Marino. Lastly, he placed his hand on the printer and patted it several times.

Fanny contemplated the scene impassively, radiating satisfaction at having found me and not in the least discerning the possible conse-quences of what she had unleashed.

Luis continued to address me: "From what I see, it hasn't exactly been a few days of holidays that you've taken, right, Blanca? Evidently you've been working hard and, moreover, without wavering from your commitment."

"That's right," I said. "And Professor Carter is helping me."

"On the other hand, that doesn't seem quite right, given the fact that he's no longer connected to this university. Nor do I understand what all these documents belonging to the university are doing in his place. In case you don't recall, these papers are restricted and should not be been taken out of the university without authorization."

Where was the Luis Zarate who had prepared cocktails at my party, who had flirted with me unabashedly at Los Olivos, who had tried to kiss me and offered me what seemed like sincere affection?

"This material does not belong to the university: it's mine," Daniel corrected him before I could say anything. His tone was bitter and forceful, so that there could be no doubt about his opinion of the department chair.

Taking a few bills out of his pocket, Luis changed his tone as he said, "Fanny, darling, would you mind going for some pizzas? Whichever ones you want, whichever you like best. Thanks, dear. And take your time, there's no rush."

When Fanny had left, we explained how those documents had come into our hands. We told Luis only about seventy percent of the truth. We mentioned Darla Stern's garage, but not the checks that were paid; we spoke to him about the distant relationship between Fontana and Daniel, but not of the thirty years that the former pupil had decided to cast his mentor into oblivion. In any case, and in spite of our effort to come across as credible, Luis had difficulty accepting our version of the facts.

"All very laudable, no doubt about it. But from the evidence I gather the following," he said, extending both hands over our cluttered table. "That all this material is part of what Professor Andres Fontana left behind in the department at the time of his death—a department that I now run—and that right now it is in the private home of an individual unaffiliated with the university and who was clearly facilitated illicitly by the researcher assigned to process it."

"Luis, please . . ." I pleaded.

"So, much to my chagrin, I believe that my official duty is to demand that all this be taken out of here immediately and, afterwards, that you draw up a report explaining this series of irregularities. A report that I'll have to send to the dean, of course."

Daniel and I exchanged another quick glance, but neither of us said a word.

"And most likely," he went on, in a tone of superiority that he'd never used in my presence before, "my duty will also entail sending the aforesaid report to your university, Blanca."

"I don't think they'll be too interested," I said with a touch of insolence.

He ignored my comment.

"And as far as you're concerned, Carter, rest assured that I'll also find a way for my report to reach Santa Barbara."

"Stop talking nonsense once and for all, Zarate, please. And make an effort to believe what we're telling you."

Luis went on as if he hadn't heard him, "I'm sure lots of our colleagues will find it amusing that the eminent Daniel Carter uses, let's say, rather unconventional work methods to carry out his research."

I noticed that Daniel's patience was reaching its limit.

"You're starting to piss me off with all these threats, Mr. Chairman."

I was on the verge of bursting out laughing. The situation was tense, yes, but also quite ludicrous. Two seasoned academics tangled up in some absurd dispute like two fighting cocks, neither of them willing to cede an inch of his terrain. Perhaps out of deference toward me, perhaps out of pure inertia, they both spoke in Spanish. They used, however, the formal form of address between them, keeping the boundaries clearly delineated.

"Take it as you wish," Luis replied with disdain.

"Since when did you develop this grudge against me, Zarate?" Daniel asked, going around the table to approach him without any physical obstacles in between.

"I've got nothing against you . . ."

"This doesn't date from our first meeting in your office, right?" Daniel asked.

I frowned in surprise, suddenly intrigued.

"That was our first face-to-face encounter," Daniel went on, "and before that we'd spoken over the telephone, remember? But there must have been something else before that—or am I wrong in assuming that?"

"We'd never had the slightest contact," Luis replied.

Daniel straightened, his arms folded over his chest, his gaze defiant.

"True, no direct contact," he said. "But we did meet indirectly. Mountview University, March 1992. Almost eight years ago. Does that ring a bell?"

"It was—"

"It was a negative report I wrote that blocked your promotion. After evaluating your curriculum vitae as an external reviewer, I was of the opinion that you were not the most appropriate candidate for the position. My subsequent mistake was to forget your name and not remember you after so many years and so many similar reports, but it's clear that I remained fresh in your memory."

The buried connections, the underground conduits through which everything can be ascertained, bewildered me.

"That has nothing to do with the matter at hand," Luis replied, trying to sound definitive. From his posture, however, I was able to tell that his tension was increasing.

"Are you sure?" Daniel prodded him. "Because, as I understand it, it was my vote that tilted the balance. And with it, you lost the position you were aspiring to."

Daniel was no longer my research assistant in worn-out jeans and faded checkered shirt. Instead he had returned to being the highly regarded academic Luis Zarate himself had described to me.

"I truly regret the adverse effects of my decision," Daniel continued implacably, "but I simply carried out my responsibility with the rigor that was expected of me. That was fair play. However, you took it as something personal. And, some years later, when I accidentally crossed your path, you found your chance for revenge."

Touché. The insolence hadn't disappeared altogether from Luis's face, but it had surely softened. He obviously didn't expect Daniel to air dirty linen. But neither was he ready to throw in the towel. Far from it.

They were still facing each other, barely a few feet apart. The jealous chairman, impeccable in his dark formal attire; Daniel, the old fox, dressed in the casual clothes of a student, ready to strike where it hurt most.

"How about we quit digging up old grudges that no longer can be settled and make an effort to be productive?" I cut in.

"Totally agreed, Blanca," Luis said. "It's not I, by the way, who has chosen to revisit events peripheral to the matter that concerns us. All that needs to be done now is to solve this . . . let us say, irregularity."

Daniel walked across to the kitchen area divided from the living room by a small counter, jerked open the fridge door, grabbed a beer, and closed it with a bang. He didn't even bother to offer us anything. Luis and I remained opposite each other, separated by the table and the barricade of material. Trying to figure out a way to wriggle out of a jam that could prove embarrassing for all parties concerned.

"In any case," Luis added, "besides the legal ownership of all these papers, I'd like to know what exactly is brewing here—because I have no doubt that, whatever it is, it goes beyond the mere cataloging of documents. And in the event that I do not receive a convincing answer, my next step will be to ask for explanations from SAPAM."

A hoarse peal of laughter from Daniel ended the standoff. Coming from behind the counter, he slowly made his way back toward the table with the bottle of beer in his hand, once more displaying a seriousness that belied his appearance.

"Don't bother, Zarate," he said, spreading his arms theatrically. "Let me introduce you to SAPAM. All that's behind it is me."

I closed my eyes for an instant and took a deep breath, trying to figure out what it was he hoped to accomplish with such a brash confession. Luis's reaction was immediate. Of course.

"That's an outrage, Carter! An infraction of any ethical code, an absolute—"

"Let him explain, Luis, please," I begged.

To my surprise, he consented. And Daniel spoke, detailing everything I already knew. Everything that, days earlier, had stirred in me a mixture of indignation and bewilderment.

"There's no more to it, Zarate," he concluded once he had outlined his setup. "And from here on, it's up to you to decide what to do."

"Obviously, the first thing I'm going to do is to inform the university of the illegality of this so-called SAPAM."

"Perfect, but I advise you to think it over carefully before you do so, because such a reaction could backfire. In the event you proceed, be aware that I'll find a way to publicize your department's inadequate management procedures for receiving funds through a bogus foundation without double-checking its origin."

"That will be nothing but a temporary blot on my record, but you'll be seen by the entire academic community as an interloper," Luis said, anticipating his argument.

"Please, can you—"

Neither of them paid any attention to me.

"Having reached this point, I don't care if what I've done is known," Daniel replied defiantly. "I'm even ready to incriminate myself before I'll let this work go unfinished."

"I'm afraid I'm not going to allow that under any circumstances."

"Please . . ." I insisted.

"What are you going to do? Denounce me? Call a notary to certify that . . ."

The bottle of beer was to blame. For being so handy. And empty. Daniel had put it on the table absentmindedly; in fact, it even left a small round moisture spot on one of the maps of San Rafael.

Only the noise of broken glass against the door got their attention. My aim was off, but it made the point. A loud shattering sound first and silence afterwards. Finally I was heard.

Chapter 40

———

Disconcerted, they turned to me. I was disgusted at the bitter verbal combat they were embroiled in.

"It's unbelievable that you refuse to reason with a little common sense."

They both began mumbled excuses.

"In the event you keep up this petty obstinacy," I went on, "the one to air all the dirty linen of the fraudulent SAPAM will be me. I've got a few more days until I leave, but I'm sure there's plenty of time to ask for an appointment with the dean and detail for him the various irregularities in my hiring process."

Neither one said a word. I took a few moments to calm myself before I continued.

"Now it's my turn to talk and you're both going to listen to me, okay? And no interruptions, please. It's clear all three of us have an interest in this business. Different interests, but equally important to each of us. You, Luis, are concerned that it follow official protocols and out of pure principle are against whoever has circumvented you as chairman, but you're not too anxious for this affair to be made public because some of the steps you've taken could be seriously questioned and your professional credibility dragged through the mud. And you,

Daniel, may have flouted Zarate's wishes and Santa Cecilia's official regulations, but you're worried that this whole project is getting way out of hand and realize that what began as an honest attempt at reconciliation and personal atonement could end up turning into a major academic scandal. And I, who have also made the decision to take on this additional part of the legacy, am not ready to throw three months of work out the window without reaching its conclusion. So, if we wish for this all to be resolved satisfactorily and in our best interests, we must each be ready to make concessions."

Zarate was the first to reply, still undeterred.

"I'm not so sure—"

"Well, you will be," I cut him short. "Don't overlook the fact that, in this whole process, which has been plagued with pitiful irregularities, you've not only involved a foreigner but a career civil servant of the Spanish state and a full professor of a public institution that, if I were to inform them of this fraud, would most likely demand an explanation from the University of Santa Cecilia."

Daniel went back to the refrigerator. Instead of one beer, this time he took out three. He handed me one and left another on top of the table for Luis. I opened mine but the department chairman didn't take his. Daniel, on the other hand, drank half of his in one gulp. Afterwards he slumped in a chair with his long legs apart and the ends of his shirt sticking out on the sides, as disgusted as I was by the whole business.

"What is it you expect us to do?" he then asked me.

There was neither friendliness nor animosity in his words. Simply the coldness of one who knows he has no choice but to obey a protocol. Luckily for me, he seemed to accept, this time around, that the protocol would be determined by me.

"For starters, all this material is to be taken out of your house immediately. As long as there is no way to prove it's legally yours, Zarate is right that it all points to belonging to Fontana's legacy."

"But you know that's not so!" he protested, depositing the bottle on the table with a dry thud.

"What I know doesn't matter. We must follow objective criteria if we are to have any shot at moving forward and reconciling the interests of all parties."

"Then everything will return to the department," Zarate was quick to proclaim, sensing he had scored the first goal of the game.

He also sat down; the only one standing now was me.

"No way. It doesn't return there because it wasn't there. My proposal is for it to stay on neutral ground."

"Where?" they both asked in unison.

No one appreciated the humor of the situation.

"In Rebecca Cullen's house. She works at the university and is friends with everyone. I'm sure she'll accept our proposal without raising any objections. She'll watch over the legacy faithfully and I'll move there to keep on working."

"By yourself?" Daniel asked bluntly.

"No. You'll continue working with me. I need you."

"No way," Zarate protested with lightning speed.

"Luis, I'm afraid you have no other option. Carter abides by the first condition, which is to get all of this out of his house because the terms of his ownership, although valid, appear suspect. Now it's your turn to make a concession. And what you're going to accept is for him to continue working with me in the days to come."

I sat down opposite them and continued.

"When this whole business of Los Pinitos is legally concluded, whatever the result, I'll no longer be here. But if—"

Some forceful knocks at the door interrupted me. Daniel yelled his customary "Come in!" but no one entered. He then got up to open it and someone loaded down with wide, flat square boxes came into view.

"Come on in, Fanny, dear," he said, assuming a cordial tone. "Those pizzas smell delicious; it'd be a sin to let them get cold."

"I'm leaving," Luis announced.

"Stay," I asked him. "We need to keep talking."

He headed toward the door with no intention of listening to me.

"I think I've heard all I need to hear; now I need to think."

"Tomorrow morning there won't be a single piece of paper here, I promise."

"I hope so."

He closed the door behind him, but I immediately opened it. He had not yet started down the stairs when I grabbed him by the arm from behind and forced him to turn around.

"You told me I could count on you, remember?"

"That was before you behaved in a way that I didn't expect from you."

"That was when you tried to kiss me and offered me your support without conditions. Or have you forgotten?"

Night had completely fallen and it was cold. I drew my old gray woolen jacket tighter around me. He did not answer.

"We've all got some reasons to feel disappointed and a lot more to keep moving forward and not look back," I added.

"But what you've done is unforgivable . . ."

"Don't talk nonsense, Luis, please." I took a step toward him. "All of this is very irregular, I know. Highly irregular. It goes beyond all possible norms and at times it even goes against common sense. Things have happened that have caught us all by surprise, defenseless, without time to react. But if you wish, there's an easy way out of this."

He did not ask what the solution was, but I knew he wanted to know.

"Stop hindering us," I whispered, coming even closer. "I've got just a few days left here, you know that. During which our only intention is to work. Rest assured that if everything ends favorably, your department will benefit greatly and it won't hurt you personally in any way."

The only light on the stairway came from a dim lamp affixed to the wall. The houses on the opposite side of the street were already decked out with Christmas ornaments: the lights on a large fir tree blinked on and off in one of the gardens, and another house had a bunch of colored bulbs strung above the window. Somewhere in the evening sky there should have been a moon, but I couldn't see it.

"Think of us all. Behind the ton of papers in the basement there was a man of flesh and blood who deserves to be acknowledged. Then there's Daniel Carter, who has not acted out of academic self-interest but rather out of a purely sentimental impulse. And then there's the business of Los Pinitos, what it means for this university and for the entire community of Santa Cecilia."

"I am not particularly interested in any of that," he was quick to say.

"Then, if during this time you've held me in any esteem, I beg that you do it for me."

When I went back inside, the pieces of glass from the bottle I'd broken were no longer on the floor. Daniel and Fanny were chatting away in the kitchen while eating pizza. Fanny was speaking nonstop while she chewed, rhythmically moving her head. "A brand-new apartment . . . my mother . . . an inheritance . . ." I thought I'd heard her say.

Daniel, meanwhile, pretended to be listening to her. Perhaps he even was, but with only half of his neurons. The other half, no doubt, was busy trying to figure out what was happening on the other side of the door as I spoke to Luis Zarate.

We'd been shoulder to shoulder for many hours, many days. Close accomplices, both seeking each other out and distancing ourselves from one another, coming close and holding back at the same time. Engrossed in an urgent task that did not allow for interference or delays even if at times our hearts might have yearned for something totally different. Getting to know each other better.

Perhaps this was the reason he was beginning to come across so transparently. I was able to guess his thoughts and I knew he was not going to talk about us, of our feelings for each other. His mind, at the moment, pointed in another direction. To the man dressed in black who at that moment was starting his car while a Spanish woman's appeal to reason continued to echo in his head.

We must get Zarate out of our way no matter what, I sensed Daniel was trying to tell me. We must get rid of him.

Before he was able to swallow his mouthful of pizza and confirm my expectation, I raised a finger in warning.

"I know what you're thinking. The answer is no way."

Chapter 41

Rebecca's large dining room table was the legacy's next destination. The same one on which we'd enjoyed Thanksgiving dinner, when we made all those toasts to life and listened to a touching appeal to compassion. Only a few weeks had gone by since then, but nothing was the same anymore. That family friend who'd come in dragging a load of memories from yesteryear, who touched us with words overflowing with affection and truth, now moved about the room brusquely, snorting as he disentangled cables, looked for plugs, and connected gadgets. I, meanwhile, was busy again unpacking a bunch of boxes and spreading their contents out in stacks while trying to find a place for everything.

In one of the boxes we'd packed in a hurry a short while earlier, the old wooden cross reappeared. I held it in my hands again, my fingers caressing its rough texture. I placed it in a corner, alone, lying flat. Don't let us down, I wanted to say, but didn't. In objective terms, that house was a five-star headquarters. With thick rugs and linen curtains that allowed for the right amount of light to come through. With fresh flowers, luminous paintings, and the lovely oak table that hosted generations of family members when they all gathered together. Without either Daniel or me openly expressing it, I knew nevertheless that we both missed the camaraderie that had brought us together in the austere apartment that we'd been obligated to leave. The warmth that emanated between us despite the sparse furniture, the naked floor, the empty walls. The current of positive energy that we transmitted to each other with a simple touch of my hand on his arm when telling him about some small discovery, of his fingers on my shoulder when asking how I was coming along. A spontaneous laugh over any little thing and that collusion that drove us to frenzied work over the surface of a simple board, forgetting for the moment the possibility of fatigue, dejection, or discouragement.

But there was no time for nostalgia. Something had changed between us with Luis Zarate's untimely arrival, and it was practically impossible to turn back the clock. Our objective was before us, not behind. There were only three days left until my departure and the deadline for the Los Pinitos project.

Toward midmorning, when we finally picked up the pace of our work, I got up to make a phone call.

"All's in order," I said simply, then listened to the person on the other end of the line for a moment and hung up.

Daniel, meanwhile, hadn't taken his eyes off the document he had before him. As if he weren't aware that I'd just spoken to Luis Zarate, as if he hadn't heard me. But he didn't talk to me until a couple of hours later.

"Are you hungry?" he asked me.

"Not yet."

I thought he'd wait for me to eat something together as he had at other times, but I was mistaken. Given my negative answer, he simply headed to the kitchen and, with the familiarity of one who knows himself on friendly territory, began to rummage around. I heard him search the fridge, tear a plastic bag, cut, split, pour, spread. A knife banged against the sink, then he briefly turned on the faucet in the manner men usually do, to its maximum. He walked out into the garden, passing through the door that once took me to meet what was left of his friend Paul Cullen.

The large dining room window provided me with the opportunity to observe him without being seen. With his back toward me, again in his worn-out jeans and a blue wool sweater. Seated on the cold stone step, the dog Macan in the distance. Eating a sandwich with his gaze fixed on the sad pool full of autumn's fallen leaves. Thinking. Perhaps of his very own presence in that same house when he was still a young professor oozing ambition and project ideas, when he still lacked an inkling of the low blows fate had in store for him. Or for all those who had accompanied him then. Thinking, perhaps, of Aurora and her infectious laugh; of his lucid and fun philosopher friend frolicking with his kids on the grass; of Andres Fontana, silently in love with the pretty Spaniard who was his wife.

Or perhaps, between bites of bread stuffed with something or other, his mind wandered much nearer: to our work together, recalling Luis Zarate's unfortunate interruption and our proximity to each other. Or turning over in his head what he took to be my betrayal.

"I've left a sandwich for you," he said on returning to his place at our worktable.

"Thank you," I murmured. I never did eat it.

After several more hours sifting through hundreds of unrelated documents, an aged cardboard folder appeared tied with a simple ribbon. Inside, a handful of loose papers. Perhaps at some point they'd been white, but now they were several shades of yellow. Between lines and phrases, we found a bunch of references written offhandedly by Fontana:

Year 1823, April 4. Altimira demands from Argüelles documents for better administering his future mission. July 10: Altimira announces to Father Señan the construction of the new mission in Sonoma. July 22: Altimira urges Argüelles regarding the construction of new installations. August 23: Father Sarria writes Altimira disapproving of the foundation of his recent mission in Sonoma for not having requested permission from his superiors.

The rebel father Altimira had, little by little, turned into the great protagonist of the story that the professor had invited us to follow. We knew the insurgent Franciscan had gotten away with the construction of the Sonoma mission. In spite of the initial reservations of his own ecclesiastical hierarchy—which refused to authorize Altimira to found that new mission—he managed to move ahead with it. The documents showed, however, that the unwavering support that Governor Argüelles had given him at the beginning slowly began to falter.

From different documents we learned that in January 1824 Altimira asked him by letter for a bell for the Sonoma mission, but Argüelles appeared not to have even responded. In the same month of the following year, 1825, he again sent him a request indicating that it would only be a loan, but it seems his plea fell on deaf ears. No one seemed interested anymore in those outdated missions whose survival he was bent on.

Altimira's trail was lost as of the summer of 1826. It was then that, tired of suffering under the father's aggressive treatment, the Indians rebelled and set fire to the mission that he had built with such tenuous resources. No matter how hard we looked and how thoroughly we went over hundreds of papers, we were never able to ascertain what became of the impetuous father immediately after the fire. It seems he never returned to the Sonoma mission.

In a letter dated March 1828 and addressed to Father Sarria by one Ildefonso de Arreguin, we learned that Altimira reappeared but soon vanished toward the beginning of that very same year, escaping from Alta California under somewhat obscure circumstances, along with another father by the name of Antonio Ripoll. Back to Spain, supposedly.

After this last brushstroke regarding the end of the Franciscan's stay on American soil, darkness descended, and we were left with only questions. Where were you, Jose Altimira, during this time? What happened to you when the Sonoma mission was burned to the ground? Where were you for that year and a half? We never asked those questions out loud, but we mentally asked ourselves a thousand times as we unpacked the boxes, not finding an answer. Why did Andres Fontana follow you so closely? What did you do once the angry Indians torched your first mission?

We added the folder to the small but growing bunch of accumulated evidence from the previous days and kept breaking ground.

Rebecca returned a little before seven. With a long striped jacket, two brown bags from Meli's Market, and a news item.

"Los Pinitos is intensifying. They've called for a new protest, they're mobilizing once more."

"But they still have nothing to latch onto. I spoke to Joe Super a couple of hours ago," Daniel said.

"Nothing at all apparently," she confirmed, raising her voice as she moved toward the adjacent kitchen with the brown bags in her arms. "But there are less than three days left for the deadline to expire and they insist on making noise until the end. Does anyone want a glass of wine?"

We both got up, ready to accept the invitation.

Without looking at Daniel, I simply asked him, "Are you planning on going?"

He raised his arms toward the ceiling and stretched, exhaling heavily like a worn-out giant.

"To the protest? No."

How comforting to feel looked after by generous hands. While we drank that first glass, Rebecca prepared dinner with her usual diligence. Tasty, hot, fortifying, served on large white crockery plates on the kitchen's rustic table. There was no need for us to agree not to talk about work: we chose to clear our heads by going over a thousand trivialities that didn't affect any of us much. And thus, for a little over an hour, the tension started to dissolve and we even managed to smile at some point.

When we were about to finish the ice cream dessert, Daniel's cell phone rang in his pocket.

"What's up, Joe?" he said, standing up and walking out of the kitchen.

He came back half a minute later with his jacket in his hand. He didn't sit down. "The students have decided to camp at Los Pinitos tonight," he announced as he took his car keys out. "Without authorization. I'm going to swing by. I'll come back as soon as I can, to try and keep working a little longer."

He didn't bother to ask me if I wanted to accompany him, nor did I propose it. The tentative closeness that we'd reestablished over dinner had vanished; his trust in me still wavered. It was not clear if we'd be able to revive either one of them.

Rebecca proposed we watch a movie together, a comedy with a happy ending or a drama by which to transport myself to some other reality. I refused the offer and continued with my work, although I did accept her invitation to stay overnight in one of her daughters' bedrooms. That way I wouldn't have to return to my apartment in the middle of the night and would feel less lonely.

In spite of having struggled on my own with Fontana's legacy for almost three months, Daniel's presence in the last stretch had been so intense that to reenter that world without him by my side suddenly felt strange. But I overcame the moment and carried on late into the night, disentangling information regarding transactions and assistance between missions: which had handed over to another two dozen chickens and three mules; which had welcomed fifteen sick converts; which had requested from the motherhouse a sculpture of a virgin, work tools for the blacksmith, or some authorization to do something. At around a quarter to two, with Rebecca asleep hours ago, the house in total darkness and in the thickest of silences, and Daniel still absent, my eyes were finally about to close, when a simple phrase in an old document snapped me out of my drowsiness.

And Altimira apologized before Your Reverence for once more failing to request permission to proceed with the new mission.

Nothing else, the rest dealt with the inventory of a bunch of small details that I could not string together, an incomplete record.

I wrote down the words on a sheet of paper. I underlined "once more," I underlined "permission," I underlined "mission." The "once more" obviously implied that whoever wrote that was not referring to the Sonoma mission, the first that Altimira founded without authorization, but to some other undertaking. What else did you do, Altimira? What else? What else? I kept repeating under my breath, patting the table, encouraging him to come out of hiding and show himself. I kept searching, eager and ravenous, but found nothing else.

I switched the last light off and climbed the stairs a good while later wondering how far the path of the erratic Franciscan would end up taking us. If indeed there was a place to be taken to.

On waking up the following morning I confirmed that Rebecca's efficiency had gotten ahead of me. In the bathroom next to the room I'd slept in, I found my toilet bag and some clothes of mine. She had a set of keys to my apartment; I'd given them to her myself, in case something unexpected happened, I vaguely thought at the time.

Daniel was already at his spot when I came down. At his back, a large painting reminiscent of Frida Kahlo's naïf aesthetics. By his feet, good old Macan lay snoozing. Instead of the previous day's wool sweater, Daniel now wore a sweatshirt with the emblem and letters of some university practically illegible from wear and tear. And as to what was inside his head, I didn't have the foggiest idea.

"You didn't come back. How did it go?" I said instead of good morning.

"Bad," he answered without looking at me. "They're hell-bent on battling it out, but with no conclusive piece of evidence to show."

"Did they end up camping?"

"More than two hundred students, next to the excavators that are there already. I'm sure they have no intention of hauling dirt just yet; they've been sent to intimidate. But I'm afraid the countdown has begun, and no matter how much noise they make, it won't be to much avail."

"Unless we are able to achieve something," I said to him, handing him the document. "Altimira showed up again last night."

Chapter 42

Wednesday rolled by unnoticed, and Thursday brought an uninviting gray day with intermittent rain. All the lights in Rebecca's dining room had remained lit from an early hour, casting clarity above us as we worked on the material scattered on the table and floor.

She had come back at nightfall. We had never even stopped for lunch, consuming instead a bottle of water, a couple of cans of Coke, three apples, and a bag of Doritos. We realized that our worst-case scenario had materialized once we got to the few loose papers at the bottom of the last box: a wrinkled receipt for some books bought in March 1969 at Moe's Books in Berkeley, a schedule of liturgical events at the Santa Clara mission, and a map of regional roads.

After that, desolation.

We'd reached the end without coming up with solid proof; we had only intuition, suppositions, and loads of loose information hinting at the truth. Father Altimira, the one we thought would end up taking us to some safe harbor, had vanished from any written testimony for more than a year without giving us a clue to what he did during all of 1827. None of the sister missions took him in. His friends among the authorities stopped mentioning him. Fontana never did find out what became of him. Based on the Franciscan's vehement and impulsive personality, the professor suspected that he might have established a new mission. Without authorization or license, without a founding charter, without a budget or backing, moved only by a faith of steel or perhaps by an ambition as fierce as it was mad. That was Fontana's dream, which infected us now as well.

"There is nothing else," I announced in a whisper.

At my wit's end before the certainty that we had exhausted everything, I flung the empty box on the floor. It fell facedown like a gloomy confirmation of the truth.

Daniel dropped into one of the chairs with legs splayed and an absent gaze. Crestfallen.

I went to lift the box to turn it right side up, but I ended up down on the floor beside it. On Rebecca's lovely flooring. Exhausted, I sat with my back slumped against the wall.

"What a fool I've been . . ." he said, his face raised to the ceiling and his eyes closed, as he ran his fingers through his hair.

"It's no use blaming yourself now. No one knew what we were going to find: we had no idea how far Fontana had been able go."

"I should have been less naïve, more realistic, and not have had blind faith in something . . . so weak and insubstantial."

"It was a risk. You went for the high stakes and lost. But if it's of any consolation, at least you've gotten half of what you sought: your teacher's legacy is no longer in the dark."

"And, most important, I should have never gotten anyone involved. Nor should I have turned to you, or confronted Zarate, or implicated the department, or . . ."

It seemed as if we were each speaking more to ourselves than to each other.

When we ran out of sentences, we started thinking. The crude reality was undeniable: there was nothing substantial for us to hold on to, nothing conclusive on which to build a solid argument to appeal the Los Pinitos project.

"Are we going to lick our wounds all night, or shall we start clearing up?"

The proposal came from me some minutes later. Return to life, return to the present. We'd failed, but I, at least, knew that I had to get

back on the move. Good-bye to Andres Fontana and his false expecta-tions. Good-bye to his old student and to his attempt at redemption; good-bye to an alien world and to some men who seduced me and carried me along for a while, but with whom, it turned out, I had very little in common. For better or worse, it was time to turn the page. It was no use lamenting; it was too late. I was leaving. I still had my apartment to clear out, suitcases to pack, matters to conclude, good-byes to say.

As at many other junctures of my life, it was time to get up and get going once more.

Up, I wished to tell myself. But instead of giving myself an internal order, the word popped out of my mouth and became an order to us both.

The great untamed one obeyed without protesting. Before I got up from the floor by my own means, he rose from his chair, came over to me, and offered his hand. Once we were both standing, without exchanging a single syllable more, we set out to pack up that chaos once again and convert the space into a regular dining room again.

He began at one end of the table, I at the other. Stacking docu-ments, piling papers. Mechanically.

"He even left behind telephone bills, but not even a clue . . ." Daniel said.

"What bills are you referring to?"

"These," he said, raising a wad of papers in the air, tied loosely with a rubber band. There were seven or eight of them, it seemed.

"Where were they?"

"Underneath this bunch of newspaper clippings. I thought you'd had a look already."

"I hadn't even seen them . . ."

"I imagine there's nothing there, but take a glance anyway, just in case." He tossed them in my direction and I caught them on the fly. "In the meantime I'll start taking this stuff out to the car."

Two business letters from Pacific Bell telephone company, three from the Federal Reserve Bank of San Francisco, one from his medi-cal insurance company, and another from a local dentist informing him of a change in his appointment date. All dated the year of the

professor's death. Maybe Darla herself picked them up from his house; perhaps she took more things: clothes, personal property, photos. And those insubstantial letters that she threw in by chance among the research papers she'd also decided to make off with for no apparent reason.

Between the envelopes, practically lost in the tedious bank and company claims, there was a smaller one. Thicker, heavier than the rest. Handwritten, for a change. *E. C. Villar, Fr.,* could be read with great difficulty on the top left-hand side corner. An old man's handwriting, I thought. *Santa Barbara Mission, Calif.*

"It's from your hometown," I said when Daniel walked back into the dining room.

"What hometown?" he asked absently, picking up a few more boxes and three rolls of maps.

"From Santa Barbara. From the mission."

I tore open the envelope and unfolded the letter. A few lines written with a shaky hand and in old-fashioned calligraphy:

May 15th, 1969, year of the Lord

My dear Professor,

After your last week's visit to our mission's archive, on replacing the records on their corresponding shelves, this fragment of a letter was left sticking out which I presume went unnoticed by you, and, unable to catalog it for lack of sufficient information, I am sending it to you as a mere curiosity and proof of my personal gratitude for your great interest in the history of our beloved missions.

I look forward to your next visit, and in the meantime I wish you my sincerest best wishes for the Lord's everlasting peace. Kindly extend them as well to the pleasant and extremely friendly Spanish woman who accompanied you to our last meeting.

A series of pictures came to my mind with powerful luminosity. An elderly archivist whose days went by immersed in files and dusty papers and whom most likely no one had consulted about anything in ages. Successive visits by a curious professor with whom he shared a common language. The pretty woman who unexpectedly appeared by his side at their last meeting, the Spaniard with her familiar accent and the quick laugh whose image remained engraved in the soul of the old archivist, who was accustomed to silence and solitude.

The letter was dated two days before their deaths. They never learned of its contents.

"Read this," I whispered to Daniel when he came back inside, ready to continue packing up.

I did not show him the Franciscan's missive with the mention of Fontana and Aurora: Why remind him of that painful story? But I did hand him the unfolded half piece of paper that the priest had sent Fontana from the Santa Barbara mission archive. Without a letterhead or addressee. Without a header or date, with half of its essence unrecoverable.

"Altimira saying good-bye to us. He shows up at a fine time, the son of a bitch," he said ironically.

It was the first time we'd seen his handwriting and signature on what seemed half of a letter that he perhaps never sent.

... and then our modest construction was the victim of the most violent action by the obstinate Indians in their heathen errors, who equipped with clubs and bow and arrows, readied to put their depraved design into practice. "Love God, children," I told them, but the heathen failed to understand such a greeting in their urge to attack. "Long live the faith of Jesus Christ and death to its enemies," I insisted, and still they didn't heed my call, which resulted in the death of seven converts, all of whom were buried among pine trees in the consecrated land of our humble mission, beneath simple slabs engraved with a Lord's cross, their Christian initials, and the year of their fatality, 1827.

*And I thus bid you God speed until the next occasion,
and may the Almighty keep you in His love and grace for many
years to come. With my best wishes, your servant who commends
himself to Your Reverence from the bottom of his heart.*

Friar Jose Altimira

A modest construction, seven converts buried among some pine trees beneath simple stones with the Lord's cross, year 1827, in the consecrated land of our humble mission.

"Our humble mission . . . We were so close, so close . . ." I whispered, biting my tongue.

He placed a hand on my shoulder and pressed it. A useless gesture of consolation.

"It's no use being sorry. Come on, let's finish packing up. We've got to make this room decent again."

Just then, his cell phone rang.

"What's up, Joe?" he said as he let go of me. Same words as last time, and the same reaction.

With Altimira's half letter in my hand and that of the archivist in my back pocket, I headed to the kitchen in search of Rebecca. That would be our last dinner, the last day I'd sit at her table, the last night I'd enjoy her warmth and affection.

"Can I help you?" I asked her, thinking that maybe by stirring the sauce for the pasta that was simmering on the stove I'd also be able to calm my uneasiness.

"Blanca!" I heard Daniel scream the minute I'd grabbed the spatula. "Blanca!" he repeated.

He burst into the kitchen, bounding over to me with a marathon runner's strides. Then he grabbed my arms forcefully and fixed his gaze on me, almost shaking me.

"On digging in Los Pinitos to make a . . . a . . . What the hell is the name for the hole you make in the ground for excrement?"

It was the first time I heard him hesitate in my language, the first time the breadth of his Spanish vocabulary turned on him.

"Latrine."

"Latrine, that's it! On digging a hole for the latrines the campers have come upon what seems like a small cemetery among the pine trees. So far they've found what appear to be three graves, but there could be more. Very simple, hardly covered by some flat stones with rudimentary inscriptions."

A cold shiver ran down my back.

"Each stone has a set of initials," he said.

"And a cross?"

He nodded.

"And a year?"

He smiled under his beard, as he had done on the days when there was sun between us.

"Also."

"1827?"

The spatula fell out of my hands and crashed to the floor with a clatter, splattering the tiles and our feet.

Chapter 43

We'd hardly slept; we both still had traces of water from the shower in our hair and a folder with documents in the backseat.

Classes and exams were over; students were waiting for grades or packing for the Christmas holiday, many had already gone home. The more combative, however, remained at Los Pinitos, camping by the humble graves of the seven converts in that territory that we no longer doubted had housed a mission, the last Franciscan mission of the fabled Camino Real. The one never cataloged, the twenty-second: the most fragile and ephemeral, which Andres Fontana chose to name Mission Olvido.

On passing by Rebecca's open office door, we gave her a silent greeting. She knew we were on our way elsewhere and that we didn't have a minute to spare.

Luis Zarate had been given a heads-up; I'd called the previous evening.

"We've got solid proof to bring forward against the Los Pinitos project," I informed him. "Everything must be tied up by tomorrow morning. My plane leaves at six in the evening, and I have to leave Santa Cecilia at two."

He summoned us at nine. We were there five minutes early.

I'd hardly had half an hour to swing by my apartment to change clothes and, while I was at it, start packing up in a hurry. Emptying out shelves and drawers with both hands, stuffing everything into suitcases without allowing myself to stop and think what I was about to leave behind.

"We want you to help us, Luis," I said when we were seated before him.

"What kind of help are we talking about, exactly?" he replied from behind his desk, which was ordered as usual with the precision of a military parade.

I did not perceive any ill will in his terseness, nor sympathy. Daniel, seated to my right, with his legs and arms crossed, listened without interrupting. I knew there was no danger from him; the beast had finally subsided. Throughout the small hours of the morning, while we struggled before my computer screen with four hands and two brains full of caffeine to write a coherent report summarizing our investigation, I was able to get his yes. Yes to letting Zarate in on it. Yes that the remaining legacy coming from Darla's garage be integrated seamlessly with the rest in the department's custody. Yes to a few more things.

"My proposal is that you join us," I then said. "That you do so as the chairman of this department, which, one way or another, in the past or in the present, we all have some sort of bond with. That you forget about SAPAM and its irregularities, that you accept Daniel Carter's part of the legacy as a donation, and that your name appears in the appeal. That you be the official spokesperson of our findings."

He looked at me with doubt written on his face, not quite believing it. And then I resumed. All at once.

"I'm asking you that you accept, in Andres Fontana's name. What we've done during the past days, even what I've done for more than three months, is an insignificant task compared to the colossal job he did. Our work has consisted of tying up a few loose ends, but the one who struggled for years to unearth this mission was Fontana. Perhaps at first he did so purely for personal reasons, sensing in the old missions a trace of his country's soul and his very own essence. But, above all, he did so as an academic, as a humanist committed to research and

352 | MARÍA DUEÑAS

the spread of knowledge, in this department, this university, and this city. When death carried him away, he held the position you hold now, Luis. And like yourself he watched over this house and its people, for academic excellence and the common good."

I then pointed to Daniel, who, leaning back in his chair, listened attentively.

"He might be Fontana's intellectual and sentimental heir, given everything that bound them for years." Then I turned my eyes back to the serious-looking department chairman. "But don't forget that Fontana's institutional heir is the one seated today in the chair he filled. That institutional heir, Luis Zarate, is you. Both of you have the moral duty to respect each other and fight for the dignity of the man whose legacy you are stewards of in equal measure."

Silence fell over the office. From the hallway and through a wall the hysterical muffled scream of a student slipped through, perhaps an irrepressible explosion of happiness at a higher-than-expected grade. Meanwhile, all three of us remained quiet.

Finally Daniel sat up and broke the silence.

"I think Blanca is absolutely right. She offers us a reasonable solution. My initial intention was to hand over the results to the platform against the Los Pinitos project and for them to decide how best to use the documentation. But she's convinced me that Fontana's voice should somehow stand on its own. And the most fitting way is through the institution he worked for." He cleared his throat before continuing. "And as far as I'm concerned, I'm sorry about my behavior. I realize my mistake and I apologize to you, Luis, for having invaded your space in pursuit of my own interests."

I wasn't too sure whether to cheer, raise a victorious fist into the air, or hug him with all my might. My plea to vindicate Fontana had convinced him to place his teacher and friend's memory above his own pride, but I never imagined that he'd express his apology in such words. With sober humility, without a fuss. He didn't stand to extend a heartfelt hand to the chairman, nor did he intone a mea culpa, but he spoke to him candidly, called him by name, and it sounded genuine.

Luis, from the other side of the desk, did not reply.

"Can we count on you, then? Here is the conclusive evidence and a written report," I said, showing him the folder in which we'd placed our findings. "We can take a look at it right now."

The department chairman finally spoke, his words loaded with ambiguity.

"Sometimes we are blinded by arrogance and are not conscious of how elementary things are. Until someone sets before our eyes the simple naked truth."

I had difficulty figuring out if that was an acknowledgment of Daniel's apology or a reciprocal apology for his own behavior. But there was no time for guessing games. Time ticked away; we could not wait.

"Then, are you willing?" I insisted.

Just as she'd done a few days earlier when she came in loaded with pizzas, Fanny again cut me off in midsentence. This time without even knocking, she poked her impetuous head through the doorway and, like an ax blow, interrupted me.

"Professor Super is looking for you. He says it's urgent."

Daniel automatically felt the pockets of his jacket and trousers. Afterwards he uttered "shit"—his spontaneous reaction on realizing that he'd left his cell phone someplace on that frantic morning after a practically sleepless night.

Next, Fanny opened the door to let the veteran professor through.

On that day Joe Super's eyes didn't show the usual bonhomie and sense of humor with which he always participated in my classes. There was no trace of the charm with which he came up to our table to greet us on the night we ran into him at Los Olivos. On that morning his eyes conveyed only worry.

"The police have come to Los Pinitos. They intend to evict the campers. Before the discovery of the graves, the judge ordered an evacuation, but the kids are unwilling to budge and things are getting tenser by the minute. If you're going to tell them anything, it's best you do so as soon as possible."

We immediately stood up and turned to Luis Zarate doubtfully, silently, waiting for his reaction. If he agreed to come with us it would be an act of blind faith, since we still hadn't been able to fill him in regarding our conclusions. Perhaps that was why he took a moment to react. Until finally, in silent affirmation, he too rose.

While Daniel drove, jolting us on the curves and running a few red lights, we explained rather hastily the particulars of our findings. Both Luis and Joe knew from the previous evening that we had conclusive evidence, but neither knew the details. The long early-morning work had allowed us to incorporate structure and coherence into our research, so we finally had a consistent account of the facts.

We reached at Los Pinitos almost at the same time that two more police cars arrived ready to join several others with their sirens and lights on. Nearby were a couple of imposing excavators standing idle as well as a large number of private cars. An enormous billboard full of advertising faces, empty smiles, and phrases whose message was beginning to wear thin had been set up there, promising exciting shopping and unlimited entertainment.

We had to walk a considerable distance until we reached the campers. There were more than a dozen multicolored tents, innumerable signs, and fifty or sixty students in sight, along with some onlookers and a professor or two. They all wore over their clothes the orange protest T-shirts that had begun to appear on campus since the demonstration.

Around them were crowds of people: less confrontational members of the platform, sympathizers and onlookers of all colors and shapes, many taking pictures. Some local television crews were among them, and at a camping table, behind a couple of large thermoses, the warrior grandmothers distributed plastic cups brimming with coffee. Others chatted away or simply watched the scene expectantly, not knowing what was going to happen.

The police had cordoned off the perimeter of what we already knew had been the mission's tiny cemetery. It was only a small rectangular area amid the pine trees, sixteen feet long, not more than six feet wide. The first thing that Daniel and I did, instinctively, was to head in that direction.

"Hey, you can't go through!" a policeman yelled from a distance. Daniel had just stooped to cross under the tape that restricted access.

In black letters on a yellow background could clearly be read DO NOT CROSS.

As if he were deaf and could not read, he offered me his hand. "Come on!" he ordered.

"You were here, Father Altimira," he said in a low voice when we came to the first grave, covered by a dirty gray stone barely one foot square, rough and irregular.

At our back we could hear Joe Super negotiating with the policeman who wanted to force us out of there.

We crouched to read the poorly marked initials, E. F., most likely scratched with no tool other than a rudimentary awl. On top of them, a humble cross, and beneath it, the year 1827. The year between the burning of San Francisco de Solano Mission in Sonoma and the return to Spain of that rebel father whose virtues did not include submission.

"What a pity Fontana never came upon them," I sighed.

"It would have been difficult: time had covered them well. Look," Daniel said, grabbing a handful of soil that had been removed when the graves were unearthed.

"What he might have found around here, though, is this," I added, taking out of my raincoat pocket the rough wooden cross we had found among the jumble of papers in one of Darla Stern's boxes.

Daniel took it out of my hands.

"It has been a good traveling companion," he admitted while contemplating it. He then looked me in the eye and caressed my cheek with two fingers. "And so have you."

"Get out of there once and for all, please!" the policeman roared.

We had no choice but to obey.

A few other members of the protest had joined Joe Super and Luis Zarate. They were all privy to the news of our findings when Joe, after Daniel's call, had shared it with them the previous evening.

"The moment to make it public has come," Daniel said.

He looked at me, raising an eyebrow. I understood him and immediately answered.

"No."

"Yes."

"Yes."

The categorical no came from me. The first yes came out of Daniel's mouth; the second, from Luis's. Both serious, convinced. I swallowed my feelings.

"On the condition that I speak in Spanish," I acquiesced after a few disconcerting seconds. "If I were to do it in English, I don't think I'd be able to convey the spirit of this story. I need a translator."

They both looked at each other.

"Go ahead, Mr. Chairman," Daniel then said. "If from now on you're going to be Fontana's spokesperson, this is a good time to get started."

The news that someone was going to make a statement quickly spread, and everyone began to crowd around us. The young Rastafarian I'd seen so many times took his drum out of a tent and struck up a good rhythm, inviting those present to be quiet.

When silence was established I began, with the voice of reason and the voice of the heart. For myself, and for those who had accompanied me on this adventure, and especially for those who'd been left behind.

"Over a period of more than five decades, a few Franciscans, austere Spanish monks, moved by an unwavering faith and a blind loyalty toward their king, traveled across the still-wild terrain of California, erecting missions in the name of their king and their God. They began in 1769 with the mission of San Diego de Alcala and, advancing by foot and on the back of mules, made their way northward through unknown territory, gradually erecting the twenty-one missions that ended up forming what would be known as the Camino Real. Their aim was to convert the native population and introduce their own civilization, and although such intentions in present-day eyes are questionable, due to the painfully high price that the native population paid in the form of sickness, submission, and loss of identity, we cannot ignore the meritorious labors performed by those men, who once upon a time crossed an ocean to carry out what they understood to be their sacred duty. They brought with them their language and customs, their fruits and animals and their way of working. And they left their indelible imprint in hundreds of names that dot the map and in a thousand little details that leap to the eye, from the color of the walls to roof tiles and vineyards and window grilles."

I made several pauses to let Luis, to my right, translate. Daniel, standing next to Joe, had moved to one side, giving the two of us the entire spotlight. Around us, more than a hundred pairs of eyes and ears looked on and listened with interest.

"More than a century and a half after that first mission was built, life's vicissitudes brought a Spanish professor, Andres Fontana, to these shores. He was moved in his later years by his discovery of the numerous echoes of his native country in this foreign land. Long since exiled by then, he decided to throw all his energies into researching what his compatriots had done here. And after a few years' work poring over old documents, he had come to believe that the fabled chain of missions founded by the Spanish Franciscans did not end with the construction in 1823 of San Francisco Solano Mission in Sonoma, as had always been thought. Somehow he knew that they'd gone farther, and he dedicated the rest of his life to finding proof that would confirm this. Unfortunately, he died before he was able to finish his work. But thanks to his effort and perseverance, we've reached the conclusion that the mission he sought really did exist. The graves that were discovered yesterday confirm that there was in fact a mission here."

After Luis had again translated, I mentioned Altimira and gave a bit of his background, including his disregard for authority in building the Sonoma mission. Then I spoke of the fire that razed it.

"Defying his superiors once more, moved perhaps by a mixture of frustration and rebelliousness or the iron will of his faith, Father Altimira, one of the last friars to arrive in California from old Spain, came by foot all the way to this inhospitable place and, without any means or permission of any kind, founded an extremely modest mission. He was accompanied by a few converted Indians, who along with him had survived the Sonoma fire and who now lie resting beneath these gravestones after perishing in an Indian attack. As you can see, nothing is left of that spare construction that Altimira erected except the remains of what was their cemetery. The survival of the mission was brief, limited at most to a handful of months. And although we don't have any record of it, inspired as we are by Andres Fontana's passionate quest, we want to believe that Father Altimira, in an evocation of his own helplessness, consecrated it to Our Lady of Oblivion, calling it Mision de Nuestra Señora del Olvido.

"My old compatriot would have been proud of all of you: for your dedication in fighting to preserve these surroundings, and for your determination to retain the integrity of this place, which belongs to everyone and which meant so much to him. Having lived intensively with his memory for these past few months, I feel honored, in his name, to express gratitude for what you've accomplished."

Luis translated in chunks, and at the end applause rang out, screams of joy were heard, and the young man in dreadlocks beat his drum yet again.

Next, Joe Super spoke and mentioned some of the technical aspects regarding the very complex legal tangle that would ensue the moment the appeal was presented. The Catholic Church could not claim ownership of the land: the Franciscans never owned the territory their missions occupied but simply enjoyed their use. But the simple confirmation of the fact that this had been missionary ground would subject the area to a special legal status as a landmark site. That, however, would have to be dealt with by experts who could reconstruct accurately what in fact took place in that setting and determine its consequences accordingly. There were, all in all, weighty reasons for optimism. The hardest work was now done.

While Joe was bombarded with questions, I could hear Daniel's voice behind me.

"A quarter to one. Time to go."

Chapter 44

———————

"**J**ust one moment."

I scanned the surrounding people in search of Luis Zarate. Joe meanwhile kept answering questions and the students shook hands and hugged one another amid laughter while they started clearing up the campsite. The onlookers began to beat a retreat to their cars; the grandmothers insisted on handing out coffee that no one seemed to want anymore; and the police, although still overseeing things, no longer created a feeling of tension. Then I saw that a group of protesters had corralled the chairman a short distance away from this commotion of movement, shouts, and babbling voices.

"Can I steal him from you?"

Without waiting for an answer, I grabbed him by the arm and pulled him along with me.

"I want you to know that I always knew you'd come around sooner or later."

"Don't think for a minute that I'd cower before Carter or that you'll end up convincing me," he declared with an ironic smile.

I did not answer him; we both knew that the definitive reason he'd decided to step up was not because of Daniel or me but rather himself.

"Promise me that you're going to do this with enthusiasm and dedication."

"And you promise me that you'll return someday. You'll be able to teach whatever course you like: Introduction to Franciscan Missions; Fontana and His Legacy 101; or How to Seduce a Chairman."

I laughed wearily.

"Let me know when you come through Madrid. A few things are left up in the air; we can still remain friends."

"Nothing has been left pending, Blanca. Everything has come to where it had to."

I stopped walking and looked him in the eye.

"Fontana would be proud to know that everything is in good hands."

I took the old cross from out of my raincoat pocket.

"Take this cross as a proof. It might be my imagination but I think Fontana found it buried around here. We've kept it with us these past few days; it has somehow been like having him close."

He grabbed it and, just as Daniel and myself had done earlier, ran his fingers over its roughness, grazing the frayed string.

"You keep it," he said, giving it back to me. "You also have plenty of road ahead of you."

I would not accept it.

"My road, no matter where it ends up going, no longer leads here. Nor does his, I don't think." I indicated Daniel's turned back with my eyes. "Now you're in charge."

I again handed the cross to him and pressed my hands over his.

"Take care of it and take care of yourself," I said without letting go of him.

"I'll try."

There were no emotional hugs or long farewell declarations; we simply pressed our hands together once more, thereby conveying a final good-bye. I somehow sensed that he would never call even if he were to visit my city a hundred times—that we'd never see each other again.

I left him among the pine trees and hurriedly went in search of Daniel, preferring not to look back.

"I'll pick you up at your apartment at two o'clock," Daniel told me, looking at his watch. "I've got to go by my place too."

The first stop was my office, where I had a few matters to attend to. The minute I opened the door I took a look around at the papers already in their boxes and the piles neatly stacked against the wall. We still didn't know where all of that would end up or who it would have to go through before it reached its final destination, wherever that would be; but there was no doubt in my mind that it would be well taken care of.

Without time for speculation, I put in my bag a few floppy disks and a couple of notepads full of information for a future report on my work. Only then did I begin to carry out my second objective, the main one.

I took the thick, outdated telephone book from a shelf and, from between its pages with their minuscule names, recovered the folded page.

Wherein oblivion dwells,
In the vast gardens without aurora . . .

I read Cernuda's poem again. Afterwards, I took out a box of matches from my desk's bottom drawer. Left over from some other transient like myself, they'd been forgotten there next to a rusted pencil sharpener and a handful of clips.

The fire took only a few seconds to consume the words.

Where I am but the memory of a buried stone amid nettles . . .

The ashes ended up in the wastebasket and among them a man's most intimate feelings.. For some vague reason, I thought that Fontana would be happy to know that someone had protected his privacy.

I found Fanny in her place, as was seldom the case, devouring a chocolate doughnut. In her eagerness to tell me something, upon seeing me, she choked a little.

"I've got something for you, Professor: a good-bye present!" she uttered between coughs.

She picked up a box from the floor. An old box clumsily covered with green-striped fabric. She'd wrapped it herself, she told me. Years ago.

"You know we're going to change houses, right? Mother has told me to start packing and I'm beginning to empty the closets."

"Yes, I've heard something to that effect, Fanny."

"Well, last night, when I was taking a few things out of the attic, look what I found . . ."

She lifted the lid of her childhood treasure chest and, between birthday cards and Bee Gees tapes, she recovered a few photos. Faded snapshots, small and square, taken with a poor-quality camera that had probably ceased to exist ages ago.

"Do you remember the day I spoke to you about when Uncle Andres took us to the amusement park in Santa Cruz? I was nine years old, but I still remember quite clearly. What I couldn't remember were these photos. I mean, I remember we took some photos, but couldn't remember where they were, because had I remembered . . ."

I'd quit listening to her after the first sentence, as soon as she held the images before my eyes. Little Fanny in a close-fitting yellow dress with an anchor in the front, with the same straight hair cut at the line of her jawbone, smiling rapturously with a plume of cotton candy in her right hand. With a man to her left. A dark man still in his fifties, with dark hair, a broad torso, and bushy eyebrows. Hairy arms, a chickpea-colored shirt half-open, and a heavy beard starting to gray in some areas. One hand on the girl's shoulder, a cigarette in the other. With a half smile, as if forced by the situation. Four photographs with very little variation. The fifth, however, was radically different. There were no longer two people posing but three. On the back of it, in the childish hand of the younger Fanny, a few written words: *Santa Cruz Beach Boardwalk, Summer 1966.* The third person in the photograph was Darla Stern, with the same Nordic dyed hair and lips as fierce then as they were now. About forty-something at the time, somewhat excessive in her tight capri pants and high-heeled sandals. Striking an artificial pose to accentuate her silhouette for the camera and with a possessive and triumphant smile on her face. My daughter and my man, she seemed to be screaming to the world. Perhaps erroneously, perhaps not.

Fontana wasn't smiling in that image; he didn't seem at ease, and maybe he was not too keen to be photographed by the stranger of whom Darla had asked the favor. But he consented and that is how he was captured in the image I was now contemplating while Fanny continued chatting away about Ferris wheels and roller coasters. I anxiously absorbed the details: the faces, the gestures. And, hovering among it all, what struck me most was his hand. On her waist. With confidence, without rigidity. Still holding the cigarette between his fingers, as if that corner of Darla's body were altogether familiar to him.

"Which one do you wish to keep, Professor Perea?"

"I don't want any, Fanny," I said, finally taking my eyes off of them. "They're yours, part of your heritage. Take them to your new house; don't ever lose them."

"But it was a present I wanted to make to you," she protested.

"My present will be that you write to me once in a while to tell me how everything is going for you."

I gave her a hug before she could reply.

"And take care of your mother," I added at the last moment. Not knowing myself, in truth, why.

• • •

Rebecca was the final stop.

"You know you have a Spanish friend again, right?"

She accompanied me to the elevator while promising to take care of whatever I was too rushed to do: return a few books to the library, say good-bye to some colleagues, empty the fridge . . .

The doors were sliding closed when she unexpectedly put her hand out to stop them. They opened again. She signaled to me, and I stepped out.

"You're back on course, Blanca," she said, grabbing me by the wrists. "The worst is over. Now consider what life has placed before you and listen to your heart."

She embraced me again and let me go.

I walked across the campus in a hurry. It was already twenty to two. I moved along at a swift pace until I reached my apartment, a thick stew of emotions bubbling inside me. The satisfaction of having attained our goal. The unexpected friends I'd just said farewell to. The uncertainty that now opened before me.

In search of serenity, I made an effort to seize on the most peaceful of all sensations. I thought back again to Rebecca, her deep-down authentic goodness. Her generosity, honesty, compassion. The way she was always ready to give a hand or keep a secret, to think of others beforehand, to never say no.

In contrast, I still had Darla's image fresh in my mind from the photograph that Fanny had just shown me. Her exaggerated attempt to come across as attractive before the camera, her haughty exhibitionism, and at the same time her insecurity regarding her power and property.

The light and shadow of human nature seen in two vastly different women. The one who faces things and moves forward, as opposed to the one who broods in resentment. Crossing the practically empty campus before the impending Christmas holidays, I was suddenly conscious that, during my last half hour spent in Guevara Hall, each woman in her own way had managed to move me. Setting aside the differences, they'd both fought in their day for a similar objective. The same one, in a certain way, that I had fought for too for twenty-five years: to see our children grow up, to have a partner close by, to build a home where the morning sunlight would come streaming in. Basic desires that had driven women since the beginning of time.

The three of us, however, had fallen into the mire at some unexpected moment: on some unlucky day all three of us had ceased to be desired. Faced with desertion and uncertainty, the lack of love and the harshness of reality, each one defended herself as best she could and fought with the weapons at her disposal. With good or evil means, with whatever the intellect, the gut, or the pure survival instinct offered.

Rebecca had had the moral integrity to overcome it, and just as she'd pointed out to me, I was forging ahead not knowing exactly where my steps would lead. Darla, for her part, never did manage. Like a poor injured animal, she took shelter in her cave without ever healing her wounds, mistaking the simplicity of human nature for a despicable betrayal or a conspiracy to destroy her. Without assuming that love is fickle, strange, and arbitrary, lacking understanding and rationality. Motivated perhaps by a fear of poverty, loneliness, or the inability to raise a dependent daughter on her own; imagining detractors where there were none, just to have a guilty face to aim her fury at; hurting herself and wounding those who never knowingly had anything to do with her misfortune.

Daniel's Volvo's horn sounded twice and with it my daydreaming came to an end.

"Are you sure you've got a plane to catch in San Francisco at six?" he asked when I came outside.

Chapter 45

The sky was cloudy as we left Santa Cecilia and took the road leading to the bay. For a few miles we remained silent, Daniel at the wheel, his eyes behind dark glasses, and I, staring vacantly out of the side window, trying to put my confused mind in order. We didn't even turn on the radio; our only accompaniment was the monotonous drone of the engine. In the end, it was he who decided to break the silence.

"Tell me about your plans. How do you intend to spend this last Christmas of the millennium?"

"I'll get my place in order, turn on the heat, go on a big shopping trip, put up a tree and Nativity scene . . ."

I spoke without looking at him while my gaze wandered erratically beyond the window. Enumerating the chores with the same lack of passion with which one takes roll call in class or makes a checklist of compulsory errands.

"Everything will be different this year," I went on. "All I know for sure is that Christmas Eve will be at my sister Ana's place; she is a hopeless host and might very well send us away with a frozen lasagna and a couple of crumbly shortbread cakes. New Year's Eve we used to celebrate at my in-laws or on a trip with some friends, something I'll no longer be doing. My sons will have dinner with their father, I suppose, so it's most likely I'll finish the year alone, watching a movie in bed from ten until the next century. One hell of a plan, isn't it?"

The landscape kept moving speedily before our eyes. The spigot of intentions open, I continued telling Daniel about my plans, finally voicing, almost six months after the deluge, what I was going to do.

"And I have to meet with Alberto; perhaps that's the most important thing. I've put my thoughts in order regarding what happened between us, and now I see it in a totally different light. I've begun to understand, so it's high time we sit down and talk."

"That's a good thing."

"You told me that once before inside this same car. On our way back from Sonoma, at my apartment entrance. Do you remember?"

He moved his head slowly up and down, his gaze fixed on the road.

"Perfectly. I told you that things always need to be given their rightful end even if it turns out to be heart-wrenching, so one can heal without leaving any scars. Had I been able to do so at the time, I would have spared myself years of anguish."

"Your black years . . ."

"My black years, those terrible years when I was incapable of taking on reality in a sensible way."

I already knew what he meant, so I didn't ask any further.

"But everything passes, Blanca, everything passes, believe me. It's hard as hell and nothing is ever the same, but in the end—and I know what I'm talking about—you rebuild yourself. You open up to the world again, you move on. This is how I've managed during the years since: teaching hundreds of classes and writing my books; making new friends and experiencing new loves; returning to Spain each year . . . Until, not even knowing how, some months back I foolishly decided to get myself into a real mess, and along with that came a skinny tormented Spaniard looking for a new place in the world. And here I am, taking her to the plane that will pluck her out of my life so that she can go and put her own life in order, not knowing what I'll do when she's no longer here."

Too much turbulence, too many mixed emotions, too many feelings blocking my ability to react. Unable to say a single word, I directed my gaze out the window.

He, on the other hand, seemed to have opened a door that could no longer be closed. Finally unwound after so many days of pent-up pressure, unstoppable, he went on.

"I remember the day I met you as if it were this morning. In Meli's Market, in the bakery section. I didn't expect to find you until the following day on campus. I'd just come back from a conference in Toronto, I'd left my suitcase in Rebecca's house, and we'd gone out to buy a few things to take for dinner to a mutual friend's house. She then, with a simple gesture, pointed out a woman in a blue shirt who was struggling to choose a loaf of bread, as if humanity depended upon that simple action.

"She touched your shoulder, you turned around, and I finally saw your face. Your hair was loose and you still had the summer's sun on your skin. You smiled at Rebecca with relief, as if her presence was something you could hold on to in order to keep from drifting. She introduced us. I told you any old thing and grabbed your hand—do you remember?—one of your hands, which are now so familiar, but back then I was struck by their lightness. A weightless hand, like a brown feather. I found you adorable from the very first instant, but how much sadness was written in your eyes. An angel with broken wings lost in the middle of the supermarket. And from that very moment I knew that I wouldn't be able to go. I struggled and in fact tried several times. But at each absence I wasn't able to stand it for more than three or four days, so I came back to stay. To help you with the legacy of good old Fontana, to find out if you'd hit upon any clues on the vague mission and, above all, to be close to you and to accompany you on your journey without the slightest idea where—together or separately—we'd end up."

I kept listening without looking at him, without interrupting that flow of sincerity.

"These have been fascinating months for me, Blanca, tremendously enriching in very different dimensions. For having reconciled myself with the past, for meeting you, for rediscovering myself. And I've done a few things I never thought I'd be able to do. I have written about my life, for example. In the loneliness of many a night I have scratched at the bottom of my memory, I've reflected and put order to myriad recollections of mine and some of Andres Fontana's too—fragments of time that I spent with him and details of his own life that he told me in pieces throughout the years. Would you grab that envelope in the backseat, please?"

It was a plain-looking manila envelope, the kind we used on a daily basis at the university to send memos between and within departments.

"It's for you, what you still need to know about my professor and myself, so that you understand both of us a bit better. So that you know what made us take the step you are now taking: to jump into the unknown without a safety net, without any certainty as to what we would find. To become the 'other,' the one who does not belong and is perhaps somewhat freer."

I put the envelope inside my bag without opening it.

"Because you know," he added, "deep down, Fontana, you, and I have a lot more in common than meets the eye. You, like us, have taken the plunge. And even though you're returning to your normal life again, nothing will be the same."

"I don't doubt it for a moment," I said sincerely. "I don't think I'll ever forget these months."

"Why don't you also write about it? About what has happened during this time inside and around you; the other lives you've come in contact with, what you've felt . . ."

"I've never written anything except academic pieces and letters to my kids when I'd send them to summer camp in England."

"I'd never done it either, and now I've realized that it's less complex and infinitely more enriching than I thought. Unlike the academic writing we're accustomed to, we can throw a little more heart and soul into it. It makes you reflect on a bunch of things, delve deeper. It creates a sense of catharsis—"

"There's the exit for the airport," I interrupted. "If you continue spouting those crazy ideas, you're going to miss it."

We reached the terminal and I checked in. There was hardly time for anything except an intense and rushed good-bye.

370 | MARÍA DUEÑAS

He wrapped his large body around me, pinning me to his chest.

"Take good of care of yourself. You can't imagine how much I'll miss you, Professor Perea."

"I'll miss you too," I said, with a knot the size of a fist in my throat. I don't think he heard me.

He then caressed my face and deposited a brief kiss on my forehead, a fleeting touch I could barely feel.

I did not look back as I headed toward the security line with my passport and boarding card in my hand. I could not bear to see him one last time. But I knew he hadn't left, that he was still standing there with his longish hair, his light beard, and his running watch. Seeing me off to straighten out my life in the country that had captivated him when he was still forging his soul, a country he'd never quite let go of.

When there were only three or four passengers in front of me, I heard his emphatic voice right behind me.

"I don't want you to start the New Year alone. I don't want you to end the century alone, I don't want you to sit at the table alone on New Year's Eve, or watch movies alone in bed, or for you to ever again go through life alone."

I turned around as if there were no one else except ourselves in the terminal overflowing with rushing people. No other passengers, no other farewells, no plane about to take off or parking lot for him to return to. As if the universe around us had run out of batteries.

"Come with me," I said hanging on to his neck.

"First straighten out your life. Afterwards, call me."

And with the aplomb of one who knows exactly what he wants, he took me in his arms and kissed me with tenderness and warmth. Solid, sure, his fingers in my hair, transmitting with his lips the taste of a man who had lived a thousand lives and had been toughened by a thousand battles as well as the great discovery of a truth.

A couple of insistent ahems forced us apart. The man in front of me in Bermuda shorts and flip-flops had just gone through the passport screening process and I was next.

He whispered one more thing in my ear as he caressed me for the last time.

"I'll be there whenever you wish."

I watched as he moved away and felt cold in his absence.

Before me was the glum face of a security agent waiting for my documents while drumming his fingers on the counter.

There were no delays; we boarded right away. Once I was seated, I devoted myself to looking out into the void from my window. Without focusing my eyes on either the vehicles or the operators that buzzed about the plane, without paying attention to the stewardesses who gave us instructions on how to put on the oxygen masks. Unwilling to think, trying to concentrate on mere trifles: what Ana would serve us for dinner on Christmas Eve, what the weather would be like in Madrid. Making an effort not to explore the unexpected twist my life had taken.

We took off. Good-bye to California, good-bye to this strange time. To a trip that had transformed my perspective on things, giving me more insight on dimensions whose reach I was still unable to gauge. I closed my eyes for the longest time, and when I opened them again only the dark night was visible out the window.

Finally I was unable to hold back any longer and opened the envelope.

My Dearest Blanca,

I've spent my entire life jumping onto moving trains; however, only two absolute certainties have struck me at simple, almost ordinary moments, catching me unawares, when my guard was lowered. One was decades ago in a pharmacy beside the Mediterranean, while looking for some remedy for an inopportune flu; the second, three months ago, when my most immediate concern was merely choosing a wine for dinner.

Different moments, different surroundings, but the shared feeling that the fullness of life was before me.

So that you know what that other time was like, here you have the rest of my past. The most recent part you know firsthand.

Yours, always,
D.C.

When the first tear fell, smudging the *Y* of "Yours," I was unable to read on. After months of holding back, unable to avoid it, I finally broke down crying. I cried for me, for them, for all of us, as the plane flew over that strange country from one coast to the other and crossed the Atlantic on a sad night that never seemed to end. For Andres Fontana and that love of his, late and unrequited, so ill timed. For Aurora, for the life she was never able to live, for her eternally preserved image in a white dress laughing barefoot in Cabo San Lucas. For Daniel's dark years, for the depth of his pain and his courage to join the world again.

For Alberto and his new course, for the future we would no longer share. For my sons: for the children they'd been, and the men they were becoming. For all of our pasts and presents, for what we were before, for what was yet to come.

It was pouring when I changed planes at Heathrow and it was still raining when we landed in Madrid. It took me only a couple of seconds to spot my sons in the arrivals area, waving and laughing, calling me loudly. Dark-haired like their father, skinny like me. With the freshness of youth written all over their faces and their entire lives before them, making their way toward me.

On reaching home I read the pages in the envelope.

Afterwards I called him and said, "Come now."

And after that afterwards, with my suitcases still half unpacked, the rooms warming up, and the Christmas tree still not set up, I traced the parallel lines of three lives and began writing.

Acknowledgments

To my friends and colleagues Malcolm Compitello (University of Arizona), Joe Super and Pablo González (West Virginia University), and Francisco Lomelí (University of California in Santa Barbara), for serving as a magnificent source of information and most valuable inspiration because of their knowledge and memories, and the nostalgic bit of half-Spanish soul they all have.

To Admiral Adolfo Baturone, Tata Albert, Juan Antonio Vizcaíno, and Juan Ignacio Ferrández, for their assistance in very different ways, which helped me reconstruct Cartagena in the 1950s and the city's connections to the United States Navy.

To Manuel Cantera and Miguel Zugasti, for their always wise revisions and corrections.

To my publishing team in Spain within Grupo Planeta, and very especially to Raquel Gisbert, Belén López Celada, and Isabel Santos, for their support, hard work, and contagious enthusiasm.

To my literary agent in Spain, Antonia Kerrigan, and to Lola Gulias, for pushing me and my books into the world.

For their splendid endeavor and wondrous zeal in bringing this Spanish story to American readers, my deepest gratitude to my agents in New York, Tom and Elaine Colchie; to my translator, Elie Kerrigan; and to my publishers, Judith Curr and Johanna Castillo, and the rest of the Atria team.

And finally, for everything, to my big family and my long-standing friends: always passionate and tempestuous, always essential.